# NEEDLE AND BONE

## TONYA MITCHELL

BLOODHOUND
BOOKS

## PRAISE FOR THE ARSENIC EATER'S WIFE

Tonya Mitchell has crafted a gorgeously gothic and atmospheric whodunit filled with surprising twists and memorable characters that I tore through in a single sitting. Inspired by a true-life crime, *The Arsenic Eater's Wife* offers proof that the darkest mystery remains the human heart.

—Kris Waldherr, author of *Unnatural Creatures: A Novel of the Frankenstein Women* and *The Lost History of Dreams*

A provocative, suspenseful gothic treat of a novel, inspired by real events. Mitchell's atmospheric prose carries readers into the past as a woman accused of murder desperately tries to reclaim her innocence and survive a harrowing betrayal. Rife with secrets, intrigue, and serpentine twists.

—Paulette Kennedy, bestselling author of *Parting the Veil*

This Victorian-era mystery had me in its grip from the first page to the last. The story is laced with suspense and shocking twists, and depicts a time when a troubled marriage left women tragically few options. A first-rate page-turner.

—Nancy Bilyeau, author of *The Orchid Hour*

*For the artists and the dreamers*

But what sustains the physician,
in the stillness of night,
in the chamber of pestilence,
in the reeking hut of a sick beggar
—in the cell of a maniac?
A moral courage, which bids him die
rather than desert his charge.

—Dr. Thomas Mütter, "Charge to the Graduates", 1851

# THE WOMAN IN BLUE
## PHILADELPHIA, DECEMBER 1841

When the night is blackest and the streets the most quiet, a seventeen-year-old girl stands at her window. One story below, a gas lamp flickers, its feeble glow just reaching the row of houses opposite. The dwellings sag against each other like aged widows, the snow upon them cloaking the peeling paint beneath. Every curtain is drawn, every pane dark. The skinny lane—iced over, slippery as a greased pole—is deserted. Still, the girl searches the shadows for something out of place: a tread of foot, a flash of teeth, a glint of eye.

Nothing.

The girl's eyes adjust inward. Her image in the glass is leached of color, her skin as pale as milk. She tilts her head, takes herself in: the curve of her jaw, the furred outline of her hair against the candlelight behind her. The single flame elongates, goes perfectly still, and then gutters as if someone has walked across the room.

It's suddenly freezing. The flame dips again and then: a face.

She turns and something inside her curdles.

A short distance away, dressed in a pale blue gown, is a

young woman. Or something like a woman—she isn't there. Not *all* there. The girl can see through her, see the candle on the table through her midsection. The woman's skirts sway, shimmy, flutter like a sheet on a line. Her slippers don't quite touch the floor.

Tendrils of panic clutch at the girl's throat and then she is pitching herself into the darkness, away from the woman, away from the light. Her elbow bangs against the door frame as she thunders into her bedroom. She closes the door, locks it fast. Puffs of air in and out, in and out.

Silence. Outside the room there is only stillness.

The girl presses her back against the door, takes in the darkness, the inky black of it. She stands for a long time, until her heart is calm, and details come into focus: the low coffin of the bed, the chair in the corner with its pile of clothes. Has she really seen a ghost? Perhaps her eyes were playing tricks on her.

But it's no use. From the chambers of her mind seep old horrors, and her heart fills with a familiar dread. Every reason, every excuse loops back to the same thought: she knows the woman in blue. Well, she *once* knew her.

She had watched her die months ago, her life bleeding out in bright pools, and she had done nothing to save her.

# PART 1

———

Lectures and books will serve
as guides and beacons,
But the goals can only be reached
by traveling the road itself.

—Dr. Thomas Mütter, "Charge to the Graduates," 1851

# ACCIDENT

## PHILADELPHIA, DECEMBER 1841

Shadows descend on a boneyard at dusk. From Annis' position in the wings, she can see torchlight flickering over gravestones and disturbed earth. The rasp of shovels against stone scrape the air. The gravediggers—two burly men of sizable girth—debate whether the woman whose coffin they're making way for died of suicide or drowning.

They banter on, shovels working, until one of them bellows, prizes something from the soil, and straightens. He brandishes his find like a jeweled crown.

It's a human skull.

"This same skull, sir," he cries with exaggerated aplomb, arm extended high, "was Yorick's skull, the king's jester."

The audience titters and young Hamlet, clad in a swirling cloak, advances to center stage.

Annis' brother, Ben, had told her months ago a propman procured the skull from one of the city's medical schools. *It's real*, he'd pronounced with morbid delight. *Real as the nose on your face.* She hadn't known whether to believe him. In the dim gaslight, it looks genuine.

The first four acts of *Hamlet* have gone off without a hitch.

Not a single mistake—not a flubbed line nor a misstep from the stagehands—has marred the performance. Still, Annis is uneasy. There's too much that could go wrong, too much Ben might be blamed for. It wouldn't be the first time he's been on the wrong side of the director's temper.

She swallows, her mouth dry. *It can't happen. It won't.*

On stage, the funeral procession approaches and Hamlet realizes it is his love, Ophelia, who's to be buried. Laertes and Hamlet come to blows, their voices careening across the stage with each feigned punch. Annis repositions herself and peers around the masking curtain. In the first row, men in dark frock coats and women in frothy finery watch, transfixed.

In the opposite wing across stage, she can just make out Ben, his hands clamped around the painted backdrop he'll slide into place for the last scene change. He nods once as if to reassure her. She nods back.

The brawl is broken up and the lights go out. Actors scurry to the wings. Annis shifts to the side to make way for the graveyard panel. She cranes her neck to see Ben push his flat into place. It wobbles, the timber frame upon which the canvas is stretched groans and looks like it will pitch forward. Someone curses behind her. The director, Mr. Simms. Annis' heart clenches. The moment stretches, tight as a bow.

And then the lights come up. The frame is in position, the actors in place. Ben has exited the scene.

Simms lumbers away in the direction of the crossover behind the stage with purposeful steps and her relief dissolves. She makes to follow him but is stilled by a hand on her arm.

"I wouldn't, Miss Hargrave." Grady, another stagehand. He's a short pinch of a man, face wizened as a dried apple, ears comically large. "Simms won't like it. It's opening night jitters is all."

It's a lie and they both know it. Simms is a viper on his good

6

days. Old Grady is doing her a kindness, warning her before she goes too far. She steadies her breath, puts her hand atop his and squeezes, then pulls away. She lifts her skirts and heads for the crossover, a dark thread twisting through her mind as she runs. If Ben loses his position...

She hears Simms' hushed words as she nears stage right.

"I said I want it *seamless*, boy! *Steady*. You've the grace of a bull. Are you daft?"

Annis pulls up sharp behind Simms. Ben's head is down, hands shoved into his pockets. He looks for all the world as if he wants to drop through the floor.

A coil of rage tightens around her throat. *He's just a lad!* she wants to scream. *Only fifteen!*

Ben looks up and meets her eyes. It's only a flash, but in that drop of time she reads him. *Utter a word and you'll only make it worse.*

Simms spins. He is scarecrow thin and bald as a turtle. His lips are pressed taut, his eyes slits. "Ah, the *sister* of this ignoramus." It's little more than a sneer. "What have you to say, hmm?"

Insults fly to her mouth: bully, toad, browbeater. Her eyes flick to Ben. His body trembles. Sweat glistens on his brow. Whom does he fear more, Simms or her?

She clamps her mouth shut and works her face into a mask of tranquility. She won't be the final stroke that costs Ben his job. Paltry as his income is, it's all they have to live on.

Simms takes a threatening step toward her and is about to launch another verbal assault when trumpets flare. They turn to the stage.

Hamlet has just agreed to a sword fight with Laertes. The play is reaching its climax. The King and Hamlet's mother, Queen Gertrude, enter with officers. Servants bring flagons of wine. The officers lower themselves to cushions as Laertes enters.

"Come, Hamlet, take this hand from me," the King announces, placing Laertes's hand in Hamlet's. The crimson stones in his crown twinkle under the lights.

Hamlet begins his soliloquy. After a moment, Simms—seemingly appeased by what he sees—turns, looks between the two of them, and strides away.

Annis steps toward Ben. She marvels again at the coltish look of him, how much he's sprouted since they arrived in the city. He hasn't quite grown into his hands and feet, hasn't yet mastered the ranginess of his limbs. And yet, he isn't clumsy. He's never been clumsy. Still, the signs he's growing into a man are more apparent each day. She is tall but at the rate he's growing, it won't be long before he's taller than she is.

He rakes a hand through his honey blond hair and cracks his knuckles. She can tell he's uncomfortable under her gaze, and so she returns her attention to the stage. The sword fight has begun. Queen Gertrude is moments from drinking the poisoned wine intended for Hamlet, moments from death. Yet the actors recede. It's the colorful flat behind them that grabs her. The scene is the castle hall, the painted tapestries on the walls so skillfully done, they look almost real. She admires the window with its stone tracery, the suggestion of a distant fogged landscape beyond.

It is *her* design on the canvas, her designs on every canvas in the play. When Ben raced home months before and told her the set designer had stormed out having had his fill of Simms, Annis had drawn each scene on paper, colored them with precious oils she'd been saving. She had painted through the night: castle ramparts, inner chambers, the plains of Denmark. Ben had shown Simms her sketches the next day, claiming them as his own just as they'd planned. Surely they would reflect well on Ben, ingratiate him to the mercurial director.

How naive she'd been. She should have known better. She feels a flush of irritation at her own stupidity for having such foolish hopes.

---

An hour later when they exit the theatre, it's all noise and confusion. The low undertone and puffed vapor of a hundred conversations fill the air as patrons clog the pavement waiting for carriages. The lamps have been lit and a brisk snow is falling. The cold is so biting Annis' scalp prickles. The ice underfoot is treacherous as they thread their way through the crowd.

She tucks her arm firmly through Ben's and tugs him toward the street corner. *How nice it would be to have the fare tonight. For a fire to be burning in the hearth when we arrive home.* She scoffs inwardly. How quickly their life has changed. To go from middle class to poverty in such a short time confounds her still. Even now, eight months on, she can scarcely believe it. It's as if the beautiful bauble she thought her life would be has been snatched from her and a faux trinket of paste put in its place.

At the curb they wait for the road to clear. Conveyances lumber past, drivers hunched over, faces muffled from the cold. Suddenly, Annis' boots shuffle out from under her and Ben pulls her up. She just manages to keep her footing, but Ben loses his, one long leg shooting over the curb into the street. He goes down hard and Annis with him. To her horror, a hackney is pulling up fast.

"Ho!" the jarvey shouts. "Mind yourself, lad!"

The man pulls on the reins. The horse slackens pace, but its hooves don't stop. Time slows and she sees Ben's leg stretched out in the path of the horse. One hoof comes crashing down on his shin. A sickening crunch. The animal rears in its traces, backstepping. Its breath fogs the air. The scene fuzzes and it's as if she's underwater. Garbled shouts, Ben going lax on her arm. Snow, too much snow.

A woman's voice at her ear. "Are you hurt, miss?"

It's enough to jolt her back to her senses. A slight man in a top hat is pulling Ben clear of the street. She scrambles on her knees to her brother. "Ben! Ben, are you hurt?" She is being ridiculous. Of course he's hurt. The man has laid him out on his back. His coat is already dusting with snow. She pats his cheeks. "Ben!"

His eyes flutter open and then his face contorts in pain.

The man in the top hat kneels beside Ben and calls into the whited air, "I need a board, something long to support the body!" No one moves. "Do you hear me? This man needs medical attention straight away! Quickly now." His eyes find a woman in a green hat hunched beside Annis, the one who'd spoken to her. "Mary, find Abbott in the queue."

A man in a driver's cap emerges from the crowd. "No need, doctor. The landau's at the curb just there."

"God be praised," the man in the top hat, the doctor, says. He takes Ben's limp hand. "Young man, we're going to move you in a moment. You'll be out of this damnable weather in no time."

There's a shout in the direction of the theatre entrance. Heads turn. "Make way! Make way!" A tall, broad-chested man breaks through the crowd. He's carrying what looks like a narrow signboard for the theatre. "This should do."

"Pancoast, thank heaven," the doctor says. "Let's get him on it, then."

The tall man lays the board alongside Ben and the two take positions at his head and feet. "On three," the doctor mutters, and they lift and lay him gently on the wood.

The crowd parts and they scuttle to the carriage, Annis

close behind. The driver flings open the door. The doctor rests the end of the board on the floor of the landau and climbs in around it. "That's right. Slide him if you can. Easy, easy."

Ben moans. She steps closer and squeezes his hand, her heart a drum. He is gloveless, his fingers cold, and she feels a spark of anger at the inanity of it, that on a night as wretched as this, he hadn't the time to put on his gloves before he'd been trampled. "I'm here, Ben. They're going to take care of you." He's to remain on the floor; the board is too wide for the seats.

She leans into the carriage. "Where are you taking him, sir? Please, I must go with him. I—"

The doctor waves her inside and motions for her to take a seat across from him. Annis steps in quickly before he can change his mind. The woman in the green hat climbs in and sits beside her.

At the door, the tall man says, "I shall tell Rebecca to take the carriage home. I'll be but a second."

"Yes, of course," the doctor replies.

In the filmy darkness of the carriage, Annis can barely see anything. Her mind can't seem to grasp it, that Ben was fine moments ago and now he is injured. Horribly so. She wants to reverse time, undo the moment when she started to fall. If she hadn't shuffled on the ice, Ben wouldn't have fallen.

A moment later, the man named Pancoast returns, steps to the footplate, and takes a seat beside the doctor.

"The Pit, sir?" the driver enquires. This rather cryptic utterance produces a nod from both men, and he closes the door, scampers atop the dickey box, and urges the horses forth.

The woman smooths a furred lap robe over Annis' legs. It seems a frivolous luxury when Ben lies in agony on the floor. He moans again and Annis blinks through tears. She can just make out his form but she can't see his face. The carriage lamps provide no light within. She is too far away to reach his hand.

The woman beside her is in the way. They pass a streetlamp. Light bleeds across the interior of the carriage: to the doctor, who's fumbling beneath his coat for something; to the man named Pancoast, who's regarding her with sympathy; to Ben whose eyes are closed, his face an unnatural white.

"Is he..." She trails off, her voice a croak. *Is he going to be all right?* She hasn't the courage to ask for fear of the answer.

The woman beside her pats her hand. "You mustn't fret. These gentlemen are doctors, Miss...?"

"Hargrave. Annis Hargrave. Ben is my brother."

The smaller man has found what he was searching for: a pocketknife. He bends down and begins cutting the bottom of Ben's pant leg. Once he's made a tear, he rips the fabric up to Ben's knee. They pass another streetlamp and the doctors peer down. The shin beneath has already begun to swell. There is no blood, at least none Annis can see, but a bruise is forming.

"A contusion and skin abrasion," Pancoast mutters.

The other doctor lifts Ben's leg slightly, running his fingers under it. "No compound fracture, thank heaven."

That neither looks relieved—they don't even glance up at her—fills her with uneasiness. "It's broken, isn't it?" she says. It has to be; she'd heard it crack.

The smaller man shoots the woman beside her a look, and Annis has the impression a silent conversation has passed between them.

"Miss Hargrave," her seat companion says, turning to her. She takes Annis' gloved hand in hers. "My husband is a professor of surgery at Jefferson Medical College." She indicates the small man who'd pulled Ben from the street. "His name is Dr. Mütter. I'm his wife, Mary." Gesturing to the tall, broad-chested man, she says, "This is Dr. Pancoast. He teaches anatomy there. Your brother is in good hands."

Annis tucks away these introductions. She must concentrate

on Ben. He is all that matters. The landau makes a left turn. Ben moans and rolls his head.

"We shall be at our destination soon, Ben," Dr. Mütter says. "Then we shall have you out of here and on a table to see what's to be done about your leg."

Though the doctor's words are authoritative, they're laced with a measured kindness.

Still, his words chill her. *What's to be done.* Might they amputate? She's heard of it before. She saw a man once on the street in New York City making his way on crutches. His leg had been cut off above the knee, his pant leg knotted at the end of the stump. He was homeless, she was sure: filthy rags for clothes, a begrimed face, wild unkempt hair. She'd turned away, embarrassed to be caught staring. *Let them not have to amputate. Anything but that.*

"Another block or so," Mrs. Mütter says. "The school isn't far from the theatre. Abbott will have us there in no time."

And then her mother's voice echoes in Annis' head as clear as a bell. *Fanciful as spun sugar, you are. You best have a straight head about your future—yours and your brother's—else the world will chew you up and spit you out.*

Annis bites a gloved finger to stanch her tears. All through her mother's illness, Annis thought her a miserable woman with a forked tongue. While that had been true at the end, it seems she'd had prescience of this very moment all along. Her mother had predicted that Annis' impulsive nature would lead to dangerous decisions that would ruin her. Ruin Ben.

Her mother had been right.

# THE PIT

## PHILADELPHIA, DECEMBER 1841

"How old is your brother, Miss Hargrave?"

The carriage swerves and she's thrown against Mrs. Mütter. Annis slides away, repositioning herself. In the inky darkness, Dr. Mütter waits for her answer.

"Fifteen, sir."

She can't be sure in the shadows, but it seems the doctor purses his lips together and nods, as if he likes the answer. He places his fingers on Ben's shin once more, feeling as he goes.

She wonders if she should be relieved or alarmed that there is no reaction from Ben. "What is it you're looking for?" she asks.

"Breakage, bone fragments," Dr. Pancoast replies. "We'll know more when we've had a thorough look at him. Ah, here we are."

The carriage pulls to a stop and the driver, Abbott, is off the box in a flash and opening the door.

Dr. Mütter drops keys into the man's gloved hand. "Unlock the door and use the prop to keep it open. Clear the steps as best you can. There's a shovel just there, and see to the lamps inside, if you will."

Dr. Pancoast alights and begins to pull the board out, Dr. Mütter pushing from the interior. Then the latter exits carefully, stepping around the board, taking the end of it and pulling it clear. It all seems to take an age. Finally, Mrs. Mütter steps down and Annis follows. The driver has done his best to clear the snow from the steps, but a crust of ice coats the surface and impedes the doctors from entering the building quickly.

Once they're inside, Mrs. Mütter closes the door and the women trail behind the doctors with their burden. Just as instructed, Abbott has illuminated the way. They move down a wide, gloomy hallway lit by gas from wall brackets placed at intervals. A chilly breeze grazes Annis' cheeks, and she shivers. Taking a turn, they pass through double doors into a chamber the likes of which she's never seen.

The first thing she notices is the large chandelier under which stands Abbott, who's using a long-handled torch and key lighter to ignite the burners. With each flare, the space reveals more of itself. It is enormous. The ceiling soars to at least three stories. Tiered rows of wooden benches encircle the room. They're broken by a bank of double length windows along one wall, panes revealing only the black of night beyond. The seats rise all the way to the ceiling, the top-most row disappearing into darkness. The area where she stands is comparatively small and feels like a stage, although entirely different to the one from which they've come.

What had the driver called it? The Pit.

The doctors are transferring Ben to a long table. Abbott has finished illuminating the chandelier. Though the burners are many in number, shadows pitch in the draft that slices through the room, the dark paneling of the stage area adding to the gloom. Lessons must be conducted here when the sun is bright, though the gaslight and the single candelabrum Abbott is now lighting indicate, it seems, that not all activity here is conducted by light of day. A large cabinet rests near the table. Through its glass panes are shelves glittering with instruments. The doctors remove their hats and coats and place them on hooks. From pegs they pull leather aprons that they quickly tie around themselves with distracted attention, their focus clearly on the patient.

She is stirred again by the urgency. Speed is an ally, but what terrors lie ahead?

With her heart in her throat, she takes a step toward the table but is prevented from going any farther by Mrs. Mütter who steps into her path, though not unkindly. "Miss Hargrave," she says, her words laced with compassion, "do come with me."

Annis bites her lip. Where does the woman wish to take her? Her place is with Ben. What if he stirs and thinks she's abandoned him? She cranes her neck around Mrs. Mütter to see what the doctors are doing, but it's no use. What isn't blocked by the doctor's wife is hidden behind Dr. Pancoast, who's leaning over the table, his back to her.

"Should he call for you, you'll be at hand," Mrs. Mütter says, as if she's read her mind. "We must allow the doctors room to do their work. I assure you, we shall sit where you can see everything."

She allows Mrs. Mütter to lead her to the six-foot wall that circles the stage. A narrow set of steps, accessed by a swinging door, admits to the first tier of seats. The bench she seats herself upon is hard and unyielding even through her cloak, and the room is frigid as iron; she can see her breath. It strikes her how small she feels in the space, how every sound—whispers, footfalls, the hiss of gas—echoes. Her eyes cast around the room. Every shadow unnerves her.

Her anxiety must be clearly visible, for Mrs. Mütter says, "The surgical amphitheater. The professors lecture here and perform surgery before the students."

*Surgery.* The word knocks against her skull. *This can't be real. I'll awaken and this will all have been a dream.* She is suddenly burning up. She doesn't know much about medicine, but opening people up—the butchery of it, the chance of infection—are harbingers of death. She wonders what the benches here have witnessed. In her mind's eye she sees patients flailing on the table, crying out in agony as doctors hold them down, their bodies opened with knives and saws as students look on. Dizziness seizes her, and it's as if a chasm yawns beneath her feet.

A hand at her back. "Put your head to your knees," Mrs. Mütter says. Her voice is far away, yet fingers press gently against her back. "That's it. Close your eyes. Breathe. If you're nauseous and feel you might be sick, let it come. There's no shame in it."

Time ekes out in heartbeats that crash in Annis' ears. Of course there is shame. Ben needs her. The sudden longing for her father is a tug in her chest. Gone four years, God rest him. He would know what to do. Papa would command the scene, comfort her, see to Ben. She isn't made for this. She's not strong enough. This is all her fault. The reason they fled New York City so quickly after Mother's death was because of Annis' recklessness. They wouldn't be in Philadelphia now—with Ben laid out on a doctor's table—if it wasn't for her.

Her and the Wolf.

Her mind trips and flashes to him—bared teeth, the black of his eyes. She begins to tremble. With great force of mind, she concentrates on the now: the press of her toes in her boots, the pinch of her corset against her ribs. *The Wolf isn't here, not in this city. He will never find us.*

Gradually, her heartbeat steadies and she's aware of Mrs. Mütter stroking her back. She raises her head, a blush heating her cheeks. Ben is suffering twenty feet away—perhaps irrevocably damaged, broken. She must get hold of herself.

The doctors are conversing in low tones. Ben's eyes are still closed. He doesn't appear to have moved.

"Has he fallen faint?" Annis whispers. She forces herself to look away and concentrate on the woman beside her. Melting snow is falling from Mrs. Mütter's hat onto her cloak, the droplets like tiny glass beads. Her lashes are long and dark, a contrast to her alabaster skin. A small mole rests to the left of her mouth. She looks young, younger than her husband by a smattering of years. Twenty-seven or twenty-eight, perhaps? A whiff of perfume swims to Annis. Tea roses.

"Most probably, from the shock," is the reply. "It's a godsend. He won't be aware of the pain."

She has the sense that Mrs. Mütter has been in this situation before. That she's been coached to distract family members from the horror of injury, perhaps death. "Will he live?" Her eyes fill with tears and the green of Mrs. Mütter's hat bleeds across her vision.

"I expect so."

Annis drags her gaze to the table. "What will they do?"

"They will set the bone first, if necessary. It's good he's not conscious. It can be painful. They will then wrap it, I think."

"So he will be able to walk then? They won't have to... he won't be lame?"

Mrs. Mütter doesn't answer and Annis wonders what it could mean. Perhaps the comely doctor's wife simply doesn't know how Ben will fair, or she does and the truth of it is not for her to tell.

Dr. Mütter is standing at the foot of the table. He leans down almost level to its surface, runs a finger down the length of Ben's damaged shin. They've rolled up his other pant leg past the knee. The doctor seems to be comparing the two. The injured limb is swollen, the skin mid-shin visibly discolored.

"No distortion of the limb," Dr. Mütter says. His words are low, barely above a whisper. "I think it's a transverse break."

"Miraculous, given the circumstances." Dr. Pancoast places his hands on Ben's injured limb, the white of his hands pale against the stippled skin. He leans down, his ear to Ben's shin, and moves his fingers over the area, squeezing lightly as he goes. "No crepitus, it seems. Yes, a clean break. If there's a fragment there, I can't feel it."

"Help me then."

Dr. Mütter takes hold of Ben's foot—they've removed his boot—while Dr. Pancoast places his hands at Ben's knee. Dr. Mütter lifts the leg slightly and, with his hands around Ben's ankle for leverage, pulls. Again, there is no reaction from Ben.

Dr. Mütter compares the legs again. "Straight as a pin, I daresay."

"That's the way."

From a cabinet drawer, Dr. Mütter removes a round object. It's not until he begins to use it that Annis realizes what it is: a rolled bandage about two inches in width. He begins to wind it around the limb in a tight crisscross pattern, starting at the bottom of the shin, over the knee, to the top of the leg. Dr. Pancoast brings a shallow basin that he's added powder and water to and stirred, to the table. With a small brush, Dr. Mütter begins smearing the liquid—which seems to be some sort of paste—over the surface of the bandage. He then applies yet another layer of bandage, working it up and around the leg the same way as the first. He then reapplies the paste.

The outline of Ben's leg is clearly discernible. It's now encased in a white sheath designed, she wagers, to keep the bone fixed in position. The doctors inspect the apparatus. Dr. Mütter runs the pads of his fingers over it. Dr. Pancoast raps his knuckles against it, as if to test its firmness.

After wiping his hands on a clean cloth, Dr. Mütter

approaches her while Dr. Pancoast busies himself with cleaning the area of debris and removing the basin from the room.

"We have done all we can for him tonight, Miss Hargrave." He is standing on the edge of the stage looking up at her. Despite the warmth of his words, there are dark smudges under his eyes. It must be after midnight. A cool breeze moves through the room again and the candles shiver. "The leg doesn't trouble me at present, but I wish to retain him for the night nevertheless. We run a daily clinic across the hall." He motions to the double doors through which they'd entered. "There's a cot that should suit him nicely. Abbott will be happy to take you home. You may return tomorrow morning with your parents at first light. I would be happy to inform them of your brother's progress."

His statements swoop through her mind and clash—Ben's leg does not require amputation (praise God) yet he must stay under watch for the night (he is not out of the woods). "Our parents..." She pauses. Dr. Mütter raises his brows. "They've passed, doctor."

"I'm sorry, Miss Hargrave. Perhaps there is a relative with whom I might discuss the details of your brother's treatment?"

She swallows. "We have no relatives, I'm afraid."

"I see." A look of compassion moves across his features.

She leans forward. "I won't leave him, sir. If he should wake and I'm not here, he'll be distressed."

"I don't mind staying on, Thomas," Mrs. Mütter says. "Miss Hargrave could use the company."

---

A quarter of an hour later, they sit in Mütter's examination room at the clinic. He had explained he had a more comfortable office with a fireplace on the floor above, but didn't want to be too far from Ben. The tiny room holds only a desk, an examination table, and a few chairs. There is no heat. Outside is the waiting area with chairs set against the walls and, in an adjoining room, a few cots. They'd laid Ben in one of them and Mrs. Mütter had gone in search of blankets. Annis was relieved Ben hadn't awakened but remarked she was surprised to find the clinic empty.

Dr. Mütter sighs. "Unfortunately, we do not offer overnight accommodation. The clinic is only open during the day when classes are in session."

Annis is struck by how fortunate it is that the doctor is staying on Ben's behalf when the Mütters could be at home in bed.

"The college board thinks there's no need," Mütter continues, "as if patients are miraculously cured when the sun begins to set." He shakes his head in irritation. "They're wrong, of course. So many of those we treat need a few days of rest under the eye of a physician before they're released. But it's not done, you see. The number of men and women piled into hackneys and sent home, their wounds still smarting, is atrocious." A ghost of a smile plays on his lips. "It will come, though, the overnight care. We'll convince the board yet, Pancoast and I."

Now that the emergency of Ben's situation has abated, Annis has the luxury of taking in details she hadn't before. The doctor must be in his early thirties—young, it seems to her, for a doctor. He has no mustache or beard, but his side whiskers give him a sophistication beyond his years. He speaks with a southern cadence, the drawing out of the vowels a long glide to the next. And his attire is expensive. No, not merely that. It borders on the exquisite. She has no doubt he is wealthy, but she's seen wealthy men about town who don't dress with the fastidiousness and aplomb this Dr. Mütter does. In the flicker of the oil lamp on his desk, the cheeriness of his cravat is the bloom of a yellow rose. The brown satin collar and cuffs of his frock coat gleam. The shirt beneath is starched to perfection. All seem incongruous to a man who works in blood and bone. And yet, perhaps it is only that he and his wife dressed for the theatre.

"What did you mean earlier by a 'transverse' break?" she asks.

His eyes twinkle. "How clever of you to remember. It means the bone has broken perpendicularly to its length, much like a branch would were you to break it over your thigh. The break occurs as a straight line and, in your brother's case, there is no indication of jagged edges or fragmented pieces—none that we could feel at any rate. All of which means reduction—that is to say, the repositioning of the bone—was easy."

She likes that he speaks to her as if she will understand him, not as if he were addressing a girl who couldn't possibly grasp his meaning. Like watercolor to paper, she absorbs his words, setting them to memory so she can relay them to Ben later.

"I must say, Miss Hargrave, your brother is very lucky. The tibia of an older man would've likely shattered and broken through the skin. Complications that would have greatly affected, to a negative degree, his recovery."

"That's why you asked his age."

"Yes. Young bones break less catastrophically in my experience, and they are quicker to heal." A bloom of hope blossoms in her chest but quickly withers at his next words. "But he is not out of danger quite yet." His eyes, a clear gray, brim with empathy. "His leg will continue to swell. The apparatus we fashioned around it won't accommodate for that, and the pressure will cause him pain. Tomorrow or the next day perhaps, I shall have to remove portions of the casing to allow for the swelling. There's always the possibility of displacing the bone again, you see. For now, it must remain immobile."

"Will he stir tonight?"

"Hard to say. If he does, I shall give him a bit of laudanum. He'll need to remain in bed when he returns home."

Annis' hand flutters to her throat. "For how long?"

"A week, perhaps a bit longer. It all depends on how he's mending. I'm not one for demanding bed rest the full length of recovery. He needs to use the limb to prevent wasting. Even so, he'll be on crutches and wear a sling for some time." Her face must mirror her anxiety, for Mütter's brow creases. He leans back in his chair and appraises her. "What type of work does he do?"

Of course the doctor would have determined, with them having no family, that Ben would be working. She hates that he has to. Ben should be training in some profession. It's what their parents would have wanted. "He's a stagehand at Chestnut Street Theatre."

"Ah, of course. What specifically does he do?"

"He moves scenery during performances. Between plays, he works at building the sets."

The doctor doesn't speak for some moments and when he does, he leans forward, his brow furrowing. "I have every confidence your brother will recover the full use of his leg, Miss Hargrave, provided he is careful. I don't advise him to move heavy things. He mustn't overtax his leg. The bone and surrounding tissue need time to heal."

At that moment, Mrs. Mütter breezes through the door with a lantern. She's carrying a stack of blankets, on top of which is a plate of apples and cheese. She sets the lantern on the desk, slightly out of breath.

"I managed to find some food in your office," she says to her husband. "And I put another blanket over Ben, Miss Hargrave. He's sleeping soundly."

"Thank you," Annis says.

The doctor cuts first the apple and then the cheese for them to share. Each bite of apple is delectably tart, a perfect match for the rich cheese. Little do the Mütters know that she and Ben haven't been able to afford such fare for months.

While she arranges one of the blankets over her lap and the Mütters talk companionably between bites, her mind ticks. If Ben doesn't return to the theatre tomorrow, he will lose his job. From the sound of it, he won't be able to work *any* job for weeks. Philadelphia is a city of hard labor, much of it in grueling mills. What kind of work can he secure that will allow him to go about on crutches? Their money will soon be gone. They won't be able to buy food or pay the rent. And they have no way to pay for the care Ben has so generously received.

She tries to suppress her fears, but they rear back at her, exposing sharp pointed teeth.

# PLEA

Annis crosses Sixth Street, hugging her cloak to her body to ward off the chill. Her left boot has a hole where the leather meets the sole and her stocking is soaked through. She wishes she was at home in front of the hearth sipping tea, feet to the fender. It's not the first time she's come to Simms to beg him to keep Ben on. She can't be rid of this task soon enough.

*Blast him and his infernal theatre.*

It is Christmas Eve morning and the world is aglitter. Fresh snow has fallen overnight, coating everything in a blinding mantel of white. A stylish four-in-hand clamors past, harnesses draped with bells. At Washington Square, she takes in the beauty of the trees sugared with snow, the lawn space yet unblemished by the trample of pedestrians. By the time she reaches Walnut, the carriage traffic has pitched the snow onto the walkway. It's choked with slush. Her breath smokes the air as a curse escapes her. Her toes are going numb.

At the corner of Chestnut and Sixth the county courthouse rises in stately brick, but its neighbor, the sprawling giant that is the Pennsylvania State House, draws Annis' attention. It spans the length of the block; its tower and steeple topping it like a hat. As a young girl she had read, nose thrust between the pages of her school primer, that the Declaration of Independence and the Constitution had been signed there, back when Philadelphia was the nation's capital.

This stretch is the heart of the city, where free Negroes jostle with Whites, where the former—despite their numerous churches, schools, and societies—still vie with mostly Irish immigrants for factory jobs and the skilled trades.

Next to the Bolivar Hotel rests the columned façade of Chestnut Street Theatre, the best the city has to offer. On the second story, two women wrought from stone, replete with flowing robes, stare down at her as she takes the steps to the entrance. A painted signboard declares there will be a performance of *Hamlet* this evening, but the building will be closed on Christmas Day.

It's deserted inside. Evergreen boughs and red and gold bunting adorn the lobby walls, columns and thresholds, but it all seems strangely out of place in the gloom with no theatregoers, costumed ushers, and cigar sellers walking the lobby. Annis takes a series of doors to the back of the building where the way opens to a high-ceilinged area where props, backdrops, and costumes cluster in disarray. Mr. Simms' office door is closed. It's too early for the actors and the stagehands to have arrived, but the director keeps early hours.

Annis knocks. Low voices within stop and the door opens. Mr. Janklow, the theatre manager, raises bushy eyebrows and rubs his chin. "Yes?"

"I've come to see Mr. Simms, sir."

Behind Janklow, Simms sits huddled over his desk. He scowls when he recognizes her. "What is it?"

She doesn't want to discuss the reason for her visit in front of Mr. Janklow. He's a nice man, but Simms isn't likely to be cordial, and she doesn't want to be skewered in the hall.

"It's about Ben, sir."

"What about him?" The scowl deepens.

She's too flummoxed to reply, but Mr. Janklow takes the cue. "I'll give you a minute," he says to Simms. To Annis he says, "You go on in, young lady."

When the door closes behind her, she approaches the desk. The room is windowless and stuffy. The only light is from two lamps on the desk that cast a glow on Simms' bald pate. What looks like an account book is spread before him. His shirt sleeves are rolled to his elbows.

Time ticks. The only sound is the director's pencil against the ledger, and she realizes Simms has no intention of giving her his focus. She wonders fleetingly if he's really forgotten her or if it's another of his schemes to belittle those who cross his path.

She sighs and clenches her fists. "Ben's leg is healing well, sir." How it grates to call him sir. "He'll be able to come back to work in—"

"I told you," Simms interjects without looking up. "There's no job for your brother to come back to. He's been replaced."

He'd told her as much the afternoon following Ben's accident when she'd come to him in earnest. *Stagehands are a dime a dozen. This city is full of men who need work.*

She takes a step closer to the desk and clasps her hands in front of her to keep them from shaking. "You'll need a set designer for your next play, sir. Ben could design the backdrops again." It's a lie, of course. She'd done the drawings, but Simms doesn't know that.

"I don't rehire. You don't show, you're off the payroll for good."

Annis has prepared for this. She licks her lips. "I could take Ben's place. As a stagehand."

This brings his attention from the desk. He fixes her with a hard stare. "A stagehand."

27

"Yes, sir."

"You."

She smooths her cloak and straightens her spine. "I'm strong. I can do it."

"I do not employ females backstage."

She manages a smile though her heart begins to race. "There's no time like the present." She clears her throat. "Sir."

His eyes rake over her, taking in every detail, and she feels like she's being skinned. "No theatre in this city employs women backstage. I don't wish, nor do I have any reason, to be the first." Simms' eyes drop to the floor. The snow she's tracked in is melting on the carpet. The hole on the outside of her left boot is visible, displaying her dingy stocking within. Her cheeks burn. "If you need employment, try the mills." He makes a shooing motion and turns back to his desk.

She swallows and shuffles in her boots. "I can design the sets, sir. Even paint the backdrops if you like." She has half a mind to tell him the truth—that it's her designs he's using now—but decides against it. He won't like that Ben lied, even if the outcome had suited him and his production. "I have artistic skill, too. As good as Ben. I can show you some sketches to prove it."

Two of them are folded in her cloak pocket: the theatre's façade and Washington Park. Carefully chosen to show her range: architectural and landscape. She considered bringing her sketch of Ben but thought better of it, considering Simms' low opinion of her brother.

He turns to her again, his expression curious. He bares his teeth in a grin and barks a laugh, slapping his thigh as though she's told him a jape. "Oh, that's rich. You think I'd hire you—a slip of a girl—as a set designer." He knuckles a tear from his eye. "Oh, Miss Hargrave. That's quite the *bon mot*."

He knows she is serious. How can he not? She is only a game to him, her pleas for employment a joke he'll forget—or worse, retell—as soon as she's gone. To think, she'd deliberately chosen Christmas Eve for her visit, thinking he would be more charitable.

"I don't see the humor in it, sir." She regrets the words as soon as they're out. They're too much like a challenge. Simms is the sort to come at from the side with deference or flattery. Direct words are a threat to a man who prides himself on always having the upper hand.

The smile slides from his face and his eyes grow stony. "You're right in that. This is no laughing matter. Women don't belong backstage. I don't hire women *period*, unless they act and only then if they are consummate professionals. You, design the flats? Do you take me for an imbecile? I wager you're as gifted at painting as I am at tatting lace."

The insult lands in her gut but she soldiers on. "I could sell tickets at the door," she says, hating herself for wheedling. "When Ben is better, he can replace—"

His chair squeaks when he leans back in it and he crosses a knee over the other. "Did you happen to read the review the morning after opening night?"

She had not. When Ben had awakened in pain at the clinic, the play had been the furthest thing from her mind. She senses he knows she hasn't read it. He's just toying with her, a cat batting a mouse.

The director rests an elbow on the arm of his chair and places his pointer finger against his temple. "Mr. Gladstone gave us a flattering review. High marks to the actors, the drama, the way the audience reacted perfectly at the right moments. Imagine my delight at reading his column, Miss Hargrave. That is, until I got to the part in which he wrote that the performance was marred only by the change of scene for the final act when the flat quivered, and I quote, 'like gelatin in the wind.'"

The air in the office is over-warm and it's hard to breathe. In her mind's eye, she sees the backdrop wobble, feels again her fear that it would topple. But it hadn't. Ben had set it straight, and by the time the lights came up...

Simms stands. He's of middling height. She's as tall as he is, yet the way he glares at her, she is swallowed whole. "Let me say this clearly, Miss Hargrave, so your little ears take it in. Your brother was replaced weeks ago, the day after he found himself under the hooves of that horse. I won't hire him again and I will never employ you. For anything. Now," he jabs his finger and steps toward her, "take yourself back through that door. If you enter this theatre again for any reason, I'll have you and your clumsy brother thrown out."

# SIGHTING

## PHILADELPHIA, DECEMBER 1841

The sun is hidden behind dark clouds when Annis returns to the street. All the way home, she fashions retorts she should've hurled back at Simms. *You self-important thug. You're not fit to clean Ben's boots! Don't shout at me, you cur. You wouldn't last a minute in the New York houses!*

She spies a portly man in a woolen tailcoat and beaver depart a coffeehouse and pitch his newspaper into a bin. When she's sure no one is looking, she scuttles to it, snatches the paper, and thrusts it inside her cloak.

By the time she's almost home, she's worked herself into a lather over Simms' churlishness. She takes a deep breath and brings her attention to the street. She needs to focus. This stretch of Seventh, five blocks from the city, is dangerous. It's dingy even in the snow. The streets branching off it aren't as wide, the houses listing and grim. Their rooms in a narrow lane between Pine and Lombard are a stone's throw from the poorest section in the city, aptly named the Infected District due to the overcrowded tenements where pestilence and disease fester. Still, the people living just outside its border live as meanly as she and Ben. The only difference is their neighbors have no qualms about working in the mills. Not if it means a roof over their heads and food on the table. The hypocrisy of it digs at her. She and Ben are no better than these people. They only balk because they'd once known a different life. A better one.

But it's gone and they'll never have it back.

At the corner, she takes a right onto Addison. Her steps slow. Two women walk in her direction on the other side of the street. Abreast of them on the opposite side, a man approaches. She's never been the victim of a mugging, but she's heard they often work in packs. Might these three be angling to take her purse? It's tucked deep inside her skirt pocket (with little money in it), but she braces herself. For exactly what she doesn't know. Her comfortable life in New York never prepared her for things like this. Should she fight? Run? Scream for help? But the women only glance at her and return to their conversation. The man continues to amble toward her, his tattered coat visible even in the weak light. His eyes—canny, narrowed, almost cruel —do not leave hers. Her heart scuds. She crosses the street to avoid him and he is soon past.

Annis' breath fogs the air. There is no one on the street. The crunch of her boots is amplified in the stillness. Pewter clouds low enough to touch cast an unnatural darkness to the atmosphere even though it's not yet noon. She knows just what watercolors to mix to make that gray—Chinese White with a dab of Payne's Gray. Or perhaps Black Lead mixed liberally with Chinese White. Then again, perhaps a bit of—

Movement two row houses down. Her thoughts disperse like pigeons to the air. A woman: she can see the bell shape of her skirts, those billowy sleeves. Oddly, she is hatless. Her bright blonde hair, parted in the middle and styled in loops at the ears, startles against the drab background. Odder still, she wears no cloak. Too poor, perhaps, to afford one but then the cut of her dress suggests otherwise. As Annis watches, her skirts appear to undulate—waving, moving—though the woman herself doesn't stir.

Annis stops in her tracks.

The woman in blue is staring right at her.

She can see the street through her bodice, the fall of her skirts. Her slippers hover a few inches off the ground. The fine details of her face are blurry, as if seen through a mist. The specter's lips move, and Annis thinks for a moment she will speak. But when that black maw opens, there is only silence.

The figure lifts her arm as if to reach for her, and Annis' blood turns to ice. Panic shoots through her. With a jolt, she springs sideways making a wide arc—heart pumping, feet fighting for purchase to avoid falling—until she is past and at her building. In an instant, she's racing up the three steps to the entrance and, once inside, shooting up the stairs the next. At the top of the landing, her boots slide on the boards, and she almost collides with the door to their lodgings. In one frantic motion, she pushes it open, scurries inside, and shoots the bolt. She leans back against the jamb with her eyes squeezed shut, pulls air into her lungs, and feels an eerie familiarity clamber over her bones.

She hasn't seen the woman in blue since that night weeks ago. Here in this very room. It's the same woman; she knows this with certainty. There is no mistaking—or forgetting—that face. There can be only two explanations: either her mind is playing tricks on her again, or the woman was really there and very real.

"What's the matter?"

Annis jumps. Ben sits at the kitchen table, his bound leg propped on a chair, a worn blanket thrown over his lap. His eyes are alert.

She works to calm her breathing as she takes in the room. There is no sign of the—what *did* she see? An apparition, a ghost, a phantom? *I've imagined her again. I'm overtired. Angry and overtired.* "Nothing."

"Is someone after you?" Ben reaches for the crutch against the wall.

When she'd left him, he'd still been asleep. He's taken great pains to dress himself. The binding doesn't lend itself to easy maneuverability. She can see in his expression that he's been anxious for her return, eager to hear how her meeting went with Simms. Proud, perhaps, to show her he could rise and attend to himself, something he hasn't been able to do since the accident.

She comes to him and places a hand on his shoulder to still him. "No. There's no need to get up." For a moment, she imagines telling him the truth. *I thought I saw the ghost of someone I watched die before we left New York.* But it's too much. He'll think she's crazy. And if she tells him everything, what would he think if he knew what she'd done, or more aptly, what she'd failed to do?

She goes to the window. One story below, snow coats the pavement. Footprints have disturbed the snow where neighbors have quit their lodgings, but the stoop a few doors down where the woman in blue was standing is free of prints.

"You were running from someone," Ben says. "I've never seen you take the steps like that."

"There was a sour-looking man on the street," she says without turning. "I thought he might grab my purse." Not the whole truth, but not a lie either. "He's gone now."

"This blasted binding. I wish I could've gone with you."

Annis turns and approaches the table, ruffles his hair, and works her face into a semblance of relaxed ease. "Don't look so glum. Nothing came of it." She hangs her cloak on a peg and runs her hands over her upper arms. It's cold as a stone in the kitchen. No fire in the hearth. They decided to save the day's wood for Christmas Day when they will unwrap their presents to each other. She places the kettle on the stove and stokes the firebox with a poker. Fortunately, there's still enough heat to warm the water, though that's all it will be—warm. She opens the tin of tea. There's enough to last through the new year, but only just. She'll reuse the leaves from her morning cup and add in a few fresh ones for Ben. The sighting of the woman has left her shaking, and she needs something to occupy her hands.

"He told you off, didn't he?" A crease mars Ben's forehead. "That's why you're acting so strange."

She considers him. It pains her he's lost so much flesh since the accident. His face is thinner, his cheekbones sharper. The weather has turned colder too, and he hasn't been outside to walk with his crutches like Dr. Mütter advised. Annis has forbidden it, frightened Ben would slip on the ice or catch a chill. Tip him further into the need for medical care they can't afford.

"I need to look for work, Ben. We can't wait much longer."

"Simms won't rehire me then?"

"No. But we expected that."

"So he's not interested in set design either."

She spoons a little fresh tea over the used leaves in the small mesh basket and places it in the teapot. "He wouldn't hear of it." She can't bring herself to tell him that Simms threatened to throw them out of the theatre if they return. She can't keep everything from him, but she can hide the worst of it.

"I'll go to him—"

She whirls and squeezes his wrist. "*No.*" It comes out stronger than she intended, and she tries again. "No. Simms won't help us. We're on our own." Annis has had her fill of that odious man today and changes the subject. "I managed to get a newspaper on my way home. I'll look through the postings. There might be something just right for me." She smiles, willing him to believe her put-on cheer. She's been looking for months, plucking papers from bins outside Independence Hall, tea and coffee shops where the swells of the city read their daily news.

The carpet weaving factories, breweries, and foundries were less likely to hire women, but the flour, cotton, and paper mills would. There were, of course, no ads for female artists. Had she really thought there would be? If only Mother, instead of schooling her in the wifely arts of embroidery and flower arranging, had the foresight to train her in useful skills—like dressmaking or teaching—she might have found work by now.

But the mills would take her in a flash. And Ben, too, once he's healed. The mill owners think nothing of working their employees to the bone. How many times had she heard their father speak of the children of New York hired for such work, only for them to be spat out later, broken and aged beyond their years? When they arrived in Philadelphia, she scoured the papers, knowing their money wouldn't last. She read of the sixty-three-cent-a-day unskilled worker pay. *Starvation wages* the papers called it. The coal-heavers, the iron workers, the sugar refinery men, the woolen hosiery and carpet makers. No, there wasn't a shortage of jobs in Philadelphia, just well-paid ones that didn't exploit laborers.

She refused to allow Ben to take such work. It would be too brutal, too cruel. And they weren't destitute. Not yet. Thankfully, he'd found a position at the theatre and changed their luck. But there's nothing for it now. Come January, she'll likely be a millworker and Ben, once he mended, would follow soon after.

It's as though her brother has read her mind. "Not the mills."

She snatches up the kettle and pours the water in the teapot, then takes a seat across from him. "We can't afford to be picky, Ben."

"Dr. Mütter said I could look for work come February. It'll come sooner than you think. I'll try the other theatres. They'll hire me and then we'll have money for meat."

Annis doesn't reply. She wonders if he believes it or he's putting on a good front for her. Lord knows she does it for him. It's not even January. February seems a lifetime away.

She pours his tea into a chipped cup and watches him take a sip. They haven't been able to afford milk or sugar for the last month. She decides to forgo her own cup and runs a finger around the rim. They have only the two teacups, a couple of jam jars, a pot, and a smattering of plates and eating utensils.

Annis suspects she's been cheated by the pawnshops where she'd sold their mother's jewelry. Those shrewd men had seen a young girl in need of cash and what had she to say about whether their prices were fair or not? There'd been no time to haggle anyway; they had needed to get out of New York.

She sold Mother's onyx choker and bracelet for rail tickets, valises, and clothing. The matching white pearl necklace, bracelet, and earrings paid the rent of their modest accommodation—a tiny kitchen, sitting area, and two tiny bedrooms—for a slew of months. There was enough left over to purchase a second-hand table with two chairs, kitchen items, a small couch that needed reupholstering, bed frames and mattresses. It had cost more than she'd imagined, even second-hand, and Ben's wages at the theatre barely made a dent.

"If it's warmer tomorrow, I want you to get some air," Annis says, replenishing his cup. "I'll take you down the street and back. It will be good for your leg, good for your blood." In the ensuring silence she hears Ben's stomach growl. She rises from the table.

"I can wait," he says. "It's early yet."

She cuts a thick slice of bread from a day-old loaf and places it in front of him. He needs nourishment to grow, to heal, and she can't even afford to buy butter. Her eyes sting with tears as she drops into her chair again.

His fingers on her hand still her and she blinks up at him.

"Don't sell it," he says. "The blue pearl. We still have some money left, don't we?"

"The rent is paid but we need wood and candles. And food, of course. If we're stingy, we'll have enough to last until the first of the year. But, Ben, the longer I wait to find a job—"

"I know. The sooner you'll have to sell the pearl."

---

They spend Christmas Day before the fire while snow falls outside. Mrs. King, one floor above, is good enough to drop by a small fig pudding they savor like gold. Annis is sorry they don't have anything to give in return. Besides the rest of the bread, a boiled potato (split between them) and tea, it is all they have. After the meal, they stretch in the kitchen chairs before the fire. Ben hands her a small parcel wrapped in newsprint. Buried within is a wooden figure he has whittled in her likeness. It's roughly six inches high and polished smooth. He's fashioned her hair in a neat bun, her best dress with the bell sleeves, her boot tips peaking from beneath her skirt.

"Oh, Ben," she says. "However did you find the time to do it?"

"Time? It's all I have these days, Annis."

"No, I mean how did you do it without me noticing? I had no idea."

He looks sheepish and shrugs thin shoulders. "You sleep like a bear. Snore too." He grins and she playfully punches his arm. "You'll have to paint it yourself. That's your skill, not mine."

"It's your turn." She slides a sheet of paper from a shelf in the kitchen and hands it to him. It's the sketch of him she's been working on, his face slightly in profile. She'd finished sketching it weeks ago and added color while sitting at the kitchen table when Ben napped during the day, exhausted from the ache of his leg.

"It looks just like me," Ben says. He holds it beside his face. "Which is the real one?" She punches him again and they laugh. His voice is soft as he brushes the paper with his fingers. "You have such talent. I wish... I hope someday you'll be able to paint as you like. When I find a good job, I'll buy you the finest paints money can buy."

When he looks at her with that boyish grin, she finds she has nothing to say and looks away.

She'd told Ben they had to leave New York because there were too many memories of their parents there, that they needed to start afresh, and he'd believed her. He knows nothing of the real reason they'd fled so quickly. She must keep it from him, for if he knew, he would despise her.

# THE MAGICIAN
## NEW YORK CITY, AUGUST 1841

Gabriel looks into the mirror. He doesn't recognize the fiend staring back. The scar on his cheek is a long vertical cord of angry puckered flesh. He briefly considered, in the days he lay fevered and healing, using face paint to mask it, but there was no veiling the raised tissue. He peers closer, turns his good cheek to the glass, and there he is, his old self. A man without blemish. He has retained a full head of black hair in his thirty-seventh year and there is no sign of it thinning. His eyes, a deep ebony, are so dark the irises are indistinguishable from the pupils. They are, he thinks, his most striking feature.

He swivels in the mirror again and the brute is back, conjured like one of his tricks. He smiles, displaying a pair of pointed eye teeth that call to mind a wolf. Perhaps he will use his disfigurement as part of his act. A two-faced Janus. Here, on one side, a charmer of audiences. Here, a beast.

The sneer fades when he considers the strangers who have caught a glimpse of him in the streets and shrunk back in horror. He is a spectacle still, but of an altogether different sort. He is no longer a skilled illusionist who turns handkerchiefs into doves.

He is someone to be feared. Despised.

Without a mask he cannot hide what is now, he thinks with a stab of fury, a part of him.

His mind whirs back to that pivotal night in his cellar: the terror in his assistant's eyes, the pleas that only served to whet his appetite. But it was his final act that brought him the release he hungered for.

But not for long. They hadn't been alone. That dirty wench had witnessed everything. That she had followed them, traced their steps in silence, required a deviousness he hadn't seen in her.

But the joke was on him, was it not? He, a gallant rescuer of souls, a man who took young ladies—alone, without family or prospects—off the streets and made them part of the magic he spun before astonished crowds. He made them special. He made them *stars*.

But, in time, they deceived him. Every last one.

There was something about the stage that brought out the corruption in them. Before long, each face—so pure at first—took on the ravaged countenance of a trollop, made plain all the more in the flood of the stage lights. Underneath the pretty faces, the veneer of charm and respectability, lurked their true natures. They revealed themselves soon enough. Did they think he wouldn't notice?

A familiar bitterness sweeps through him. All women are immoral. Creatures of deception. As lewd and sinful as Eve. He'd learned as much from his own filthy tramp of a mother.

*That worthless, diseased bag of bones.*

His vision dims and he is seized with vertigo. He has been living in a frenzy, eating irregularly and drinking more. The desk and the bed beside it pitch. The floor undulates. When the room settles a moment later, it is the whiskey that beckons. Only it has the power to calm him. He splashes a finger into a glass, knocks it back, and wipes his mouth with his sleeve.

He must focus. All depends upon it. The bitch had cut him, sliced him open like a ripe melon. In that one desperate thrust she had ruined everything.

If he is to find her, he must use every ounce of his intellect.

The weeks have slid to months. His room is little more than a cesspit off a blackened alley in the filthiest part of the city. He doesn't trust the hag running the boarding house. Her eyes are too curious. He hasn't had a proper bath in weeks. Ah, but to have a maidservant.

No, he needs a whore. Someone on whom he can sate his desires. It's been far too long.

His crotch tightens and he thinks of the wench: her honey-colored hair, the perfect bud of her mouth. It's not lost on him how he relishes his need to both possess and destroy her, wants her for his own yet loathes her in equal measure.

He pulls on his frock coat and downs another shot of whiskey. Then he is stepping out the door, steadying himself on the jamb before he staggers into the night. The moon is a smudge tucked behind a veil of clouds, but it is enough to light his way. He brings up the lapels of his coat to shield his face, a reflex in the months he's been hiding.

He's walked no more than a block when he sees two tarts leaning against the wall of the alley. When they spy him, they saunter his way, beckoning him with the sway of their hips.

"Evening, sir," the taller of the two says. She's nothing more than shadows, but the smell of her—body odor mingled with cheap perfume—hits like a clout.

"Some company tonight?" the other says, sidling up. "No need to pick. A nickel for us both."

The moon comes out, spills over them like milk, and he sees neither of them are young: hollow cheeks, thin lips bracketed by lines. Too old then for a bawdy house and almost certainly diseased. The second reaches for him and he shrinks away.

"Aw, will you look at that, Polly," she says. "We've a shy one." She takes a step closer. Her voice is as rough as a crone's, coarse from hard living. Just as his mother's had been. "We knows just how to take the edge off. We'll make you feel right."

Gabriel will not waste another minute with these filthy strumpets. He makes to step around them, but they misread him and start to laugh.

"Is you a virgin, sir?" the tall one called Polly asks with a giggle. "No shame in it. Though it's a rarity in these parts." She laughs again, and he can hear the loose sputum in the back of her throat.

Revulsion moves through him. It reminds him of his mother, that sound. She was always poorly, racked by cough. He blinks away the memory and finds the other woman leering up at him. She's missing a tooth. "Oy, maybe he's a queer one, Poll. Prefers your own kind, does you then?"

There is a resounding crunch as his fist connects with her nose. The crone wheels back but manages to keep her footing. Gabriel's knuckles smart and he glowers down at them. He is a great illusionist. They aren't fit to scrape the shit from his boots.

"You bastard," Polly shrieks. "You broke 'er nose!"

The moon is still out. He lowers his collar and gives them a good look at his scar. "Beat it or I'll do worse." They stumble back, then pitch into a run.

He wends his way west toward the Hudson River, past crowded taverns and cheap lodging houses. The farther he goes, the stronger the reek of sewage. Brick buildings give way to listing wooden structures and pavements scattered with trash. As he nears the wharf, the odor of decaying fish brings memories that flash: bodies wrapped in burlap, the soft splash as they entered the water.

He'd done his best by them. They had only themselves to blame.

So far has his star risen, it is a shock to him at times that he came from this world. That the squalor and starvation were the beats of his first sixteen years. Once he realized he needed to cut the ties that tethered him—and oh, how freeing *that* had been—his life had begun anew. He shrugged off his old existence like a filthy garment and replaced it with a new one. It took time, but he rebuilt himself, each rendition better than the last. And now, if it weren't for the wench, he'd still be living on custard and fine wine, mystifying audiences with ease.

His mind slips away to a decade-old memory: Augustus. His mentor, his friend. Seated regally in his royal-blue frock coat, the firelight playing on his ridged cheekbones and graying beard. A cold, cold evening and the remnants of a roast duck picked clean between them. Gabriel feels it then, the old horror sliding into place. That night still lives within him and he despises it. His life had been a prologue up to then, and afterwards? His life really *began*. Gabriel closes his eyes and when he opens them again, he is himself.

He steps around a cluster of barrels and sees movement in his periphery. A man in a sailor's hat pisses against a wall, his body teetering from drink. A loud belch followed by humming threads the air.

*Fool.*

It is dangerous here, black as pitch when the moon vanishes. Any unsuspecting soul is easy pickings for ruffians. He wouldn't put it past the thugs who roam here to use the man as a ruse to distract him. But Gabriel is no buffoon. The foulness of the air has roused him, the haze of the whiskey thinned with each step. He thumbs the handle of the blade in his trouser pocket, poised to use it at the slightest provocation.

The brothel is tucked off an alley, situated where seamen

looking for entertainment can find it easily. He'd happened upon it a week ago during one of his nocturnal ramblings. The neighborhood alone deems the harlots far below the quality he's used to—another thing the wench has taken from him. He can no longer frequent his regular haunts. He must be careful. The police are surely hunting him.

A woman—presumably the madam—is seated at a desk in the entryway.

"May I help you?"

Gabriel steps towards her, doing his best to hide his face. His hat is pulled low, his collar up, his scarred cheek averted. He searches for something in her expression that conveys she is working with the law. It would be clever of the authorities to employ a madam or two to help ferret out a French magician. For this reason, he's dropped the fake accent.

"I have someone particular in mind," he says.

"Oh? You've been here before? I don't recognize you."

"I've just arrived in town. Maud's was highly recommended." A lie, but better to play to her vanity so she will give him what he wants.

His words have the desired effect. Her lips curl. Her teeth are good, but she is past her prime: hair too red to be natural, cheeks rouged to convey youth. Still, the swell of her breasts in her low cut bodice is not unappealing. "You've come to the right place. Maud at your service."

She offers her hand and, with carefully concealed disgust, he deposits a tiny kiss on a gloved wrist. "I require a young girl, not more than sixteen or seventeen. Skin like cream. Hair neither blonde nor brown. The color of honey." A pull in his crotch. How the memory of her undoes him.

With a nod, Maud excuses herself to find who he is looking for. In another minute, he is following her down a narrow corridor where behind a door, a young girl waits. It excites him to think what he has in store for her.

For now, he will abide a substitute. But he will find her. He's already begun his search. The method of tracking her down came upon him in a flash, as much of his inspiration does.

So simple in the end.

Before long the wench will be his.

# COSMORAMAS AND CURIOSITIES
## NEW YORK CITY, MARCH 1841

Five months earlier

The omnibus is crowded and over-warm, even for a chilly March afternoon. Annis' window seat affords her a view, if not protection from the pungent aromas issuing from a few riders. A combination of musty wool, sweat, and something sharp she imagines is whiskey or gin. A man in a filthy brown coat turns in his seat and meets her gaze, a stare as strong as touch. His face is hardened from the sun, his hair unkempt. She drops her eyes, her cheeks heating. This is what comes from her willful nature. These teeming streets are a far cry from their respectable middle-class home in Greenwich Village. What else did she expect?

If her mother knew she was here without a chaperon she would punish her severely, not least with her acerbic tongue. She should be at her mother's sickbed, not spending time enjoying herself. But she needs a break from the bleakness at home and today—at least a part of it—is hers. There's nothing that's going to spoil it.

The omnibus turns onto Broadway and passes an upholstery shop, a furniture warehouse, the branch of the British College of Medicine with its long bank of curtained windows flanked by shudders of hibiscus blue. Two women emerge from a wig and curl shop, batting away a dog who sniffs their skirts then dashes off. The rude ogler notwithstanding, she wonders why she's never ventured out on her own before. She doesn't need a destination to amuse her; the cog of the city is enough. The people, the smells. And the *sounds*. Hooves striking cobblestones, the clatter of wheels, the cry of vendors. Who would have thought that for ten cents a ride, an omnibus could provide such a show of vigor. Of *life*.

The conveyance slows the farther south they progress, the grids of busy intersections thick as molasses. The rude man alights at Reed Street, and she relaxes. At the next block, the lush green of City Hall Park stretches to her left. In the distance, the spire of St. Paul's pierces the heavens like a dagger. The omnibus stops at Ann Street, and Annis jostles off with several other passengers.

Just across the way is a four-story building proclaiming itself in bright yellow letters SCUDDER'S AMERICAN MUSEUM. A small line has formed at the entrance. Before she loses her nerve, she dashes across Broadway. At the door a signboard proclaims:

OVER 150,000
Natural and Foreign CURIOSITIES!
ANTIQUITIES and Productions of the FINE ARTS!
OPEN FOR PUBLIC VIEWING!
FANTASTICAL SHOWS
including
LA GRANDE MARVEILLE and the LEVITATING LADY!

She waits outside, standing between two gentlemen and a young family of five, and is soon through the door. Inside, a portly man with ginger side whiskers stands behind a counter selling tickets. She waits for her turn in line, then drops fifteen cents into his palm. He hands her a green stub and gestures to a wide doorway with a sign above it announcing the entrance to the first hall.

As it's a Saturday afternoon, the hall is crowded. Still, it's evident it's well-appointed in handsome dark wood that stretches from floor to ceiling. Behind glass cabinets and curious cages, animals of every kind stare back. They've been stuffed with such skill, it is only their immovability that declares them lifeless. Some are perched on branches, others on the ground. Many are poised as if in flight, running, or simply resting.

She moves on, her attention drawn to an enormous bird. It's taller than she is. Its body cavity is as big as a laundry copper, its legs and neck comically long and narrow. *The African ostrich is noted for its stupidity*, she reads. *When it decides to conceal itself, it plunges its head into the sand*. She claps a hand to her mouth and smiles.

She weaves through the crowd, wondering at the craftsmanship, the meticulous details of armadillos, moles, gophers, and sloths. How the taxidermist must set to his work as seriously as she takes to her own sketches and watercolors.

She ascends the stairway to the second hall. Awaiting her are displays of butterflies, owls, a leopard and, surprise of surprises, an elephant. Oh, how huge its ears, how princely its tusks.

Time suspends. On the third floor, people stand around a low glass case. A snake twists along the bottom and the crowd murmurs. *Eighteen-foot Burmese Python, weighing over 200 pounds*. Its pink tongue flicks as it moves, its eyes mere slits.

The next creature isn't living, but she finds it far more

remarkable. Standing inside a small cage is a lamb with two heads. Annis marvels at its tiny hooves, its large brown eyes (of glass, she is certain). *The two-headed animal is the sign of a bad omen. This rare phenomenon isn't just a curse on nature, but to all who look upon it.* A laugh bubbles up in her throat. The imagination of Mr. Scudder and his museum!

She steps to a guillotine. Its wooden frame is empty save for the blade at bottom that rests on the neck of a woman in repose. Strapped to a narrow platform, the lady is clad in a gold brocade gown, her head adorned by a powdered wig. Her terror is so evident, Annis half expects her head to drop into the leather basket beside it. How vulgar the display, yet she is unable to look away. It's the very grisliness of it—the thin red line at the woman's throat—that attracts her.

On the other side of the display, a man with dark hair meets her eyes. Her glance is only a brief one, but she registers the fine quality of his burgundy frock coat and the curl of his mustache before she moves away.

She's reached a set of broad windows where a series of mirrors hang in handsome gilt frames. Small round convex ones reflect the room behind her and feel like passageways to another life. The largest is vertical and full length with angled mirrors at each side. *The reflecting mirror affords the viewer the desirable but uncommon advantage of seeing his or herself as others see him.* Annis steps closer. Her coat and bonnet of sapphire blue draw out the same color in her eyes. The honey curls at her ears are just visible beneath the brim of her hat.

In the side mirrors she sees what the placard references: herself as others see her. And what does she see? That her small, upturned nose is like her mother's and she is tall, taller than she would wish, and—

A figure steps behind her and their eyes meet in the looking glass. She whirls. It's the man from the guillotine display. Her heart thuds. She feels caught out, vulnerable without a chaperon. Her thoughts flash. It is unseemly to be approached in such a way, for a strange man to stand so close.

He makes a deep bow. "Pardon me, madame. I did not mean to startle you."

His words are laced with a thick French accent. He is perhaps thirty or thirty-five years of age. She marks again the fine cut of his coat with its buttons of gleaming gold. A white rose peeks from his breast pocket.

"You didn't startle me." A lie, but she can already feel her fear evaporating. He isn't the poorly dressed man on the omnibus who'd stared, but a gentleman.

He raises dark brows. "No? *Tres bien*. I could not live knowing that I frightened such a fine lady. May I introduce myself? My name is Gabriel Marchand." He smiles. A flash of white teeth. He takes her gloved hand and raises it to his lips.

The license of it. Annis blushes to the roots of her hair. He had called her madame. A lady. She stands up straighter. Perhaps she's older than she looks. Why not? She could be twenty or twenty-one. For a fleeting moment she wonders how to conduct herself the way an older woman might and comes up with nothing. She's no good at this. She bites her lip and wonders how to excuse herself.

"You are enjoying Scudder's Museum, *oui*? It is a marvel, is it not?"

"Yes, sir. I mean, yes. It is. There are many wonders here."

He raises an ebony walking stick and points to the wall behind her. "I find the reflecting mirrors quite illuminating. I could not help but notice your own interest." Marchand steps forward and indicates a mirror next to the vertical one. "Come, tell me what you see."

She positions herself before the mirror. To her astonishment, she is not herself. Her reflection is... warped. Her head is elongated, her nose and mouth a vertical smear. Her body is thin as a toothpick though at the bottom, her ankles bow out like balloons. She goes up on her toes and back down. Her body warbles, and she laughs. "What sort of mirror is this?" The placard is no help. It merely reads, *A Masquerade Mirror*.

Marchand's face in the glass is as twisted as her own, his eyes dark pools. "It is a distorting mirror. Its surface is curved in places, *oui*? Not so flat as it appears. If you have been to a *carnaval*, you might see a looking glass such as this. It is great fun to imagine oneself in such a way. Because we know, naturally, that this mirror reveals what we are not."

"What we are not?" She's not sure she's following him.

Marchand nods, his black shoulder-length hair falling forward. "Twisted. Disfigured." He steps closer and breathes into her hair. "Vile."

He smiles in the mirror, his teeth elongated. There is something about them that calls to mind a wolf. She swallows, the fancy gone, and lowers her eyes. "Thank you for introducing me to the masquerade mirror, Mr. Marchand," she says with more courage than she feels. "I must find my family." She bids him goodbye and heads for the stairs.

Running a hand along the banister, she climbs, aware of a slight tremor in her limbs. The final hall is what she's come to see—Scudder's collection of art and something called 'cosmoramas.' At the top of the stairs, an arrow directs her through a doorway into another large salon. Artwork adorns every surface. From gold frames, famous personages stare back at her.

She pauses before a small oil on wood by Raphael. *Saint George and the Dragon c.*1506. She admires the verdant trees, the glinting armor of the soldier, the cape that bellows in tufts behind him. How is it Raphael managed to add such texture, such depth? She is suddenly overwhelmed by despair. She will never be instructed the way Raphael would've been in his day, apprenticed to a master artist.

She remembers Papa's efforts to keep her dream alive, the precious paper, charcoals, and tube paints he would give her on her birthdays and Christmas. He'd even hired Miss Hutchinson to instruct her once a week in the art of sketching and painting. Though he'd only thought her drawing a hobby he could foster, he'd believed in her. Mother, on the other hand, was a different kettle of fish. When Papa died, she had put Annis' lessons to an end. She'd thought her daughter's aspirations a ridiculous delusion.

With a sigh, Annis moves along the wall, her eye landing on an enormous canvas ahead. It's a painting, but it must be at least forty feet long and over eight feet high! This must be the cosmorama. Several patrons stroll along it, looking into curious lenses placed here and there. A sign proclaims it to be the Chateau Versailles. Across the room against the opposite wall is another vast canvas, the chateau's gardens. She places her eye against the nearest lens. The image depicts a magnified perspective of the fountain in the foreground of the palace, so enlarged she can see the tiny ripples on the surface. Oh, the play of blues that shapes the water! At this level, she can see the strokes of the brush, the way the artist worked the details that, taken in at a greater distance, all but disappear.

She moves down the canvas, waiting for her turn to see through each lens. Some are so high there are steps up to them. When at last she comes to the end, she works her way down the other canvas, marveling at both the intricacy in which the chateau's gardens were designed, and the way the painter used, if she's not mistaken, French Green, Rose Madder, and Indian Yellow to create the plants and flowers.

It is more than just casual viewing. She is *learning*.

As she passes into the hallway, she sees a signboard for the lecture hall. Standing beside it is Mr. Marchand. At the sight of her, his brows arch. "Ah, my distorted friend," he says. She nods, walking past him before he can detain her. "One moment, *s'il vous plait.*"

She turns. He is standing so composed, so gentleman-like, she can't help but smile. After all, he's given her no reason to be discourteous. "Yes?"

"I have something for you." He reaches behind her ear and when he withdraws his hand, he opens it to reveal a red carnation in his palm.

Her mouth drops open. "How...?"

"Ah, you see, we parted too soon." He swirls his hand. When he opens it again, the flower is gone. "I am a man of great marvels." With his walking stick, he taps the signboard beside him.

Now Appearing
LA GRANDE MERVEILLE!
Don't Miss the Master of Magic
Shows Daily on the Even Hour

Below the words is an illustration of Marchand, his mustache crimped into two sharp curls, his walking stick brandished like a sword.

"You're a magician."

"Bah. 'Magician.' Such a limiting word. You have before you, madame, La Grande Merveille." He bows. Once again, his hand comes up to her ear, and when he pulls it back, a small piece of paper rests in his palm. He inclines his head. "Take it, please. It won't bite."

It's a reproduction of the signboard with ONE FREE ADMISSION stamped at the bottom.

"Monsieur Scudder insists I give away a few free tickets to

whomever I choose, *oui*?" He shrugs. "If you don't like the show, you have paid nothing. If you do, well, then I have astounded you with my marvels."

She peers down at the ticket. It's harmless enough, but she needs to get home. "Thank you. You're very kind."

He nods. "You may come any day. Rain or shine."

She turns to go, but he lays a gentle hand on her wrist. "You forgot something, madame."

Her brow furrows. What can he mean? She expects him to magic something from her ear again, but he only smiles.

"You haven't told me your name."

She hesitates for a moment. "Annis. Annis Hargrave."

"Ah, Miss Hargrave. Have a lovely day. And do send my regards to your," and here he leans in and winks, "family."

# BAUBLES

## NEW YORK CITY, MARCH 1841

That afternoon, Annis sits on a chair next to her mother's bed. The room is stifling, the air giving off a faint scent of malaise—fusty linen, the sweet smell of laudanum the camphor doesn't quite mask. The curtains are closed. Gaslight flickers from wall sconces on each side of the bed, casting shadows across her mother's ravaged face.

"Would you like some sunlight, Mother, or perhaps some fresh air?" She's only been in the chair an hour and already it seems like an age.

Her mother looks askance. "How many times must I tell you? The sun isn't good for my eyes. It gives me a headache."

Propped against downy pillows, her mother stares with dull eyes, the bruise-like circles bracketing them a sign she's been too liberal with the laudanum. Annis suspects it's to blame for her head pain but says nothing. She can scarcely believe a year ago her mother was still directing servants and making social calls. It was a small miracle her vitality returned after the sudden death of Annis' father from the Panic of '37.

Her heart skips the way it always does when she thinks of him. Gone four years, nearly to the day. The financial crash that throttled the city destroyed his stationer's business. He died at home of a heart attack that spring. One of the servants found him seated at the breakfast table, head to one side as if he'd drifted off to sleep. The front page of the morning paper lay before him. With its lurid headline of the crash, the words had as good as reached out and squeezed his heart until it beat no more.

His death was a blow to them all, but her mother took it the worst. The fire in her died. She rarely left the house. She faded to a ghost, drowning in melancholy. The house grew quiet, and she refused visitors. Eventually, after a span of months, she recovered and came back to them. Her mother's voice (so cultured with its British accent), her laughter, her pianoforte music flowed through the house again.

She approached life with a new vigor, bought gowns and satin slippers for herself and Annis; shirts, trousers, and caps for Ben. She refurbished the front parlor: hung new wallpaper, bought new furniture upholstered in bright pinks and burgundies, sat for an artist to have her portrait painted that now holds court above the mantel. While Annis was relieved to see her mother brought back from the cliff of grief, she wondered what her father would have said. Mr. Nettles, who managed their accounts, must have given her mother license to spend as she liked—perhaps to bolster her recovery.

Yet there was something not quite right to Annis' way of thinking. Her mother would leave in the afternoons for hours. *Shopping*, she would say when she breezed in laughing, *merely shopping*. Yet she couldn't quite look at Annis when she said it. How much buying could one do week after week? Some days she came home with bags and hat boxes. Sometimes she did not. It troubled Annis that she was never asked to accompany her. She couldn't help but think something dreadful was happening. But the more she tried to shrug it off, the more this thought seeped into her, like water to a sponge.

The heaviness that crept into her mother's lungs masqueraded as a common chest cold and went ignored. Until, after months of progressive symptoms—hacking cough, exhaustion, fever, and eventual wasting—her illness showed itself for what it really was: consumption.

As the disease progressed, so did her mother's irritability. By the time she began to languish in bed more hours than she was out of it, she was impossible to appease. The servants left, one by one. The pianoforte grew furred with dust. Grates were no longer blackened. Rooms took on the stale, moldy scent of disuse.

Articles from the house disappeared: crystal goblets, plate ware, Tiffany lamps. Even her father's humidor (how could she?). It was odd and unsettling to Annis, but all her mother said was they were things they didn't need so there was no reason to keep them.

It was a curious unfolding Annis didn't understand, this passionate acquisition of things, and the quiet, almost surreptitious, dispersal of others.

Her mother clears her throat, shunting Annis back to the present. "Where is Ben?"

Annis had always been the apple of her father's eye, but it was Ben who filled their mother with joy. "I sent him out for bread, Mother."

"Why?" Her blue eyes sharpen. "Martha will do it."

"She's overburdened as it is."

Martha, in the Hargrave's employ as long as Annis can remember, is the last of the servants to remain. The old woman is spread so thin doing the tasks that couldn't be neglected—cooking, washing, fetching—she has no time for errands except for a weekly trip to the market. Lately, the poor woman has taken to working half the day on Sundays, her traditional day off.

"Overburdened." Her mother makes a shooing motion with her hand. "Well, if the rest of the servants hadn't left, we wouldn't be in this position."

It is a fiction her mother insists on perpetuating—that the maids left for better opportunities and not because their mistress stopped paying their wages. Despite Annis' attempts to understand the state of their finances with her father gone and her mother ill, the latter refused to tell her anything. Her mother insisted the household accounts were her sphere.

A log falls in the fireplace sending up a shower of sparks. The room is as hot as Hades and Annis itches to leave. She hates the cloying oppressiveness of it, the olive wallpaper with its leering cupids, the heavy carpet with its loops and whirls that have always made her faintly queasy.

Her mother takes up her silver hand mirror and inspects her face, a finger tracing the prominent line of a cheekbone. She's lost so much flesh these last weeks she looks ten years older. She sets the mirror down with irritation and looks for something to pick at. "Stop looking so sour."

"I'm not sour, Mother." *I'm concerned about what will become of Ben and I.* She swallows and looks away. She doesn't like to take her mind down such a morbid path, but what does their future hold with her growing worse every day?

"Where did you go today, Annis? Martha said you left this morning."

Details leap, bright and sharp. Mr. Scudder's giant cosmorama, the worlds within it she'd seen through the optic glasses. "I took a walk."

"Not by yourself?"

"Who else? Ben was with you."

"You shouldn't be walking the streets. What will the neighbors think?"

"That I was out for air. It was a fair enough day." *Which you'd see for yourself if you'd let me open the curtains.*

Her mother smooths the sheets over her lap. "Bring me my gems."

Annis steps to the dresser. On its surface sits a walnut box with a mother of pearl inlay. She brings it to her, perching herself on the side of the bed. Lemon verbena, her mother's signature scent, wafts to her and is quickly smothered by the sickly-sweet pall of laudanum.

Her mother opens the lid, lifts each jeweled piece, and lays it on the coverlet. The three-piece white pearl set: necklace, bracelet, and matching earrings; the gold heart-shaped locket, which bears the images of Annis and Ben; the onyx choker and bracelet. Last is the blue pearl necklace, the finest of them all.

Instead of laying it with the others, she holds it out to Annis. "Put it on me."

Annis hesitates. Her mother only wore her finery when she was going out.

"Surely you realize my time is coming to an end, Annis," she says, closing her eyes with a sigh. "The least you can do is obey my wishes, however foolish they may be." Her eyes open and dare Annis to argue with her.

Chastened, Annis unlocks the clasp and fastens the necklace around her neck. Her mother leans back against the pillows and appraises it in her hand mirror. The pearl is big and roughly tear-shaped, though it isn't smooth. Its pits and ridges wink as if it holds a secret. When she was a child, Annis had asked her mother many times to place it in her palm simply to feel the weight of it, to catch the flickers within its depths. In the gaslight, the pearl's surface flashes purple, green, pink, and yellow. Colors within colors, worlds within worlds.

"I can almost believe when I wear it that your Papa is still alive." Her mother's expression goes distant. "He used to love to put it on me. He told me how beautiful I was whenever I wore it."

He had purchased it years ago during a trip to Wales. It was rare, quite out of his price range he would say later, but he'd bought it cheap. The jeweler wanted it gone. The man told him in hushed tones and a slide of the eyes—Papa was so good at acting it out—the blue pearl was as cursed as it was rare. The tale only added to its allure.

A rattling sigh escapes her mother, and she tugs a handkerchief from her sleeve and coughs into it, bringing up blood. "My mistake was only putting it on for special occasions. When you're staring death in the face—"

"Mother!"

"What? Does it pain you? You always were too soft for your own good." The beauty of the moment has snapped like a twig. "When your days eke out and you know there are few left, you wish you'd worn the best dress. Bought the hat. Donned your favorite necklace and wore it down to breakfast."

*This is why you spent so much. Because your time was running out.* No, that wasn't right. The spending came first. Then the sickness.

"I have few regrets for the things I did, only for the things I didn't. The places your papa and I could've traveled. The dresses I might have had."

Her mother had come from a family of wealthy ship builders in Kent, England, of some renown. But when she'd married Annis' father against her parents' wishes, they'd disinherited her. The marriage had been a happy one, but Papa (God love him) took a firm hand with expenditures. His business flourished, but not to the extent it brought an income her mother had been accustomed to before she married.

Annis smiles through tears. "Papa loved you so, Mother."

Her mother remains still, with her eyes closed so long Annis wonders if she's fallen asleep.

"Please tell me you've written Uncle Desmond," she says finally. "He'll take you. I know he will. My brother is a hard man, but soft on the inside. You will love England. Buckets of rain, but you'll get used to it."

Annis wipes the tears from her eyes with the heel of her hand. "I shall never get used to it. Nor will Ben."

Her mother's eyes flutter open. "You've no choice, foolish girl." She begins to put the jewelry back in the box. "You have written him? Told him of my fate?"

"Not yet."

A hand snatches her wrist. "Annis, you know as well as I that Papa's family is gone. There is no one else."

"I don't understand why *you* don't write—"

Her mother's hold tightens. Annis hates her when she's this way. Hard and cruel. "I have told you. Desmond will have far more sympathy for you and Ben than he'll have for me."

It's not the first time she's said this and each time, Annis wonders what her mother has done to make her own brother so harsh.

"Take this," her mother says, dropping the soiled handkerchief into Annis' palm, "and run along. These discussions tax me."

There is nothing for it but to put the handkerchief among the soiled linen and leave the room. The sun is awash in Annis' window when she enters her bedroom. It's dressed in pale pink, but even the cheerfulness of it doesn't quell the dread in her heart. She sits down at her writing desk and takes up a pen.

A memory plays through her mind. Uncle Desmond's first and last visit to New York. He'd strode into the parlor and raked his eyes over her parents, then fixed them on her and Ben. She had only been seven or eight years of age and she'd hidden behind Papa's leg. Annis remembers little of that visit, but she does recall his coolness, how afraid of him she'd been.

There is nothing now but the cold reality of her mother's prognosis, the knowledge that her life and Ben's hang in the balance.

She dips her pen and begins.

> *Dear Uncle Desmond,*
>
> *I write to inform you of bad news. Mother has taken ill with consumption. The doctor does not know precisely how much longer she has, but says she is in the end stages of the disease. Ben and I have no other family to rely on for support. Mother says, out of the kindness of your heart, you will take us.*

It's a lie. Hadn't she seen there was no kindness in her uncle? If he refuses to take them, they will have nowhere to go.

She crumples up the page and casts it across the room.

# ENCOUNTER

## PHILADELPHIA, JANUARY 1842

Annis sits on a bench in Washington Square, her sketches and watercolors stacked in neat piles beside her. She cups her gloved hands around her mouth and blows into her palms, her breath just enough to bring feeling back into her fingers. The old year had gone out in gusts and flurries, but the new one had begun in ice that turned to snow. When she awakened cold and stiff this morning to see the sun for the first time in days, an idea sprouted like a green bud shooting through snow—a niggling that perhaps she could avoid millwork for another few days, maybe a week. Now, without a single buyer for her art, she's ashamed. No, angry. What a fool she is to have such lofty thoughts.

Sleigh bells ring out clear and sweet around her, as if poking fun at her naiveté. Ladies and gentlemen are turned out in their winter finery. The paths have been shoveled for walking and couples parade the square, faces angled to the sun. A passel of boys pitch snowballs at each other, their hoots puncturing the air. She watches a gentleman help a lady out of a sleigh, the woman tucking her arm through his before her hands disappear inside a fur muff. What Annis wouldn't give to have one now.

When her mind ticks to how much it might bring at the second-hand stalls on Market Street and the choice cut of beef she could purchase for the transaction, she's appalled by the turn of her thoughts.

A small gust kicks up a cloud of snow, ruffling the pages of her art and threatening to send them flying. She holds them down, brushing the snow from the top-most ones, frightened the flakes will run the colors. To the surface of the thin board propped against the bench, she's tacked some of her best work: the façade of Chestnut Street Theatre, the park-like landscape of Washington Square, a clutch of ships on the Delaware River. Their corners lift and shiver as another gust rushes at her.

A bewhiskered man with graying hair approaches, squinting at her through his fogged pince-nez. He comes closer, plucks the glasses from his face, and rubs them against his coat. After placing them on his nose again, he bends to inspect the watercolors on the board.

"Fine work." He smiles, revealing even rows of yellowed teeth. "Who is the artist?"

"Myself, sir," she says.

He raises grizzled brows as if he doesn't believe her. His eyes slide to the pictures. "They are rather... primitive."

The lack of the morning's turnout has soured her, and she finds herself unable to curb her annoyance. "They were 'fine work' a moment ago. Would you rather I tell you my father painted them?"

"Did he?"

She pauses. "Yes, sir. He's ill. The pneumonia has him in its clutches." Indignation burns in her chest, and she places a hand there as if to steel her misery. She puckers her lips like she's on the verge of tears. "We need the money for kindling, sir. It's been frightfully cold without a fire."

He watches her sideways through shrewd eyes. "I'll take the boats for five cents."

"Ten, sir. My father won't have it sold for less."

"Seven."

She fumbles out of her gloves and removes the sheet from the board, her anger simmering. She is almost loath to give it up. It had taken her hours, perched on a low wall and scanning the harbor, getting the hulls just right, the shadows on the water where the masts blotted the sun. She wonders if he will frame it, where it will hang.

She holds the paper just out of reach. "Eight pennies and it's yours."

With a scowl, he drops eight coppers into her palm and shuffles off.

Her stomach rumbles and the wind moans. A couple wanders by. They give her sketches a casual glance and saunter past, the woman's laughter smacking into her like a fist. Is she ridiculing her? Is she someone to be scorned, despicable in her desperation? Her temper flares again, and she picks up the stack beside her and shuffles through them, looking for a replacement for the board. Most of her subjects are small things, odds and ends easily found in and around their lodgings: a cup and spoon, her shabby boots, a stray cat with a misshapen ear curled on a stoop. Though each has honed her skill for detail, for composition and perspective, she wonders at her own inanity for trying to sell them. What person would pay for a picture—no matter how well-crafted—of a pair of tattered boots?

A crunch of snow brings her gaze from the pages. The gentleman and the lady with the muff amble toward her. With a sudden pang, she realizes she knows them. Her cheeks heat and she feels caught, like a mouse in a box trap.

"Why, Miss Hargrave," Dr. Mütter says. "What a pleasant surprise." The doctor and his wife step to her, their breath fogging the air, their smiles warm. "I trust your brother's leg is mending?"

"Yes, doctor." Her stomach flutters with embarrassment. What must they think of her, peddling her art in the square like a common bone-grubber? If the Mütters find it unseemly, they don't show it.

"Have him stop by the clinic this week. I'll have another look at that leg."

She remembers how out of sorts she'd been over Ben's accident, how the doctor and his wife had shared food with her and remained with Ben until the morning, never complaining once.

"Oh, we couldn't trouble you, doctor," she says. "You've already done so much as it is." Dr. Mütter has already seen Ben twice since he applied the binding to his leg. Once to cut and remove vertical pieces from the case around his leg (to allow the leg to swell and the skin to breathe he said), and another to equip him with a crutch that allowed him to walk. The doctor never asked for payment, and she gave none. As awful as she felt about it, it pales in comparison to the sickness in her gut when she thinks what might have happened if the doctors hadn't been at the theatre that evening. Would she have even tried to get Ben to the hospital knowing they had no money to pay for a physician's care?

"What do we have here?" Dr. Mütter says, bringing Annis from her thoughts. He scans the board. Mrs. Mütter steps closer, pretty in a russet coat and bonnet.

"Just some things... I drew," she manages to say. Each word buries her deeper in the mire of her poverty. She has the urge to dash off, leave every one of her pieces to the birds for the shame of it.

"Why, Thomas," Mrs. Mütter exclaims, "our Miss Hargrave is an *artist*."

Annis' heart warms at the word 'our,' the inflection of 'artist,' but the thought scatters when she sees the two exchange a knowing glance. What can it mean? Are they, too, laughing at her?

"May I?" Mrs. Mütter says, gesturing to the artwork in her lap.

There is no mockery in her eyes, only kindness, and Annis hands the stack over. Dr. Mütter takes the other. They consider each page, their eyes roving each one with interest. The doctor indicates a rendering of a robin she'd sketched from her windowsill. A charcoal representation only, but Annis likes the way she'd drawn the proud breast of the bird, the thin sticks of its legs.

They stand before her an agonizing few minutes, Annis reading their faces for a hint of... *anything*. Other than Ben, Papa, and her teacher, Miss Hutchinson, no one has ever really seen her work. She feels exposed in a way she's never quite been before. It matters to her that they like her pictures, but worries they are only being charitable. After all, her last patron had called her watercolors primitive.

"Look at this, Thomas," Mrs. Mütter says. "The way she's captured the cat with its tattered ear."

Annis had liked the irregular shape of it, how it contrasted with the other. It was just an old stray, but there had been something about its imperfection that appealed to her.

"Extraordinary," the doctor murmurs. "Who taught you to draw, Miss Hargrave?"

"My father employed a woman for a time to teach me, after I expressed interest."

"Well, I commend your father and your lady instructor. You are very talented." He stares down at the sketch of the cat. "I would like to buy it. It would be a welcome addition in our home, don't you think, Mary?"

Again, a look passes between the couple and Annis could swear they are having a different conversation than his words convey. With an encouraging nod from his wife, the doctor turns to her and drops silver into her palm. He then says, his eyes dancing, "Miss Hargrave, forgive my boldness, but I would like to speak to you about a job at the college. Would you be willing to see me tomorrow at my office?"

Annis gapes at him. Her ears buzz. Has she heard him right? She is dimly aware of replying in the affirmative, of him giving her instructions to meet him the following day, and then they are stepping away.

She doesn't register how generously he's paid her until she counts the coins after they are gone.

# MARVELS

## PHILADELPHIA, JANUARY 1842

Dr. Mütter had been hesitant to say much about the particulars of the job, only that she was to meet him at a quarter to noon and use the same entrance as before, where the main lecture halls of the college were located at the corner of Tenth and Sansom Streets. Once there, she was to ask for directions to his office. The doctor would explain to her in more detail what position he had in mind, though he assured her it consisted primarily of drawing, a job he felt certain she had the requisite skill.

The following day, she arrives promptly. A posting on the wall announces the faculty. Some half a dozen names wink at her from shiny silver plaques, two of the names familiar.

## DR. THOMAS MÜTTER
## CHAIR OF SURGERY

## DR. JOSEPH PANCOAST
## CHAIR OF ANATOMY

A young man, cravat askew, is heading to the exit.

"Excuse me," Annis says. "Can you direct me to Dr. Mütter's office?"

He pushes his spectacles up the bridge of his nose with a forefinger. He can't be more than a few years older than herself. "Up the steps," he says, indicating a stairwell at the end of the hall. "Six or seven doors down on the right. Name's on the door."

The student saunters off and she follows the way he's directed. She passes the closed doors of the Pit, doors to the left indicating the clinic, and the dissection room. She reaches the last one at the end of the hall marked STORAGE and takes the stairs. Another hallway flanked by doors, most of them shut. When she reaches the one with Mütter's name affixed to it, she knocks. It opens with a flourish and the doctor beckons her in.

His office is unlike anything Annis has ever seen. Shelves and bookcases line the walls, chock-full of strange and curious things: skulls, sections of bones connected with twine, masses floating in pickling jars, what look to be medical instruments. Books, so many books. *A System of Anatomy Volumes I and II* by Caspar Wistar. *Culpeper's Complete Herbal, and English Physician. Leçons Orales de Clinique Chirurgicale.*

From the walls hang colorful illustrations: *Musculature and Blood Supply of the Abdominal Wall, Bones of the Human Body, Anatomy of the Inner Ear.*

She wants to inspect everything—run her fingers over the spines of the books, imprint the details on the blank pages of her mind, but Dr. Mütter is waiting. When she pulls her eyes from a plaster of a human hand and turns to him, she finds he is watching her.

He gestures to a chair across from his desk. "Please."

Annis settles herself. The doctor is dressed in a frock coat of deep aubergine, a pale green cravat at his throat. Every bit as fine as the clothes he wore the night of Ben's accident. A fire pops in the hearth. Above it hangs an oil painting of a sprawling white home with pillars. She is arrested by the skill of the painter, how the light and shadow are depicted on the façade.

"Sapine Hall," he says, his expression turning somber. "My childhood home. You have detected my southern inflection no doubt? I was born in Virginia. My parents and brother died within a few years of each other when I was very young. I was given to my grandmother to raise. When she died not long after, I was sent to Sabine Hall, the home of a distant relative. I was seven."

"I'm sorry," Annis says. "It must have been..." She struggles to find the right word.

"Difficult? Yes." He makes a pained face. "My family does not have a history of good health, I'm afraid." A sigh. "Well, you haven't come to hear my sorrows. Tell me, what do you make of the objects in my office?"

The question surprises her. That it matters what she thinks. "I find them interesting and rather... unconventional."

"Do you find them worrisome?"

"Worrisome, sir?"

"Unpleasant, frightening. There are many who consider such things unsettling, to say the least." He gestures behind him to a full-scale human skeleton she's somehow missed, strung together with twine and hanging from a hook. "Being in the presence of such oddities makes some people, shall we say, flustered? My grandmother would have said they give one the dithers."

"I'm not bothered by them, sir. I find them rather fascinating." And she does. What must it be like to work amid such things, to know the workings of the human body?

His eyes twinkle and a small smile claims his mouth. "That's very refreshing, Miss Hargrave. Very refreshing indeed." He brings his palms together on his desk and considers her. "I should like to give you a test. Something to sketch. You may take as long as you wish, but I ask that you conduct your work here in my office. When you are done, I'll have a look at your sketch. If I'm happy with the result, I shall tell you more of the job I wish you to undertake. Does that sound amenable?"

Her heart skips. *A test.* What if she fails? What if she ruins the only chance she may ever have to use her skills to earn a living? Her hands are suddenly clammy. She presses her palms against her thighs and rubs them down the length of her cloak. She's certain sweat is forming on her brow. "Yes, sir."

"Well then." From a drawer in a dresser behind him, he produces a slender bone about fifteen inches in length with bulb-like ends. Whether it is human or not, she cannot say. But it doesn't matter. If drawing this is what will get her a job, then it could be a bone from the devil himself and she wouldn't care a whit. "This is all I ask you to sketch."

"I've brought my charcoals, sir."

"You needn't use them unless you prefer to." From the same drawer he withdraws sheets of paper and a small pouch. "Everything you need is here." He smiles as if to reassure her. "If you need more paper, you can find it in this drawer. I have a lecture down the hall in a few minutes. I shall be back in an hour's time. You may sit at my desk if you wish. Does that suit, Miss Hargrave?"

She nods and in another minute, he's closed the door behind her and is gone. She comes around to the other side of the desk and upends the pouch. From it fall a few graphite pencils, lengths of charcoal, and a rubber eraser. She removes her cloak and takes a seat. The bone isn't heavy when she lifts it. She brings it to her nose. No odor. When she runs a finger down the length of it, she finds it dry and porous.

But how to draw it? Horizontally? At an angle? Add shadow? What perspective would show her skills in the best light? She has the sense he's leaving this bit to her, that it's part of the test.

For the next forty-five minutes she does one sketch after another, erasing errors, fine tuning lines. She decides to depict the bone from different angles, using the charcoal to dot its surface to show texture and shading. The fire snaps in the hearth. She has just completed a third rendition when doors in the hall outside begin to open, and footsteps and low conversations sift the air. A class has ended and another begun. With the graphite, she fashions a close up of one of the ends, detailing the two rounded points, and a third ending in a ball-shaped cap.

When Annis has finished, she rises and warms her hands by the fire. The skulls grin from their shelves and she imagines them telling her she's done a fine job. *Commendable work, Miss Hargrave.* Then her mind careens to the opposite, that she's mistaken their smiles for leers and they see her for what she really is: an unskilled artist with no promise. *Primitive, indeed. The doctor won't be humbugged by the likes of you!*

Annis bites her lip and approaches the desk. Has she depicted the bone admirably? She casts about the room as if to find the answer somewhere hidden among Dr. Mütter's curiosities. Her eye falls again on the large print of *Bones of the Human Body.* Lines to each indicate the name by which the bone is called. She is comparing what she's drawn to those of the leg when the door opens.

"Ah, Miss Hargrave," Dr. Mütter says. "How went your sketching, hmm?"

"It's a tibia, isn't it? The bone my brother broke."

The doctor's lips curve in a smile. "Most astute of you." He comes around to the desk and Annis sidles to the chair opposite. She watches him study her work, his silence picking at her every insecurity. The skeleton sneers.

*I've done a poor job. That's why Dr. Mütter isn't speaking.*

After another moment, he gestures for her to sit once more. "How do you think you did, Miss Hargrave?"

The question catches her off guard. "I... I don't know, sir."

His brows rise in surprise. "Don't you?"

"Isn't it your opinion that counts?"

He takes a seat and, resting his elbows on the armrests, steeples his fingers. "Do you think you've done your best work?"

She lowers her eyes to the surface of his desk. "Yes. No. Perhaps... perhaps I should have done more versions?"

From a desk drawer, he takes out a sheaf of papers. He sifts through them, pulls out what he's looking for, and lays it next to hers. It's another sketch of the tibia, and rather poorly done.

"And this one, Miss Hargrave?"

She doesn't know what to say. And then it comes to her. *This is part of the test.* "The proportions are wrong. It's too slender and the ends too large."

He rummages through the pile again and withdraws another sheet. This tibia drawing is an improvement over the first, yet it has none of the details—the shading, the hint of texture to the surface—she added to her own sketches.

"And this one?"

"Better."

"How?"

"The balance is correct. It's more symmetrical than the first."

"Ah." The doctor places a finger on the first sketch. "This one was the work of a man I employed last year. This was *his* test and he only did one representation. He was my initial attempt at finding an artist for the college. I knew it wasn't perfect, but I thought, with time, his renderings would improve. That, much like a doctor and his surgical work, the young lad's skills would advance with practice. Unfortunately, they did not.

He didn't seem to have much interest in getting any better, in fact. I had to let him go. A nasty business, but there was nothing else for it."

She waits.

"This one," he indicates the other, "is much better, as you said. My fears were quite allayed when this fellow performed my little test. I thought I had my man at last and Jefferson College its artist. And yet, he failed to add the details you did. He was, when I think back on it, rather too prideful in his executions." Mütter strokes his chin. "I was looking for an artist, but I failed to take into consideration something else, something beyond their artistic skill. I failed to consider how they would *feel* about the subjects I asked them to draw. It was a grave blunder on my part.

"You see, Miss Hargrave, there are things here which are quite abnormal. Such as the hands with gout in preserving fluid just there, and a tumor of the stomach in the jar beside it."

She glances at them and back at him.

"I am referring, of course, to the strange and unexpected. It is more than bones the artist must sketch. It is these peculiar specimens the artists—the former ones I hired—took opposition to. They found them grotesque. 'Abominations' is how one of them put it." He quirks a brow. "Your sketch of the cat I admired yesterday. You drew it with its imperfection. *Despite* its imperfection. The withered ear. Why?"

She shrugs. "It was lovely the way it was sunning itself."

"And yet, it was flawed."

She hadn't seen it that way. She'd wanted to get the execution right, yes. But there was something else. "I suppose I drew the cat because the ear made it different. I rather liked that."

"Working here will require more than artistic skill, Miss

Hargrave. You must be able to stomach the rarities you will see, in specimen form and in the living flesh."

It takes her a moment to grasp what he's telling her. "Your patients, you mean?"

"Yes. I specialize in surgery, particularly the removal or reconstruction of the abnormalities of my patients. Those who come here are labeled by many as 'monsters.' People with tumors and cysts of the body, those born with misshapen limbs, even those who have been so badly burned they are scarcely recognizable."

"But you work to... fix them. If you can."

"It is my aim to do so, albeit at times with less than satisfactory results. I am discovering still. Jefferson is as much a learning college as it is a teaching one. Patients come from great distances to see if we can help them. The point I wish to make plain, Miss Hargrave, is that I failed to ask my former artists if they were comfortable working in the midst of such patients." He watches her.

"I wouldn't be skittish, doctor. At least, I don't think so. And the things here," her eyes sweep the room, "I don't find them dreadful at all."

"Very well." Dr. Mütter places the artists' sketches back in the drawer. "Now then, I should like to tell you more of the job you would be required to perform, were you to accept my offer."

Does he think she will not? The thought is so absurd, she wants to laugh. But then he doesn't know how close to the street she and Ben are.

"I have, over the course of my career, formed a collection. Some are quite rudimentary, such as the tibia. Others are not. These are quite extraordinary—marvels, I call them. Some of them you see here. They are unusual. Rare. It will be your job to document them so they will remain for future generations."

"Might the specimens remain themselves for future generations?"

"Certainly," Dr. Mütter says, running a hand down his silk cravat. "But it is more than that. Renderings of these curiosities can spread further than the mere objects ever could. The sketches could be gathered into printed collections, surgical manuals, treatises, and the like, and reproduced for physicians and their students far and wide. Much can be learned from their study, you see, which is why I've been gathering a collection."

She swallows; her heart is a drum. Her work distributed to a broad audience. It's enough to make her dizzy. She wonders if she's dreaming, if he will laugh and tell her it's all a joke.

"Naturally, I would provide, at Jefferson's expense," Dr. Mütter continues, "all the supplies you need: paper, pencils, charcoals. Paint and brushes, too, as some of the items are best presented, I think, in color. You would have your own area in which to work with plenty of light, and I only require you to work when the school is open, Monday through Friday."

"How many of these marvels are here, doctor?"

"Ah, you are wondering if there is enough work to keep you busy. Ha!" He leans forward, clasping his hands together. "Rest assured, there is enough here to keep you busy a very long time."

"Months?"

"Years. Perhaps I failed to describe how large my collection is. The objects in this room are but a sample. They are presently kept in storage in what will one day be—soon, I hope—the college's museum. Now then, shall we discuss particulars? I am prepared to pay $6.00 a week."

Her breath catches. Has she heard him wrong? The sum is above what the mills pay for sixty-hour work weeks. Yesterday she'd glimpsed an ad in the *Public Ledger* for girls to work in the match factory for $2.50 a week. Servant girls earn even less. She bites her lip. Mother always said if something looked too good to be true, it was. Could Dr. Mütter be like the Wolf, a fiend in sheep's clothing? She hazards a glance at him and bites her lip.

"I assure you I am in earnest, Miss Hargrave. I paid the same sum to the previous artists. We've already established their skill is mediocre compared to your own." A pause. "Would you like to think on it?"

"No," she says, a little too quickly. "I'll take it."

He smiles. "Excellent. The academic year started only a few weeks ago. It's a good time to begin. I gather you can start first thing tomorrow?"

"Yes, sir."

A few minutes later she is again on the street. She can scarcely believe her luck. How quickly their fortune has turned. To think, they'll be able to afford better food, clothing. Paints for her and whittling knives for Ben. As she plods home, she feels detached from herself, airy and shimmering, and the world seems a brighter place.

# LETTERS

## NEW YORK CITY, JANUARY 1842

Gabriel is adrift on the tendrils of a dream. The sway of Maud's hips as she leads him through a dark corridor, the door opening into a small airless room. The girl is young. The thin chemise barely covers her, and he is pleased. Her loose honey-colored hair arouses him, but as he steps to the bed he sees the chemise is dirty, her hair hangs in greasy tufts. The eyes are wrong—too dark, too canny. Face paint applied like spackle. She skims his coat from his shoulders and says something foul—words she's been taught to excite, to tantalize. She smiles, revealing a cracked tooth. He cringes.

The scene shifts and Gabriel lies next to her in bed. She runs a finger down his left cheek and doesn't shudder. His face is whole and unblemished. The girl grabs his crotch and laughs when she finds him flaccid. It's never this that summons his passion, never the coupling that he's after. Not in the traditional sense. Gabriel presses against her, breathes in the body odor of other men. He almost retches until he remembers he's come prepared. It only takes a moment to reach for the knife. With one hand he stifles her scream, with the other he slashes. His cock is granite and then he is shuddering in ecstasy, spilling himself, buoyed by the warmth of her blood, those blank eyes. Another one saved.

He awakens with a start. His room is lit only by the embers of a dying fire. He rakes a hand through his hair. The dream has been recurring since his visit to Maud's brothel months ago. After killing her, his passion spent, he wiped as much blood from himself as possible and left through a window. Just as he supposed, only a few of the papers mentioned the murder, and they soon dropped the story altogether. A whore was a whore after all.

Still, he must be cautious.

An old memory floats to him. His mother's face ravaged by illness, her confusion as he crossed the room to her. *Gabriel? What is it? Why do you look at me so?* She sat up in bed, pulled the tatty bed sheet to her chest. Then, a horrified dawning crept over her as she took in his sooty face, smelled the smoke coming off him. *What have you done?*

He sits up and swings his legs to the floor. Memories of his mother often swirl when he wakes, intrusive as a fly. They always leave him in a black mood.

The first time he discovered his mother's spot in bed empty he still had his milk teeth. He was five, six? The sheets were still warm from her body. He'd known he was alone as soon as he awoke, and fear had clamored over him. His mother never left him by himself, certainly not at night. Where could she have gone? She returned at dawn singing softly to herself, jingling coins in her pocket as she fell into bed. A sharp odor clung to her—something piney and pungent. Gin. He hadn't known it as such then, but he would soon enough. His mother didn't stir until noon the next day, and when she did, she wouldn't look at him. She washed herself with more vigor than he'd ever seen her display and then pulled the money from her dress pocket and told him to buy food.

It happened the next night and the next.

Before these nightly episodes, his mother had been a seamstress. Gabriel's earliest recollections were of her sitting at a window, a pile of bright fabrics beside her, needle flashing as she mended, let out waists, replaced buttons. But when influenza gripped her as it often did, it laid her low for weeks. It frightened him. They had only each other and he was never more aware of how tenuous their lives than when his mother lay sick in bed. She slept round the clock when she wasn't wracked by cough or spitting up phlegm. When her health improved, she pulled him through the streets, his young legs barely able to keep up. She would rap on the doors of women who gave her work, or dressmakers who might need an extra hand. More often than not she was sent away empty-handed. With no new work and a good deal of it delivered late when she took ill, her customers sniped and sent her away.

*There are too many seamstresses looking to fill their children's bellies*, she'd tell him. *I can't compete when I'm abed.*

They moved regularly, in time with her sicknesses, each neighborhood filthier, each room smaller and more despicable than the last.

Gabriel knew it wasn't mending that took his mother out into the dark, but he was afraid to ask what it was. He was fearful that if he did, she would cease whatever it was she was doing that filled her pockets. The food they could afford would disappear. There would be no coal to keep them warm, no hand-me-down clothes to replace the ones he always seemed to be growing out of.

For a time, his mother's midnight excursions made things better. They had money for rent, food, and fuel. But the illnesses that affected her sewing business also laid claim to the coin she earned for her nocturnal work. When she was too sick to go out into the night, they would starve. Sometimes for weeks. She would eventually get better, but the healthy times between bouts grew less.

As the years progressed, she ate less and drank more. She spent most of her days in bed. When he turned ten and learned what she was, rage began to build in him. He asked her once to stop. *You can return to your sewing*, he exclaimed. For a moment, she was her old self, his loving mother who tended him with care. Then she laughed. *With my eyes? The time for that has long passed*. She was drunk. Her breath reeked of spirits.

It sickened him. Not merely because of what she was doing, but how it began to change her. His mother's cheeks grew hollowed, the purple crescents under her eyes deepened. Bones jutted from her skin. She formed a curious rash on her limbs and a wound on her nose that refused to heal.

The worst of it was that she pretended she worked at taverns open until the wee hours of the morning, a fiction that only stoked his anger.

In a few short years, his mother couldn't go without drinking for a day and spent much of her time in bed. He hated how she mewled at him to buy her gin. He detested how she left their lodgings in dresses with low-cut necklines and rouge, face paint liberally applied to hide the ghastly lesion that had begun to erupt on her nose.

A log falls in the hearth and returns him to the room. Gabriel laughs dryly. All women are cunning and deceitful. His mother had just been the first to show him.

He runs a hand over his face. His mouth is parched and he still wears his boots. He steps to the mantel and strikes a match. The room flickers as the candle's wick catches. In the mirror beside the desk, his eyes look strained, his face haggard. Dark hair skims his shoulders. His mustache needs trimming. He traces a forefinger down his scar and shivers. The room has gone cold. Crouching on his haunches, he stirs the embers with a poker and puts on another piece of wood.

His mind spills back to that fated night, the one that resulted in him being here, in reduced conditions, forced to hide. The honey-haired wench had fled the cellar as he cried out, his body buckling, hands coming to his face in agony. Blood, so much of it. He staunched the flow with handkerchiefs, pressed them to his searing cheek. The memory of the pain is still so sharp, it brings on the pounding agony, the feel of his lifeblood ebbing away. He rises and steps from the hearth, palm pressed to his cheek, expecting to see it streaked crimson when he pulls it from his face.

In the chaos of the aftermath—even as he bled and bled, and dizziness threatened to overcome him—he disposed of the body. He can't remember his assistant's name. Georgina? Gail? He wrapped her in burlap tied with rope, cleaned the cellar floor, then dropped her into the Hudson a block away, the bricks tied around her waist sealing her doom. He then returned and threw his things into a valise. Time had been of the essence. The Night Watch would be on him soon enough.

And so he ran.

Gabriel knew that if he was to survive, he needed stitching up and soon. There were few options. A respectable doctor would've asked questions. He needed someone who had the skill but wouldn't alert the law. It dawned on him then: he knew a seamster, a Sodomite who made him costumes in his early days as a magician (garish frock coats and striped trousers. Cheap and distasteful but he was green with no eye for elegance then). Luck was with him. Big Tim still resided off the Bowery Road, plying his trade from the second floor of a molly house that disguised itself as an inn. Gabriel pounded on the door and Big Tim flung it open, eyes like saucers when he took in the sight of him. The cur wanted no part of aiding him (too much blood, he didn't want any trouble) but when Gabriel threatened to bring the law down on him for being a molly, he surrendered like a child. The stitches were far from even, and he'd been feverish with infection for days when he collapsed on Big Tim's couch, but the man had cleaned his wound, fed him, and kept his trap shut.

For days, Big Tim fetched the city papers for him, and Gabriel, when he was well enough to sit up, scoured the broadsheets for news of a dead woman fished from the river, waited for the pound of constables at the door. He wondered if he could escape unscathed, for the wench had surely run straight to the authorities. But there was no likeness of him printed in the papers, not a word that the magician at Scudder's Museum was wanted for murder. By the time he left Big Tim's, he was well enough to find lodgings nearby, in the hovels of Five Points where he could lay low.

He looks around the dingy room, the grimy walls with its flaking plaster, the grubby floor. No one would expect him here. He'd masqueraded as a Frenchman for years; they likely think he returned to France. Still, doubt plucks at the edges of his mind. He cannot be too careful.

It is then he sees the envelope that's been shoved under the door. It's from Providence, Rhode Island. With anxious fingers, he rips it open with a knife and brings it to the light.

> Dear Mr. Jape,
> I received your inquiry regarding the blue pearl necklace. We have no such item among our stock for pawn or sale. Such a singular piece would have come to my attention. I shall write you at once should it enter our premises, but I really cannot go as far as to supply you with the address of the customer who might bring it in. We pride

*ourselves on the privacy of our clientèle. I am sure, upon*
*consideration, you will understand.*
    *Sincerely,*
    *T. Prescott*
    *Proprietor, Prescott Jewelry & Pawn*

The words blur and for an instant, he cannot make sense of them. It's like this when he is enraged, the clouding of his vision as if a dark veil has been pressed to his eyes. A holdover from his childhood when his mother returned from whoring too drunk to stand.

He blinks and the words sharpen themselves. In one smooth motion, he crumples the note and flings it into the fire. Another dead end. And yet, he is onto something; he's certain of it. The wench will sell the pearl soon if she hasn't already. He feels it in the marrow of his bones.

He has already exhausted every pawnshop in New York City. He expanded his search to Stamford and Albany. When that yielded nothing, he wrote to pawnshops farther afield—New Haven, Hartford, Providence. Each attempt resulted in a return letter of polite condolence, all saying no such necklace had come in, most refusing to give him the address of the client who might bring it forth in the future.

The whiskey bottle winks in the candlelight, beckoning him, and Gabriel splashes a shot into his glass and knocks it back in one. The liquid singes all the way down. He takes a seat at the desk, consults the directory (such small type it really is absurd), and sets his pen to paper.

    *Dear Mr. Kiersley,*
    *I am in search of a silver necklace with a rare single*
*blue pearl. It is in the shape of a teardrop, with a pitted*
*surface that reflects the light. I believe it may come into*

*your possession soon if it has not already. I am prepared to
pay handsomely for it.*

Gabriel leans back in his chair and considers the words.
They lack teeth. Perhaps it is only that he's sent so many letters
to so many establishments, the lines have become too familiar to
him. He must *think*. What words would convince *this*
pawnbroker to dash off an address as soon as the necklace
appeared without the slightest hesitation?

After a third shot rests in his stomach, Gabriel picks up the
pen once more, the whiskey buoying his deception.

> *The necklace was a gift from me to my lady wife but
> was stolen from our home by a conniving maid. It holds
> great sentimental value to me, sir, for my wife perished not
> long ago. I have but a daughter remaining and wish most
> fervently that the necklace be restored to me so that I may
> present it to her in remembrance of her dear mother. I beg
> you to write me immediately if you have encountered it or
> should in future, and send me the address of the duplicitous
> girl who brought it to you. I pray you will be circumspect in
> the matter and not raise any suspicion, for I will not rest
> until the item is returned to me and I have seen the face of
> the wench who so cruelly robbed us of it. Again, you will
> receive a generous reward for your actions.*
>
> *In gratitude,*
> *A. Jape*

Gabriel leans back. It has the right tone: enough urgency,
light on demand. Too much of either might overplay his hand.
He is especially proud of his nom de plume. A lie held within a
play on words. He is shocked sometimes by his own brilliance.

The pearl will lead him to her. It's only a matter of time.

Either the wench is not yet desperate enough or she has fled the city. His money is on the latter. Clever of her to run, but not so clever that she can't be found.

He folds the letter, careful not to smudge the ink. He addresses the envelope to Kiersley & Sons, Samson Street Pawn of Philadelphia, Pennsylvania.

# UNMAKING MONSTERS
## PHILADELPHIA, JANUARY 1842

Annis sits at her easel below a window cut into the ceiling, what Dr. Mütter calls a skylight. To think, the doctor thought the artistic cataloging of his marvels so important, he'd ordered a rectangle removed from the roof for better light. The very idea! The light on clear days is unparalleled. She wonders what the former artists made of it, if they were as awed by it—and the paints and brushes, paper and pencils he has so generously provided—as she is.

The skylight is only slightly less extraordinary than the studio. She can scarcely believe she has her own place to draw, and she's being paid so handsomely to do it. It isn't large, but the easel and stool, worktable and shelves are perfectly suited for the space. It was once part of Dr. Mütter's office, but he'd had it walled off with its own door and added the skylight. Sometimes she can hear him speaking through the wall or leaving his office. Some days she doesn't see him at all.

It's been three weeks since she drew the tibia. It seems an age ago when they were running out of money and hope. Now, every morning she's anxious to get to Jefferson College to draw and every evening ends with the realization that—even as she rubs the ache from her shoulders from bending at her easel all day—she's finally living her dream.

When she arrived the first day, the shelves in the studio were full of the things she was to sketch. Still, her hands shook and her voice trembled for fear the doctor would change his mind and send her home. *If they don't sit nicely while you capture them,* Dr. Mütter said, *you are to let me know straight away and I shall give them a firm talking to.* She laughed and knew the doctor was putting her at ease. Later, as the light bled from the day, he knocked and presented her with her own key to keep her studio locked at night.

She is awed still by the array of the things she has rendered, some dozen or so objects of varying size and shape, such as the articulated bones of the hand, an encysted tumor suspended in liquid in a jar, a colored waxwork (called a *moulage*) of the parts of the inner ear. She drew most in graphite and charcoal. To the wax model she added watercolor to match the original, for each component—the earlobe, the canal, the spiral shaped cochlea— was shown in a different hue to stand out from the rest. The doctor was impressed with all of them; he made not a single change. She'd done so well, he tasked her with bringing her subjects from the storage room herself and replacing them when done. At the end of each week, she collects her work and leaves them on his desk.

She rises from her stool and stretches, her spine popping. Out the window, slate clouds scuttle across the sky and Samson Street bustles. A mother walks her children around a half-frozen mud puddle. A wagon trundles by. The owner of the sweet shop wipes his windows clean. Directly below, a clutch of students leave the building, probably headed to the nearest pub for a meal and ale.

*How freeing to be man*, she thinks. *To study any discipline, to enter a public house and eat and drink without fear of sullying his reputation.*

But really, hasn't she embarked on her own discipline of choice and eaten until her belly is full these last weeks? With her earnings they can afford the best of foods—coffee, milk, cream, thick cuts of meat—and there's enough left over for sugared sweets and toffees. Their last days in Greenwich Village, when her mother's sickness held them in its thrall, they hadn't eaten as they do now.

Last week she purchased a new coat for Ben and a pair of boots for herself. Best of all, her brother can afford to be picky in finding a job—something that appeals to him. Lately, she's been thinking about an apprenticeship for him, though she knows little about how to set one in motion or to what trade Ben should apply. She must speak to him about it.

Annis turns from the window, rubbing her upper arms. The one disadvantage of her studio is that it has no heat; she must dress in layers to stay warm. The constant chill has dried and roughened her hands. She considered applying tallow to her fingers to ease them, but how would she hold her brushes steady? And, of course, there are the wet specimens in glass jars that could easily slip from her grasp.

On her worktable rests such a jar. Inside, suspended in fluid, is a foot. A child's or a woman's, given the tiny ankle. Next to the pinkie toe is a small fold of flesh, a sixth toe. It's next in line to sketch, but the room is frigid and her limbs stiff from sitting at her easel so long. She snatches up a painted wooden model of a set of teeth and opens the door.

She is often reminded, when she leaves the seclusion of her studio, that she is a rarity here. Tucked behind her door, she's in her own world. Outside it, she is a stranger in a foreign land.

The young men study things she knows almost nothing about. She's never attended a lecture or puzzled over the pages of an anatomical exam. But they, she thinks with a pang of something like pride, have likely never brought something to life on paper, or considered how much Rose Madder to add to Chinese White to make the perfect shade of pink.

She comes to herself when two students approach from the other end of the hall. Just as they pass, the tallest of them grins at her and winks.

Annis feels her cheeks heat. The men break into laughter, but she doesn't dare look back. Presently, she finds herself following a trio conversing in loud tones. When she hears Mütter's name, her ears prick.

"You mustn't miss any of his talks," the one on the right says. "He's by far the best. Mütter's not merely a lecturer, he's an orator. He *likes* his students. He invites them to participate in his lectures."

"Not like old Meigs," the one on the left in a gray frock coat says. "The man makes obstetrics dull as dirt."

She doesn't know what obstetrics is, but they appear to be talking to the man walking between them in a navy frock coat.

"Sorry to disappoint," the man in gray says, "but if you want to know anything about the more titillating parts of the female anatomy, you aren't going to hear it from Meigs. He reduces them to boring bovines."

Snorts and guffawing, and then the one on the right says, "You can't help being a first year, Stickles. But if you miss even one of Mütter's lectures, you're an idiot."

"I second that," the other agrees. "Pure entertainment. I'd attend them again if I wasn't so busy." They stop before one of the side doors that let into the Pit, and the one on the left squeezes the shoulder of his navy-coated friend. "Mütter may be good, but his examinations are a beast. Take good notes."

The two amble off, their conversation lost to her. The remaining student disappears through the door.

With a flash, Annis decides to sit in—just for a moment—to see for herself what the students are talking about. There's another door behind her, one which admits to the highest tier of seats. She'd mistakenly come upon it the other day, thinking it led to one of the building's exits.

Annis retraces her steps and pauses before the door. Would Dr. Mütter mind her listening in? Before she loses her nerve, she wrenches open the door. Just as she supposed, the bench that runs the length of the back wall is empty. To her relief, no one pays the slightest attention to the female clutching a wooden model of a jawbone with teeth making her way to a seat.

She notices instantly what the darkness had hidden the night of Ben's accident: a central skylight and bank of windows set high on the far wall. In the afternoon light, the space seems less intimidating though no less big.

Below her around the circular ring, students fidget and talk to their neighbors in low tones. The space is comfortably warm from the bodies of perhaps two hundred students. Wood creaks. Stacks of books litter some of the benches, top hats resting upon them. The odor of mud, wet wool, and sweat touch her nose. She can only imagine what the Pit must smell like in warmer months.

Her focus comes at last to the stage. Centered on it is a table upon which rests a cube-shaped object covered with a sheet of calico. Beside it, a lectern.

One glance at the surgery table off to the side brings back the awful night Ben lay on it as the doctors worked. She's relieved when one of the double doors opens and Dr. Mütter steps through, papers in hand. The pupils settle and the room quiets. Mütter is dressed in a frock coat of French blue, his cravat a flamboyant green and white stripe. She has come to expect his fastidious dress. He doesn't care a whit about standing out. In a room full of men dressed nearly identically in somber blacks and grays, it seems a smart choice. Yet if the students who were talking outside are to be believed, the doctor's reputation alone puts him in a class by himself.

"Good afternoon, gentlemen," Dr. Mütter says, pivoting in a circle to address the room. He receives a murmured 'good afternoon' back and grins. "As you've heard several lectures thus far on the developments of surgical procedures in the last few years, I would like today to speak of the type of surgery in which I specialize."

The room buzzes. Students exchange glances. Someone in the upper tier snorts.

"You've seen the men and women who wait at the clinic to be examined. There's quite a line that forms some days, yes? Many of them have commonplace complaints—fever, cold. Measles, perhaps. These we address with rudimentary care, the type every doctor is trained to treat. But you have also seen others, those with physical peculiarities."

More buzzing. He waits for the room to quiet again.

"Dr. Pancoast and I deal almost exclusively with these cases and are making strides—as well as other physicians in this country and abroad—in correcting these afflictions. You will likely see, in your own careers one day, such patients. Today, I should like to tell you a story from my own humble beginnings as a student in Paris and a case brought to my attention there."

Mütter steps in the middle of the stage next to the table. With a flourish, he whisks the drape from the object upon it. A collective intake of breath sucks the air from the room. Inside a square glass case is the head of a woman. It isn't real. Even from a distance, Annis can see there is no preserving fluid, and the features have the distinctive details and coloration of the *moulages* of beeswax in storage one floor below. Though the skin, hair, and eyes are lifelike, these aren't what draws the eye.

A thick brown horn protrudes from the woman's forehead, curved in an arc toward her chin.

"I present to you Madame Dimanche." Mütter rotates the wheeled table to give every observer a view of the face. "I purchased her—that is, this reproduction of the head with its distinctive horn—in Paris while I was studying there. One of the first of my collection. I had very little money at the time. I was a rather poor medical student, as it happened. I barely had enough funds to sail home, as I recall." A titter goes up. "But when I saw her for sale in a shop specializing in reproductions such as this, I did not hesitate."

Annis feels a warmth spread through her, as if she's taken a sip of her mother's claret. She feels as if she's on the verge of being told a captivating story. She isn't the only one; there's not a sound in the room.

Mütter rests a palm on the glass. "Madame Dimanche was not a woman of high birth or education. She was a French washerwoman, I was told. I wonder what must have gone through her mind when a brown nub first appeared on her forehead. It took years—six as a matter of fact—for the horn to grow to the length you see now. As the story goes, she learned of a surgeon practicing what the French call *les chirurgies plastiques*. He told her he could rid her of it and he did. Admirably I'm told, but not before the doctor saw that a wax model was made of her for study."

He steps to the wall and looks up, hands behind him. "I should like you all to close your eyes. Go on, do as I say." Annis presses her lids closed, a thrill moving through her. "Imagine the job you do—your very livelihood—comes from taking in laundry from others. You live in a small village where everyone knows everyone. You do not have the luxury to hide away behind a gilded door while servants dress you and bring you food. No, you must ply your trade publicly, before others. You must come to collect their soiled linen, wring and hang clothing on a line visible from the town square. Imagine your embarrassment, your extreme discomfort, when you see others—on whom you rely on to eat—mock or degrade you because surely anyone cursed with such a deformity is a freak, a villain. They jeer and spit at you in the street. They laugh in your face.

"Except those who make the sign of the cross when they come upon you because you are a thing to be feared. You are to them a monstrosity. *A horror*. With each passing year, the horn on your forehead grows. There is no disguising it. Can you feel what that must be like? The isolation, the despair? If you do not, I submit to you that you are not trying hard enough."

The doctor pauses so long, Annis cracks open an eye. No one moves and she's aware of how still the room is, how much Mütter clutches them in the palm of his hand.

"Now, imagine you hear of a doctor who can, perhaps, end your nightmare. A doctor who will remove the heinous thing that makes you a pariah, an outcast, an imbecile. Imagine meeting this doctor who tells you he will operate—free of charge —for the sake of learning. Imagine him promising to rid you of the thing that has cast you a monster. Imagine putting so much hope in him, that you do not care if you survive the surgery. Imagine your misery so profound, you would risk dying to remedy the nightmare that is your life. You care nothing of the pain the surgery will require. What of it? If pain will make you normal, then so be it."

The only sound is the echo of Mütter's footsteps as he paces. Annis is rapt. She is part Madame Dimanche, part spectator and she doesn't know which moves her most.

"Now imagine lying on a surgical table and not knowing if you will sit up after the doctor has completed his task. You may very well die whilst under the saw and knife, but you endeavor to persevere because you want a chance at life. *A normal life.* You will do anything to be whole again. To be detested and feared no longer.

"Imagine you do survive. Picture yourself, after a short recovery, walking down the street and meeting the eye of every critic who hooted or scowled or cowered in your presence. Imagine yourself no longer different. No longer lonely. No longer considered a beast."

The moment hangs, pulled by a thread. Annis visualizes walking through a village smiling, waving as people smile and wave back. No more tears. No more pain.

A loud clap from Mütter brings her around and he says, "You may open your eyes."

Murmurs sift through the room, the students jostle. The doctor considers them, as if to plumb the heart of every man present. There is a vulnerability to him Annis hasn't noticed before and she thinks, *This is why the disfigured come to him. He understands them, what's inside them.*

"I have been accused," Mütter continues in a voice so low she must strain to hear, "of collecting deformities to profit from them. Parade them as atrocities of the human form. These accusations have come from some of the men on the faculty here, as a matter of fact. But these men miss the point, or rather, do not understand mine.

"I do not collect these so-called abominations to exploit those who endured life with them, but to use them as lessons. Lessons to remind us that our differences—a clubbed foot, a cleft palate, a horn protruding from the forehead of a French peasant woman—can be remedied. They should not separate us but bring us together in our shared humanity."

Something swells in Annis' chest. She is struck with the realization that she's in the presence of a masterful orator, just like the students had said. Every eye in the room is pinned on Mütter, each ear bent to hear what will next spill from the doctor's lips.

"Now then, when you graduate from Jefferson Medical College—that is, *if* you graduate." He quirks a brow and the room guffaws. He waits for the noise to settle. "You will see patients who are ill, diseased, dying. And yes, perhaps disfigured. In my experience, those without abnormalities—the vast majority in other words—are frightened by these individuals. Some even believe these unfortunates are shunned by God Himself. You must remember, gentlemen, they are human. Do they not walk among us? Are they not alive and breathing? You must never forget it takes courage to be a good physician, but it takes humility to be a better one."

The Pit is as silent as a church.

Mütter steps to the lectern, clears his throat, and shuffles papers. "I shall now turn to a discussion on tumors of the body. I expect you to take copious notes from henceforth and—"

Quietly, Annis gets to her feet and leaves the Pit.

---

The hallway is empty. She makes her way down to storage. Inside the large room, crates, shelving, and cabinets are placed haphazardly. The smell of sawdust is heavy. Sunlight streams through a wall of vertical windows. Dust motes swirl. Dr. Mütter told her this space would one day be the college's museum, but things are in such disarray, it's hard to envision it.

She deposits the model on the shelf where she found it. Though there is no order here, she's carefully working her way through specimens some students have been unpacking near the windows. The light is golden and beautiful, draping the room in a warm loveliness. She roams, skirts swaying, until she is standing before a cabinet with panes. It's difficult to see what's inside; the glass is dirty. She opens one of the doors and uses the sleeve of her gown to buff it. There. Better. On the shelves before her are small skulls. Written in ink on the top of each is the age of the child: three months, fourteen months, twenty-one months. They are arranged in ascending order, each skull larger than the last. What affliction had each child suffered? How had the parents bore the death of such tiny fragile beings? She cannot grasp it, the pain of losing something as precious as a child.

A shiver sweeps through her. She is surrounded each day by the pieces of people who have passed, yet none of the specimens she's drawn thus far made her feel as sad as these do.

She is closing the cabinet when she notes her breath fogging the air. Her mind clambers around the significance of the sudden drop in temperature. Something moves in the glass. Another shiver and she realizes what—*who*—it is.

The woman in blue.

The same dress, the same bright pop of hair, the same filmy translucence that sets Annis' teeth on edge. The woman stares at her with an earnest gravity. For an instant, Annis thinks to stand her ground, that perhaps her mind will right itself and see that *there is no one there*. But when the woman's mouth gapes and she sees the dark tunnel of her mouth, Annis loses her nerve.

She spins. With horror, she realizes there is no escape; the apparition hovers between her and the door. She can only stand there, rooted in dread as the apparition stretches out her hand. Annis backs up against the cabinet, heart thudding. Her eyes flick around the room. There is no other way out, no other door but the one she can see through the fitted bodice of this wretched *thing*.

A sound in the silence. A creak of wood. The apparition

hears it too, for the woman turns, skirts billowing with movement. The door is opening. Then two things happen at once. The apparition disappears and a figure advances into the room.

He stands for a moment in the shadows and her heart is a drum. The Wolf. The dark-haired, onyx-eyed villain with the lupine teeth. He's found her at last. The realization is like a bolt sliding into place. She has always known, somehow, that he would.

Her mind fizzes and she feels what little control she has leeching from her. There are only the tiny skulls behind her, but if she can manage to reach for them—she doesn't dare turn her back—she might fling one at him in defense.

He steps forward. A shaft of sun slashes him on the diagonal, half his face in shadow. It isn't possible for her to be more ossified than she is. Her limbs will simply not *move*. She hasn't the strength to cry out. But as her eyes cast over him, something isn't right. His proportions are wrong. He's larger, taller. His hair isn't the shoe polish black of the Wolf's. At the same time she registers this, she sees the mask. The lower half of his face is covered by a strip of cloth. Only his eyes are visible.

She can't make sense of it. The man she fears may find her is not this man. She should be relieved. Yet he's a threat.

Annis swallows and finds her voice at last. "If you lay a hand on me, I'll scream. I'll bring a hundred students down on your head. See if I don't." The eyes above the kerchief widen, blink.

To her surprise, he shuffles to the side and sweeps his arm toward the door, as if to say, *Very well. Take your leave.* He looks down, places his hands behind his back, and bows his head in submission.

She isn't stupid. He means to grab her as she leaves. And

yet, he moves to the side even more, giving her plenty of room. He dips his head. Yielding.

Well, she can stand here all day trembling or she can save herself. She takes a tenuous step towards him, but he doesn't move. With a rush, she races past him, pulls open the door, and flies from the room.

# THE LEVITATING LADY
## NEW YORK CITY, APRIL 1841

The sky is robin's egg blue. Spring has flung itself open and travelling down Broadway in the omnibus, Annis sees evidence of it everywhere: the daffodils and tulips bobbing from window boxes, the light striking the buildings, the warmth of the sun on her arm. The world is coming alive. The conversations of the vendors on the streets are louder and more jubilant. The ladies tripping down the avenue are dressed more radiantly with a jauntiness to their step.

When she gets off the omnibus, the air wafting from City Hall Park is pungent with the smell of earth and new grass. The line at the entrance to Scudder's Museum is long, but she thinks nothing of it because she is here, finally. For a month, the memories of her visit threatened to spill from her like pennies from a purse. Twice she almost told Ben. Each time, the words —*you should have seen the python. And the lamb with two heads!* —withered in her throat. There is no joy at home with her mother worsening, only the pall of death. Is it so wicked to have Scudder's all to herself? Sharing it would diminish its wonders, perhaps because it is, in part, the secret of it that Annis finds so exhilarating.

She pays and enters the first hall. Up she climbs, floor after floor, until she's standing at the entrance to the lecture hall where she'd spoken with Mr. Marchand. From her pocket, she withdraws the ticket he conjured from her ear with the smoothness of a dance step. It's half past the hour; she's missed much of the show. Her mother had been especially talkative this morning, relaying to Annis her memories of growing up in England (her coming out, the quintessential English garden, and so on) and Annis only half listened, the possibility of getting to Scudder's to catch the two o'clock show dwindling with each reminiscence. The man standing just inside the threshold plucks the paper from her fingers and gestures for her to advance inside.

The theatre is three quarters full. She takes a seat in the back. On stage, a young woman lies on a chaise, her blonde hair blazing under the gaslights. She is blindfolded, hands folded neatly on her stomach, slippers crossed at the ankles. Marchand, clad in a velvet burgundy tailcoat, walks among the seats closest to the stage where the light flickers over those seated.

"Who is next?" he calls with theatrical aplomb. "Who will test my powers to transcend thought?"

There's a murmur through the crowd.

He stops before a woman seated on the aisle in a plumed hat. He gestures to her arm. "May I?" Pulling at her fingertips, he slides a cream glove from her hand. Without turning, he says over his shoulder, "What article have I here, Greta? Do you know?" With a sheepish grin to those seated nearby, he says, low enough for everyone to hear, "Ah, I forget myself. I must think precisely on it." A titter from the ladies as Marchand presses the satin to his forehead with one hand and presses his temple with the other, eyes closed. Annis thinks perhaps the blindfold is transparent, but Marchand is keeping his back to the stage.

The assistant, Greta, moves her head from side to side in

mild torment. "I'm thinking. It's coming. I see..." Marchand does not stir. He still has the glove to his forehead, and his eyes remain closed. "Something of a woman's. Is it a glove?"

The crowd erupts in surprise. "Correct again, my dear Greta." Marchand returns the glove to the woman, gives a small bow then straightens, saying, "Shall we do another?"

A man two rows up calls, "I've got something for you!"

Marchand steps to him. The gentleman, perhaps to foil Greta into thinking it is his own belonging he's offering up, takes a fan from the woman seated beside him. "Ah," Marchand says. Again, he calls to his assistant from over his shoulder. "What article is this? Tell us, won't you?" Again, the fan is pressed to his forehead and Marchand seems to go into a sort of trance.

Greta raises a palm to her forehead. "I see... a brooch? No, no. A fan. Yes, a fan."

A burst of applause. Marchand returns the fan and makes his way to the stage. He removes Greta's blindfold and the two bow in unison. They are opposites—Marchand is tall and slender, dark brows crowning onyx eyes; Greta so tiny with her fair hair and frothy dress of light blue tulle. In the dance of the lights, they are as exciting as anything Annis has ever seen. They take a second bow to thunderous clapping.

"Now, now," Marchand says, palms pumping the air. "We must have quiet for my next feat." The noise settles. Marchand has the audience eating out of his hand. "For the final act, I shall perform what I call the ethereal levitation!"

A ripple from the crowd, a smattering of applause.

"For this trick," Marchand says, "I shall need two stools and a wooden plank."

Two men scurry from the wings, each carrying a stool they place on stage about four feet apart. Two more enter with a long plank of wood, which they rest atop the stools to from a sort of bench.

"My assistant will now stand on the plank."

Greta lifts her skirts a little and, with Marchand's help, steps up. She's now facing the audience about two feet from the floor.

"I will now place two posts into recessed holes in the plank." With help from the stagehands, Marchand places each in position so they stand vertically on either side of Greta, just brushing her skirts. The posts are square, flat at the top, and perhaps six inches in diameter.

From one of the stage men, Marchand takes a brown bottle, which he lifts high. "Ladies and gentlemen, I have here a vial of ether. Do you know what it is?" The crowd murmurs but not a hand raises to answer him. "No one? Very well. Ether is a compound that was discovered many years ago. It is—"

"A damn good time is what it is!" a man cries boisterously.

The audience explodes in laughter.

Marchand's eyes find the man in the crowd. "Ah, you are referring to the so-called ether frolics popular in the last decade?" He chuckles. "Indeed, I myself partook. And why not? Such a lot of fun inhaling the fumes in the company of one's friends!" Marchand stumbles around the stage as if drunk, saying as he does, "The dizziness, the gaiety from but a few inhalations."

The crowd erupts at his antics then Marchand sobers. "Physicians today use it to relieve spasms, scurvy, and such. But in *my* hands, ladies and gentlemen, ether does more. With the transcendent power of thought I have just demonstrated between myself and Greta, I can, with ether as my aid, achieve something quite extraordinary." He holds the bottle aloft again. "Ether, specially procured for me at its highest level of concentration, will enable Greta to go, upon inhaling it, into a deep, if brief, sleep."

With a showman's flourish, Marchand removes the

stopper from the bottle and holds it even higher. A smell wafts to Annis, sweet as syrup. The audience shuffles in their seats. The odor isn't unpleasant but there's something about it that unsettles her. She feels almost violated. "Rest assured, ladies and gentlemen, you cannot inhale enough from your seats to succumb. You are quite safe." He gives an exaggerated wink to the ladies in the front row, and giggles go up.

"Now, I will demonstrate for you the magical properties of ether!"

The gaslights dim. The audience is in total darkness. Only a small spotlight illuminates the stage. With a few brisk strides, Marchand stands before Greta. "My assistant will now spread her arms and rest them on the posts." Greta obeys. "Follow my hand." With his pointer finger raised, he moves it from side to side and Greta's head swivels to follow. He then places the bottle under her nose. "Inhale."

Greta takes a deep breath. In the next instant, she goes limp, eyes closed in apparent slumber.

"That ain't much of a trick!" someone yells from the back.

"She's faking!" another shouts.

Marchand's eyes widen as he spins. For a second, he looks ferocious, almost angry, but then his lips curve in a smile and the moment is gone.

"There is another rather mysterious property to ether." His voice has crept to a whisper. There's not a sound in the room. His eyes flash, the whites of them flaring. "With the aid of ether, I have the power to make Greta *float*."

Marchand turns and removes the right post from beneath Greta's extended arm. It remains in position. He moves to the other side. With his pointer finger, he drops Greta's head onto her right arm. Once more he moves to Greta's other side, the one unsupported by the post.

"Shall we see how light my assistant has become by the magical property of ether?"

He bends and, with his hand on Greta's slipper just peeping from her dress, shifts her legs right and up until her body and arms are parallel with the bench. A woman gasps. Whispers fill the theatre. The swell of her skirts hang below her body. She is now floating horizontally above the plank, her only contact the single post that seems to be supporting her weight.

A sense of wonder comes over Annis. The pole could support Greta's weight perhaps, but not from such a strange angle and not without a good deal of balance and strength—and she's asleep. Or pretending to be.

Marchand grabs a large hoop. He places it at Greta's feet and moves it along her body to show there are no strings helping her float.

Annis' mouth goes dry. She's never seen the like. This is no flower conjured from an ear, no head of a lamb fused to another to make it look real. This is, this is...

Marchand then steps again to the left, the side with the post still intact. With the toe of his boot, he taps the stool under the plank. "Shall I remove this?"

Murmurs from the crowd. A woman in the front row covers her eyes. Stepping behind the plank, Marchand kicks the stool from beneath it. Miraculously, the plank remains horizontal. Annis cannot believe her eyes. How is it the plank remains horizontal without the stool beneath to hold it up? A crescendo of applause reverberates around the room.

Annis' mind works, looking for the answer to how he's doing it. She doesn't believe in magic, not really. It's all tricks and sleight of hand. But what she sees doesn't make sense. How could a single post support a woman in such a way?

Greta's head moves, and she begins to stir. Marchand raises a finger to his lips and the clapping ceases. He replaces the stool, nudges Greta's legs back to their vertical position, and sets the post beneath her arm again. He pats her cheek a few times and Greta's eyes flutter open.

In another minute, Marchand is helping her down from the bench. The duo bow in unison once more and the crowd is on its feet. The applause is like a thunderclap. Hoots of praise, whistles. The crescendo shakes the floor.

When the curtain falls, Annis feels a constriction in her chest. To come back to reality, to the real world where illusion and miracles do not exist, is a bitter pill she must swallow all the way up Canal Street.

It's late afternoon by the time Annis returns home. Dr. Moody's carriage is waiting at the curb. Inside, the house is cold. The doctor is coming down the stairs, his face grim.

"Miss Hargrave," he says with a curt nod. He sets down his case. The judgment in his eyes is as sharp as a blade. He raises his chin and looks down his nose at her.

The house, so quiet, gathers itself around them. As if... The blood drains from her face. "Is she...?"

"She is changed from yesterday. I think your mother is rather ready to go."

It makes no sense. Mother was her old self—feisty and irascible as ever—when Annis left. "I don't—"

"The fight seems to have gone out of her."

Annis doesn't believe him; she wants to tell him how it is. That her mother courts his pity because it feeds her vanity. That when he isn't here, she is a dragon, sharpening her claws to nip them with.

"You said it would be months." Annis can't help disliking him. He was the physician who arrived at the house after

Martha found Papa dead in the breakfast room. His face, his very presence, reminds her of all they've lost and have yet to lose.

Dr. Moody purses his lips, one hand rasping over his beard. Behind his spectacles his eyes are a cool, assessing gray. "And perhaps it will be. There is no set time to these things. But her breathing is labored and she has no appetite. It could be weeks, perhaps only days. I cannot be clear enough about the delicacy of her condition, Miss Hargrave. You should be present as much as you are able. As I said, your mother seems to have prepared herself for the end. When patients do that, it usually means..." He trails off, his meaning clear. "Have you...?" A pause, as if he is unsure whether to continue. "You have made arrangements? A relative—"

"Yes, Mother's brother in England." Her mood seesaws from anger to despair.

They step to the front door, and he gathers his coat and hat from the hall tree in the corner. "Very well, Miss Hargrave. But have a care. She is frailer than I think you realize. I shall return tomorrow, unless you summon me beforehand." He dips his head in farewell and steps from the house.

When Annis has closed the door behind him, she rests her forehead on the smooth grain of the wood and closes her eyes. She should never have left the house.

With a sigh, she turns and passes shrouded furniture, their forms like inert ghosts. There's no need to maintain rooms no one occupies any more. After her father died, her mother had his study shut up. The house had become smaller, quieter, less itself. Now it has shrunk again. As if its chambers are perishing too, room by room.

Ben is sitting beside the bed when Annis enters. Relief sweeps over him when he sees her. He may be Mother's favorite, but even he has struggled to keep her spirits up.

"She's been sleeping awhile," he says.

"Laudanum then."

When his eyes flick to the bed, it is fear Annis sees. She hates that their mother's condition has aged him, that he's no longer the easygoing boy he was when their mother was well. She wonders if either of them will ever be whole again. Or happy.

"Go along then," she says, batting his arm. He raises his brows. "I had some time to myself, Ben. You need yours. You've earned it. Go, before I change my mind."

Annis stirs the fire, adds another log. The bed chamber is over-warm as usual. She settles herself in the chair. When she glances at the bed, she's surprised to see her mother's eyes open.

"'Earned it,' Annis? Am I a job then? So tedious?"

"This is difficult for him, Mother."

"And it's not difficult for me?" Her eyes move over her. "You've been out again. God in Heaven. What will people think with you bounding about without a chaperon?"

The same tired argument. Annis refuses to respond.

Her mother is suddenly wracked with cough. Her body convulses and she leans forward and hawks into a handkerchief. Annis has seen it a hundred times, but the doctor's words worm their way through her mind and she notes how pale she is, how slender her arms in her white nightdress. Perhaps Annis' daily ritual of tending to her has blinded her from the progression of the disease.

*The fight seems to have gone out of her. I think she is rather ready to go.*

The words clamp their claws around her and Annis is suddenly ashamed.

She comes from the chair and sits on the edge of the bed. "Would you care for some water?" Rising, she pours a glass from the pitcher and takes a clean handkerchief from the dresser drawer. The soiled one her mother hands her is heavy with blood. Annis deposits it in the pail next to the bed and starts to help her back against the pillows.

"No," her mother says. "The chamber pot. Quickly."

Annis slides the pot from beneath the bed and helps position her mother over it, gathering the folds of her nightdress in one hand, helping her balance with the other. Gradually, she lowers to a squat. Her mother's legs are as thin as sticks, and she barely has the strength to maintain her balance.

The stench of urine and body odor is sharp, but Annis is careful not to flinch. It's times like this when her own strength withers. What kind of daughter is she to leave her mother for hours with only Ben to look after her? What if Dr. Moody is right and she only has days to live?

The thought is punctuated with another ghastly rasp from her mother's throat and she's seized again with another fit that upsets her balance. As Annis flails for the handkerchief, it is all she can do to keep them both upright.

"I shall wash your hair and give you a bath tomorrow," Annis says, as she eases her back into bed. She carries the chamber pot to the door and leaves it at the threshold.

When she returns, she considers her mother's wan color, her greasy graying hair. This shrunken woman isn't her mother. She can't be. When Annis speaks her voice has a forced cheeriness that rings hollow. "Would you like Martha to bring you anything, some broth perhaps? I can ring for her."

"I won't leave you with much, but you'll get on," her mother says as if she hasn't heard. Her eyes are closed and her voice gravelly, dredged from deep down. Annis has no idea if this is true. How can they know when their future is tied to a man they barely know who lives a world away? "Have you heard from him? Have you heard from my brother?"

"Not yet."

"He'll send you passage for the trip." Her mother's eyes move behind her eyelids left to right and back again. "You have told him? He knows of my pending demise?"

"Yes, of course," Annis says. She'd had no choice but to write him.

"Don't go spouting off to him about painting, do you hear? He won't have it. Women do not concern themselves with such things. He'll find a suitable husband for you soon enough, but not if you fill his head with nonsense about the need for your *art.*"

The way she says 'art.' Like it's a dirty word. Resentment settles in Annis, and she sighs with displeasure.

Mother cracks open an eye. "You make that sound in front of your uncle and he'll turn you over his knee." She coughs all of a sudden, brings up phlegm, then sobers just as quickly. "You best have a straight head about your future—yours and your brother's—else the world will chew you up and spit you out, Annis."

"Since our future rests entirely with Uncle Desmond, Mother, I think it's him who'll be in charge of it, not the world."

A dismissive wave of a hand. "Enough. Bring me my gems." Her mother's eyes are open now, and her gaze misses nothing. Her mind still works and interprets and assesses, that particular skill she has to consume Annis with a look.

The disease may be rotting her from the inside, but her mother won't die until she's ready. Annis knows what Dr. Moody does not. Beulah Hargrave is as unrelenting as hardscrabble, persistent as winter. She will not meet Death until she deems it's time. Her mother will wait until they've heard from Uncle Desmond at least. It's enough to bring some relief to Annis and the heaviness inside her lightens a little.

She brings her the box of gems and watches her mother set each piece on the coverlet. The blue pearl is last. She lifts it from the box and lets it dangle from the chain where it swings like a pendulum, pits and grooves flashing.

"Would you like me to put it on you, Mother?"

Her mother's eyes are glassy, her pupils shrunk to pinpoints. "All of them. That's what I want."

"All of them... you want to wear them all, you mean?"

"When you bury me—"

"Let's not speak—" Annis begins.

Her mother's face twists with distaste and she closes her eyes again. "I want them all."

Annis doesn't understand. "All, Mother?"

"My gems, fool girl. I want them all with me. In the grave."

# STILL LIFE

## NEW YORK CITY, APRIL 1841

A few days later Annis and Ben sit in the parlor with Mr. Nettles, the family attorney.

"A most dreadful situation," he says, glancing down at the papers in his lap. He is too big for the tiny, upholstered chair. "Troublesome in the extreme."

From a gilt frame over the mantel, Annis' mother stares down in oil-embellished hauteur. Beside Annis, Ben fidgets on the sofa like his trousers have caught fire.

Everything had happened so fast. Their mother had passed less than a week after Annis' trip to see Mr. Marchand's magic show. In the days before her death, she'd been in and out of consciousness, her brain fevered. At the end, she'd been hardly there: just morphine and a foul odor, and Annis and Ben had sat clutching each other in speechless horror. Dr. Moody hadn't left the house. Martha had hovered at the threshold of their mother's room like a transient—pacing, talking to herself, adrift in her own thoughts.

Annis can't quite believe it. How can a person be living one minute and not the next? How could her mother be gone? But all the signs had been there. Her mother had known she was slipping away—her queries about Uncle Desmond, her instructions of how she was to be buried—and Annis hadn't seen. How could she have believed her mother's stubborn rancor would keep her alive?

"If you please, sir."

Annis snaps to attention and the three of them turn in unison. Martha. She takes another step into the parlor. Her eyes skim first Ben and then Annis. When they land on Mr. Nettles, something hard comes into them, as if she's bolstering herself for battle.

Mr. Nettles peers at her over his spectacles. "Yes?"

"It's just that Mrs. Hargrave, bless her, said she'd leave me something. 'Recompense' she called it, for staying on."

A cog slides into place. *Of course*, Annis thinks. This is why Martha remained when the rest of the staff fled. Her mother's body hasn't left the house and already she's been reduced to numbers.

Mr. Nettles frowns and removes his glasses. "Mary—"

"Martha. My name is Martha." The cook wraps her shawl around herself and raises her chin. Her gray hair is slipping from her cap in spots.

"Martha," Mr. Nettles says, "I'm afraid that's not the case."

The corners of the cook's mouth press down. "I know what you're thinking—I'm lying. I'm making it up to fool you. I'm not." She turns to Annis then back to Mr. Nettles. "I know the missus had debts. I'd have been deaf, blind, and dumb not to know, wouldn't I? But a promise is a promise."

"Your loyalty to your late mistress is commendable but I'm afraid she made no such allowance," Mr. Nettles intones.

Annis feels her chest burn with shame. Mother must have made no provision for the cook in her will. She never meant to give Martha a cent.

"I see how it is," Martha hisses. "I worked for months

fetching and carrying, keeping her comfortable, doing more than any one person could and for nothing. I even prepared her for burial, I did." Annis can't look at her. She knows it's true. "Well, I'll be taking my leave. I'll not spend another minute in this house with the likes of you." With a scorching glare directed at Annis, Martha storms from the room.

When her footsteps recede, quiet settles over them. "I suspect you knew nothing of this?" Mr. Nettles inquires.

"No," Annis replies. "Mother never mentioned it. She refused to discuss anything money-related."

Her heart scuds. Yesterday she'd crept into the dining room where her mother lay swathed in black bombazine awaiting the undertaker. She waited in the silence for her to wake, as though her ashen pallor, that drawn mouth, weren't enough to convince her she was dead. *This is grief*, she'd thought. *The obstinate refusal to let go. Let* her go. In the maw of death, her mother looked even older, and Annis hadn't the courage to touch her, to lay her hand on her mother's chest and feel the stillness there.

"I'm afraid that was by design," Mr. Nettles returns darkly. He straightens the stack of papers. "It was your father's instruction in his will that, upon his death, all bills would be routed to me. The mortgage and some other monthly expenses I duly paid. Your father left, while not a large sum upon which the three of you could depend, a moderate one that, with proper budgeting, would last until your mother passed at a respectable old age."

A creeping unease sweeps through her, spreading to her edges. *How much did you waste, Mother?*

"She was aware of this, of course," Nettles says, adjusting his spectacles. "I explained it to your mother after Ambrose— your father—died. However, it is now appallingly clear that she was racking up bills at her dressmakers, for furniture, fripperies and the like. She instructed these businesses to send bills directly to her. As a result, I have known nothing of her exorbitant spending until now. Had I known, of course, I'd have put a stop to it." For a moment, Mr. Nettles' gaze is lost out the window, as if he's playing back his instructions to her, wondering where and when she decided to gammon him. "Your father left the matter of your own inheritance to your mother. In hindsight of course, he didn't know she would pass so soon. Some months ago, when her consumption persisted, I drafted up a will as she wished, leaving everything to the two of you."

His voice is tender, but the undercurrent of something else runs beneath it, something black and threatening.

"I didn't know then about the state of things—that bills I knew nothing about were going unpaid. It wasn't just a matter of overspending, you see. Your mother was... well, I don't know how to put it delicately. She was gambling."

Annis' heart gives a hard knock. Her guilt for finding some time to herself, her grief and fear, and her mother had been gambling away her and Ben's future.

"Now that her debtors have learned of her death—you can thank the papers for that—I've received a flood of correspondence, which is how I learned of her habit. A ladies faro club if you can believe it. She appeared to have lost large sums at times. More than she could pay."

Those solo shopping trips. The disappearance of the crystal and plate ware. "How much?" Annis whispers.

"I shan't disclose the sum to you. You have enough weighing on you as it is." Mr. Nettles' eyes soften, and he comes forward in his chair, his face earnest. "I shall see that every penny available will go to any outstanding bills."

The sun darts behind a cloud and the parlor darkens. Long ago, she and Ben put on a play in this room before guests. Papa lowered the gaslights to set the scene and the evening was special, like a dream. There was animated chatter and laughter.

Her mother served cake after, and the day turned like any other. No one knew this future lay ahead of them. That death had been waiting to pounce.

"With the sale of the furnishings and proceeds from the house, I believe I shall be able to pay off your mother's debts. However..." Mr. Nettles looks pained, as if he can't quite bring himself to impart more bad news. "I'm afraid, after everything is paid, there will be no money coming to you. Every cent must go toward relief of the debt. As I said, it is a most dire situation."

From the corner of her eye, she sees Ben turn to her. She should take his hand, tell him it will be all right. But she can't. She doesn't know it will be.

"I understand you have an uncle from your mother's side, yes?"

The sound of the hope in Mr. Nettles voice makes her eyes prick. She clears her throat and blinks back tears. "Yes."

"He is aware..."

"Uncle is on his way. We expect him any day." There. She has said it. There will be no taking it back now, even if she wants to.

"Ah, thank heaven," Mr. Nettles says, relaxing as much as he can back into the chair. "Imagine my fear when I thought..." He waves a hand, as if to shoo away his words, and then his lips lift in the first real smile Annis has seen since he entered the house. "Of course he will take you. You are his beloved niece and nephew, after all. Splendid." His eyebrows collapse into a furrow. "Good news, that is, on the heels of tragedy. Nothing will replace your mother."

Annis snatches a look at Ben who stares at her, his forehead creased with confusion. *Say nothing*, her eyes say. *Not a word.*

Annis sits on the window seat in the parlor overlooking the street. Across the way, a maid steps through a wrought-iron gate headed for the grocer, a basket on her arm. A carriage grinds past. A dog barks. The normalcy of it all stirs Annis' anger, that the world can go on spinning with Mother gone and their future uncertain.

She'd lied to Mr. Nettles. Uncle hasn't written to say he was on his way to them. He hasn't written to declare his intentions to foster them at all.

They have two weeks to vacate the house. Mr. Nettles explained it must be readied for sale. She had assured him that Uncle Desmond would see they left the house on schedule and that if his arrival were delayed, leaving them with nowhere to go in the interim, she would send him a note and he would see to temporary accommodation.

She'd been surprised at how easy it had been to deceive him.

She gnaws at a fingernail. Panic has settled in her like sediment. They have no inheritance, no home, and no family on whom they can depend except Uncle Desmond. She can't fathom what their lives might become in the care of a man who seemed to loathe them years ago.

She isn't sure Uncle Desmond will take them. For months, she's tested the idea of it, like pressing a tongue to a molar and finding it decayed. There is something odd about her mother's refusal to write her brother on their behalf. Annis has the unshakable sense that Uncle Desmond dislikes Mother for more than marrying Papa all those years ago when her family forbade it.

What if his letter doesn't come before they must leave? Surely Mr. Nettles will discover her lie when he puts them up in a hotel and Uncle never arrives. Why, *why* had she deceived him? It occurs to her then that she is like her mother in her deception. Some unseemly part of her runs in Annis' own veins.

A flash of movement out the window. The postman is stepping to the door. She runs to the foyer and crouches before the letter box. The little brass hinge squeaks open and letters slide through and drop to the floor. She scoops them up, turns, and there is Ben.

His hair needs washing. One of his suspenders has slipped from his shoulder. Her brother has reached the point where the strain of relentless dread has pressed in on him. His body moves independently of his mind—he sleeps, dresses, eats, but the light in him is gone. She knows this because it is the same with her. As their mother's death approached, they've grown more silent, as if they're afraid to tread on the other's thoughts for fear of cracking the delicate veneer holding them together.

His eyes speak a question and they stare at the stack of letters in her hands. "I don't know," she says. "We'll look together."

They settle in the window seat. Most of the correspondence is bills. Some are stamped with the word OVERDUE in lurid red. Martha, it's now clear, had been instructed by Mother to snatch them up to keep her from discovering them—another deceit. Earlier Annis found stacks hidden in Mother's wardrobe and handed them over to Mr. Nettles before he left.

The last envelope bears a foreign postage mark from Kent, England. She doesn't trust herself to look at Ben, lest she see her own terror mirrored back.

She breaks the wax seal and unfolds the letter. In a trembling voice, she reads aloud:

> *Dear Annis,*
> *How it saddened me to receive your letter and on such a grievous subject. Consumption has rushed many a Stoddard to an early grave. Your grandfather is long gone and your*

*grandmother died years ago—both from the same disease that strickens your mother now. Oh, the irony of fate!*

*Do you know, when it was clear your grandmother was dying, that I sent letter after letter beckoning your mother to her bedside? That I crossed the ocean to entreat her, as it was our mother's dying wish, to come to her so that she might be forgiven, her heart lifted by glimpsing her only daughter one last time? You may have been too young to remember my visit. Well, imagine my disgust when your mother wanted assurance, before she stepped foot on a steamer, that she would be left in your grandmother's will. I refused to give it—how could I when it was clear her motive wasn't love, but greed? Your mother refused to return to England with me—even at the most strident urging of your father! Well, I knew then it was my duty to see that Mother left her not a farthing!*

*But my sister's wickedness did not end there. Did she tell you that soon after the death of your father, I learned through my solicitor that she had sought to purchase a horse and carriage using my name as a pledge for the loan? I informed her in no middling terms that if she persisted, I would bring litigation upon her. Do you know of any of this? No, I do not imagine you do. Had she informed you it would have surely revealed her as the calculating, selfish woman she is. Or perhaps you do know and care not. Perhaps the apple does not fall far from the tree.*

*You ask if I will take you, you say it is my sister's most fervent wish. Ah, but the tables have turned, have they not? I am the sole heir to the Stoddard fortune. I have no wife or children upon whom to leave my wealth. I have ample funds to provide you and your brother the best life has to offer. But it is not a question of money—it is a matter of principle.*

*I don't know how long my sister has to live, but when the time comes, I hope she sees what she has wrought. You can tell her plainly that upon her death, I will not assume the role of guardian for you or your brother, nor will I send a single pound for your upbringing, whatever that may be when you are orphaned. You may think me cruel, but mark my words, one day you will thank me. For it is through hardship and tenacity that the phoenix rises stronger from the ashes.*
*—Uncle Desmond*

Shock rolls through Annis in waves. He cannot be this heartless. Yet is there a single line that doesn't ring true?

"What's to become of us, Annis?" Deep hollows haunt Ben's eyes, and he looks as if the slightest push will bowl him over.

"I don't know. We shall be sent to the Orphan Asylum maybe," she says. "Or perhaps the poorhouse." She bites her lip to keep herself from crying and tastes blood. She will not fall into the pit of self-pity.

"Mr. Nettles will know what to do, won't he?" Ben blinks. His eyes, as big and blue as her own, well with tears. "Mightn't he see we're adopted?"

She places her hands on his upper arms. "No one will want us, Ben. We're too old. And if, by miracle, someone does, they won't want us *both*. We shall be separated."

A lone tear travels down Ben's cheek, and she hates that she has made him cry. She hugs him to her, breathes him in—jam and flannel and boy. "I'll think on it. We must stay together."

She glares at her mother smiling from her gilt frame and it takes everything in her not to hurl the portrait into the fire.

———

In the bottom of the night, Annis rises from her bed. She lights a candle and slips from her room. Earlier, she'd drifted through the house, fingers trailing the walls, the door knobs, the windowpanes. With each passing hour, cords of panic wound tighter and tighter around her throat. She can feel them pressing still, threatening to stop her breath.

She treads down the stairs in her bare feet, one hand skimming the banister, the other holding the candle. Shadows pitch against the walls as she opens the dining room door and enters. The smell of lilies touches her nose. Sent by Dr. Moody two days ago to mark her mother's passing. Beneath the flowery scent is something cloying.

Her mother's body is beginning to turn.

Annis sets the candle down. Her mother lays on the table, hands folded at her chest. She doesn't look asleep in death as Papa had; Mother looks... cross. What right has she to look vexed? It's she and Ben who must pick over what remains of their lives. Annis tells herself she's come to look upon her mother one last time. To mark her features and commit them to memory, and, if she's honest, to find that her love for her still remains. It is there, yes. Beneath the shock and anger.

She pauses for a moment, heart pounding. She imagines Uncle Desmond's disgust at her intentions. But there is no risk of him catching her here and anyway, what choice does she have? Still, Annis hasn't the stomach for this. She can't do this horrid, unseemly thing. But when she considers never seeing Ben again once they enter the poorhouse or seeing him adopted and whisked away to a place she would never know, her resolve thickens.

She starts at the hands. Unbuttons a sleeve and pushes back the delicate black lace there. Her mother's wrist is cold and unyielding, but the pearl bracelet rotates easily around the bone to the clasp. It's off in an instant. On the other side, she repeats the process for the onyx bracelet. The pearl earrings are next, then the cameo brooch.

Of the necklaces, only the gold locket is visible. How to get at the clasp? She follows the chain with her fingers, rotates it to reveal the catch. When it is at last unlatched, she places it on the table with the rest.

The remaining pieces are under the dress. Annis' hands go to the back of her mother's neck. She winces when her fingers brush the cold, rigid skin. The collar is frilled and high. She must undo the tiny round buttons at the back. She fumbles again and again, trying to make sense of the fabric and loops, her fingers almost numb in the chill of the room. Just when she believes she'll never manage, the last button comes free. A whiff of something foul hits at the loosening of the collar and she sucks in a breath and holds it.

The filmy darkness feels almost alive—poised, watching, ready to laugh or hiss or rebuke her—but she refuses to turn back now.

She sees the onyx choker first, but the pearls are in the way. She rotates them as she had the locket chain and fiddles with the clasp. She curses the shadows; she is barely able to see the mechanism. She leans in. Yes, it is just there. After a few tries, the pearls come away in her hands, as does the choker.

Now for the blue pearl. When she unfastens the hook from the eye, she tugs the delicate chain from beneath the dress with care. It's slow going. She doesn't want to break it, and the pearl is heavy. Even in death her mother is reluctant to surrender it. Yet a minute later, it, too, is in her hands. She takes a step back.

*It's done, Mother. There's nothing left to take.*

She surveys the tiny cache. All the shiny baubles that decorated her mother's life. She'll fetch the walnut box with the pearl inlay from her mother's room to keep them in.

Annis is about to snatch up the candle and go when she hesitates. She fingers the gold locket, brings it to the light. Inside it, her and Ben's miniature likenesses stare from tiny frames. Without another thought, she fastens it back around her mother's neck. If she can't be buried in all her finery, she'll at least have a little something of them.

Still, guilt saws at her.

She entered the dining room a daughter but leaves it a thief.

# OFFER

## NEW YORK CITY, APRIL 1841

A week later, Annis walks down Maiden Lane, her legs already cramping with fatigue. The omnibus dropped her at the western end of the street, blocks from her quarry. Still, it's a glorious spring morning. Sunlight glances off window displays of mirrors, medicines, hats. The air is not yet threaded with horse dung and the noxious smells from the market. The farther she goes, the louder the traffic. All around her, activity bubbles. A man in shirtsleeves yells at a leather-aproned boy. A rangy dog lifts a leg to a gas lamp. Steam from a horse's nostrils puffs to the sky. She sidesteps a couple sauntering arm in arm toward her and narrowly misses dousing her boots in a puddle.

Twice she'd come here with her mother who proclaimed Maiden Lane the best place in the city for jewelry. They'd ambled from window to window, noses to the glass, hands arced above their eyes to cut the glare staring at treasures winking from velvet. Rings, necklaces, watches. Rubies, sapphires, diamonds. It had seemed a delicious way for them to spend time together, when her mother was her happiest and most indulgent.

Now Annis wonders if those visits were predestined to aid

her in their present conundrum. In the next instant when a soft breeze kisses her cheek, it feels like a Heaven-sent message from Papa: *Yes, my dearest girl.*

When the shops give over to displays of precious stones and metals, Annis knows she has arrived in the heart of jewelers' row. She isn't particular in her selection; one jeweler is as good as the next. A bell rings over the door when she steps into a shop lined with glass-fronted counters. A man with white whiskers adjusts his spectacles and frowns at her. She steps to him and wishes now she'd worn her hair up and put on a better dress. She is a girl here, ridiculous and naive, playing the role of a young woman badly.

She clears her throat. "I have a necklace."

The man says nothing for a full minute. His eyes narrow and flick behind her, probably wondering where her chaperon is. "And?"

Annis fumbles for the chain at her neck and tugs until the blue pearl is free of her collar. She displays it in her palm, learning over the counter slightly. It glitters like a multi-faceted blue-gray eye. She is always amazed at how heavy it is, an indication, she is sure, of its novelty and worth.

The whiskered man picks up a glass and peers through it, studying the pearl. "An exquisite piece. Quite rare. How may I be of assistance?"

"I'd like to sell it." She'd almost tacked a 'sir' at the end, but decided it would make her sound young and inexperienced. She is a customer here like anyone else; there's no need to fawn.

Whiskers lowers the glass and frowns at her like she reeks of something foul. "May I ask how old you are?"

She straightens and feels a flare of indignation. "You may not."

Outside, a cart clatters by. A horse bellows. She has the sudden urge to flee the shop but stands her ground.

"Miss...?"

"Hargrave."

"Miss Hargrave." He glowers down at her with a raised brow. "I am a seller of fine jewelry, not a buyer. I also, on occasion, repair and clean pieces that require it." His eyes flick to the necklace at her breast. "May I ask how you came into possession of this?"

"It was my mother's."

"I see."

He doesn't believe her, not with the narrowing of his eyes, that set to his mouth. Does he think she has stolen it? Her heart squeezes. That's exactly how she felt when she snatched it from her mother's neck.

"I suggest you return this to whomever it belongs, Miss Hargrave." A warning.

Annis tamps down on her anger and does her best to collect herself. "That's impossible. My mother—" *Was buried three days ago.* She clamps her mouth shut. The jeweler will not understand. He isn't worth her time. She gathers her cloak about her and tries to give him a withering look. Instead, her eyes brim with tears. She blinks them back and steps from the counter. "Never mind. I shall take my business elsewhere. To someone who *believes* me."

She stomps to the door, prepared to make a magnificent exit but is stilled by his words.

"I suggest you take it to any number of pawn shops in the city. There's not a man on jewelers' row who'll buy it."

She doesn't flatter him by turning. Instead, she squares her shoulders and steps from the shop with her head high.

By the time she reaches City Hall Park, it's near noon. Her feet ache and she is over-warm from the exertion. The experience at the jewelers has distressed her. The ride home in a hot, crowded omnibus no longer holds allure. How can it be that a few weeks ago it had seemed a fresh and novel thing?

Across Broadway, Scudder's Museum has the pull of a magnet. She aches to lose herself in the cosmoramas and oil paintings, to thread her way through the curiosity cabinets and gawk all over again. But she hasn't the time and anyway, it's selfish to spend money when they have only the smidgen Mr. Nettles gave them to last until Uncle Desmond's concocted arrival. After an hour or two in the museum she will exit its doors, and the puzzle of their lives will still be there to fret over.

She sits on a bench along the rim of the park to wait for the omnibus. Behind her, children gambol on the grass. A vendor screams, "Pickles a penny! Pickles a penny!"

When she hears her name, she thinks at first she's imagined it.

"Hello, Miss Hargrave!"

She turns. Ambling toward her, swinging his walking stick, is the magician, Marchand. He is dressed in his usual attire: black trousers, a frock coat of rich burgundy velvet. In the noonday sun, his skin is as pale as snow.

"What a delight to encounter you here." He steps to the bench, bends at the waist, and brings her hand to his lips. "*Rebonjour.*" His slender curl of mustache tickles her knuckles. Her cheeks heat. Marchand's eyes are dark and curious, and she has the sensation that if he looked long enough, he would plumb all her secrets. "La Grande Merveille at your service."

His French accent polishes his words to a shine. She pulls her hand away and doesn't stand, but she smiles a little. "I remember, Mr. Marchand."

He smiles, his teeth long and fanged like a wolf's. He

straightens, leans a hand on his walking stick, and crosses an ankle over the other, the toe of one boot to the pavement. It is a showman's stance and she remembers the drama of his act, the spotlights, the attention of the crowd.

His eyes fall to her neck. "What a striking jewel."

She looks down. She's forgotten all about the pearl. It winks cunningly from her cloak. "Thank you. My father gave it to my mother years ago." She grasps it with her fingers. In the bright sun, it twinkles like a star. "Blue pearls are quite rare." Perhaps it's that the day hasn't gone as she had hoped, or that she's tried so hard to stay strong for Ben, but her eyes fill with tears. She looks away, horrified he has seen.

"Oh, my dear Miss Hargrave. May I?" Marchand gestures to the bench. She nods and scoots to one edge.

He sits, white gloved hands resting atop his stick. "You are upset. I don't mean to pry. However, sometimes it is easier to speak of one's troubles with—how do you say? A stranger, *oui?*"

His eyes are kind. And he's right. Who else is there to unburden herself to?

"My mother passed last week."

He clutches his chest in horror. "*Mon dieu.*" He makes the sign of the cross. "How unfortunate. My condolences to you and your family, madame."

A sob bubbles up her throat. She swipes at her eyes with the tip of her glove. Now that the tears have started, they won't stop. "Somehow, I never believed she would go. It was consumption. She was sick a long time, but she was strong and very stubborn. I didn't think she would allow it. How silly of me."

"Your father must be—what is the word?" His lips purse. "Of a heart broken?"

"Heartbroken, yes." She sniffs. "I mean, no. He isn't. Papa is dead. He passed four years ago. It's only my younger brother and I now."

Marchand's eyes spark. "Only? You must have relatives—"

"No. There is no one." *Except a rich uncle who won't have us.*

He watches her. "It pains me to see you so alone. Is there no one to come to your aid?"

"I must find a job, Mr. Marchand. My mother spent more than we had. There's nothing left for us to live on. She left us nothing." Annis hadn't thought to bring a handkerchief. She pats her nose with the hem of her cloak. "My mother had a few pieces of jewelry that I... kept." Her mother's voice snaps in her ear. *You stole them, Annis. Tell the man you stole them off my body as I lay dead.* She clenches her teeth for a moment and goes on. "I must sell Mother's jewelry. It's the only way we'll be able to live until I find suitable employment."

He looks at her questioningly, and she knows what he is thinking. What suitable employment exists for a girl with no skills?

"I'm too old to be adopted, Mr. Marchand," she continues, "but Ben may not be. He's fifteen. Someone might want him. I can't bear him going to the Orphan's Asylum either." Another sob escapes her. She stiffens, then straightens, embarrassed by her lack of etiquette. She must get hold of herself. "We can't be separated. I couldn't bear to be alone, to be without him, you see. I... you might think it silly, but I'd like to be an artist one day. To make my way painting, if I can. Mother always thought it... well, never mind."

His eyes dart and narrow and hunt and catch. "There is much resolve in you, Miss Hargrave. I think..." He pauses, looks away, then swivels to her again. "I think perhaps there may be an opportunity for you. Yes, yes. If you would consider it."

"Oh?"

"I have an assistant who helps me on stage—"

"Greta, the levitating lady." He raises his eyebrows with an expectant air, and she rushes to explain. "I've seen your show. I enjoyed it very much." She hiccups and her face blazes. The tears are burning salt tracks down her cheeks. "I don't know how you do it. It's quite enchanting."

"Ah, you used your free ticket," Marchand says. "I am flattered. Well, on the matter of the opportunity. As it happens, Greta will only remain my assistant another few days. She has informed me she is moving on." He licks his lips. "You are younger than she but old enough, I think. You might make an excellent replacement, if you are so inclined. It is a paying position, of course."

Marchand smiles and there is something playful in it, almost derisive. Oh, what is wrong with her? *He's only being kind.*

"But I can't... I don't know how your acts are done. I haven't Greta's skill."

Marchand's lips pull into a grin and he chuckles, as if a joke exists between them she doesn't quite comprehend. "My dear Miss Hargrave, I shall teach you."

Her chest blooms. He will pay her. Between the jewelry and what she will make as his assistant, they might have enough to live on.

"But theatre is not for everyone," he says with a scowl. "It takes careful application and a certain amount of *l'art dramatique*. And you wish to be an *artiste*, so perhaps theatre is not your, what is the expression? 'Cup of tea'?" He flexes his fingers on his walking stick, studies his gloves.

"But you can teach me, you said. I could do it."

He sniffs and gives a shrug. "*Oui*. But as I say, it is not for everyone. You must be serious."

She shifts on the bench, leans toward him. "Oh, but I am, Mr. Marchand."

He turns to her, his eyes glittering. "Scudder's Museum is closed tomorrow as it is Sunday. Come to the lecture hall where

I perform. Noon, shall we say? I will leave the back door open for you. You can have a look around and see if you think yourself suited for such work. We can discuss your wage, assuming we are both amenable to you taking the job." He winks. "I might even reveal how a trick or two is done."

Annis' chest swells. She can't believe her luck. "I shall be there, Mr. Marchand."

The omnibus nears. The children rush to queue at the corner. Annis stands and dips her head in farewell. "Noon then," she says and moves away. Just before she boards, she waves to Marchand who is still sitting on the bench. He nods solemnly, hands atop his cane.

It isn't until she is seated and moving up Broadway that she realizes she never asked why Greta is leaving or where she is going.

# PART 2

---

Thus strangely are our souls constructed
and by such light ligaments are we bound
to prosperity or ruin.

—Mary Shelley, *Frankenstein*

# PAWN

## PHILADELPHIA, FEBRUARY 1842

The pawnshop has gold lettering on the windows and black striped awnings. Annis steps inside. The merchandise looks well organized, if of varying quality. Porcelain sets adorn tables, candlesticks and other bric-a-brac line shelves. Jewelry sprawls like pirate's treasure inside oak cabinets before the windows.

A middle-aged man with a hooked nose and a blond beard comes from behind a curtain in the back. He watches Annis take in a silver tea service on a table.

"Something you're looking for, miss?"

"I have something I'd like to pawn." The words seem to shrivel in her mouth, and she feels caught out. What does she know about the business of pawning? Has she even used the word correctly?

She is certain she catches a smile quickly swallowed. Already, he knows how green she is. He'll swindle her if she isn't careful. The pearl is the last of the jewelry. All the rest had been sold for train tickets, rent, furniture, food—all the things that have kept them afloat since they arrived in Philadelphia.

This transaction is different. If she's clever, she'll see the pearl returned to her and then it will never be out of her hands again. It means too much to her and Ben. It's more than a gem. It's the story of their parents—Papa's discovery of it, his shrewd bartering to have it, Mother's proud display of it whenever they went out of an evening (and later when she sickened and did not). The pearl was the embodiment of their marriage, the rare, interminable quality of it, and Annis no more wants to part with it than she does her precious paints.

But she'll have it back only if she's smart.

"Let's have a look then," he says. His face is as bland as white bread, his tone bored.

She steps to the counter and pulls the blue pearl from the neck of her dress. After unfastening the chain, she places it on the counter between them. In a flash, his demeanor changes: he tenses, stands a bit straighter.

"The blue pearl..." Barely breathed. Little more than a murmur.

It's as if he's been expecting it. But that can't be right. It must be its beauty. The pearl has a way of taking its beholders ransom.

The shopkeeper gathers himself and pulls a candle from a surface behind him. Under the light, the pearl flickers like the surface of an ocean under a thunderous sky: gray, aquamarine, green, violet. The man wets his lips, glances at her, back to the pearl. She's learned to read the mannerisms of these brokers. Poker players, all. He is excited but keen not to show it, else he'll have to part with more money for her to relinquish it.

She casts around while he fusses over it. There are no other customers. The noise from the street is hushed, the air threaded with silence. There's an inherent seediness to the shop. The floorboards need lacquering and the walls, what she can see of them, are thirsty for paint. She notes a tiny chip on the lip of a pitcher. The mismatched, pocked rims of teacups that rest on the counter. All placed where the light is poorest.

"Mr. Kiersley at your service, Miss...?"

"Hargrave."

He absorbs the details of her—her face, clothes, hair—like he's reading words on a page.

"A most rare specimen," he says.

She smiles inwardly at his choice of words. It makes her think of Dr. Mütter and his collection.

"How did it come into your hands?"

The question surprises her. The other pawnshop owners she sold to never asked. "It was my mother's. A gift from my father." The broker looks askance so she continues, her face hot. "It's cursed. That's the story anyway. The man who sold it to my father said it has a way of attaching itself to its owner and bringing bad luck." She thinks of her mother—her desire to wear it even in sickness, her premature death—and wonders if there's something to the curse.

"I am prepared, Miss Hargrave, to give you a thirty-day loan."

"How much?"

"Sixty dollars, plus twenty percent interest. That's a total of—"

"I know what the total is. It's worth more than that." He would never give her the pearl's full value; he wouldn't be a good businessman if he did. But she glares at him nevertheless to show him she's no fool.

"You have a different sum in mind?"

Kiersley's polite demeanor unnerves her. Never in the sale of any of her mother's jewelry has a broker's deal been negotiable. In each case, the shop owner barked out the sum he was willing to pay and that was that. Annis could take it or leave it and, given her naiveté and desperation, she agreed to each sum. The tables are turned now—a testament to the pearl's worth.

"I don't need to borrow that much," she says. "Thirty dollars will do, and at half the interest. And I should like sixty days to pay it back." She'd decided on the sum beforehand. It's a little more than a month's wages. She's been looking in the papers for new lodgings in a better neighborhood and needs the money to secure a place, once she finds one. It's a surprise for Ben—a new home, closer to where they work with more room. Perhaps a few new dresses for herself and some shirts and trousers for Ben. With what she's earning at the college, she'll be able to pay the loan back easily.

Still, worry saws at her and she bites her lip. Since they left New York, the pearl has been a fall back just in case she and Ben end up on the streets. What if she never sees it again?

"It's a fine piece, to be sure," Mr. Kiersley says. She doesn't like the way he's looking at her, the way his pupils have shrunk to pinpoints. "I'll cut you a deal," he says. "No interest."

She stares at him. The statement is counter to everything she knows of pawnshops. Buying items for far less than they're worth and earning interest off the backs of the destitute are the cogs that keep brokers in business.

"I understand your hesitation in parting with it."

"I'm not parting with it. I shall return for it in sixty days."

The shopkeeper winks and spreads his arms in defeat. "Who am I to quibble with a fine young lady. I'd sooner run myself through than see you leave in a flap." He leans into the counter. "You're a shrewd woman. I'll not only drop the interest, I'll give you the sixty days."

There is something too easy in his manner. What is she missing? He must think she won't be able to pay it back, in which case the pearl will be his.

*It will never be yours. I'll get it back if it's the last thing I do.*
"Very well, we have a deal."

"One stipulation." He raises a pointer finger. "I'll need your address."

She nods and he gathers paper, inkpot, and pen and begins scratching out the terms. There's an energy coming off him, as if he's made the deal of his life. She can't wait to return and make a payment in full—no interest!—and watch him grimace when she repossesses the pearl.

She's brimming with smug delight when a movement over Kiersley's shoulder arrests her attention at the same time a blast of chilly air moves over her skin. Something stirs in the murk of the shop's curtain. Loops of hair, a pallid face. The woman in blue. *Greta.* The stuff of her dress pushes against the shadows. She's as close as she has ever been. Annis lets out a tiny whimper and feels a rush of horror. Under Greta's chin, along the pale marble of her throat, is a red horizontal slash.

Annis feels the blood drain from her face and lowers her focus to the wood grain of the counter. She feels boneless, as if she will sink to the floor.

*She isn't there. There is no one there.*

"Miss?" The proprietor taps her wrist with the pen.

Annis blinks, forces her attention on the paper he's slid in front of her. She hastily signs her name and is handing back the pen when he says, "Your address. Below your signature, just there. We've no deal without it."

She obliges and then he's laying notes in her palm. Though she keeps her eyes trained on her hand, she can still see Greta bobbing on the edge of her vision. A nightmare just out of reach.

It takes every bit of courage not to pitch herself out the door.

She leaves Kiersley & Sons of Samson Street Pawn, wondering vaguely why he was so insistent about her address. But the notion slides away and is replaced by a singe on her back, the burn of Kiersley's—or is it Greta's?—glare as the door closes behind her. When she's past the shop windows, she begins to run. She doesn't look back.

---

The days turn and Annis is a fit of nerves. Her mind cannot rest. She startles easily and sleeps poorly. A dozen times a day, Ben asks if she is well, what it is that disturbs her.

*I don't know what you mean, silly boy.*

*It's nothing.*

*I had a nightmare, is all.*

If Annis is to retain her sanity, she must put Greta from her mind. But the more she tells herself this, the more the woman occupies her thoughts. And so dread covers her like a second skin. Ben hadn't known—still doesn't know—a thing about Greta, about why they left New York in a dizzying spin. *I can't abide another minute in the city where we lost our parents*, she'd told him. He believed her and they'd discussed it no more.

In the evenings when she's making dinner, stoking the fire, dressing for bed, her thoughts loop. Has her guilty conscience conjured a chimera or is Greta real? She vacillates constantly, wavering between the belief that Greta is a figment one minute, and real the next. At night, Annis drops exhausted into bed only to find that her sleep is fitful—if she sleeps at all.

Twice Greta appeared in moments of anxiety: when Annis looked out on the street for the Wolf, and when she'd returned home from her meeting with Simms in which she knew, without work, she and Ben would soon be homeless. Might her fevered mind have imagined Greta then? But the incident at the pawnshop was different. She'd been pleased with the deal she'd struck with Kiersley. And at Jefferson in the storage room weeks before she'd merely been selecting her next specimen to draw. She wasn't anxious, she'd been *curious*, studying the tiny skulls lined in a row. But then the masked man had appeared. She remembers well how terrified she'd been. Had the menace of him brought on that terrifying, gossamer form? No, she'd seen Greta's reflection in the glass *first*, hadn't she?

If Greta is real, it's revenge she wants. She knows this as sure as night follows day. Annis had failed to save her, failed to act at all, and Greta has come to even the score. In the dead of night (how the pun pricks at her) Greta creeps, the red wound at her throat bright as a scarf. Her bloody fingers reach from the darkness toward Annis and each time she awakens soaked in sweat, coiled in blankets wound around her like serpents.

By day, she absorbs herself in her work at the college, drawing and painting for hours until the light in her studio dies with the day. Dr. Mütter is happy at the growing pile of sketches and watercolors she places on his desk. But he, too, has started to regard her more closely. Whenever she has chanced a look, she's seen the tender concern etched on his face, his lips puckered with worry. She wonders, like Ben, if he will ask outright what it is that troubles her.

But what happened to Greta is a secret she can never tell anyone. She must keep it to herself. No one can ever know.

# REQUEST

Several days after she pawned the pearl, Annis walks down the hallway at Jefferson College toward her studio. In her hands is a small box of kidney stones. Beneath its glass lid, recessed and nestled in cotton, are what look like pebbles of varying size and color. She can't wait to weigh the objects in her palm, work her thumb over their surfaces. The careful study of specimens have a way of ordering her thoughts. By day's end, as long as Greta doesn't appear, her mind will feel like a cupboard that has been tidied and, if she's lucky, sleep will come.

As she nears her door, a man approaches from the opposite end of the hallway. It's the man from the storage room. He wears a neckerchief drawn over his mouth as before. She tenses, expecting Greta to coalesce, but the corridor remains empty.

As it happens, he arrives at Dr. Mütter's door the same instant she arrives before her own. He is close enough to touch. They stand, their movements arrested, focused on each other.

Everything else recedes. He is the giant she remembers: broad shoulders, body thick and muscled. She is tall for a woman, but he is tall for a man. Her belly flutters and her emotions swim.

How peculiar, it seems to her in that moment, that she no longer fears him. Quite the opposite. She is curious and... captivated.

Her cheeks heat and then a strange thing happens. He smiles. Annis can't see his lips for the kerchief, but she can tell by the way the cloth shifts and the crinkles deepen around his eyes. And those eyes, such a luminous green! She swallows, her mouth suddenly parched, her face hot. The mortification is enough to spur her to action. She turns the knob and rushes into the sanctity of her studio, closing the door fast behind her and leaning back against it.

She wants to think on it more but hears his knock next door and Dr. Mütter's muffled 'come.' The door opens and closes. Low rumbles of conversation. The wall isn't so thick. She's often heard snatches of conversation, usually between Dr. Mütter and his friend, Dr. Pancoast, or the higher pitch of students speaking with the doctor. But she hadn't been particularly interested before.

She creeps to the wall, presses her ear against it.

"...surgery... preparation... important." Dr. Mütter.

The response is a deeper timbre that sets her stomach dancing again. "...time... out of work... must resume..."

Dr. Mütter replies. "...two weeks... artist... woman..."

Annis moves from the wall. Did the doctor just mention her to this man? She puts her cheek to the wall again but can't make out anything more.

She steps to her stool and sits down, opens the lid of her Osborne Superfine Watercolors box and straightens the paint cakes in their slots. She picks up a brush and chews on the wooden end. All the while she replays the incident in her head: the bigness of him, the neckerchief, the startling green of his eyes. Among the cakes, the Terre Verte and Sap are too warm and dark to do them justice. But the Verdigris, that singular green that copper turns with age. Yes, it's the best fit.

She places her palms to her cheeks. How ridiculous he must think her for blushing crimson, for her obscene words she now regrets. *I'll scream. I'll bring a hundred students down on your head. See if I don't.* All her lofty thoughts about the patients here, yet she'd treated the masked man like every ounce the monster.

Dr. Mütter's door opens, and she hears footsteps retreat down the hall. The man in the neckerchief is gone. She startles at the sound of knuckles rapping on her door. She brings the box of kidney stones to her lap to occupy her hands. "Come in."

Dr. Mütter steps into her studio. "Good afternoon, Miss Hargrave."

The doctor doesn't visit often, but it's always a treat when he does. He is a favorite among the students, often calling out to them by name in the hallways. It's something she's never seen another doctor at the college do. Most of his peers, at least from what she's witnessed, seem to treat students with hostile disdain —as if an unfortunate condition of teaching students is the students themselves.

"I wonder if I might have a moment of your time?" The doctor's smile is warm, and she finds herself relaxing. She is pleased he thinks to *ask* if he can speak with her, something he has every right to do, in a space he has every right to occupy.

Today he is dressed in a frock coat of burnt sienna. His waistcoat is equally ostentatious, if a shade or two lighter. A yellow cravat (closer to Orpiment than Ochre were she to mix it) is tied at his throat.

"What can I do for you, doctor?"

Dr. Mütter leans back against the worktable in the center of the room and crosses his arms. "I've come to ask if you would be willing to broaden the scope of your work here." He reaches for the tin of brushes beside him and stirs them, taking one out and running a finger over the bristles. "Dr. Pancoast and I have leapt upon a new project. We would like to publish a book of surgery for the college. A sort of manual, if you will, of methods to repair various aberrations—the kind we treat at the clinic.

"Its principal aim is to aid the students. On a broader scale, we wish to make it available to other physicians who do such work. We're only in the beginning stages, but it will need illustrations which will then be made into engravings for the book."

Annis is intrigued. "You wish me to sketch the abnormalities, sir?"

"Yes, and the results of their correction or removal—whatever the case may be—following surgery. You've seen the types of imperfections of which I speak."

She's witnessed those who hobble into the building with crooked limbs, those who've been badly burned, children with misshapen lips and noses. Her heart had gone out to all of them. To live in such a way, miserable under the cruel stares of others, is a fate she wouldn't wish on anyone. It's a feeling that has only strengthened in the weeks she's been here.

"I would be honored to help."

His face lights up. "I am glad to hear it, Miss Hargrave. You are proving to be an instrumental part of our work here. For some of your sketches, there is an interim step between the before and after results I should like you to draw." His hands come up and he slices the air with an invisible knife. "Where incisions should be made and tissue resected." He makes a weaving motion with his hands. "How the skin is to be stitched. I do not require you to attend the surgeries for these. I can explain them to you well enough for you to show them adequately."

"Of course. I shall do the best I can." Something occurs to her and she bites her lip. "It's just that, I'm not sure..."

"Yes?"

"Will they allow it? For me to draw them, I mean? The patients seem... bashful. Angry too, some of them." She remembers a man just yesterday she'd glimpsed entering the clinic. One of his shoulders was hunched and askew. It looked as if the bones had broken and never been reset. He'd glared at her, demanding she look away. She had, but not until she'd given him a smile. As if to say *I don't take offense to you. You're not a monster to me.*

"Very astute of you, Miss Hargrave. You're right, of course. Many have been treated abominably. In my experience, those living under the curse of looking different either react with shame or fury when they feel curious eyes on them. I don't blame them in the slightest." He deposits the brush back in the tin. "I shall prepare each patient before I send them to you. Then, if they are willing, I shall explain that their surgery is to be documented in a book—with their permission, of course—and that they must sit for you for the purposes of illustration before and after surgery."

"Prepare them how, doctor?"

"Ah," he says. "Let me explain. Most doctors don't ready their patients before they undergo the knife. In my experience, physicians scarcely speak of the procedure at all. My methods are different. I want my patients to know what to expect. I have found the more I prepare them for what lies ahead, particularly regarding pain and recovery, the better the end result."

"The surgeries for this book," Annis says. "They are difficult?"

"All surgeries are difficult, Miss Hargrave," Dr. Mütter says gravely. "For two reasons. One, the probability of infection is high. We don't, at present, know exactly why that is, though I hope soon enough we shall know the answer. The other has plagued physicians for years and one that's become something of a personal challenge to me. It involves the skin. It's rather vulgar for the delicate ears of a young lady—"

"Please," she says. "I'd like to know."

"You are certain?" She nods. "Very well. It may indeed inform some of your sketches post-surgery." He takes a deep breath. "When the skin is removed for surgical purposes and reattached it is often rejected. What at first looks pink and healthy," his face twists, "becomes yellow, then green, and finally, necrosis sets in. That is to say, death of the tissue. It becomes a rather malodorous, festering wound."

"Back to infection."

"Yes. However, while I was a student in Paris I was introduced to a novel concept. Surgeons there found some success in leaving a portion of the skin *attached* and then stitching it back over the wound. When they did so, they achieved a higher rate of success. It is this procedure that I'm perfecting here at Jefferson."

"And this procedure is a common one?"

"It depends on the abnormality. For burn victims, it is especially helpful. But, as I say, it needs further study." He crosses one ankle over the other and cocks his head, gray eyes shining. "Word has spread about our clinic. I am seeing more and more people. From as far afield as Illinois, thus far. My work is a matter of rescue, Miss Hargrave. For many, coming to me is the last resort. Some have even contemplated death rather than go on living. Imagine how their lives will change."

Something stirs in Annis. She imagines flipping through a manual—*a book*—in which engravings of her sketches appear. Dr. Mütter's work at the college is essential and she's assisting him in it. *You see, Mother? My drawings are important. I am making a difference.*

"Now then," Dr. Mütter says, "I've just had a meeting with a young man I've scheduled for surgery. He has a facial tumor he covers with a cloth tied around his face. You might have seen him about. Mid-twenties, perhaps. Tall fellow. I asked him to have a look at the cabinets in storage as I'd like him to make more for our museum. He's a furniture maker." She cannot meet his eyes. Instead, she makes a show of opening the box of kidney stones and placing each in a row on her work surface. "I have taken the leap of telling him about you."

She glances up. "You have? I... he is prepared to sit for me then?"

"Forgive me, I should have spoken with you first before I discussed it with him just now. Cart before the horse as they say. Mary would have my hide." A chuckle. "But I hoped you would be amenable to the surgical sketches and, as you've fortunately agreed, I should like you to sketch him next week."

Her insides twist. The man here. In her studio. Close enough to sketch.

Dr. Mütter comes off the table and peers down at the stones. He takes one, tosses it into the air and catches it. "Wretched little things. Small enough, but they create excruciating pain when they pass." He looks up. "His name is Nathaniel Dixon. I have already begun to massage the tissue on his cheek to relax the muscles. I expect him to be a bit embarrassed to reveal the tumor to you, Miss Hargrave. He was with me the first time I asked him to remove his neckerchief. He's suffered with the tumor since he was a child. You must do your best to relax him, if you can. I fear all the patients I send your way may be uncomfortable revealing to you what they have worked so long to hide."

"Then I shall do everything I can to put him and the others at ease," Annis says. *I know what it is to keep something hidden.*

There must be something in her face that mirrors her

thoughts, for the doctor takes her measure. "Of late you have been..." He tries again. "Is there something on your mind, something that troubles you?"

He's noticed her jumpiness, the way she looks over her shoulder wherever she goes because she expects Greta to appear. "No."

"Well, if there were, I hope you know you can confide in me."

There is a small silence while Annis works to make her face as blank as parchment. "I do, sir."

He searches her face. "Well then."

In the next instant, he is gone.

# THE MAN IN THE MASK
## PHILADELPHIA, FEBRUARY 1842

Outside Annis' studio, students tramp past: a cacophony of footfalls, hoots, and laughter. Floorboards groan, doors creak and slam until all is silent, and the next class begins. It is the ebb and flow of the college on a regular day, something she has grown as accustomed to as the beating of her heart.

Except today is different. Today is the day she is to sketch Nathaniel Dixon and every thud outside her door sets her on edge. She's waited for his knock all morning.

She can't seem to focus for more than a few minutes at a time, and so she half-heartedly occupies herself with menial tasks: tidying the contents of her box of paints, moving specimens around on her worktable, cleaning her brushes with bristles of sable and fox. When the sun hangs directly over the skylight, it is noon. It's the best time to sketch, the light strong and lit with gold. Yet, the blue rectangle of sky seems to mock her, ridiculing her anxiety, taunting her with perfect light that will be wasted if this stranger who has somehow transfixed her doesn't show.

There is a small modicum of comfort in knowing Dr.

Mütter hadn't promised his patient would come at a particular hour. Strictly speaking, Mr. Dixon isn't late.

Still, she paces and bites at her nail, skirts swishing against her legs. She took extra care in arranging her hair this morning. It's braided in a single fat plait and tucked in a loop at the nape of her neck. Long curls hang on either side of her face, a fashion she's glimpsed on respectable ladies of the city. With the money from the pearl, she ordered a few new dresses but as those won't be ready for a few weeks, she is dressed in her best frock of indigo blue with a scalloped bodice that emphasizes both her diminutive waist and long torso.

When the knock comes, it's as if her heart has been plunged into ice. She smooths her skirts, gathers her shawl about her, and whisks open the door.

Nathaniel Dixon stands straight and tall, dressed in a coat of worsted gray wool with a scarf flung around his neck. His hair falls to his forehead in a riot of loose brown curls. Half his face is obscured by a deep blue neckerchief. Fisted in one hand is a cluster of red berries with bright green leaves. It trembles when he holds it out to her. She takes it gingerly and blushes to the roots of her hair. She drops her eyes and steps aside to let him enter.

"Thank you. Please come in."

When she has closed the door and turns, she has the sense of the room diminishing. The hulk of him. He is over six feet tall. Broad too: wide shoulders, a vast chest. The iron hardness of him excites her. She is tiny in his presence. His green eyes dart from her vacant easel, to her box of paints, to the items on the worktable. They settle on her for a fraction, then roam again, as if reluctant or unable to find purchase. In that instant, she understands that he is as nervous as she is. The realization gives her a much-needed rush of courage.

"You may take off your coat," she says. "There's a peg just there by the door."

While he removes his things, she upends a tin of brushes and places the berries in it. They are lovely. Has he unearthed them from his garden, brushing the snow off the tender leaves this morning, or did he purchase them from the market? She wonders at their import, what it means. But these thoughts only make her heart skitter, and so she takes a deep breath and wills herself to behave like a professional artist and not a silly, foolish girl.

She steps to her easel. Her graphite is already laid out next to it. When he moves to the worktable once more, his features are burnished gold by the light above. That color renderings aren't needed for Dr. Mütter's book is a disappointment. How she would love to bring out the red highlights in his hair, those startling irises, the deep burgundy of his flannel shirt. He is dressed like a tradesman, his clothes clean and of good quality. A furniture maker, Dr. Mütter had said.

She positions her stool beneath the skylight and beckons him to sit. He has removed his gloves and she finds that his hands are large, his nails clipped and clean. He rubs his palms up and down his thighs, as if to steady himself.

Now that he is sitting, she's taller than him though not by much. She clears her throat and wills herself to appear calm so that he will respond in kind. She clasps her hands together.

"My name is Annis Hargrave, Mr. Dixon. I know Dr. Mütter asked you to come so that I might... capture you for his book of surgery." A silly word, capture. As if she plans to ensnare him. He merely nods, once. A clipped movement that seems to underscore his unease. "I don't think your sketch will take that long today. No more than an hour at most. Does that suit? Is there any place you need to be?"

He shakes his head and Annis bites her lip. She knows he can speak; she'd heard him next door. Perhaps she should do less talking and more *doing*. She takes a deep breath and reaches out to him with both hands, meaning to untie his neckerchief in back. His hands come up and clamp around hers so quickly she gasps. A jolt of electricity at his touch. They are so close. His hold is tight, but not cruel. His chest heaves.

He's angry. She has already made a mistake.

"I'm sorry," Annis says, and she is. She takes a step back and he releases her. Unwilling to meet her gaze, he stares at a spot behind her. What if he leaves in a huff? What will she say to Dr. Mütter? She remembers how Nathaniel had smiled at her last week. He'd seemed relaxed. Almost... flirtatious. What was so different then?

*He was wearing his mask. He doesn't feel confident without it.*

She clears her throat again. "Did Dr. Mütter tell you that you are my first patient, Mr. Dixon? I waited for you today and I was so..." She digs at her thumbnail and can't quite meet his eyes. "Nervous." She hazards a glance and looks away. "Mostly, you see, I sit here alone and draw any number of things for Dr. Mütter. I'm drawing his collection." His brows raise in surprise. "That's why I was in the storage room that day. I was replacing something I'd finished and choosing another."

She gestures to her worktable where a gangrenous hand floats in preserving fluid inside a jar, and a papier-mâché model of an eyeball is mounted to a post. "They stay silent, Dr. Mütter's wonders. They don't complain. He joked once about that. He said if the specimens protested, he would give them a talking to." His eyes flick to hers and away but there's a lightness she hasn't seen since he came through the door. "They're not people, of course. They're just things. That's what makes me nervous. With you, I mean. It's easier for me to draw things that are inanimate. People are different. They have thoughts and feelings. They care about what they look like, how they're portrayed. I don't want to disappoint them." Her heart is scampering but she goes on. "I don't want to disappoint you."

To her horror, her eyes fill with tears and she turns to her easel lest he see. She gathers her shawl again and touches a length of graphite, moving it around with her finger. "My first sketch—of a person that is—was my little brother. It took me a long time. It was agony for us both. He hated staying still."

Nathaniel makes a small movement. The cloth over his mouth rises and the skin around his eyes crinkles. A smile.

"My father was the first person to believe that I had talent. He wanted to foster it, if only as a hobby. When we lived in New York he employed an artist—Miss Hutchinson—once a week to teach me how to draw. It's not much in the way of professional training, but it was enough for Dr. Mütter to take an interest in some sketches of mine. He gave me a test not long ago." She gestures next door. "Right in his office. I was terrified. I need to work, Mr. Dixon. My brother and I are on our own. If he hadn't given me the job..."

Her voice breaks and her eyes burn. She'd meant to tell him something of herself to gain his trust, not blubber in front of him. But he is looking at her now, interested in what she has to say.

"It's important what Dr. Mütter is doing, Mr. Dixon. I'm not just saying that because it's my job to sketch some of his patients for his book. I want to be... a part of it." She takes a step closer. He immediately rises, turns from her, swipes a hand through his hair.

"You're not a task for me, Mr. Dixon. Not *merely* a task. You are a man who has an unfortunate growth I'm told can be—*will*

156

*be*—removed. Dr. Mütter wants to give you a life you want. One where you don't have to wear a mask."

He turns to her, his brows knitted, and gives her a brief, stabbing glance before he looks away.

She steps to him, wrings her hands. "I promise I will not react in horror at what I see. I'm not squeamish. That's why Dr. Mütter trusts me with his patients." A thought occurs and she rushes on. "I... I promise, if you don't like my sketch—if it doesn't represent you in the way you wish to be seen—you may dispose of it. You may dispose of any of the renderings I draw of you."

Dr. Mütter has given her no such license, but she doesn't care. She can't bear for Nathaniel Dixon to be unsatisfied with her work.

When he turns to her there is something akin to longing in his gaze, a weary strain she understands.

"Will you trust me, Mr. Dixon?" It is only a whisper.

It is Nathaniel who unties the neckerchief. After taking a seat on the stool once more, he reaches back and draws the cloth from his face. Annis is careful not to glance at the tumor first. He is marking her every reaction, and she wants to show him that it is the last of her observations. It's not difficult; there is much to admire. His nose is long and straight, his jawline angular, as if wrought from stone. Together with his fine brows and startling eyes, he is near perfection.

Then she takes in the details he has hidden for so long. The tumor on his left cheek is bigger than she thought it would be: the size of a plum. Oblong and light purple in color, rising from the surface of his flesh like a boil. In itself, it is not so monstrous. However, the skin around it is stretched taut, so much so that his lips on the left side ride up in a half sneer. It's this that is startling. In the eyes of the unsympathetic, it makes him look a fiend.

He watches, as if daring her to say something now that she's taken her fill.

She lifts her hand. "May I?"

His only response is to close his eyes.

Gingerly, she glides her fingers across his cheek until they come to rest on the lump. "Will it hurt if I—"

"No." His voice is deep, coarse from lack of use.

She presses a fingertip to it, eager to show him she's willing to touch him, to touch *it*. She wants to. The scent of pine, sawdust, and leather waft from him. Utterly pleasing and wholly male. For an instant, her breath catches, so transfixed is she by his scent. She shakes her head to clear it, grateful his eyes are still shut, for she is certain her cheeks are aflame. She mustn't let him think she is shaken by what she sees. In truth, she isn't.

The tumor gives a little under the pressure of her finger. It isn't hard, but not soft either. "Can you feel it?"

When his eyes flutter open, she realizes how close they are again. She is standing in the V of his legs.

"Your touch? Yes. It's not... unpleasant." His voice is educated, syrupy. The air feels loaded. The walls shrink. Annis is certain Nathaniel feels it too, but then he is clearing his throat and pulling away from her. "The doctor has worked for weeks to loosen the muscles." He moves his palm over the raised skin. "He has asked me to massage the area myself at least thrice a day. He means to improve the circulation of the blood before surgery. It has worked. I have more feeling in my cheek. Almost as much as I feel in the other."

"When is your surgery to be?"

"Wednesday."

Annis takes the graphite in her fingers and begins to sketch, starting (as she always does) with the eyes. She feels him watching her, but concentrates on her work and soon, the graphite and her hand become one. Gradually Nathaniel's eyes, brows, and nose take shape on the paper. He has a small mole at his right temple in the shape of a heart. Where his lips are stretched to accommodate the growth of the tumor, a few teeth are visible.

"What do you do, Mr. Dixon?" She already knows but she wants him to tell her. To be comfortable enough to tell her.

"Other than walking about town with my face obscured frightening children?"

His tone is light, and she can't keep the corners of her lips from lifting. Her heart flutters when Nathaniel's do the same. "Yes, other than that."

"I'm a furniture maker. I have a shop on Marble Street. I live by myself above it."

The scent of pine and sawdust then. And he isn't married. Pieces of him slide into place.

"Do you like it, making furniture?"

"I like working with my hands." He stretches them out, flexes them. There are callouses on his fingers. "My father was a carpenter. Following in his footsteps is all I ever wanted to do."

"He must be very proud."

A pause. "He might be, were he alive. He died, along with my mother, in the cholera outbreak of '32. I was eighteen and an only child."

Her hand stills. "I'm sorry."

He presses his lips together. "What of your parents? You mentioned New York."

"My father passed years ago of a heart attack. My mother died of consumption last year. My brother and I moved here."

"Family here then."

"No." She can't bring herself to tell him of her mother's expenditures that left them destitute, of Uncle Desmond's cruelty.

"You moved here without knowing anyone?"

"Yes. We needed..." *To stay alive.* "A change."

They talk of Philadelphia, of Independence Square and the wharf, Chestnut Street Theatre, Ben's broken leg and how it led to her propitious meeting with Dr. Mütter.

When she is finished three quarters of an hour later, she detaches the sketch from the easel and lays it on the worktable. They stand looking down at it, their arms almost touching. She has captured him well—the blunt edge of his jawline, his intense eyes, the dark tangle of hair that crowns his head. It is only the raised snarl of his lips and the rounded mass rising from his cheek that mar his features. She has drawn these truthfully without minimizing them. Nathaniel does not speak for some moments. Her stomach knots. *Perhaps he will dispose of it after all.*

"If you don't like it..." she begins.

"It is exceptional," he replies at the same time.

When she turns to him with a laugh it dies in her throat. His jaw is set, his face red. "Your *work* is exceptional," he says low. "*I* am a disgrace."

"You are not. I, I have seen worse." She wishes immediately she could take it back. It is the flimsiest of compliments, if a compliment at all.

He remains staring at the paper, his face shuttered. Her mind grabs for words, anything to ease him, but all that comes to mind are lines that are overly familiar. *You are beautiful. You have the finest of features far exceeding most men.* Seconds beat out. The air in the studio is warm and she is sick with the frustration she feels on his behalf.

"It will soon be remedied," she finally manages to say. "I have every faith in Dr. Mütter."

A cloud passes over him, as if he is thinking ahead to the surgery, as if tethered for an instant to the horror that awaits him. But then he blinks and comes to himself. She thinks he is going to say something more, but the hallway fills with noise. The delicate bubble between them is broken.

He reties the neckerchief, grabs his things, and leaves without another word.

# UNE CHIRURGIE PLASTIQUE
## PHILADELPHIA, FEBRUARY 1842

Annis sits in the highest tier of the Pit, her insides churning. It's mid-morning, the best time to exploit the natural light. It spills through the easterly windows, draping the stage in amber hues. Still, the gaslights flicker above and the candles of the candelabrum have been lit. Center stage is a sturdy wooden chair. On the table beside it, surgical tools glitter malevolently: knives, a hook-shaped instrument, forceps (she recognizes them; she sketched a pair last week), scissors, and other instruments she doesn't recognize.

Students are crammed shoulder to shoulder on the benches, notebooks balanced on laps. There is a cheerful, animated energy to the room that belies the serious nature of what they are about to witness. She wants to stand and rage, hurl her words to the ceiling so they rain down like arrows, piercing each man to the bone. *This is not entertainment for your sake. This is a man's life!*

When the door at the back of the room opens, the chatter peters out. A man of medium build with a white shock of hair is the first to enter. Dr. Pancoast follows, long legs reaching the chair in a few quick strides. When Dr. Mütter and Nathaniel enter, a buzz fills the room. Nathaniel isn't wearing his mask. Even from a distance, the tumor is easily seen—purple and misshapen, thick and raised, faintly shining.

*He is so much more than this*, she thinks.

Students crane their necks for a better view, whispering amongst themselves. She cannot think their behavior is due entirely to their interest in a surgical lesson. The disfigured man on stage is a spectacle, and they are to see him cut, resected, and sutured.

Her heart goes out to Nathanial, now seated and staring at the floor in front of him. He has not yet regarded the audience focused so acutely on him. Why would he, knowing the faces he'd see staring back? Does he not already feel the burn of their eyes, the bald scrutiny that's as bold as touch? How despicable to be an object of curiosity, to know such pain and suffer it publicly.

Dr Mütter steps to the edge of the stage and looks to the tiers. He's dressed a tad more somberly in an aubergine frock coat. With his hands clasped behind him, he proclaims in a booming voice, "Gentlemen, we have for you today the removal of a cystic tumor of the cheek." Murmurs sift through the Pit. Mütter cocks a brow and frowns, something she has seen him rarely do. "Calm yourselves. As you know, I ask for two things only when you come before me to witness surgery. The first is your silence. I must communicate with the doctors and the patient, and I cannot do so amid the blathering of two hundred students. Secondly, I ask for your respect for the patient. In this case, Mr. Dixon." He gestures behind him where Nathaniel sits, his stare still directed at the floor. "I will not tolerate *outbursts of any kind*."

This last is delivered with such derision, it must have occurred before. Annis' mind reels. What comments have been hurled at the stage while patients suffered the horrors of surgery?

"This includes," Mütter continues, "questions during the procedure. You may present them to me later if you wish. It is my conviction that surgery prioritizes the patient above all else. Even at a medical college. The need to be swift to lessen the stress and pain is paramount. If I am too quick for your eyes or positioned in a way you cannot see my hands, there will be other opportunities." He skewers the students with his gaze and, having compelled every man to hang his head in silence, says darkly, "One further thing. Should anyone need to vacate this room for, shall we say, sensitivity reasons, you must do so quickly and quietly. Is this clear?"

Some of the students must have had difficulty bearing surgery—the blood, the instruments, the cry of the patients. Two weeks ago, Annis heard a man scream. She had paused at her easel and listened but heard nothing more. Still, something awful had skittered over her bones.

Mütter introduces the white-haired man as Dr. Norris, a visiting physician who now stands behind Nathanial busying himself strapping Nathaniel's chest to the chair. Dr. Pancoast affixes similar bands around Nathaniel's wrists, tethering him to the arms of the chair.

"He'll take the whiskey," a student in the row in front of Annis whispers to his neighbor. "He looks brave enough, but they all cave in the end." A snicker.

"Can you blame him?" the boy beside him replies. "Were it me, I'd be in my cups singing like a bird. Anyway, Mütter advises against alcohol on account of it coming back up and prolonging surgery."

"Advises, sure. But there's the bottle, under the chair."

The other pauses then says, "I'll bet you he won't drink a

drop. He's strong as a bull. I think he's got the courage to match."

A guffaw. "Idiot. The brawny ones are the biggest milksops of all."

Rage swells within Annis so intense, she has to look away. And then, just as quickly, dread creeps over her. The skin around Nathaniel's tumor has come alive due to Mütter's regular kneading of the tissue. How is Nathaniel to deal with the pain without whiskey to deaden it? Would he go against Mütter's advice to remain sober? Perhaps he's already had a few drinks. She wouldn't blame him.

The doctors put on leather aprons. Mütter removes his coat, rolls up his sleeves, applies his own apron, and washes his hands in a basin. He then takes a clean linen square, dabs it in a bowl of water, and cleans the left side of Nathaniel's face. He instructs him to lean his head back so it rests against Dr. Norris' chest. Taking a step closer so his patient can see him clearly, he says in a low voice, "I will proceed as we discussed. First, I shall cut around the base of the tumor. Try, if you can, to remain still and relax as much as possible. I shall be as quick as I am able, but if you need a break, tell me and we shall stop for a time."

With a nod from Mütter, Pancoast hands over a knife. It flashes for an instant. Nathaniel goes rigid in the chair, his eyes wild. Does she imagine the moan issuing from his lips, the quick rush of air? She is up and making her way down the aisle before she is aware of what she's doing. Her boots tap loudly against the boards, magnified in the silence.

She finds the steps that let down to the stage and approaches the doctors.

Dr. Mütter's brows raise in surprise. One hand holds the knife, its point raised to the ceiling. "Miss Hargrave."

"I've no business here, I know," she sputters. Benches creak.

The moment hangs, stretched tight as a bow. "I thought Mr. Dixon might like a hand to hold."

Whispers drift through the tiers. She is bathed in light from the windows, the students veiled in murk. She feels truly on stage now, as if playing a role without having rehearsed her lines. There is no going back; what's done is done. She thinks then that they will banish her, that she will lose her job and be the talk of the school. *The girl who dared take the stage to hold a monster's hand.*

Mütter and Pancoast exchange a glance. Dr. Norris looks furious, as if her presence is absurd and will tarnish their work.

A movement from the chair. "Yes," Nathaniel says, his voice pinched. "Please."

He directs this at Mütter, and something in the doctor changes, as if a new resolve comes over him, a windfall he has not heretofore seen. His lips break into a grin and then he is beckoning her to stand to Nathaniel's good side. Annis covers his tethered hand with her own. She positions her face above his and smooths the hair from his brow. In that drop of a moment, he is a man laid bare to scrutiny, humiliation, and pain and she wants to weep because of it.

With a curt nod, Nathaniel acknowledges he is ready.

Mütter announces he will make the first incision at the base of the tumor. This he does with a quick, shallow slice. Nathaniel flinches. Pancoast, at her periphery, dabs a sponge to the cheek. Mütter continues cutting. Sweat beads on Nathaniel's forehead and he begins to shake. Pancoast hands her a cool damp cloth, which she places on his forehead.

"If you wish to take a break, bat your eyes," she whispers.

Nathaniel does not move.

Time drags. Sweat forms on Annis' body. It's too hot in the room. Too close. Her corset is a vise. Her feet pinch in her boots. And yet they are nothing to the pain Nathaniel must be feeling.

She squeezes his hand again, brushes her thumb over his forehead. He closes his eyes, as if her touch is a balm. But how can that be with a knife to his face?

After what seems an age, Mütter says, "I have completed the cut around the tumor. Now, I shall carefully prize it from the underlying skin." More sponging from Pancoast. The water in the bowl must be bright with blood but she will not take her eyes from Nathaniel. "Just one last section," Mütter says. "Stubborn, but I almost have it." Nathaniel closes his eyes and moans. He is shaking more vigorously now, straining against the bands, trying to keep still.

"Dr. Mütter, a break if you please," Annis says. It's more a command than a request, but she doesn't care.

Dr. Norris huffs and she gives him a piercing glance. *Let you go under the knife and see what it's like.*

"Of course," Dr. Mütter says. "Nathaniel, I've removed the tumor. You are free of it." Annis darts a look at Mütter and catches his wide grin. But she can't see the area in which he's been working for Pancoast is blotting it with linen. "It came away cleanly. You are through the worst of it. Do you wish for a shot of whiskey?"

A small shake of the head.

"Good man." To Pancoast Mütter says, "Water."

Pancoast hands her a clean sponge. "A few drops into his mouth."

She does as she is told and relief washes over Nathaniel, his upper body relaxing, if only a bit. But it's soon done and Mütter does not wish to tarry long.

"I have left a portion of the skin attached and will now place it back over the site of the tumor," Mütter tells his audience. "I have here silk thread and a suturing needle. I shall start at the widest section and begin to close the wound." To Nathaniel he says, "I shall make quick work of it, young man." He squeezes his shoulder. "If you aren't the hardiest patient ever to grace this stage, I don't know who is."

Mütter's movements are but a blur. It is Nathaniel who is her focus. She searches his eyes for clues of heightened discomfort, but he seems to have renewed his resolve. Mütter is true to his word. He works so quickly, she scarcely knows how the students track his movements.

"God in Heaven, the man's ambidextrous," Dr. Norris says in a hush.

Pancoast chuckles. "What, you haven't heard within the hallowed halls of Jefferson how gifted Mütter is in that regard? He makes the rest of us look like first-year surgeons."

"Practice, gentlemen," Mütter says quietly. "I abhor open wounds. They are a harbinger of infection. Using both hands means I can do twice the work in half the time." After a tick of silence, he says, "Now, I believe, we are quite done." He cuts off the last of the sutures with a flourish, then inspects his work. "Yes, I believe that will do. You may dress it, Pancoast."

Mütter steps back and wipes his hands on a clean towel. "I shall finish addressing the class. The doctors will lead you back to the clinic where you can rest. I should like you off your feet the rest of the day."

Annis unbuckles Nathaniel's wrists and helps him to get up. He allows Pancoast and Norris to help him through the door. Annis stands before them wringing her hands, unsure of what to do. Should she follow? Will they bar her from entering the clinic?

It is Mütter who decides the matter. Coming to her, he whispers, "Well, what are you waiting for? I believe that young man would be happy to see you at his bedside." He winks and turns, and begins to address the students.

Annis won't likely get a second invitation. She hurries through the door to the clinic.

# REPLY

Gabriel strides down Cross Street in the infected pustule that is Five Points, a place of buckling structures, rotting front doors, and putrid refuse spilling into the streets. The air is sharp and cool, the rags pinned to lines strung across alleys wave faintly in the breeze. He passes the Old Brewery, one of the dirtiest tenements of the city where people dwell ten or more to a room in conditions rife with disease. As if to prove the point, a woman on the second story upends a bucket of shit onto the street and Gabriel sidesteps to miss it.

A man pulling a rag cart turns to stare but looks away when Gabriel pins him with a glare. He can, he thinks with amusement, make himself appear formidable when he wishes. A decade on stage hasn't softened him; he's as volatile and dangerous as the thugs who roam the streets here.

Beside a pile of broken cobbles, a boy pokes a dead pigeon with a stick. Gabriel recognizes the sunken eyes, the sharp angles of him. An old memory shimmers. Running, running as fast as he can through the filthy streets to avoid the taunts of the boys in the neighborhood. Hurled words with sharp edges: *Dim wit. Whoreson. Bastard.*

The image swirls to another. His mother taking his chin in her palm. *Pay them no mind.* She wiped away his tears with her thumbs and spoke words that would change the course of his life. *Your father is a wellborn man of education. A great magician who thrills audiences far and wide.*

Gabriel looked for clues his mother was joking and found none. The peeling walls that caged him, the grimy window through which he glimpsed the blighted world, disappeared. He saw instead his father, a man he fashioned with a curling mustache and immaculate clothes. A man of stature and means who was not from the hovel in which he and his mother clawed to survive. His chest swelled with pride. He, Gabriel, was the product of a great man.

*A man who could conjure wonder.*

Wasn't that what magicians did, made audiences gasp and gape? He saw one once when he snuck into a traveling show off Market Street. He was amazed to watch a caped man pull fake flowers from a top hat and an egg from a girl's ear. To be the son of such a man!

*You're the spitting image of your pa*, his mother told him that day. *Find him. He'll take one look and know you're his. Then our luck will change.*

She told him something else to aid him in his quest: his father had a missing index finger. An odd detail, but it only added to the mystery. For years after, he would make up stories in his head of how his father had come to lose it. These imagined scenarios—he'd been in a duel, wrestled with an alligator, been struck by lightning—kept him up at night, each version of how that finger had been severed bringing his father alive.

It didn't occur to him then to ask why his father was a stranger to him. Gabriel only knew, once he found him, everything would be different. His father would see his own face staring back at him and exclaim, *Is that you, Gabriel? How I've missed you and your mother.* In his mind's eye, once his father clapped eyes on him, he would insist he and his mother become a part of his life.

To think, no more slum living, no more nights of gnawing hunger. They would live in a fine home in a fine neighborhood. His father might even take Gabriel under his wing and train him in the craft.

But Gabriel had to find him first.

From that day forward, he sought his father's face on show posters, handbills, and broadsheets. He'd never learned his letters, but it didn't matter. Advertisements for illusionists, shamans, soothsayers, and other virtuosos of the trade were almost always depicted with showy illustrations. In draping robes or pointed hats, the headliners leered from the paper like the shrewd masters they were. How well he remembered poring over the marquees at theatres and the discarded newspapers he pulled from bins, hungry to spot the mysterious father he'd never known. When his mother had extra money, Gabriel attended the circus at White Street and Broadway, searching the tents for a lanky, dark-haired man who looked like him, but grown.

When new theatres opened and the circus moved up Broadway, he continued his quest. In the dip and whirl of New York City, there was always entertainment. Performers were always on rotation. Some men in the illustrations resembled Gabriel just enough for him to believe he'd found his father, but once Gabriel saw them in the flesh (trickier for the pricey uptown venues. He'd wait at back door stage exits where the acts left in carriages to get a look-see) he was always disappointed. The eyes and hair might've been dark like his own, but when it came to the fingers, they were all accounted for.

With each passing year, his feet grew wearier and his hope began to curdle.

Still, he searched.

When he was nine, he started as an errand boy at the docks, fetching and carrying, doing any task that put coin in his pocket. His only refuge from those punishing days was sleep. He would drop into bed filthy and withered as his mother took off into the night.

A dog's bark shunts him back into the present. He kicks at the feral beast as he turns left onto Mulberry. There is an air of unrest along this stretch. The tenements overflow with men, women, and children who track his steps, silent and watchful. He takes out his knife to show his lust for destruction, that he won't hesitate to use it.

A whiff of rotting meat stirs another memory. His attention on the street remains sharp, even as his mind trips back to the past. When he was eleven, he began working in a slaughterhouse near Washington Market. His job was to collect bones—stripped of flesh and sinew—into barrels that were then sold to bone manufactories for sugar refining. He hated the screams of the cows, the stench of blood and entrails.

One day, after Gabriel had been working at the slaughterhouse for about a year, he climbed atop the fence that surrounded the cow pens. He'd worked ten hours straight and stank, but he didn't want to return home yet. He'd gotten used to staying out until dark to avoid his mother. He withdrew a heel of bread from the pocket of his breeches and watched the crowd go by as he ate. There was always a sea of bodies streaming past headed to the market. He glimpsed a grubby boy stop a man on the street. The man was dressed like a swell—a gray topper and matching frock coat—and he wondered what an urchin had to say to such a man. He then realized, given the man's gestures, the boy was asking for directions. Gabriel felt his lips split into a grin. No one knew this stinking side of town better than a street urchin.

It was the first time he laid eyes on Dabney. He was older than the other boy, but his togs were just as ratty. He approached the man from behind, veered alongside him, brought his hand to the swell's pocket, and lifted his wallet clean out. He didn't break a stride. Now that the deed was done, the smaller boy thanked the man and he and Dabney strode off in different directions. The man resumed his walk, none the wiser. Pickpockets were ten a penny in the city, but he'd never actually glimpsed one.

It was so expertly done, Gabriel was fascinated.

The next day after work as he headed home, he saw Dabney ambling down Fulton, cocksure as you please. He followed him for blocks, until the streets grew less crowded, the carriage traffic thinned. Dabney rounded a corner and Gabriel followed only to stumble into him as he turned. At once, Dabney took him by the collar, smashed him into the brick wall behind him, and got up in his face.

"Why're you following me, eh?" Dabney said.

Now that he was close, Gabriel took his measure: ginger hair, blue eyes, a face as coated with filth as Gabriel's. They looked about the same age. "I saw you yesterday at the slaughterhouse. You stole that swell's wallet."

Dabney narrowed his eyes. "What's it to you?"

"I want to know how you did it." Gabriel shrugged, his collar pulling, for Dabney continued to grip him. "I'm poor, same as you."

Dabney looked at him as if to gauge the truth of it then released him, pushing off Gabriel's chest as he did. "Everyone here's poor. You work for the police?"

"I'm a bone picker at the slaughterhouse."

Dabney laughed. "Now that's a pleasant job, ain't it?"

"I hate it." Gabriel thought again of the offal, the stench on his clothes that had become a part of him. "I figure you got more from that dandy's pocket than I'll make in a year. You could teach me."

Dabney hawked and spit, his smile disappearing behind the wrist he dragged over his mouth. "Tell you what, meet me here tomorrow, same time, and I'll show you a few tricks, eh?"

Gabriel showed up the next day. The alley was empty, though with the light slanting the way it was, he couldn't see too far down it; it disappeared into shadows. He leaned against the brick and considered what to do. When a quarter of an hour passed, he decided to leave. He'd been duped, that's all there was to it.

As he pushed off the wall and turned, something hit him from behind. Hard. Gabriel plunged to the ground. When he sat up, a large stone lay beside him. When he drew his hand from the back of his head, it was streaked with blood. Movement behind him. A troupe of boys emerged from the shadows and surrounded him.

One of them was Dabney. "Stand up," he said.

Gabriel pulled himself to his feet. None of the boys were bigger than he was, but he was outnumbered six to one. The first strike was Dabney's, a blow to the face that sent him flying. He landed on his rear. A kick to the ribs followed, then another. After that, it was a whir of limbs, of punts and wallops that dimmed his vision. He fought back at first, or tried. But it only winded him and brought on jeers. In the end, he lay in the dirt curled in on himself. Only then did the boys stop.

Dabney leaned down and spoke into his ear. "First rule and the last you'll get from me. Never turn your back on a dark alley."

They began to walk away. Gabriel pushed himself to a sitting position, the world tilting around him. "Wait," he said.

With their grimy clothes and scrawny frames, he might have been one of them. He *wanted* to be.

Dabney's chin tipped up. "What? You want some more?"

The moment ticked. Gabriel's eye was beginning to swell shut and his head throbbed. The others grew bored and walked off, but Dabney remained.

"My mother is a whore." He didn't know why he said it. It had just spilled from him; ugly words Gabriel had never dared speak to anyone. And yet underneath the shame, he felt... a release. He spat out blood and got to his feet, swaying as he did.

Dabney snorted. "So? What's it to me?" He wasn't judgmental, wasn't disgusted by what Gabriel had confessed. He simply took it in stride.

When Dabney turned to go Gabriel spoke again. "My father is a magician." *That* got him; Dabney paused in his tracks. "I've been looking for him everywhere. My mother says he's a gent."

Dabney looked at him strangely, as if trying to gauge his reason. There must have been something in Gabriel he liked, for he jutted out his hand and introduced himself. Years later Gabriel would recognize it for what it was: the beginning of his own rebirth.

He chuckles, low, and takes the bend in the road. A second later he ducks into a crowded tavern and takes a seat in a corner. A barmaid approaches and he orders what's on offer: a stew with beef and potatoes, and a pint of ale. When the soup arrives, there's a film on the surface and no trace of meat. Similar to the fare he was used to supping on with Dabney all those years ago and just like that, his mind is heaving memories again.

Dabney took him under his wing that very day. He taught him how to pickpocket. First, on unsuspecting victims of the lower east side, then in neighborhoods uptown where ladies and their gents shopped. Next came theatres and music halls where the crowds made it easier for him to melt into the melee once he'd fleeced them. Gabriel made so much more as a cutpurse than he had at the slaughterhouse, it was laughable. He never returned. There was too much money to be made by thieving and he was good at it.

But then, is he so surprised? Is he not light of hand? He places his spoon in his palm, flicks his wrist, and the spoon is gone. His knack for subterfuge runs in his blood. As for Dabney, he became like a brother. He understood Gabriel. His ginger-haired friend had no family of his own and lived on the streets. Gabriel heard him say once of his own mother, *Well, least you got one.*

When the day's thieving was done, Dabney helped him look for his father. He believed as much as Gabriel did that he was out there somewhere. The more Gabriel scoured theatres, circuses, and dance halls, the more that world tugged at him. He would fit in these places; he *knew* it.

At night he began to work in cheap houses that drew low, rowdy crowds—laborers and sailors, mostly. There was no job beneath him because he was where he needed to be for the next step of his scheme to unfold. He polished seats, mopped stages, scrubbed floors. He watched, he listened, and grew accustomed to the kind of acts that drew people. He would know the right opportunity when it presented itself.

Four years later, after working a series of jobs at as many venues, he met a French magician named Augustus.

He worked first as his stagehand, moving scenery and props during performances. He was a drudge, a grunt. He fetched Augustus's food, brushed his clothes, polished his props. Gabriel saw that he became Augustus's most reliable worker. They traveled to the cities of New York—Albany, Buffalo, Kingston, and more—and for the first time Gabriel saw the world outside New York City.

Augustus's specialty was his act in which he pretended to read minds. He would stalk the audience for a trinket and his assistant (a pretty young thing Augustus found on the streets) would lie blindfolded on a sofa and name it. A year later (after working with an iron craftsman in Brooklyn), Augustus introduced the Levitating Lady trick. It was his greatest triumph. He did it all with the air of a charming Frenchman. He impressed with his acts, seduced with his words. The crowds loved him.

What amazed Gabriel most was how easy the deceptions were. The real magic, he discovered, was the gullibility of a rapt audience.

Between bookings Augustus taught him how to read and do sums. He had a natural ability and was a quick study. When he was alone, he practiced speaking as Augustus did, with a heavy French accent. It was like trying on a new set of clothes: it made him feel different. Important. All the while he packed and carried, traveled and watched. He learned Augustus: how he projected his voice, used his cape and wand, made the audience laugh. He studied how to pull rats from hats, pennies from handkerchiefs, daisies from ears. The trick was to make it all look easy while hiding the false bottoms, the decoys, the sleight of hand.

He slurps at his stew and a darkness comes over him, a feeling of falling. He is shunted into a familiar room with a dying fire. Augustus in his royal blue coat, seated in an upholstered chair. The roast duck between them, the smell of cloved oranges in the air. Augustus's mouth moves but Gabriel can't hear what he's saying. They're important, these lines, but the more he tries to grab at them, the more elusive they become. And then Augustus pours wine, laughs. Shadows move on the walls, the fire glows in the hearth.

A ringing in his ears, the tunneling of his vision, and Gabriel snaps to attention in the tavern.

He takes a long pull of his ale. Cheap and watery. He should be in a satin tailcoat at Delmonico's, eating an exquisite meal paid for by a rich admirer of his show. *Such a wonder you are, Monsieur Marchand. How do you do it? I don't suppose you would tell me your secrets? No, of course not. You conjurers must keep it close to the vest, I wager.*

Gabriel orders a double whiskey and shoots it down. Orders another. Soon the tavern slips in and out of focus.

A clot of men enters and they take a seat at a table, their chatter boisterous as they settle. Near the hearth, two tarts in heavy face paint sit atop a man's lap, hands roving over the lapels of his coat. He whispers words Gabriel doesn't catch, and the girls tilt their heads back and cackle.

Beside the bar, a young woman stands alone. His gaze moves on then snags back. She's dressed in a pale blue frock—much too fine for place like this. She stares at Gabriel as if to catch his attention. A thought niggles. Has he seen her before? Something isn't right, something about her dress, the face. He pushes the heels of his palms to his eyes, rubs, and tries again. She looks sheer, as if... Gabriel shakes his head and blinks. The whiskey is making him fanciful. He scans the room to see if anyone else has noticed. When he looks again, she is gone.

When he leaves the tavern, it's nearly dusk.

---

Up the narrow flight of stairs he climbs. A twist of the key, and he's inside his room. As he is making his way to the desk, his foot treads on something soft. He lights a candle. Resting inches from the door is a letter, no doubt pushed there by his nosey landlady. He rips the envelope open with his bare hands.

*Mr. Jape,*

*I have news regarding the pearl necklace you inquired about. As it happens, a young lady came into the shop today with it. I am certain it is the rare jewel you described. It is now in my safekeeping as is the lady's address. I shan't part with either, however, until I am in receipt of the 'generous reward' of which you spoke. Upon agreement of the sum, I shall be happy to deliver both into your hands.*

*Nigel Kiersley,*
*Kiersley & Sons,*
*Philadelphia*

All Gabriel's imaginings crystallize. A familiar turbulence stirs within him: red-hot anger and a ferocious burning desire. He grabs his quill, stabs it into the inkpot and writes so furiously, he is forced to crumple the paper and begin again.

*Kiersley,*

*I leave for Philadelphia on the morrow. Rest assured you shall receive more than satisfactory recompense for your trouble.*

*I remain,*
*A. Jape*

He has found her at last.

# NEW PATIENT

## PHILADELPHIA, FEBRUARY 1842

Annis tidies her work area until it gleams. It surprises her how content she is sweeping the floor, buffing the worktable, cleaning the window. Perhaps it's because her tiny studio is the only space that's ever been entirely hers.

Earlier, she'd cleared the room of Dr. Mütter's specimens. She didn't want them upsetting the visitor she's expecting. The only object resting on the table is the cluster of berries from Nathaniel. They are beginning to droop in the brush tin. When the time is right, she'll take them home and press a few stems between the pages of a book to preserve them.

Thoughts of him bring on a blissful giddiness. She can barely think of him without a flutter in her stomach or a smile on her face. How quickly he has come to dominate her thoughts. Nathaniel seems to have filled a chamber in her heart she never knew existed. How is it she has only known him a smattering of days?

During the hours he lay resting in the clinic, Annis split her time between sketching and dashing to him when she could afford a break. How his face lit up when she arrived, how firmly he grasped her hand when she sat with him. At regular intervals, Dr. Mütter came by to see if he was comfortable, to check on his dressing, to make sure the stitches were clear of infection. Each time his patient improved a little more, and the doctor promised that in a few days Nathaniel would have no need for the bandages. Infection would still be something the doctor would keep an eye on, but all looked well for a complete recovery.

The last time Annis visited, when the day was winding down and his release was imminent, Nathaniel took her hand and kissed it. The feel of his lips on her skin sent a hot current through her. She hadn't known what to do, where to look, how to behave. Nathaniel had smiled, pleased, it seemed, at her momentary discomposure. Which had, of course, sent another delicious thrill through her.

Soon he will meet Ben. Annis spoke highly of her brother while Nathaniel lay listening. It was only natural he asked to be introduced. Nathaniel will see, she is sure, Ben's new-found confidence, for fate has turned in his favor. Ben has found work at Walnut Street Theatre and his leg is as good as new.

Annis can scarcely believe that a month ago, their lives had been in tatters. Her new reality has taken on the quality of a dream—glittering, diaphanous, an experience outside of life. At night she is sometimes struck by the notion that it will all end badly, that the world she holds in the palm of her hand will be fleeting, then gone. But she tells herself she's being ridiculous, that her fears are behind her and nothing can take away their good fortune.

*Not even you, Greta. You're nothing but a figment.*

When she finishes the last swipe at the window, she steps back. The glass is clear and void of streaks. Outside, fat snowflakes drift to the street under a bruised sky. The light dusting that fell overnight has muffled the street noise, another boon to this perfect day. She makes a mental note to stop at the sweet shop across the street to purchase some sugared almonds for Ben.

She is affixing a piece of paper to her easel when a knock sounds behind her.

"Yes?"

A woman peeks around the door. "Miss Hargrave?"

"Miss Santos? Please come in."

The middle-aged woman who advances into the room walks with a pronounced limp. Her skirts sway as she approaches the worktable, her slim frame rocking with the effort. She is dressed in a coat of brown wool that's been patched in places.

"Call me Mariah."

Annis helps her out of her things and says, "If I'm to call you Mariah, you must call me Annis."

Mariah offers a pretty smile. "What a delightful name." Her skin is smooth and as white as cream, and sets off her dark hair and eyes.

"Thank you for coming," Annis says. "My sketch won't take long. I shall get you out of here in no time." She doesn't like to think of the older woman falling in the street on slick ice. She's slight and her gait is precarious as it is.

"You mean on account of my clubfoot, I suppose," Mariah says with a titter. "Goodness, I've walked in weather fouler than this and for more winters than you've been living." Those dark, eager eyes take in the room. "What a cozy place. Is it yours?" Annis nods, pride filling her. "Where shall I...?" Mariah's voice tapers off and she points to her leg.

"Would it be too much for you to sit on the worktable and place your foot on the stool?"

"Not at all." With some help from Annis, Mariah hops to the table and lifts her skirts. Her legs are clad in heavy wool stockings. On her right foot is a well-made leather shoe that is misshapen. Her shin is so slender, it makes the twisted lump at the ankle more pronounced. "I assume you'll want my foot bare?"

"Yes. I'll need to draw it without any encumbrances."

"Well, I suppose as the doctor's artist, you've seen a good many of these."

In truth, Annis has seen many patients hobble in and out of the clinic, but she's never seen a clubfoot up close. Mariah, however, doesn't appear the least bit wary of Annis' scrutiny. So different than how it was with Nathaniel, but then a foot is easier hidden than a face.

"Born with this, I was," Mariah says as she pulls the shoe off. "Couldn't find a doctor in Ohio who could mend it, and didn't my father search for one, and then my husband, for years." She strips off her stocking to reveal a bulbed ankle, the foot badly twisted and rolled inward. There is no discernible heel.

Annis picks up her charcoal. "You've come all the way from Ohio?"

Mariah tucks a strand of black hair behind her ear. "Cincinnati, yes. I wouldn't be able to afford the inn where I'm staying if it weren't for the doctor doing the surgery for nothing. Don't mind a bit about his students looking on, not if he can correct it." Her brown eyes twinkle. "He's a kind man, Dr. Mütter, even if he does wear the most outlandish clothes. 'Course, if he can cobble my foot back together, he can wear tar and feathers for all I care." Mariah's lips curl in a mischievous smile and Annis can't help but laugh.

She begins to sketch, starting with the top of the shin, making long strokes down to the swollen ankle.

Mariah leans back on her hands and regards her foot. "Do you know, I've longed all my life to run. I know that may sound crazy, but it's true. Now I suppose I shall be delighted to simply walk properly. But I mustn't be too positive, even about that. It's what my Henry says. 'You mustn't get your hopes up, Mariah.' He's right, of course."

Annis makes a loop to form a toe and adds the tiny nail. "Clubfoot is one of the most successful procedures they do here. The doctor and his friend, Dr. Pancoast, are masters at surgery. I've seen one myself."

A look of alarm flits across Mariah's face and Annis chides herself for being so callous. The word *surgery* is enough to conjure horrific images even in the most fearless of patients. Before she knows what she's doing, she launches into Nathaniel's story. When she finishes with his recovery in the clinic under Mütter's careful eye, Mariah's face is placid again.

"What a relief for that young man." Mariah sits up straight, tilts her head and regards Annis curiously. "Did he have the tumor as a child?"

"Yes. It began growing when he was quite young."

"Children can be so vicious," Mariah replies, her voice soft. "That was the case with me. As I got older, it was easier. Not because the jeers lessened, but because I'd grown accustomed to my lot. By the time me and my Henry married, I didn't give a fig about what others thought. I still don't, but my leg aches when it rains and I've the most fearsome pain here." She points to the side of her foot where the skin is rough and calloused from bearing her weight.

"My husband..." Mariah's eyes fill with tears. "He's endured no end of cruelty on account of this wretched thing." She glares down at her limb and then juts her chin at Annis. "He's a shoemaker. Don't think I don't see the irony in it. He takes such care in the shoes he makes for me. But there's no skill that can hide the ugliness of this pathetic stump." She scoffs through her tears, wipes them with the hem of her sleeve. "Do you know there are people who refuse to come to him? They travel fifty miles to the next shoemaker because they think I'm cursed. A *freak*. When I come back whole, his business will be the better for it." She sobers and smiles a little. "Thank you for telling me of the man with the tumor. It's good of you."

The day ticks. Students tread to the next class, the snow continues its lazy descent, and they speak of Dr. Mütter, Jefferson, and the book Annis is illustrating for the college. When her sketch is complete, Annis rotates her easel. Mariah nods but says nothing. When she has put on her stocking and shoe once more, she hops off the table. She turns for her coat and stills herself, turning back to Annis.

"I lied. I've never grown used to it." Her lower lip trembles. "All those years of cruelty and stares."

Annis takes Mariah's hand. "I don't blame you. You've lived a life with a burden far greater than a twisted foot." The older woman smiles through her tears and an understanding unfurls between them.

She helps Mariah into her coat. "Your surgery will be quick work and you'll be headed home a new person."

Mariah reaches up and sets her palm against Annis' cheek. "What a treasure you are. I shall see you again when I've had the surgery. I pray my foot will look very different then."

They embrace for a long moment. Suddenly, Mariah stiffens and pulls away. Annis tracks her gaze to the empty shelves in the corner. A chilly stir of air lifts the sketch at the easel and is gone.

As if something had been in the room a second before and vanished.

The hairs on the back of Annis' neck bristle. "Did you see something, Mariah?" She is clutching the woman's upper arms now, pressing into the flesh. Anything to snap Mariah to attention—she's still staring transfixed into the corner. "Was it... *someone*?"

Mariah's eyes are wide as she turns to Annis, but she blinks, shakes her head, and the moment evaporates. "It was nothing. Nothing at all."

"But—"

Mariah lurches to the door, her face as white as chalk. Her every movement brims with the urgency to leave the room. It's all Annis can do to watch her retreat down the hall, wondering if Mariah has glimpsed what Annis has been seeing for weeks.

The ghost of Greta.

Despite Annis' wish to flee her studio to avoid another encounter with Greta, she forces herself to remain. Her gaze flicks again and again to the corner. If Mariah saw Greta, then Greta isn't a delusion. The understanding that she isn't losing her mind is quickly eclipsed by the knowledge that Greta—the ghost of her anyway—is undeniably genuine. Not physical, but substantive nevertheless.

*Enough of this. I have work to do.*

The hallway is deserted. It's late; there is only one class left before the students head home. Out the windows across the hall, daylight has drained from the day, the clouds so leaden they appear to droop, exhausted, on the tips of the barren trees. Not the best light to work in. If it's too dark when she returns to her studio, at least she'll have fetched some things to work on tomorrow.

She traipses down the steps, turns left, and enters the storage area.

"We shall need a good—" Dr. Mütter stops mid-sentence and turns. "Ah, Miss Hargrave."

He is standing several feet from the entrance. Next to him, clutching a notepad, is Nathaniel. Annis' heart is a drum. It's the first time she's seen him without his bandage.

"Miss Hargrave," Nathaniel says, dipping his head in greeting.

"Come to collect one of the marvels, have you?" Dr. Mütter queries, his tone light.

"Yes." She nods a greeting, glimpses the warmth in Nathaniel's eyes. "I'll come back at a better—"

"Nonsense," the doctor says. He waves her closer and gestures with open arms to the room. "I was just telling Nathaniel of the museum that shall soon grace this place. There's much yet to do, of course." He turns to Annis. "You are aware, I think, that Mr. Dixon is a furniture maker?"

"Yes," Annis says.

Dr. Mütter's eyes shift from her to Nathaniel, and she swears there is a glint of mischief in them. "I suppose you learned much about each other when Nathaniel was at the clinic. So good of you to look after him."

To relieve Annis of her discomfort or perhaps his own, Nathaniel coughs and says, "You were saying, doctor? About the cabinets?"

"Yes, yes." Mütter steps farther into the room. "I've collected many things over the years, many of them intended for display behind glass. We shall need at least a dozen more cabinets. I've set it all out in my mind—where the bones are to be, versus the illustrations and wax models. It shall be very organized."

The doctor approaches a seven-foot cabinet with glass doors. "You could reproduce this, I assume? Its dimensions, the shelves inside?"

Nathaniel is already sketching on his pad. "Of course." He runs a finger over the grain. "Oak. You wish for the same?"

"I know nothing of wood, I'm afraid," Dr. Mütter says. "I work in a very different medium." He smiles at his little joke. "If it's oak, oak will do."

Nathaniel nods and jots a note. "I shall work up an estimate for twelve cabinets like this one once I've taken the measurements."

"Good," Dr. Mütter replies. "I shall have to share everything with the board, naturally. They will want to know the expense. In for a penny, in for a pound, as they say."

"Of course," Nathaniel says. "I know a glazier who would be happy to supply the glass. As for the installation—"

Annis lets them talk and picks her way through the room, past crates exploding with sawdust, and mysterious heaps under sheets. She finds what she's looking for on a dusty shelf: a doctor's bag with an old surgical kit inside. She's been working through most of the instruments around it, many of them dull and rusty from years of disuse.

When she makes her way back up the row, she finds Dr. Mütter gone. Nathaniel is finishing taking measurements of the cabinet. She has the sense he's been slow at it and has waited to catch a word with her. The light through the large bank of windows is muted, but she can clearly make out the stitches and incision marks on Nathaniel's cheek. The sneer is gone; his lip no longer rides up on one side. The softness of his lips contrasts with the sharp angle of his jaw. Standing so tall and poised, he could be a sculpted David. The thought makes Annis' heart beat faster. Michelangelo depicted David in the nude! She drops her eyes and bats a wisp of hair from her face.

He remains silent so long, she darts a look at him. "What?"

"You haven't done it properly." He reaches out and tucks the wayward lock behind her ear.

"Your face. It's healing." She winces. Of course it's healing. Why does his proximity reduce her to a simpleton?

"I've you to thank for that."

"Me? What for?"

"Visiting me when I lay in pain."

"You said you felt no pain."

"I didn't. Not when you were there." The words are as intimate as a caress. "Dr. Mütter said you may sketch me any time, now that the bandages are off. I'd like to get started on the estimate for the cabinets right away, but may I come to you tomorrow? Sometime in the afternoon?"

"Of course."

He walks her back to her studio, neither in any hurry to reach it. By some silent stroke of a clock, students pour into the hall, laughter and footfalls careening off the floor and ceiling, shoulders knocking against Annis as she battles against the sea tide. At once Nathaniel takes her hand and draws her behind him. He is good deal taller and broader than most and, in deference, the young men make a wide arc around him. It brings a private smile to her lips. When they stop in front of her door, she is trembling. The hall has nearly cleared. She's struck by the memory of their first time together at her door, when he'd been about to knock on Dr. Mütter's.

"Until tomorrow afternoon, then," Nathaniel says. He still clutches her hand. She is struck with the intensity of his gaze, as if he is saying more than goodbye. When he'd come to be sketched, he'd had a hard time looking at her. She likes the change in him, even if her stomach bubbles. And then she is wishing he would kiss her right there in the hallway. Would it be too much? Is she wicked to want it?

"I'd like to know what it is you're thinking when your eyes do that," Nathaniel says and she wants to die. "They are a most beautiful shade of blue."

She knows in that instant she has never met anyone like him and never will again. The thought is at once liberating and terrifying. When he bids her farewell a second later, she is still trying to find an adequate response to his compliment.

# ARRIVAL

## PHILADELPHIA, FEBRUARY 1842

Gabriel swirls the amber liquid in its snifter, takes a sip, and sets it on the table. He'll say this about Kiersley: the man knows his brandy. Well-aged and rich, with notes of vanilla and candied fruit. A far cry from the gut rot he's been drinking in the slums of New York City. He folds his hands together on the table and considers the man seated across from him. With his coiffed fair hair and hooked nose, the chap has an air of privilege about him. But there is a wiliness too—mostly about the eyes and his not-quite-tawdry suit of clothes—that sets him firmly in the world of pawn.

"She told me the pearl was cursed, you know," Kiersley says mildly.

Gabriel covers his surprise by taking another drop of brandy. "How creative."

Kiersley shrugs. "Customers lie all the time. Usually about the worth of the item they're selling." He lifts his drink, the bowl of the glass seated in his palm. "There was, I think, something of the truth about this former maid of yours. I think she believed it, the curse. Though it strikes me as odd."

Gabriel raises a brow, his restraint thinning. "Oh?"

Kiersley's eyes twinkle. "If the pearl is as cursed as she believes, I wonder why she wants it back."

So the wench hadn't sold it. She'd only wanted a loan.

Kiersley tips another splash of brandy into their glasses. When the cork is replaced, he leans back and hooks the crook of his arm around the back of his chair, languid as you please. "It's an exquisite piece, to be sure. Rare, as you say. But she stole it from your... how did you put it? *Lady wife.* I wonder why the chit didn't simply sell it immediately in New York. Why come all the way here to pawn it? And why the devil would she want it back?"

Kiersley clearly hopes to ensnare him in a lie. At the very least, he's making it clear he doesn't believe a word of his story about a theft. "It is as you say," Gabriel says simply.

Kiersley's languor slips and for a moment he's off his game, his curiosity laid bare. "How so?"

Gabriel grins, the sort of leer that makes him look lupine. "Customers lie all the time."

Kiersley's indifference returns with a thin smile. "Ah. I will remind you, Mr. Jape, that in this," he gestures to Gabriel's letter laying between them, "you are a customer."

Gabriel leans in. "Then let us get down to it instead of wasting time on the fanciful tales of maids," he snaps. "I am not a patient man. Show me the necklace."

"I've yet to hear a price," Kiersley intones. He rolls the stem of his snifter between his thumb and forefinger but doesn't take his eyes from Gabriel.

"I won't discuss payment until I see what I came for." Said with teeth so the fool will know he means business.

Though Kiersley works to keep his features bland, his cheeks flush with color. He pushes himself to his feet and approaches the desk at the back of the room. Gabriel was careful to arrive late in the day when the shop was near closing. Upon identifying himself, Kiersley locked the front door and directed him here, the small room behind the curtain, where they could haggle over a drink. While Kiersley takes a key from his vest pocket and unlocks the desk drawer, Gabriel scans the area. It appears to be a combination of office and storeroom. Behind Kiersley is a door that almost certainly opens to the alley behind the building.

When he returns to the table, Kiersley has in his grip a burgundy velvet bag. From it he pulls a large teardrop-shaped pendant attached to a thin silver chain. He sets it between them. Gabriel is disappointed. In the weak gaslight, the pearl is as gray and ordinary as a stone. It had looked more extravagant months ago. Magical even.

But it is inconsequential now. He'd used it to find her and that is all that matters.

Gabriel picks it up. It's heavier than it looks, the surface pitted and opaque. Then, quite to his astonishment, the pearl catches the light, shimmers, and goes dark.

*Strange.*

Gabriel rises, walks to the gas sconce on the wall and holds the pearl to it. The iridescent colors within come alive. Its depths, he thinks wildly, store a million inner worlds. Tiny fragments of light and color seemingly explode from it, as beguiling as a showman's trick.

"Ten dollars," Gabriel says without looking up.

A laugh behind him. "Do not take me for a fool, Mr. Jape."

Gabriel returns to the table, seats himself, and dangles the pearl from its chain where it flashes intermittently in the lick of the gaslight. A cuckoo clock in the shop chirps the hour as if to remind him that time is eking away and his prey is deliciously close. "Name your price then," he says.

"Sixty. Cash."

Gabriel nods as if he is satisfied. He's enjoying this game

that Kiersley hasn't guessed. He then drops the necklace into his other palm. He closes his fingers around it, rolls his wrist and reveals his palm once more. It's empty.

Kiersley shoots to his feet, his face crimson. "Now, look here—"

"You drive a hard bargain, Mr. Kiersley," Gabriel says. "Now sit down."

"I—"

"*Sit down.*"

Kiersley obliges, but only just. The gleam in his eye is gone, replaced by anger. "You common th—"

Before he can finish, Gabriel reveals the necklace once more with a flick of his wrist. "Thief, you were about to say? I jest with you. I dabble in sleight of hand from time to time." He chortles and drops the necklace into its velvet bag then pushes it across the table to Kiersley. "Now, before I leave to get you the cash you require—you don't think I'd run around the city with that much on me, do you?—I need the second condition of our bargain. The young lady's address."

"You may have a look at it only," Kiersley says between clinched teeth. "I shan't give it to you until the money is in my possession."

"Wise of you."

From the inside of his breast pocket, Kiersley pulls a sheet of paper. He unfolds it and dangles it close enough for Gabriel to see the description of the pawned item, the signature and address at bottom.

"Excellent," Gabriel says. "I shall be back in a half hour with the funds." With casual ease, he drains his glass while Kiersley stands waiting, nostrils flaring. When he rises at last, Kiersley leads him to the alley door, just as Gabriel expected.

With a twist of the deadbolt, Kiersley opens it and bids him through. With one foot over the threshold, Gabriel turns. "Just one thing more, Nigel. May I call you Nigel?"

The pawnbroker glowers at him, his face tight with rage. "What is it, Jape?"

"I promised you satisfactory recompense for your trouble," Gabriel tells him. "Here it is."

He plunges the knife deep into Kiersley's belly, ripping downward as he goes. Kiersley's face contorts and blanches, his eyes bulge. He looks down at himself, at the handle of the knife whose blade has been driven into him. A second later, he stumbles backward and falls, oozing a fountain of blood.

Gabriel pockets the little velvet bag and plucks the paper from Kiersley's breast pocket. He feels for a pulse. Finding none, he withdraws the knife and whispers into the dead man's ear, "What's the saying? 'If you lie down with dogs, you get up with fleas.' So apt a phrase, that. Except in this case, of course, you won't be getting up."

Gabriel heads for the door, but at the last minute, he dashes back and seizes the brandy from the table. It is too delectable to go to waste.

Whistling to himself, he heads down the alley.

# PURSUIT

## PHILADELPHIA, FEBRUARY 1842

Gabriel wakes before dawn and leaves his rattrap of a room. The streets are deserted as he moves his way south. He can still feel the remnants of the brandy threading through him. Though the air is misted with fog and the silence thick within it, his steps are light and his spirits high. He was elated to learn, upon finding the wench's lodging house last evening, she lives no more than five blocks from the inn where he's staying. The knowledge thrilled him. To know, as the night came down and the city slept, that she lay in slumber not far from him felt deliciously propitious.

By the time he reaches Addison Street, the fog is thinning and dawn is beginning to break. He positions himself between two row houses, a space too narrow to be an alley but wide enough to hide him and provide an unobstructed view of the string of houses across the street.

Shutters open. A dog barks and is answered by another. A smattering of lodgers emerges and step gingerly to the iced pavement, heads bent against the cold. Gabriel shivers when a breeze picks up, tinged with the faint odor of refuse. Now that the sun is rising, it's clear this stretch of block isn't squalid, but it dangles by a thread: the brick is grimy, the casements around the windows in need of paint. The wench has sacrificed the blue pearl to live and managed to keep herself from the slums, but how is she to come by the money to buy it back?

A swell of anticipation fills him. He will know the answer soon enough. No secret remains hidden from him, not if he desires to know it. He has found her at last, just as he had his father.

And just like that he is away, his mind spilling memories.

A tavern near Corlears Hook. The place crowded and smelling of oysters and stale beer. He sat down with Dabney and as Gabriel cast around, he landed on a man seated at the next table. He remembers him so vividly: dark shoulder-length hair, thin nose, irises black as coal. His clothes were shabby: his cravat was in need of washing; the cuffs of his coat were worn. When Gabriel saw his left hand, he knew. As he watched, the man—no gentleman he, not here in this thieves' den chock-full of thugs and whores—swung his gaze to him.

The stranger took him in. And grinned. It seemed to Gabriel that it was his own self—aged thirty years—staring back.

"Ah, you've found me," the older man said. His upturned lips held no benevolence, only ridicule.

Gabriel stood so abruptly his chair overturned. The noise in the tavern stilled. He was dimly aware of Dabney turning in his chair, his, *Christ Almighty, if you ain't the spittin' image.*

"You're my father."

"Well, thanks be to God. You're not as thick as I feared."

His father raised his glass to Gabriel and the tavern burst into laughter. Gabriel wanted to strike him down, but he merely swallowed, his tongue too big for his mouth. "She said you were highborn. Educated."

A tart at the bar cackled. "Our Gabe? He's as common as they come!"

*Our Gabe.* His mother had named him after this scoundrel, a man who'd fled before he was born.

The tart crooned again. "But him's educated, all right. Not a finer swindler at cards!"

The crowd hooted.

Gabriel watched him rotate his whiskey glass with the tips of his fingers, long and so very like his own. "You were never a magician," he breathed, his face burning. "That was a lie too."

His father chuckled. "I had an act for a short time in my youth. Flimflam, easy trickery. But I didn't take to it. 'All work and no play' and all that rot. Your mother was my first assistant. Though not my last." He winked.

The tavern roared again, everyone in their cups, it seemed, but Dabney and himself. Gabriel was keenly aware that the tightening of his throat, the prickle of heat behind his eyes, was his dream evaporating. All those years searching, wanting, aching. All for nothing. *Nothing.*

His father lifted his drink again. "Give my regards to the old girl, will you?" He shot back the whiskey, licked his lips when he was done. "She was a fine woman." For a moment, his father's face sobered and he looked wistful, as if he were combing back the years. But then the look was gone and he was beckoning the barmaid over for another.

Gabriel took a step towards his father. "She's a whore," he spat. "Tell her yourself."

The shock on his father's face was quickly masked, but Gabriel saw it nevertheless.

Dabney grabbed his arm. "Come on, Gabriel. There's nothin' here worth stayin' for."

"Unless, of course, you'd like to buy a round," his father called as they left, the laughter cutting as the door shut behind them.

Gabriel was in no mood for company and Dabney finally

sauntered off into the night. Gabriel's rage stayed with him, so when he stood across from the tavern and watched for his father (how the very word made him cringe), he followed him home and a plan took shape.

He's torn from his reverie by the sound of footsteps. A couple. They eye him warily as they pass. He must be careful; his recollections are making him sloppy.

For the next twenty minutes he stands alert, his senses honed to every stir and footfall. A ginger cat scurries past. Crows alight on the chimney top of the wench's row house. A door opens and a young woman emerges.

His heart seizes.

She's guarded against the cold, clad in a heavy coat and scarf that all but obliterates her features, yet he recognizes her honey-colored hair peaking from beneath her hat, her delicate profile. Gabriel wets his lips, his hands balling into fists. He is filled with the sudden urge to fly at her, to see her lips part in horror at the sight of him.

But now is not the time. His plan cannot be hurried, not yet. His attention snaps to the man behind her. A lover? Anger blooms in his chest but quickly dissipates. He is young, more boy than man. There is a similarity to their profiles, their manner of walking. A cog slides into place. The brother. She spoke of him at the park months ago. *I must find something if Ben and I are to make a go of it.*

Gabriel crosses the street and follows them, keeping a half block back. Along Seventh Street the foot traffic is already heavy, and he must work to keep the two in sight. Wagons and carriages trundle down cross streets. The cold nips, its teeth sharp. They turn onto Walnut, walk another two blocks until the boy waves goodbye and enters a theatre on the corner while the wench continues straight.

She turns right at the next block and disappears. Gabriel

cannot lose her. He quickens his step. She is disappearing into a three-story building on the left when he rounds the corner.

He walks to a shuttered sweet shop across the street, his mind working. He cannot make sense of it. The sign on the building proclaims it a medical college. Why would she have gone inside? Using his scarf to full advantage, he tucks himself into the recessed doorway of the shop. It is then he sees it—a small plaque over the door marked CLINIC.

With renewed interest, he studies those who enter: a man with a pronounced limp, a woman with the emaciated pallor of consumption, a wincing boy with an arm that hangs at an odd angle sandwiched between two adults who scuttle him toward the entrance. Gabriel watches for a quarter hour, so intent on the peculiar assortment of people, he no longer feels the cold. Yet the more he sees, the more the reason for the wench's presence here eludes him. The people entering the school are sickly, many of them disfigured. The wench had shown no sign of either. But then again, her coat could be obscuring a disease that lies beneath, mightn't it?

His thoughts flash and disgust settles in his ribs. *The pox.* Cupid's disease, Dabney had called it. The Great Imitator. She has come down with it. This is why she'd pawned the pearl. How else could a girl survive—

Behind him, the shop door creaks open, and a waft of burnt sugar touches his nose. A man with a handlebar mustache glares at him through the crack. "We're closed."

"Forgive me," Gabriel says, all manners. "May I inquire as to the clinic across the street?"

The man's gaze snags on the scar peaking from his scarf. "They take people like you, if that's what you're asking." He starts to close the door.

Gabriel plants the toe of his boot over the threshold. "People like me?"

"Monsters, miscreants." The man's lip curls in a sneer. "Now remove your foot before I break it and don't be darkening my door. Freaks are welcome *there*, not here."

Gabriel's curiosity is too aroused to react with malice. The door slams. When he turns, a young man in an expensive topcoat is looking at him. He is nineteen or twenty perhaps and carrying a formidable stack of books that look as if they might topple.

"McGrady's a tough sort," he says by way of apology. "He'll go on and on about the freaks, but he's happy enough when us students form a line for his toffees."

Gabriel's mind spins with questions. "You're a student?"

"Second year. I'll be a physician soon enough." He smiles. "Say, if you're looking to have that scar remedied, Jefferson's the place. The University of Pennsylvania may be older, but it's not the superior of the two." The young man's chest swells like a robin's and Gabriel lets him talk, praying the dolt will give him something of use. "Dr. Mütter's the best surgeon in the city, bar none. And he'll perform it—surgery that is—free of charge if you agree to allow his students to attend the procedure. He trained in Paris, you know. What the French call *les chirurgies plastiques*."

"Is that so?" Gabriel says. His eyes flick to the door across the street.

"The clinic is all Mütter's doing, as he's the chair of surgery. Well, there's obstetrics and materia medica of course, and the usual cases of influenza and measles and such, but it's his reconstructions that make it what it is. People come from miles around for those. You've only to enter the clinic and a doctor will have a look at you." He turns and eyes the entrance. "Though it looks to be a very busy morning. You'll have to wait to be seen."

Gabriel's attention turns to the student. "Thank you. I shall let you get to class."

"Of course." The student moves off and waits for a carriage to pass. When he looks back and sees Gabriel hasn't moved, he calls, "If you have any doubt of his skill, you should know he's making a book of his surgical procedures. It's to have illustrations. For the medical community at large of course, so that physicians beyond Pennsylvania can..."

The student prattles on and Gabriel's attention wans. He wants to be free of him so he can focus on the building, determine his next move.

"...hired a young lady to do them. I hear she's quite good with the patients and—"

Quick as lightning, Gabriel steps to him. "A young lady?"

The student smiles, his breath fogging the air between them. "A quite accomplished artist I'm told. Quite *avant garde* of him to hire a woman, but that's our Dr. Mütter."

"She is young, no more than twenty?" Gabriel asks. "With honey blonde hair?"

The young man sobers. "Why do you ask?"

Gabriel shoots him his most ingratiating smile. "She is my niece. I've come a long way to see her. I wanted to make sure I've come to the right place."

The student's eyes widen. "Why didn't you say so, sir? It is indeed the right place. You'll find her studio next to Dr. Mütter's office."

Gabriel beams. "Thank you, again. You've been most helpful."

The student nods and turns to cross, but Gabriel stays him with his hand. "I ask for your circumspection in the matter. She doesn't expect me you see, and I'd like to surprise her."

"I shan't say a word, sir."

He is so close. Sweat covers him, and his body shakes with want. Yet he must be patient. If he is to catch her, he must know her movements, understand her surroundings. As he suspected by the people entering through the clinic door, the entry hall of the college is crowded. He slips in easily, finding himself in a wide passage jostling with students and patients. No one suspects he doesn't belong, nor does anyone inquire as to the nature of his business. He learns quickly that the clinic resides in a set of rooms to the left of the entrance, to the right a room with closed double doors is marked THE PIT. From the echoing chatter coming from within, it sounds like a large lecture hall. A group of students rush past him to climb the stairs at the end of the passage and, as the hall is emptying and he doesn't wish to be spotted alone, he slides through a door marked STORAGE.

He is not prepared for the vastness of the space. For three quarters of an hour, he walks among the crates and boxes lifting lids, unrolling specimens wrapped in fine linen, peaking inside glass cabinets filled with artifacts. Skulls and bones. Instruments and tools. Wax and plaster models. A most curious assortment, one he finds delightfully macabre.

He hears the tread of students again and slips from the room and up the stairs. Here he finds, as he walks among the stream of well-dressed young men, classrooms where lectures take place and farther down, the offices of the teaching physicians, each marked with a nameplate. Dr. Mütter's office is three quarters of the way down. Beside it is a door marked STUDIO. His heart pounds. The wench is on the other side, he is certain. To his chagrin, both doors have a keyhole. They will almost certainly be locked at night. He chuckles. Becoming well versed in the inner workings of locks was one of his favorite pastimes in the days with Dabney when they broke into homes high on the thrill of thievery.

He's caught off guard when the hallway clears. A door marked SUPPLIES opens with a twist of the knob. Stacked neatly on shelves are paper, tins and tubes of paint, bundles of brushes, pencils, and graphite. To his delight, the space is large enough to accommodate him. Darting a look both ways to make sure he is unobserved, he steps inside and pulls the door nearly closed. Through the tiny crack he has a view of the studio door.

There he waits.

The woman who knocks at the wench's door is comely: dark hair swept into a neat bun; skin unblemished though she isn't young. There is something of the countryside about her, perhaps it is the cut of her coat, which is weathered but clean. Most notably, she walks with a slight limp. When she is bid to enter, the door doesn't afford a look into the studio, but the sound of the wench's voice—a light timbre he well remembers—is enough to bring a rush of desire to his loins. He breathes in the smell of paper and graphite, and it is like being wrapped in the essence of the wench herself.

Time stretches. Class ends and another begins, marked by the passing of students in the hall. In the gloom of the closet, his mind works. How to get his wench alone? How to ensnare her so that escape is futile?

When the studio door opens sometime later, Gabriel sees her at last. His most vivid imaginings have failed to capture her beauty in full. She stands at the threshold, one slender hand on the jamb. A thick plait of golden honey falls over one shoulder. Her dress of burgundy brocade and wool accentuates her tiny waist. Oh, how perfect her mouth, how intelligent those vivid blue eyes! It takes everything in him to keep from trembling.

Then it comes to him. He's been the prey all along. She has led him here as surely as she's led him by the neck with a rope. It is *he* who's fallen victim to her wiles.

*The filthy, craven slut.*

"You shall be mended in a few months' time," his vixen says to her visitor, their hands clasped together.

"No matter how many times I see it, I can't quite believe it's mine." The other glances down, lifts her skirts a few inches to reveal a foot wrapped in heavy bandages.

"You must write and tell me how you're getting on, Mariah. Promise?"

"I will. I shall be dancing a jig come summer."

They embrace and then the woman moves off while Gabriel watches the wench blow a kiss and wave, calling, "I shall miss you."

"And I shall miss you, dear Annis," is the faint reply.

*Annis.* He hasn't considered her given name for months. She's taken on the guise of a quest, a thing to be found. And here she stands. How proud she must be to have eluded him! The arrogance of it. Anger bubbles within him, hot as flame.

*You haven't escaped me. You've merely delayed the time of your reckoning.*

Just as she closes the door, Gabriel's mind flashes on what he must do. *Of course.* The true joy of making her his lies not just in the final moments, but the steps he will lay leading to it.

He's quick to slip from the closet and take the stairs down. He almost loses the black-haired woman when she turns down the street. He follows her to a small inn a few blocks away. She limps up the dim stairwell to the second floor, Gabriel trailing after. It's easy to mask the creaking of his steps in the clomping of her own. It is only when she reaches her door and inserts the key that she stills and looks back the way she's come.

"Who's there?"

Gabriel doesn't stir. Crouched in the shadows, he is the darkness itself. After a few seconds, the woman disappears inside her room.

Now that he knows where he can find her, he retraces his steps to the college. There's more to discover and his hunt isn't over.

Yet.

# WORKSHOP

## PHILADELPHIA, FEBRUARY 1842

Annis runs a finger along a plank of wood on Nathaniel's workbench. Despite its lack of varnish, it's as smooth as silk. Lumber and woodworking tools rest on every surface. The floor is littered with sawdust, the air leaden with the pungent scents of naked wood and varnish. She hadn't figured Nathaniel's workshop would reveal so intimately the man himself. Here is where he creates, where his *medium*—as Dr. Mütter had called it—is cut, sanded, carved, and lacquered. Turned into something useful and beautiful by the skilled mastery of his hands. Nathaniel had told her his living quarters are above, and she wonders if she will ever see his kitchen table, his books. The mere thought of his personal things—Nathaniel's woolens, his bed—make her face burn.

"Say something," he says. He's perched on the corner of his desk, one leg hitched up, the other planted on the floor. Nathaniel's hands are clasped, fingers entwined, and he's dressed in dark brown trousers and suspenders, worn leather boots. Annis imagines if she were to trace her fingers over his chest, the faded shirt of blue flannel would be soft to the touch and give off the scent that is so irrepressibly *him*. Pine, sawdust, and leather. The corners of his mouth twitch. "What are you thinking over there?"

"Why?"

He comes to her and cradles her face with his hands. "You're blushing. To the roots of your hair."

How ensnared she is by his gaze. She swallows and when she speaks, her voice is as small and fragile as a child's. "I'm not used to being in the company of a man. Not by myself."

His green eyes dance. "We've been alone in your studio."

*Yes, and I was just as unsettled then.*

Nathaniel tilts her face up to his. "We are a rather boorish sort, aren't we, us men?"

"Entirely uncouth and uncivilized. You frightened me to bits in the storage room."

"Will you ever forgive me?"

"Never. You shall be atoning for decades. Perhaps centuries."

"I shall spend my life making it up to you." Her heart flutters at his words. Does he mean it? The fluttering intensifies when his eyes dip to her lips and his smile vanishes. "I think you know you're safe with me, Annis."

*It depends on what you mean by safe.* Yesterday she'd drawn him in her studio, showing the results of Dr. Mütter's surgery—the tumor gone, only the incision lines showing where the doctor had cut to extract the mass. She was disappointed the time had flown so quickly, even as his proximity tied her stomach in knots. Nathaniel had spent another twenty minutes with her after she'd finished, and they'd arranged for her to come here after work the next day to see his shop.

She thinks of him constantly, can remember every time he's touched her in dizzying detail. Does he feel as passionately for her as she him? She'd been so distracted, she'd yanked the sketch of him from her easel and hidden it in a pile of other renderings. Out of sight, out of mind.

Now, she finds herself curiously awkward around him. She's terrified he can read her thoughts, that he knows how important he's become to her. Mother had always warned her that her reputation was always at stake, that men couldn't be trusted. Annis must always be chaperoned for this reason, for a fallen girl—by deed or innuendo—was a ruined one.

Annis doesn't think Nathaniel has it in him to be anything other than what he's shown her, but she'd thought the same of the Wolf. Shadows move across her mind: the glint of the knife, the mustiness of the wardrobe, Greta's scream. She shivers and steps away.

"Annis?" Nathaniel watches her, his brow furrowed. "What's the matter?"

She trails a finger along a table edge and changes the subject. "You asked what I'm thinking." She steps to a stout piece of furniture of chestnut brown, its surface shiny with varnish. "That's lovely."

"The design was my father's. Secretaries were his most sought-after pieces. I've been making my own modifications here and there." Nathanial steps to it and draws down a panel that transitions to a surface for writing. Nestled in the space above are a series of intricate drawers with gold pulls. "I work primarily in mahogany, but I've inlaid rosewood and yellow poplar against the darker wood to bring out the details of the drawer fronts."

Annis runs a hand down a vertical column with gold piping, its twin gracing the other side. "This work here," she fingers the top of the column finished in decorated metal, "is exquisite."

"Gilded bronze. And the feet too."

"Who is it for?"

"Matthew Newkirk, a railroad magnate. He has quite a mansion on Arch Street."

"It must have cost a pretty penny."

"Yes, but as you've noticed, it's a complex piece." He raises a brow. "Philadelphia teems with furniture makers, most of them German. The big shops turn out several pieces a day for the more ordinary items: standard tables and chairs, chests. Some are purchased for installation in conventional working-class homes, some are sent by ship or rail elsewhere. These craftsmen employ legions of apprentices to churn out such work."

"But you don't."

"No. I'd need a host of workers for that. I prefer to specialize in finer pieces. Bookcases and cabinets primarily."

"Like the ones Dr. Mütter needs for his museum."

"The cabinets for the college will be simpler and won't take as much time for me to make. The ones I fashion for the upper classes have far more ornamentation and are of higher quality woods, and they can afford them." He steps to another sample with round tapered legs and open panels that reveal shelves. The glass hasn't yet been inserted in the doors. Though it's lacking stain, it's plain to Annis it will become another exemplary work. "I'm known for bookcase bureaus like this, with burl if I can get it."

"Burl?"

"The whirl patterns in the wood." He drags his fingers over a drawer. "See? The stain brings them out beautifully. Burl is wood grain that's grown in a deformed pattern. It's a knobby sort of growth on the tree due to disease of some sort." His hand dashes to his cheek, his expression darkening. "Not unlike my tumor, I suppose."

She works to keep her face straight. "I see nothing now but a face in need of a straight razor."

His eyes widen and then he realizes she's jesting. "Are you offering to give me a shave, Annis?"

"Most certainly not."

"With the skill of those hands of yours, I'm sure you'd be rather crack at it."

"You shall never know."

She lifts her chin feigning disdain, his low chuckle as pleasing as his touch. She takes in the workshop. At first glance it had looked cluttered, but she sees there is clearly order to it: on one side there are parts in various stages of cutting and sanding, on the other, assembled items requiring only the final touches. The tools hanging from pegs along the back wall are arranged in neat rows. She steps to his desk where a stack of paper rests. She fans through them. "There are some fine renderings here."

"My attempts at making minor adjustments to my father's designs. And that's quite a compliment, coming from you."

She smiles but doesn't look up from his drawings. He's indicated measurements on each and scrawled the types of wood in the margins. "How do you decide what kind of wood to use?"

"Oftentimes a customer will request it, especially if it's a piece meant to match a set."

He waves her over to his workbench and sets her down on a round stool. He places himself behind her and reaches forward, his forearm grazing her wrist. When he speaks, she can feel his breath at her cheek. "Have a look at this. What do you think?"

The bit of wood in question isn't stained. "There's a pattern in the grain. Not swirls, but... stripes."

"Tiger oak. The effect is produced when a log is sliced to expose the grain in such a way. It's rather distinctive when stained. And this one?" He places another sample before her.

"Not much of a grain. It has a red hue compared to the other."

"That's because it's cherry."

"Are you going to school me in all manner of woods, Mr. Dixon?"

He spins the stool around so fast to face him her head spins. "I'd much rather school you in something else."

The thud of her pulse in her ears is so loud she fears he can hear it. "Oh?"

In one smooth motion, he grips her waist and lifts her, kicks the stool away, and sets her on the workbench. It's so easily done, Annis feels as weightless as a doll. She's never felt so tiny, so cherished.

He leans in and rests his hands on either side of her. "I should very much like to kiss you but I don't want you to behave as you did over there. That shiver unnerved me. I don't want to disconcert you, yet I fear I have." Annis drops her eyes. "You're doing it again." He lifts her chin with a crooked forefinger. "You're just as beautiful when you're petulant."

"I'm not petulant." She bites her lip. How to explain the Wolf, the trickery she fell for? It's too much. She squeezes her eyes closed to blight the memories.

"Annis? I've lost you again."

Her eyes flutter open. He is so close. So big and handsome. She takes him by the collar and pulls him within an inch of her face. "Kiss me. Please."

It is glorious, the union of their lips. At first, Nathaniel is tentative, as if testing her resolve. When she responds in kind, he presses harder, his mouth opening, tongue teasing past her teeth. Her own shyly meets his. The kiss has the desired effect. So lost is she in it, she can't think of anything else. His ardor brings his hands to her back, and she is dizzy with the thrill of being enclosed in his embrace, her hands in his hair. She wants more, yet wonders if the heat of it, of him, will catch her afire. She doesn't care. Let her burn if this is what it is to be raptured. Her skirts won't allow her to place her thighs around him, but she wants to. Needs to. To bring him even closer, she angles her legs to one side. There is tension in her nether region, the secret place where her sex throbs with need, an ache she knows only he can relieve. She feels it in him, too; the need, the urgency.

He moans softly, scoots her closer, her backside now half balanced on the edge of the workbench and half cradled in his palm. She wants to die with the ecstasy of it. She is almost completely in his arms, swallowed up by the hard mass of him, and it is more pleasure than she has ever felt in her life.

Her hand comes around to caress his left cheek and he startles, pulling away a little.

"How stupid of me," she says, her eyes coming open. "Did I hurt you? Heavens, you're still healing."

He takes her hand in his, kisses it tenderly. "It isn't that. Annis, you must know. There's a chance the tumor may return. Perhaps more than one. It is not unheard of."

"And you think I'll fly to the hills in horror? Run from the 'monster who terrifies children in the streets?' If you think I care a jot about that you don't know me very well."

Her words don't bring him the relief she expected. "You realize I will have a scar?" he says. "That I shall never be free of the wretched thing? It's branded me forever. Dr. Mütter said facial hair won't grow where he cut the skin."

"I should think that would be less work for your straight razor then." She traces the line of the incision lightly with her fingers, elated she's made him smile. "We all have scars, Nathaniel. The ones outside are just more visible."

He brushes a curl from her brow and rests his forehead against hers. "I doubt any such thing pertains to you. You are perfect. Inside and out."

He leans in to kiss her and she is caught up again, warmth threading through her all the way down to her toes.

And then suddenly, behind him, movement. A telltale shimmer. And it's freezing.

*No.*

She lowers her face and presses it to his chest. It cannot be. Not at such a precious, golden moment. Her chest constricts and she wants to cry.

Nathaniel coaxes her face up and she's stung by the concern in his expression. "You must tell me what troubles you." He leans away, taking in her face, marking every curve and line. "Something's on your mind. Tell me what it is."

Annis' eyes flick past him. Bobbing before the secretary, slippers hovering above the ground, is the translucent Greta. She is more disturbed than Annis has ever seen her. The same blue dress, yes, but her features are different, wilder: her face is contorted with emotion, her movements frenzied. The raw severity of it makes the red slit at her throat all the ghastlier. And then Annis sees it: the blood that begins to soak her skirts. As she watches, the dress becomes a bright crimson mantle of horror. Greta stamps a foot, and the black cavern of her mouth opens like some terrible abyss.

*She is... yes, she's screaming.*

The ghastly apparition turns to the shop window and points, as if to show Annis something outside. But there is no one there, no one on the street. It all happens in the flash of an instant. In the next, she is gone.

"What the devil?" Nathaniel says, turning. "Is there someone there?" He whips back around. "You're white as a sheet. What are you looking at?"

Annis can't still herself. Her body quakes and her palms are clammy. She must face it: with each ghostly sighting, her apprehension grows. Greta's materializations are plucking at the seams of her, unraveling her stitch by stitch.

*Perhaps that's the point.*

"What point, Annis?"

Has she said it aloud? Her gaze flicks to him and away. How can she tell him her secrets, things so dreadful, she keeps them shut inside herself?

Nathaniel places his hands around her upper arms, lowers his face so it is even with hers. "Annis? Please."

Silence fills the workshop. She can't look at him. A word about the woman who haunts her, about the man who took that life so viciously, would alter Nathaniel's perception of her irredeemably. He would never understand why she'd been fool enough to trust a *fiend*; never understand how her need for self-preservation was greater than her will to protect another.

It is into this awkward stillness that Ben enters. He breezes through the door and takes in the shop until his head swivels and he spots them. How strange they must look: Annis perched atop the worktable, Nathaniel's hands still grasping her forearms.

"Hello?" Ben's smile turns to bafflement as he takes in the tension between them. "Have I... is now not a good time?"

Nathaniel moves away and Annis slips from the table, the spell between them broken.

"Not at all," Nathaniel says. "You must be Annis' brother. Quite a resemblance." He steps to Ben and proffers a hand. "Nathaniel Dixon. I hear you might like a turn around my shop."

Ben shrugs, a sheepish grin tugging at a corner of his mouth. "My sister is always looking for ways to keep me occupied. It's a trait she inherited from our mother. 'An idle mind is the devil's workshop' and all that." He assesses the space. "Speaking of workshops, what a place you have here. I had no idea."

Nathaniel sets to taking Ben around, showing him the lay of it, remarking on his work, the tools, the designs on paper that come to life in wood.

Annis stays at the fringes, her mind absorbed elsewhere. Nathaniel will want an answer to her odd behavior, and she has no idea how to rebuff him. He'd seen something dreadful in her expression he won't forget. She could tell him everything, come clean with Dr. Mütter, too. *I see the ghost of a dead woman everywhere I go.* They'll think she's crazy. If she does tell them, she'll lose everything—their good opinion of her. Even her position at the college.

When she hears her name, her attention is shunted back to the room. Nathaniel is questioning Ben about the wooden figures he's been working on at home.

"She told you that?" Ben's head swings to her. "Well, it's a hobby really. They're not very good. I'm improving, I suppose."

"But you like to whittle?"

"I like the feel of the wood," Ben replies. "I like to make it something."

Nathaniel is pleased. She can tell by the knowing nod he gives her brother. Nathaniel's eyes find hers and she knows they're thinking the same thing. Ben likes to work with wood, to shape it, just as Nathaniel does. Perhaps there is a future for him here, one far better and more gratifying than theatre work.

A half hour later, at dusk, when she and Ben are bound for home and the chill snaps at their noses, her mind ticks. Every shadow and alley lurks with the potential for Greta to materialize, to shatter what's left of her nerves. Ben chatters about the shop, ignorant to the dark turn of her thoughts. A few blocks from their home she can't shake the impression that someone is following them. She turns.

"What is it, Annis?" Ben says, coming to a halt.

"I'm not sure. I think..."

There is nothing save a gas lamp not yet lit, the gnarled branches of the tree at the curb. *Greta has left me afraid of my own shadow.*

Ben tugs at her sleeve. "Come on. I'm famished. A warm fire would be just the thing on an evening like this."

They resume their steps and Ben his babbling. On he goes— the size of the shop, the number of saws alone, would Nathaniel give him wood scraps for his whittling?—but between his words Annis hears the distinct fall of footsteps. Greta, she is certain, has never followed her, only appeared *before* her. Which means Annis is overwrought; it's only a pedestrian headed home as they are. *And Greta doesn't make sound. Even her screams are silent.*

Annis' last thought before they take the steps into their building is that her madness is a weight she must carry, and she will endeavor at all costs to keep it hidden.

# SNATCHED

## PHILADELPHIA, FEBRUARY 1842

In thick darkness, Gabriel climbs the stairs to the second floor of the inn. At the top, he rubs his hands together. All has gone according to plan, every step unfolding without a hitch. It's fate, he is sure, that the wench will so easily, so undoubtedly, be his. It had occurred to him in the closet at the college that terror is best meted out in teaspoons, not ladles. Tonight, he will lay the groundwork that will lead the wench to *him*.

It had been quick work to pick the lock below (there really is no mechanism he cannot master), easier still to climb the stairs with no sound to betray his presence. The tawdry establishment —smelling faintly of stale beer and pork fat—is shuttered for the night. It pleases him to the brim that nary a soul—not the lodgers nor the innkeeper—is aware he lurks in their midst and yet here he is, a wolf in the shadows.

It's not the first time Gabriel has marveled at the ease with which he walks among the unsuspecting and catches them unawares. But then, he thinks with a low chuckle, he possesses a cunning unrivaled in his fellow man.

Behind the door across from the woman's room a boarder snores in his sleep. Another touch of fate. The noise will cover any sound he makes picking the whore's—for she most certainly is now, he's certain—lock. While the moonlight had aided him in gaining access to the inn, there is nothing but viscid darkness here. From a pocket of his coat he withdraws a matchbox and lights a match. The flame sparks to life and into the escutcheon he thrusts a tiny pin. He waves the match out; he doesn't need his eyes for this. In less than a minute the latch bolt springs and he's inside.

Moonlight from the window hazes into the room, the filmy curtains doing little to mask it. The bed rests in the corner and he can just make out a form on it. From the folds of his coat, he withdraws a lead pipe and, coming to the bed, raises it. In one quick strike he brings it down upon the whore's head. A low moan, then silence. With quick fingers he shoves a rag into her mouth and binds her hands and feet with rope. After lifting her from the bed he retraces his steps, leaving the inn as silently as he entered it.

The wheelbarrow he's filched waits in the alley beside the inn. He settles the whore into it and pulls a tarp (also filched) over her, careful to tuck in her limbs. His lip curls at the bandage wrapped around her ankle. The doctor may have rid her of some physical abomination, but there is no cure to bring a strumpet to rights. They are all the same: lewd, disgusting, rotten to the core.

The streets are deserted at so ungodly an hour, yet Gabriel avoids the gas lamps, keeping to the darkness. His breath puffs before him like a ghost, the cold seeping into his bones. He is at the school in less than fifteen minutes, slightly winded from the exertion. The clinic door is already open; he started the night here first and put his pin to quick use. A wise decision, for he didn't want to dally at the building's entrance overlong once he'd snatched his quarry, as a gas lamp at the curb illuminates the entrance more than he would like.

Last evening he'd observed the building for hours and seen not a single watchman stroll the block. Another turn of destiny! He'd taken the opportunity to explore the school. With a lantern held aloft, he'd seen the clinic with its rows of empty beds, the anatomy room with its malodorous corpses shrouded under sheets, the surgical amphitheater in its cavernous gloom. He'd loved it most of all: the theatrically of it, the size.

He'd climbed the stairs, walked nearly the length of the corridor and picked the lock of the doctor next door to the wench's studio, the one for whom she draws. Inside he'd found a curious assortment of books, bones, and specimens. When the lantern light had fallen upon a head enclosed in glass, he'd started. But his temerity turned instantly to silent laughter, his shoulders shaking with the absurdity of it. A woman with a horn projecting from her forehead! An exquisite piece of work certainly, yet if these are the type of patients surgery is performed on, they're hardly worth the doctor's time. Degenerates, all. With a disgusted sneer he'd left the chamber, closing the door behind him.

The *pièce de résistance,* his *trouvaille,* awaited. With tremulous fingers, he'd put his pin to work again and entered the wench's studio, the lantern light spilling over surfaces, shadows jumping at the walls. He'd stood a moment, taking it all in: worktable, shelving, easel and stool, brushes, a small wooden paint box within which nested lozenges of paint. Oh, the pleasure he'd felt in that confined space knowing his wench spent time here, hours of it. Closing his eyes, he'd inhaled and the essence of her had come to him. Lilac unquestionably. And something else. The piney undertone of turpentine, likely for brush cleaning. It had taken all his resolve to leave the space as it was, touching nothing. He was careful to lock both doors when he left, leaving no trace he had been there.

He leaves the wheelbarrow tucked behind a bush near the

entrance and hefts the whore over his shoulder. With one hand, he opens the door. A breeze greets him as he steps inside. It's as cold as a mausoleum within. Fitting for a place that houses its own cadavers.

At the end of the hall he ascends the stairs, his legs cramping with the effort. In the months he's been hiding and drinking more than he ought, he's lost strength. Stamina, too. Still, while his star might have dimmed since he's been laying low, he feels more alive than he has for months.

Down the corridor he scuttles with his load, taking no care to remain silent as there is no one here to deter him. There is just enough light from the gas lamps on the street that shine through a few windows to make his way.

At last, he is at the wench's studio. He unlocks the door, lays the whore down on the table, and fetches the lantern he'd hidden last evening in the closet across the hall. He strikes a match, holds it to the wick, and the studio fills with dim light. It looks much the same as it did before. His wench is fastidious with her things.

"Something we have in common, my dear," he whispers. In the silence, there is something monstrous in his voice that pleases him.

Now, placement. Where to pose the whore for maximum effect?

Upon the table, perhaps, as she is now? Hmm. She will be seen before the wench is fully into the room. No. She must close the door and be alone when she sees his handiwork. He lifts the whore and places her on the floor, sitting her up against the easel.

"Ah, you see? I offer you, my dear wench, my own exceptional work of art."

The whore hasn't moved, but Gabriel has accounted for this. He withdraws a tiny flask of smelling salts and uncaps it, waving it under her nose. The sharp scent of ammonia assaults him, but there is no response from her. He slaps her cheeks and is rewarded with a low groan.

"That's it, that's it. Wake up, my little minx."

The whore's eyes flutter open, take in Gabriel crouched before her, then the room with its stuttering lantern light. Blood is caked in her hair. A ribbon of it has dried on her cheek. She shrinks back, the gag pressing at her mouth. Her shoulders shift, and she attempts to look behind her.

"Tied, I'm afraid," Gabriel says, and he is impressed by the smoothness of his voice. "You've nothing to fear." The whites of her eyes flair when he traces a finger down her cheek, and she spies his scar. "Do you know where you are? You should. You're at the medical college. You've been here before, yes? I've seen you here myself. We are in our friend's studio, you see?" He gestures to the room. "I've arranged a little surprise for her. Something she will like very, very much."

The whore makes a sound again, notes her feet are bound, implores him with her eyes. "Ah, I can't free you. But I promise I shall soon. You have my word." From a pocket of his coat, he withdraws a bottle of whiskey. "Let us drink to you, hmm? For being such a brave little thing and coming along for my surprise." He takes a pull, feels the burn in the back of his throat. "Our friend will very much like what I—we—have in store for her. I know her quite well, you see." Another sip, a longer one. "Did she mention she is acquainted with a great magician? La Grande Merveille of New York City?"

His prisoner shakes her mop of black curls. "No? You are certain?" Gabriel leans in closer. "If you lie I shall be forced to hurt you." The whore shakes her head again, vigorously. "Very well," he says, waving a hand. "I was only jesting. You mustn't take me so seriously." He chuckles but inside, the knowledge singes him. The wench has said nothing of him, not even told the story of what happened months ago in his cellar. But then, she had quit the city in fear, and that is something. He considers the whore, the wary way she watches him, the way his mother used to do. For a moment, he thinks, *I'll kill her now*, but he steels himself.

"Here," he says, bringing the whiskey near. "Take a swig to set your mind at ease."

He eases her face up, moves the gag to one side, and attempts to splash some of the liquid into her mouth. But it runs down her cheek when she jerks her head away.

"Now look what you've done. Let's try again, shall we? I only want to calm your nerves while we wait for our friend, you see? You really must obey me. I will untie you and remove your gag if only you do what I say."

This time, she allows him to coax her head back and, after he's shifted the gag a bit and pours, she swallows. The whiskey has soaked into the material, the smell sharp but not unpleasant. Gabriel smiles. When he's lowering the bottle from his own lips again, she wavers before him. There are two of her. His stomach lurches and he shoots to his feet, thoughts ricocheting. His head pounds. He hasn't had a thing to eat for... he can't quite remember. The room dips, blurs. He rubs his eyes with the heels of his palms.

When he pulls his hands away, he sees it: the sheet of paper pinned to the wall. It hadn't been there last night, he is certain. He grabs the lantern and steps to it, his fist bunched at his side. It's a sketch of the man he'd seen the wench with earlier today. Even with the lines of scarring on his cheek, he is a ruggedly handsome. Younger than Gabriel and altogether different in physical makeup. Tendrils of fire root deep within him, red hot and ferocious.

Earlier, he'd followed the wench from the college to the man's place of business and there, through the window, Gabriel had seen them together. His hands all over her. It had enraged him, just as all the girls he'd once employed had. How many men have there been? The wench may have fooled some, but not him.

*I know what you are. A filthy slut, a jezebel. Just like my mother.*

As he'd crouched at the window peering in, watching the man and the wench—*his* wench—paw at each other, a thought had marched across his mind: *I'll kill him.* But the brute was large and wouldn't easily be overpowered. It would take time to learn his habits, his weaknesses. The more Gabriel put his mind to it, the more he'd realized it was best to stay the course.

He whirls from the wall, his insides still ablaze, and recognizes the sensation for what it is: his rage pawing to get out. Beneath the easel his prisoner watches him. In two strides he comes to her and squats. She tries to push away but her bindings prevent it.

"Now, now," he cajoles. "Be still. All will be well."

He will enjoy this part. All his potential lies before him, and he will not let the moment go to waste.

# TOUR

## NEW YORK CITY, APRIL 1841

Just as Mr. Marchand had said, the back door of Scudder's Museum is open. Once inside, Annis climbs to the fourth floor and finds the lecture hall. On the signboard at the entrance, the magician grins at her as if he knows why she's here. Somehow, it seems like it's been more than a few weeks since they first met. But then, her mother's death has plunged their life into turmoil and not even time seems itself.

She tugs open the door to near darkness. A single spotlight illuminates the stage. There's just enough light to see the seats in front. She's making her way slowly down the aisle when a figure steps from the gloom.

Annis jumps. "Mr. Marchand. You frightened me."

"Ah, Miss Hargrave. Forgive me, I meant no harm." In the shadows she can see almost nothing of his face. "Follow me," he says. On stage, the props for the levitating lady trick are in place: the two stools supporting the wooden plank, the square vertical posts that rise from it. Annis can't take her eyes from any of it.

Marchand laughs softly. "By all means, have a look."

Annis circles the plank. Everything seems just as it was when Greta floated so ethereally above it. The only thing missing is the assistant herself. Annis comes around to the front again.

"Ah," Marchand says, his attention at her neck. "Your mother's necklace. Such a captivating piece."

Annis fingers it, feeling its pits and ridges. Today she is certain it's a talisman of good luck. She refuses to believe it's cursed.

"Well, madame," Marchand says, indicating the plank, "would you like to know how it's done?" He winks. "I shall tell you if you promise to keep it our secret."

Under the gaslight his skin is pale, his eyes dark, his crimped mustache twisted at the ends. He's dressed in shirtsleeves rolled to the elbows and she wonders vaguely what he was doing here before she arrived.

Marchand advances to the plank. "If you recall, I explain to the audience the magical properties of ether while Greta stands between the posts. A misdirection, Miss Hargrave. While the attention is on me, Greta's right hand, concealed by her skirts, is working to release a mechanism within the post just here." He pushes something behind the left post, the one that had supported Greta. There's a soft click and a long vertical metal piece slides out about half the length of the post. It's wider at the bottom and cupped, almost like a seat. "When I ask Greta to extend her arms, the hidden support is already in place." He guides the piece up until it's parallel with the stage where, with another faint click, it stops.

"It's a sort of ledge for her to lie on," Annis breathes.

"Yes," Marchand says, his eyes dancing. "Concealed by her skirts."

"And the stool you kicked from under the plank? Why didn't it fall?"

"Ah," he says, a pointer finger raised. "The stool I remove is a regular one, but the other is made of heavy iron. When the plank is put in place—carried in by two men—the stagehand inserts a small metal knob underneath it into a hole on the top of the stool, easily done by using his body to shield the knob from the audience. The plank itself is no ordinary piece of wood. It's solid iron *covered* with wood. When I kick the left stool free, the plank stays horizontal because it's attached to the other stool that's supporting its weight, along with Greta of course."

He demonstrates, giving the left stool a shove. The plank remains vertical.

"So the stool was never supporting the plank."

"*C'est exact,*" Marchand replies with a chuckle.

"The ether had nothing to do with it," Annis says. "I didn't think it did."

"Right again. The smell you no doubt noticed didn't come from the bottle I opened. It was produced backstage by a stagehand pouring ether on a hot shovel."

Annis blinks. "It's so simple once you know how it's done. I wonder how I didn't see it."

Marchand chuckles again. "As it is with most magic tricks, madame." He regards her, hands on his hips. "Would you like to stand on the plank? Come, give it a try."

He quickly lowers the support and slides it back into the post then helps Annis up. She stands facing the seats, the first two rows lit faintly, the rest disappearing into darkness. It's hard to get a sense of the size of the room.

"How does it feel, madame?"

"I... I don't know." She imagines every seat full, all eyes on her. Does she have the skill, the courage to perform before a crowd?

Marchand removes the post on her left and sets it on the floor. "Feet together, *s'il vous plait.* Now, keeping your right arm at your side, try to feel for the mechanism. No peeking."

Annis' fingers probe the back of the post and feel nothing.

Just when she's ready to give up, she finds a small, raised notch. She pushes it and feels something brush against her skirts.

"*Parfait!* You are a natural, I think." Marchand's eyes blaze with delight. "Extend your arms out to your sides. Good. Now get a feel for how to position yourself so that when I tap your foot, you'll be nestled against the support. Are you ready, madame?"

Annis' mind trips. What if she falls?

Marchand bends and lightly nudges her feet left, one hand outstretched to prevent her from rolling off. "Lean your body into it. Your weight will help it move."

Her feet leave the platform and her stomach roils. She has never been so terrified and exhilarated at the same time. In the end, it takes dozens of tries for her to get the feel of it, until she is at last 'floating' above the plank as Greta had. When at last they stop, Marchand helps her down from the plank. He whisks two chairs from the wings and sets them facing each other under the spotlight, indicating for her to take a seat.

"I think, Miss Hargrave, with more practice and training in the other parts of the act, you might prove to be a suitable assistant." He crosses one leg over the other. "It all depends on what your own wishes are in regard to the position."

She swallows. "I must find something if Ben and I are to make a go of it." *There is nothing untoward about being a magician's assistant. Greta is a perfectly respectable young lady.*

He frowns and purses his lips. "You have not been turned out of your home, I trust."

A tear travels down her cheek, and she wipes it away. "Not yet. But we must leave soon. It's to be sold to pay off my mother's debts."

Marchand shakes his head. "Such a pity. But I should like to help. A kind girl needs a friend she can trust." His face breaks into a smile. "I am prepared to pay you thirty cents a day, six days a week. And should you show improvement, I might perhaps pay more. Not bad money for a young lady to earn her keep, *oui?*"

In truth, she has no idea. The weight of her situation presses in on her and she is suddenly very tired.

"In the matter of your living arrangements," Marchand says, leaning forward in this chair, "I have a solution. Allow me to arrange for you to take over as tenant of Greta's *appartement*. I found it for her myself. A lovely, if small, set of rooms on Primrose Street. I look after my people, you see. It is a nice place in a respectable neighborhood. Modest, but suitable."

"I could… afford it on the wage you're paying me?" She's embarrassed by how little she knows. What if he's deceiving her? *Stop being so suspicious. He's trying to help.*

Yet something in him seems to have shifted. His mouth is turned down, his geniality gone. "Greta did well on what I paid her." He drops his eyes and considers his nails, one brow cocked. "As I said, a modest accommodation to be sure, but livable."

"And Greta, Mr. Marchand?" He stares at her. "You haven't told me why she's leaving."

"A personal thing, she said," Marchand answers coolly. "I did not pry."

His words are almost clipped. She's upset him, questioned his good will. Still, she presses on. "And my brother? Can he stay there too, where Greta lives now?"

"Your…?"

"Ben, my brother."

"Your brother." He looks at her for an interminably long time. "Yes, of course." He waves a hand. "Room for him, too."

"When would you expect me to start?"

"In a few days, no more."

Annis bites her lip. "May I think on it, Mr. Marchand? It's a big decision. I shall have my answer to you in a day or two."

A muscle in Marchand's jaw ticks. His smile doesn't meet his eyes. He gets to his feet. "Naturally, but I really cannot extend the offer more than two days. The position will go very fast."

"Yes, of course."

She rises and bids him goodbye, making her way back through the dark theatre, down the steps and to the street, all the while wondering at his change in mood.

# THE CELLAR
## NEW YORK CITY, APRIL 1841

The next afternoon, Annis waits for Mr. Marchand at the museum's back entrance. It is early evening, the air sharp and laced with a cool breeze. Her only company is a man slightly older than herself. He paces, his brow hidden beneath the brim of his cap, hands thrust into his pockets. He stops frequently to check the exit door then resumes his steps again. In the enclosed space of the alley, she feels his frustration. Or perhaps it's unease. Then again, perhaps it is her own unease needling through her. Her stomach hasn't been right all day.

She has decided to accept Marchand's offer to be his new assistant. Last night when she'd come home, she'd been uncertain. Her mother would never have allowed it—a girl from a good family, working? Unconscionable. Even Papa, who'd always adored Annis and satisfied her every whim, would've opposed it. A proper girl should marry. Have children. But those dreams began to unspool when Papa passed and further unwound when Mother lost herself in gambling and died. There is no relative to come to their rescue, no beau to whom Annis has been introduced to whisk her and Ben from the threat of poverty.

Which means only one thing. It's up to Annis to save them. And she can, if only she's given the chance.

A firm resolve had settled on her as she'd gone to bed last night. Despite the churn of her stomach, the second guessing even now, there is nothing tainted or disrespectful about an unwed young lady being an assistant on stage. She told herself this a dozen times on the omnibus. She understands now that Mr. Marchand had been a bit cool yesterday because her questions implied she didn't trust him. How could she have anything but faith in him when he's only been kind and wants to give her a job? She's been given an opportunity—more than her mother or Uncle Desmond gave her—and she will take it.

Maybe Marchand will employ Ben too—to work backstage perhaps, or put in a good word for him at the museum. Why not? They are young and their lives just beginning. They will live in Greta's lodgings and when the time is right, they will move on when they please. Most especially, nestled deep inside her, is the seed of her long-held dream, the one she can't let go: to one day make a living as an artist.

The young man coughs and Annis steps away, settling against the shaded wall of the building across the alley. After a few minutes, the door opens and out come a few of the stagehands clad in black. Following them, in a top hat and gloves, is Marchand. Beside him is Greta, the woman who'd floated so ethereally above the stage.

Marchand offers his arm to Greta, and with sure steps they begin to stride away.

Annis pushes from the wall but halts when Marchand is assailed by the young man. "You are the magician?" he inquires, his voice quavering.

Marchand makes to move past with a sneer on his lips, as if the fellow is a pesky fan and he hasn't the time. He is almost...

cruel. She feels an odd beat inside her, like a disharmonious chord of music.

"Please," the man says, placing a hand on Marchand's arm. "I would like a word with you."

Marchand ticks with impatience. "I do not sign autographs outside the museum, young man. Now, if you will step away."

"I want no autograph. I believe my sister was once in your employ. Her name is Lucy."

Marchand straightens, sizing him up. "*Vous vous trompez.* You are mistaken. I know of no one by that name." He attempts to direct Greta around the man.

"I think you do, sir," the man says, stepping into their path. "I've been looking high and low for her for months. Yesterday I came upon a woman who says Lucy lived in her building on Primrose Street, though she hasn't seen her in a long time."

*Primrose Street.* The words ripple through Annis' mind. Hadn't Marchand mentioned it yesterday?

The man talks on, his words a rush. "Lucy told the woman she worked for the magician at Scudder's. I saw your show, sir." The young man swallows and to Annis' surprise, tears fill his eyes. He turns to Greta. "You're his assistant now."

"Yes," Greta says. "I'm so sorry. You must miss your sister terribly." She reaches out, a dainty gloved hand squeezing his wrist. "I'm afraid you've been misinformed. I live on Primrose, but there's no Lucy in my building. You must have spoken with Mrs. Carson. She's a frightful busybody. I think she's confused me somehow with your sister."

The young man's face falls and he looks between the two of them. "But she was so certain."

"I'm sure she was," Marchand says, brushing off the man with a sweep of his hand. "But as I said, I know of no one by that name. Perhaps she was referring to another magic act in the city. There are a good many."

"She might have used a different name," the young man mutters to himself, then snatches at his hat and rakes his fingers through his auburn hair. "She went off on her own one day after we'd argued. We have only each other." His voice breaks but he continues on. "She said she was going to find work. I never saw her again. That's not like her, not like her at all. Lucy was of average height with red hair." He searches Marchand's face for a spark of memory. "Perhaps she's moved on from her employ with you? No harm done. If you'll only tell me where she's gone—"

"I have nothing to tell you, young man," Marchand says, his strident tone careening through the alley and smacking into Annis. "I have never employed a red-haired girl in my act nor one named Lucy. Of that I am certain." He lifts his cane menacingly. "Now you really must desist. You are upsetting my assistant."

Though his face blooms red, the man nods and steps back. The duo saunters off arm in arm, leaving the fellow alone with his anger.

Annis feels as if she has eavesdropped on a private conversation, but her curiosity is too aroused to leave it be. When the young man pulls his hat back on and stalks off in the other direction, Annis follows Marchand and Greta.

———

For three blocks Annis trails them at enough distance to stay undetected, but close enough to hear snippets of their conversation. Their words sift the air, comments about the show (so crowded today) and the weather (unexpectedly cold for spring). Greta's dress—the same light blue Annis had seen her wear during the show—peeks beneath the hem of her coat. Beside her, Marchand is almost comically slender, his legs long and spindly. They halt at last at a cross street and Greta turns. "Thank you, Mr. Marchand. I shall see you tomorrow."

He nods and his eyes narrow, one hand twirling his cane in circles. "I have ordered dresses."

"Sir?"

Annis tucks herself behind a bin and peers around it. It's the closest she's been to Greta. The magician's assistant is older than her, mid to late twenties perhaps, and very pretty. Large, blue eyes, pleated blonde hair arranged in loops at her ears.

"They've only just arrived," Marchand continues. "They were meant to be a surprise, but alas," and he sweeps his top hat from his head and bows, arms wide, a sheepish look on his face, "I confess I am unable to keep them a secret until tomorrow. Would you be so good as to accompany me home? You can have a look at them to see if they suit, *oui*? I shall toss what you don't like."

Greta bites her lip. "I could see them tomorrow?"

"Yes, yes, *bien sur*," Marchand says, straightening, his tone cool. It reminds Annis of how he'd behaved yesterday when their meeting had come to a close. "I shall bring them to the museum. How silly of me. You should get home to your young man."

Greta's lips turn down. "Young man? I don't have one, sir."

"Oh? Well, forgive me. A thousand pardons."

Greta toys with her gloves. "But I could have a look now, I suppose. It would be nice to have a few new dresses. For the show, I mean. The dresses *are* for the show?"

"Of course," Marchand replies, a hand splayed at his chest. "For what other purpose would they be?" He blinks and says somberly, "If you decide to come with me, I shall order a carriage for your journey home so you won't be walking home in the dark. One can never be too careful."

An invisible vise squeezes itself around Annis' abdomen.

Something isn't right. Greta doesn't need dresses. She's leaving the show. That's what Marchand had said. She was moving on. Annis searches the magician for some sign that he's jesting, that he's lying or being disingenuous, and finds only a gentleman earnest to show his assistant a kindness.

*Greta must have changed her mind about leaving.* Still, apprehension has sunk its hooks into her and won't let go.

"Very well, Mr. Marchand." Greta's smile is rapturous. "I shall come with you."

With evening shadows lengthening around every turn, Marchand stops before a modest, slender brick home. Instead of taking the steps to the front door, he indicates for Greta to follow him around the side of the house.

Seeing Greta hesitate, Marchand steps to her. What words pass his lips Annis is too far away to hear, but they result in Greta following him. Annis steps quietly to a large tree flanking the curb. From this vantage point, she sees Marchand unlock and swing wide the doors of a large bulkhead against the house.

"There's just enough light to see the steps, *oui?*" Marchand says. "Down you go. Watch yourself."

He assists her with a proffered hand but doesn't take the steps himself. Greta disappears into the cellar, her voice filtering up a few seconds later. "It's frightfully dark."

"I'll fetch a lantern and be right back," Marchand calls down. "In the meantime, remove your coat. The dresses are there, I assure you. You shall be delighted, I hope."

Marchand turns and Annis shrinks back behind the tree. At the clatter of his boots on the porch, she peeks around and watches him unlock the front door. As it closes, she hears the unmistakable sound of his whistle, which cuts when he shuts the door.

She must act fast before Marchand returns. Lifting her skirts, Annis races to the bulkhead and plunges herself down the steps. The smell of damp earth assaults her instantly. As her eyes adjust in the dimness, she finds she is in a small low-ceilinged cellar. A stained, battered worktable rests in the center of it, Greta's coat on its surface. The cement floor is stained the same brown as the table. A large wardrobe rests against one wall. Greta stands gazing into it, turning at the sound of Annis' steps.

"Who are you?" she asks.

"That's not important now," Annis whispers, terrified to raise her voice lest Marchand hear. "I followed you, but we haven't much time. Greta, did you tell Mr. Marchand that you can't be his assistant any longer, that you're leaving?"

Greta pulls in her chin. "No. Why would I do that?"

Annis looks to the steps. The light is going. In another minute they won't be able to take them up without feeling their way. "I don't think it's safe here. And to answer your question, Mr. Marchand told me yesterday I could have your job because you're moving on."

"You must be mistaken—"

Annis comes around the table and seizes Greta by the forearms. "What did he say to you? To get you down here?"

A pause, as if the older woman is deciding how much to tell. "He told me he didn't want to ruin my reputation by taking me through the front door because the neighbors might see. That it was best—"

"We've got to leave now."

"But the dresses—"

"Where are they?" Annis hisses back. She looks in the wardrobe. There's nothing there but a bucket, a coil of rope, and what looks like folded burlap. There is nowhere else in the cellar the dresses could be; curiously, it's almost empty. "He said they'd be here, but they aren't. For some reason, he's lured..."

The sound of whistling fractures them both. They freeze

and look at one another. Annis brings a finger to her lips. She is climbing into the wardrobe when she hears the bulkhead doors slamming shut above, the bolt sliding home.

Silence.

She doesn't think Marchand heard them, but she can't be sure. Inside the small space, she works to calm her breathing. Whatever his plan, Marchand has barred Greta from any chance of escape. She shudders at the sound of footsteps above, the punch of boots on stairs. Marchand is making his way down to the cellar from inside the house. A door is unbolted. Hinges creak. Through a slender crack in the wardrobe, Annis sees the flicker of light. He's brought the lantern.

Marchand is in shirt sleeves rolled to his elbows. He sets the lantern on the table.

"Sir," Greta breathes. "The dresses. They, they aren't here." Her voice is uneven. In the garish twist of the light, Greta is terrified, hanging on to the hope that she hasn't been deceived. To Annis' horror, her eyes flick to the wardrobe.

Marchand doesn't seem to notice. He steps around the table, his back to Annis. "I have played a trick on you, my pet. Surely you know by now the dresses were a ruse."

"I, I don't understand, sir," Greta says.

"No, I don't think you do." He chuckles, the note so high and irregular it sounds like a girl's. He places his elbows on the table and folds his arms as if this is a casual exchange across the bar of a pub. "Do you know what my mother was? Have a guess. Please."

"I don't—I can't say, sir."

"Ah, Greta. That's the problem. You have no imagination. My mother was a whore. Just like you."

Greta shakes her head, her mouth agape. "No, sir. I'm not. I swear it."

He begins to step around the table, and Greta moves in turn, keeping it between them. "I watched you struggle in the street. I offered you finery and you couldn't help yourself. No, you could not keep yourself from the flashy trappings of a tramp. That's what whores do. They decorate themselves to draw attention."

"Please, sir. I beg you. I'll tell no one of this, I promise. Just let me go."

Marchand continues as if he hasn't heard. "I chose you because you were attractive and pure, but you toyed with me. You changed, just like the others. You couldn't keep yourself chaste."

"I am not a whore, sir."

Marchand's hand slams down on the table. His face is white, his eyes shining like dark wet paint. Annis trembles, hugs her arms to herself. This is a dream. She will wake up; she will wake up and find—

"I have seen you preening in the mirror," Marchand says. He continues his slow circle around the table. I've seen you rouging your cheeks."

"I merely thought to look my best, sir." Greta is crying now, tears snaking down her face. "If you didn't like it, you should have—"

"How many men have there been, hmm?"

"N-none, sir."

In the flickering shadows, Marchand is monstrous. "My mother was dying of the pox. It ate at her, destroying her face. She withered away to nothing, but I saved her from herself." He licks his lips. "I can save you too."

Greta blinks and considers him. "Save? That's... good, sir."

"Ah, you agree. Excellent."

*No*, Annis thinks. *It's a trick.*

"I should... like that very much." Greta wrings her hands. Her eyes cast around the room and flick to the wardrobe again. There is a sheen of sweat on her forehead.

"Come to me then," Marchand beckons. "If you desire to be saved, come to me."

"I, I don't—"

"*Now.*" His eyes flash, his mouth a grim line. When he speaks, the words press through clenched teeth. "I will not tell you again."

Trembling, Greta begins to step to Marchand. Annis' thoughts roll. *Run. Fight. Scream. Flee.* If Marchand's back was to her, she might surprise him but what then? She has no weapon. She feels around for something she can use, her fingers finding only the burlap, the rope. Nothing hard or sharp. If she comes to Greta's aid, how much time will she have to fly from the wardrobe before Marchand comes at her? *Not long enough.*

"That's it," Marchand coos. "Closer, pet."

When Greta is two steps away Marchand lunges, grabbing Greta's arm and pulling her against him. Her hat falls to the floor. "Good girl. You have chosen well."

Greta whimpers. Marchand smells her hair and runs a hand over it. She shrieks and tries to get away, but he just laughs. He clamps a hand around her throat, pulling her back against his chest. Greta stills and presses her eyes closed. "Ah. Now you see sense, don't you?"

Greta sobs quietly but nods.

Stealthily, Marchand pulls a knife from his trousers and lays it on the table.

Just as Annis decides to leap from the wardrobe and spring for the knife, Marchand grabs it. In that instant, Greta's eyes open, locking on the knife.

"Save me!" Greta screams, the depth of it filling Annis with terror. "Oh God, please save me!" Greta turns to the wardrobe.

"Your shyness doesn't fool me." Marchand's voice is soft and oily. "And your screams are music to my ears." In one swift motion, Marchand slashes. Annis turns to ice. Her mind can't make sense of what she's seeing: Greta's split throat; a fountain of red; the woman falling to the floor; and above it all, Marchand's look of rapture. He's getting a perverse pleasure from it. He shudders; his eyes closed in... euphoria.

Seconds beat out. Annis can't see Greta anymore; the table is in the way. Marchand steps back, staring at the floor. "There, you see? I have saved you. Filthy whore."

A ripping sound. Marchand has torn a strip from Greta's dress and is cleaning the knife with it. When he's finished, he looks down at himself and tuts softly. "Look what a mess you've made."

There is something in the bland way he says it that makes Annis quake anew. She presses her palm harder against her mouth, but she can't control the sobs threatening to overtake her. Her heart pounds, her vision warbles as tears well. She places her other hand over her mouth but to her horror, a tiny whimper escapes.

Marchand straightens, listening. His head rotates to the wardrobe. He takes a step toward it and another until he stands before it. He raises the knife.

Annis can't breathe.

He yanks open the door and Annis launches herself at him. She grabs at the hand holding the knife and propels herself from the wardrobe, using her weight to force him back. He stumbles against the table, buckling for a moment. It's the chance she needs. Her teeth clamp down hard on the hand with the knife, and he roars as he releases it.

Annis steps away, knife aloft, but Marchand lunges. With all the strength she has, she stabs the blade into Marchand's left cheek, dragging it down, down through the flesh.

Blood seeping, running. Running down his face. He screams and sinks to his knees, hands at his face. Screams again. Annis doesn't hesitate. She finds the door and clatters up the steps, falling twice. She finds herself in a dim kitchen. She races through it, crashes into furniture, shatters glass. Hands feeling for the front door.

When she finds it at last, she tears through it and plunges herself into the night.

# PART 3

———

Hell is empty and all the devils are here.

—William Shakespeare, *The Tempest*

# THE RED GRIMACE
## PHILADELPHIA, FEBRUARY 1842

The morning after their tour of Nathaniel's workshop, Annis and Ben trod up Seventh Street. The sun is little more than a pale suggestion in a low, muddled sky. When they reach the theatre on Walnut, Ben waves goodbye and Annis continues on. For the remaining few blocks, she's careful to keep her head down to foil any of Greta's attempts to spook her.

*Take that, ghost.*

And so it is that she nearly collides with a man near the clinic door as he's descending from a carriage.

"Look sharp, young lady." The culprit stretches out a hand to waylay her, then, recognizing her, doffs his top hat. "Why, Miss Hargrave. What a pleasant surprise."

"Dr. Pancoast. Good morning."

A waft of cinnamon comes to her—the doctor's effort to stall the stench of decay from attaching itself to him. By end of day, the spice will be replaced by the sweet, sickly smell of decomposing corpses. During dissection, the students are encouraged to smoke to mask it, yet Annis has caught the scent —a thick fug of meat on the turn and stale cigar smoke—outside her studio on many occasions.

Pancoast extends his arm toward the entrance. "Please." As they step through the door he says, "I shall put down my things and come to Mütter directly. He's to show me your sketches thus far for our book. Oh, not to worry, Miss Hargrave. He says your work is coming along wonderfully. We're going to discuss how best to arrange your renderings—in the chapter they pertain to, or in the center of the book as a collection."

He nods and steps away while Annis heads for the stairs. The hall is empty; classes don't commence for another hour, but she's eager to get started on a specimen she'd taken from the storage room yesterday (*human skull with extensive caries from tertiary syphilis*, according to its label).

As she steps inside her studio, a strong metallic odor hits like a clout. The skull on its miniature plinth stares in abject terror from the worktable, teeth bared, forehead pocked with holes. She leans in, sniffs. The iron smell isn't coming from it, yet she is seized by a sudden all-consuming terror. She's certain she has smelled the stench before.

Her attention drops to the floor. As she takes in the lurid stream of red coming from beneath the table, she tells herself it isn't real. This is Greta, Greta sucking away reality and swapping it with the night Annis can't forget: the Wolf's shirt blazing in the lantern light, Greta's screams, the blood. Slowly, Annis comes around the table and follows the red to a widening sea.

And then she sees the body.

Mariah sits at the base of her easel. Her throat has been slashed from ear to ear, the arc a lurid red grimace. Her face is tinged an unnatural white, her mouth parted like a wound, but it is her eyes that pull at Annis. They stare through her, empty and dark. Above her, pinned to the easel, is her latest sketch of Nathaniel.

Revulsion races through her and she screams. Back through

246

the door she runs, sinking down against the wall. She rides a dark wave of fear, pitches in the swell of it, body convulsing. Images: the Wolf's head rotating to the wardrobe, the slash of the knife across Greta's neck, his animal scream as she plunged the knife into him. She leans forward and is sick.

With each panting breath, each jagged beat of her heart, thoughts flare.

*He has come.*

*He's here.*

*It can be no one else.*

Shouts, running. Someone at her ear, bending, touching her. She starts and pushes away, scoots farther along the wall.

"Miss Hargrave, what has happened? Miss Hargrave?" Mütter. She can't look at him. Her eyes flick to her studio, the abomination within it.

Mütter disappears inside it. Someone runs toward her from the opposite end of the hall. Dr. Pancoast. His face is full of questions.

"Miss Hargrave, are you ill?"

"Pancoast," Mütter calls from her studio. "I need you here."

Annis' thoughts skitter. Mariah gone. Murdered. Never to be reunited with her husband again. How, *how* had he found her? How had he managed it? All these months of freedom, of feeling out from under the pall of him. The last thought brings her awareness up sharp. The hall is so still, so silent, yet the Wolf is close, she can feel him. Does he watch her now? Her heart gives a hard knock. Bile rises in her throat, and she vomits again.

She must get to Ben, run before the Wolf catches her. But when she tries to lift herself from the floor, the world spins. She is attempting to stand again, stomach curdling against the sour stench of vomit, when Pancoast and Mütter cup her elbows and coax her to Mütter's office. They deposit her on a chair before the cold hearth and, sensing her torpor, speak in low tones.

She is vaguely aware of Dr. Pancoast departing, Dr. Mütter banking a fire. The catch of flames. Mütter busies himself at his desk then he's bending beside her. "Miss Hargrave, my wife will be here soon to look after you. In the meantime, take this."

His voice sounds far away. When she turns, the glass he holds is out of focus as if seen through a prism. Gently, the doctor takes her hand and places it around the glass. "You've had a horrible shock. Drink. It will fortify you. I'm certain a constable will need to speak with you before long." She sips with distraction, though the bitterness of the liquid clears her head a little. "Forgive me, Miss Hargrave, but I must ask." Gentle, now, his voice. A worry in it. "Have you any idea who might have done this?"

Annis turns to him. She cannot speak, cannot endanger him, for the knowledge of the Wolf will almost certainly bring ruin upon him.

She meets his eyes with a courage she doesn't feel and shakes her head.

Sometime later—she can't say how long—Annis comes to herself. She still sits before the fire, still holds the glass though it's empty. She can't say where her mind has been, what dark thoughts have crept through it. Gradually, details unfold: Mary Mütter sits beside her, Mütter's door is open—she can hear him speaking from her studio. Pancoast is there, too. She hears his, "I heard her scream as I was making my way from the ground floor and came running."

She closes her eyes to steady her mind. What's important is to get away. The Wolf will have no interest in the people she cares about if she vanishes. He will try to follow her, but she'll be more careful this time. Before she does anything, though, she must remain calm. The urgent need to flee will look suspicious.

"She was most certainly slain here." Pancoast. "The amount of blood is indicative of that. There's the smell of whiskey on the gag. She was forced to drink it, perhaps, to slow her faculties. Though the blow to her head would have likely rendered her unconscious."

A reply she doesn't catch in a voice she doesn't recognize, then: "Another? In the city?" Mütter. Annis sits up in her chair.

"Yes, doctor." The stranger again. He must be the constable. "The method wasn't the same—a knife to the gut, I'm afraid, but given the violence of it and the type of knife I think was used, I wonder if it could be related somehow. It occurred at a pawnbroker's shop on Samson Street three days ago. Man by the name of Nigel Kiersley of Kiersley & Sons. Does the name mean anything to either of you?"

Murmurs in the negative.

Annis' thoughts trip. Mr. Kiersley the pawnbroker. The Wolf traced her here by the necklace. He'd seen it that day in the park and later when she'd met him at the lecture hall. They had spoken of it, and he'd admired it. She never could have imagined the blue pearl would lead him to her. Because of it—and her naiveté—Mariah had become a pawn in his game.

Next door, the mention of Nathaniel startles her.

"Are you feeling better, my dear?" Mary pats her wrist. Annis doesn't stir.

"A patient of mine," Dr. Mütter says. "I tasked Miss Hargrave with sketching him before and after surgery."

"Curious it was found above the victim. Very curious indeed." The rustle of paper, as if the constable has pulled the sketch from the easel. "Does he know Mrs. Santos? They were both patients you say."

TONYA MITCHELL

"I think it unlikely," Mütter replies. "Mrs. Santos doesn't—didn't—live here. She's from Ohio."

Annis stands and takes a step towards the door.

"But Dixon has been here, to the young lady's studio?"

"Of course," Mütter replies. "But there's nothing unusual in it. Miss Hargrave has sketched a number of patients. Naturally, she does so in her studio."

"Yet his is the only sketch hanging here. What was his, er," a dry cough, "deformity, doctor? There's a mark here on his cheek."

"A tumor. I removed it a short time ago." A pause, then, "Mr. Dixon is a fine young man, constable. He is a furniture maker in the city. In fact, I hired him to make curiosity cabinets for the college museum."

"Oh? Dixon has admittance to the college?"

"Not insomuch that he has a key, no."

Annis' heart thuds. Mary stands beside her. Two statues frozen in time; ears pricked to what is unfurling in the next room. Then Mary's hand moves, perhaps to pacify her or draw her attention away from the interrogation on the other side of the wall. But Annis moves her arm away, shoots Mütter's wife a look that communicates she is listening and will not be deterred.

"But he knows how to get around?" the constable asks. "To the clinic, here, and your office."

"Yes, but no more than any other patient."

"This museum, where is it?"

"It does not exist at present," Dr. Pancoast offers. "For now, the collection is housed in the storage room on the ground floor near the clinic."

"And Dixon has access to this?"

Annis can't stand another minute. She can't fathom entering her studio, so she takes a deep breath and calls, "Dr. Mütter, I am ready to speak to the constable." She runs her hands over her

250

hair and down her skirts, her courage withering when she sees the sympathy in Mary's eyes.

Dr. Mütter is the first to step through the door, followed by Pancoast and the constable. The space is small for so many, so Mary and the doctors move to the desk in the corner while the constable steps to Annis. She doesn't miss his survey of the room, the mixture of alarm and disgust on his features as he takes in the skeleton hanging on its hook, the horned Madame Dimanche, the lithographs of body parts.

The constable, gray whiskered with spectacles perched on his nose, licks his lips. "You are Annis Hargrave, the artist?"

"Yes."

"I'm Constable Bradcliff. I have some questions for you. Are you able—"

"I'm fine, sir. Please proceed."

He lifts his chin, considering her. "Very well. What time did you discover the... make your discovery?"

"Just after seven." He makes a note in a tiny green book. "I don't usually arrive until eight am when classes commence, but I arrived early to get started on some work."

"Dr. Mütter tells me you knew Mariah Santos."

She swallows, tears welling in her eyes. "Yes. I met her when she came to me to be sketched prior to surgery. I sketched her again after her procedure a few days ago."

"Did she give you any reason to think she might be in danger?"

"No. She was planning on leaving Philadelphia today and returning home to Ohio."

"Do you know where she was staying?"

"An inn in town. She didn't say which." A pang in her chest. Annis hadn't thought to ask.

He thrusts Nathaniel's sketch at her. "You are acquainted with this man?"

"Yes." Annis feels her face go hot.

"When was Mr. Dixon last in your office, Miss Hargrave?"

"Two days ago."

"The same day as Mariah Santos?"

"Yes, but that has nothing to do—"

"He was the last patient you sketched, after you'd done the same for Mrs. Santos?"

"He was, but—"

"Tell me," the constable says, his pencil poised above his little book, "did you notice anything out of place? Anything disturbed or taken?"

*The Wolf moved Nathaniel's sketch to the easel.* Yesterday, she'd fished it from the pile of renderings and tacked it on the wall after Nathaniel left. If she tells him this—that the paper was moved to the easel—he will think Nathaniel did it, that he placed the likeness of himself directly above the ruined Mariah as if to indicate he was the killer. How can she think otherwise after hearing his line of questioning next door? But declare the real culprit now—after months of silence, moving, building a new life—and they will question why she never went to the authorities in New York, why she consorted with the Wolf in the first place. *Because no one would have believed a smooth, well-mannered Frenchman could do such a thing. And I had no proof.*

"Miss Hargrave?"

She straightens her spine, takes a breath. "No, nothing was touched. I'm sure of it."

His eyes rummage over her as if searching for something lost in the crevices of her. "What is he to you, this Mr. Dixon?"

Blood heats her cheeks. Sweat prickles under her arms. "He is... I..." She swallows. "I am fond of him."

His smile is quick. "Fond." Behind the constable's spectacles, his eyes shine. "Mightn't he, as a means to demonstrate to you his strength and prowess, commit such a—"

"That is quite enough," Dr. Mütter says, stepping from his desk. "I resent, and I'm sure Miss Hargrave agrees, the impertinence of such a question."

Bradcliff raises thick brows. "I have struck a nerve it seems." His eyes flick to Annis. "Very well, I shall desist. For now. Of interest to me, Miss Hargrave, is how the murderer got in. You have a habit of locking your studio when you leave?"

Safer territory. She has no reason to lie about this. "Every evening."

"You are certain you locked it when you left yesterday?"

"Yes."

"And you said, doctor, that every physician has a key to the clinic door. How many to Miss Hargrave's studio?"

"There are but two keys," Mütter says. "I have one, Miss Hargrave the other."

*He picked the locks. For a master of deception, how easy it must have been.*

"Interesting," the constable mutters. "A school full of patients with unusual, rather *unnatural* physical characteristics who may, shall we say, have committed any number of crimes—"

"Look here," Mütter says, his lips white. "I resent, again, the implication that our patients, by virtue of their appearance, are criminals."

"That's right," Pancoast says, thumping his knuckles on Mütter's desk. "This is a teaching college for doctors and a clinic for patients who need medical assistance. Nothing more."

"Nothing more?" The constable's tone is so strident, Annis wants to strike him.

*You priggish, pugnacious fool.*

"I know the types who frequent your clinic, doctor. Do you think it a secret? Jefferson is well known for opening its doors to the... unconventional, if I'm to use a nice word for it," Constable Bradcliff barks. "But I wouldn't call a savage murder committed under this roof nothing." He turns to Annis. "There has been another knifing. While the city has its share of slayings, most aren't as brutal as Mrs. Santos's." He watches her but she doesn't flinch; it's a tactic to break her composure. She won't give him the satisfaction.

"Nigel Kiersley was found gutted to death three days ago in the back of his pawnshop. It doesn't appear to have been a robbery, at least as far as we can tell. Nothing looked disturbed. And while the method of murder wasn't the same, such violence seems too significant to be mere coincidence. Miss Hargrave, do you know Kiersley or his shop?"

"Why would I?" Annis says. "I've nothing to pawn." She will, one day, go to hell for lying. But if these men were her, a woman under no man's protection pursued by a madman, would they not do the same—flee before the villain came to strike her down?

*Perhaps it's already too late to escape.*

"Well then, Miss Hargrave." Constable Bradcliff folds her sketch carefully and thrusts it in his breast pocket. "I'll need your address for further questions." He hands over the book. "Please stay clear of your office until we have removed the... Mrs. Santos." He turns to the doctors. "I thank you for your co-operation. I trust, with a careful investigation, we shall find the culprit. A wise choice closing the school today. I suggest you avoid the press. More often than not, their involvement only makes our job harder. In the meantime, I should like a list of every student and doctor affiliated with this college and every patient who has darkened its doors in the last two weeks."

Dr. Pancoast scowls. "To what end, constable?"

"A link between one of them and Kiersley, for starters. Perhaps Mr. Dixon has such a link. His connection with

Jefferson College intrigues me and the fact he was in Miss Hargrave's studio two days ago where this atrocious crime was committed cannot be ignored. Nor, of course, can his image be, resting directly above the victim. Now, if you will excuse me, ladies, gentlemen."

The constable dips his chin and departs. In the ensuing silence, the fire pops but the room has gone cold.

It is Mary who breaks the spell. "Annis—Miss Hargrave—I think, given what's happened, it would be wise if you went home with me today. You could use someone to look after you. I'm sure, after some rest—"

"I have my brother, thank you," Annis says. "I shall be fine." She knows no such thing but wills herself to smile, to pretend her words are true even as panic pools in her stomach.

"I cannot insist you take my wife up on her offer," Dr. Mütter says quietly. "I *do* insist, however, you take a few days away to recuperate. I can't think of a better place than our home to do so. You and your brother will not have to worry about a thing."

"He's right, Miss Hargrave," Dr. Pancoast says.

She wrestles with her predicament. It will look odd if she denies her need for protection, though it's been couched as rest. She knows how peculiar it is that her studio has been chosen—out of all the rooms, all the nooks and crannies here  by the murderer. She's been singled out. "Very well. I'll speak to Ben. I'm sure he won't mind a change of scenery for a day or two. He's working at Walnut Street Theatre. I'll take a cab to him now. We shall come to you this evening after the last performance, once we've packed a few things."

"Nonsense," Mary says. "We shall have our driver, Abbott, fetch you about eight o'clock. Does that suit?"

She nods once, her gaze lingering on Dr. Mütter. There is concern in his eyes. For her, yes, but the college too. It can't be good for Jefferson's reputation to be the site of a heinous murder.

But there is something else in the doctor's expression, a mixture of curiosity and unease that, had no one else been in the room, might have led him to ask her again if she knows who might've done this terrible thing.

Dr. Mütter suspects she's hiding something.

# NOTE

## PHILADELPHIA, FEBRUARY 1842

The sign affixed to the entrance states classes have been canceled and the clinic is closed, yet the street churns with people. Annis spies a mother with a screaming baby perched on her hip as she tries to quiet it. Another, with a patch over one eye, scowls at the entrance as if looks alone could cast open the door. Scattered among the needy are the students—easily distinguishable in top hats and fine worsted coats—their animated conversations sprinkling the air. Among them, there is an atmosphere of excitement, of mystery. Can news of the murder have reached their ears already?

Heart in her throat, Annis rakes the crowd for a man with dark hair and eyes, a lupine smile. She doesn't find him, but her relief is short lived. At the curb is a covered undertaker's wagon. Of course. Mariah's body hasn't yet been removed. Annis wishes she could accompany her, see that her body is cleaned and watched over until her husband arrives. She owes her this. It's her fault Mariah—sweet, kind Mariah—has been so viciously murdered.

Some clockwork inside her advances another notch—the

shocking, shameful slaying of a woman and Annis must flee to save her own neck. Again.

A few students approach as she descends the steps. They stop when Dr. Pancoast appears at her side and, leading her toward the street, attempts to hail a cab for hire. While they wait, the doctor, flushed with temper at the students, tells them to go home. There is nothing to see, nothing to hear. With any luck, the college will open its doors on the morrow. The crowd thins and Annis can breathe again. The last thing she wants is to be peppered with questions.

A hackney coach stops at the curb. After helping her in and paying the driver, Pancoast instructs the man to take her to Walnut Street Theatre, rapping once on the vehicle before he steps away. As soon as it's in the street, Annis redirects him to Nathaniel's address. In the bump and rattle of the cab, her thoughts wrestle. How long has the Wolf been in the city? What will be his next move?

She peers through the grimy window, passes narrow houses and crowded shops. Pedestrians walk the street, oblivious that the Wolf moves among them. A Frenchman with an air of grace. A man of magic. A killer.

She understands now why the pawnbroker had been so amenable to the terms of their agreement, so particular she provide him her address. Kiersley had wanted her, at whatever the cost, to leave the pearl with him.

Now he is dead.

She digs in her purse, fishes out what money she has. Not near enough. She should have foreseen this, kept a stash of clothes and money in her studio just in case. She's grown too content, too happy and careless. How naive she's been, how lazy.

She and Ben must leave the city. Every minute counts. Still, she can't leave Nathaniel without saying goodbye. Her throat tightens. The telltale prickle of tears, the fierce longing for what could have been seizes her like a fit. But she won't come undone. She forces herself on the now: the cold biting at her ankles, the flex of her fingers in her gloves, the in and out of her breath that fills the cab.

She is alive, that is something. What if the Wolf had been waiting, poised to strike in her studio this morning? He could've killed her in the space of a heartbeat. Instead, he announced his presence. To say *see what I have done. Mark my power, my cunning.* He is toying with her. Mariah was a move in a longer game, one of revenge he will dispense at his own pace. Annis' every countermove must be carefully considered if she and Ben are to escape with their lives.

There is a hackney in front of Nathaniel's workshop when she alights from the cab. Otherwise, there are no other carriages on the street; it doesn't appear she's been followed. She asks her driver to wait and enters the shop. Her heart wrenches at the sight of Constable Bradcliff.

"Annis," Nathaniel strides to her, seizes her forearms. "Thank God you're safe. The constable told me what happened. It's a miracle you're alive."

A perfect response: a man deeply concerned and grateful she's come to no harm. Does Bradcliff see his goodness? That there is nothing in him that could do such a thing?

"I had a feeling I might see you, Miss Hargrave," the constable says, "seeing how fond you are of Mr. Dixon."

There is accusation in his words, a flippant suggestiveness. An idea dawns bright as a bauble.

"I came to tell you, Constable Bradcliff, that Mr. Dixon could not have killed Mariah Santos."

"Oh? Don't tell me, you're too *fond* of him to believe him capable."

"I was with him last night. All night. Here, above his shop."

Bradcliff's eyes walk over her, and she feels as if she's been pinned and mounted. "You failed to mention this at the school earlier. Why?"

Nathaniel sucks in a breath. "Annis—"

"We were in the company of others," she explains to Bradcliff. "Surely you can understand." Her gaze lingers on him long enough to see that he does. She turns to Nathaniel. "I won't have you suspected for the sake of saving my reputation. It's true, isn't it? I was with you last night." A challenge. If he professes the truth, he will label her a liar and bring himself under more scrutiny. She sees by the softening of his features that he won't betray her.

"It's true," he replies. "Miss Hargrave was with me."

"You didn't say so a moment ago."

"I wished to protect Miss Hargrave's reputation."

There is a beat of silence in which Constable Bradcliff searches the two of them for the lie. Then he closes his notebook, the resounding *snap* as satisfying as the scowl on his face.

"I will take my leave, Mr. Dixon," Bradcliff says. "Miss Hargrave." He starts for the door, then wheels. "You are advised to stay in the city, Mr. Dixon. I'm not finished with my questioning and I would hate to find you gone."

"Naturally," Nathaniel says. "I shall help in any way I can."

As soon as the door closes behind them, Nathanial pulls her close. "Please explain to me what just happened. I'm innocent. The investigation will prove this whether you vouch for me or not."

"You don't know what he's thinking," she replies. "The sketch of you was on my easel, directly above Mariah's body. When I left the studio yesterday, it wasn't. I left it tacked to the wall."

Nathaniel's brow furrows. "The sketch was moved? Why?"

"Because it makes you look guilty. To Bradcliff, it looks like you're claiming responsibility. The killer wanted him to draw that conclusion." She watches his mind tick, try to make sense of what she's telling him. "I don't mean this unkindly, but Bradcliff thinks because of your... your—"

"My tumor?"

"Yes. He thinks there's something in you prone to violence. That, combined with you knowing your way around the college —even building the curiosity cabinets for Dr. Mütter—that you've done this. Or he strongly suspects it."

Nathaniel releases her and steps away. "He searched my wagon and my rooms above. Whatever he was looking for—a bloody knife or clothes, I imagine—he didn't find." He studies her face. "Have you any idea what this is about?"

Such a simple question. *And the Wolf takes no prisoners.*

"Of course not," she says. "Did you think I would?" Feigned indignation. She hates herself for it.

"It's only that you seemed so upset yesterday. I thought..." He runs a hand through his hair. "I thought perhaps you were frightened or that someone was harassing you. Forgive me." He comes to her again, folds her into his chest, rests his chin on the top of her head. "I'm happy you're unharmed. You mustn't go home. Not until the constable knows more. You could stay here with me, you and Ben."

It's the worst course of action. Anyone linked to her is fodder for the Wolf. Annis inhales him in, relishes the feel of him. They are down to moments now. "The Mütters have asked us to stay with them a few days. I'm going to Ben at the theatre. After the show, the Mütters' driver will pick us up."

"Thank heaven."

"Nathaniel." She draws away from him so she can see his face. "Everything will be well. You must believe that."

"I'm not sure I do. I have a bad feeling. Something isn't right. Why you? Why your studio?"

She shivers before she can stop herself. "Let's not speak of it now."

"Of course. You're tired, I'm sure. How unpleasant this day has been. Allow me to escort you to the theatre."

"*No*," the word is out too quickly, said with too much force. "My hackney is waiting just there. See? I shan't be on the street, but perfectly safe in a carriage. And we'll do the same, Ben and I, when we leave the theatre. Take a carriage."

"I still don't like it."

"We shall be safe with the Mütters, Nathaniel." Then she is pressing her lips to his, running her hands through his hair, distracting him.

She will imprint on her mind every detail. Remember this moment—*him*—always.

---

Annis can't get to the theatre fast enough. She's already lost valuable time. She can't think where the Wolf is now—there is no one pursuing her carriage that she can see—but he will have thought through what her next steps will be. Perhaps he thinks she's finally told the police about him and he must hunker down for a time to evade detection. It's possible. Or he's waiting near their lodgings to grab her from behind and into an alley. But she isn't fool enough to go home.

Chestnut Street is choked with traffic. By the time the hackney turns at Ninth, the vehicles are at a standstill. She almost steps from the carriage to run the rest of the way, but stills, her hand on the door. It would be easy to accost her here in front of the National Theatre or Peale's Museum where foot traffic moves in thick clots. The night will come early due to the leaden clouds and it's overcast as it is. In such poor light on a street full of the sounds of horses and pedestrians, it would be easy to muffle her screams. No, she'll remain in the hackney, even if it kills her to keep still.

Twenty excruciating minutes later, she steps from the vehicle and races through the theatre door. The lobby is empty of patrons. The play has already begun. Annis isn't as familiar with the layout of this theatre as she was the one on Chestnut. How to find a door to the back? She approaches a uniformed usher at a door and inquires how to get backstage.

"Not allowed, miss," he says, puffing up his chest.

"I must see my brother." She stares at him. "It's important."

"You're not allowed backstage, miss. Not without a pass. But you can buy a ticket, if you wish. Though there are only mezzanine seats remaining and only in the back."

Her temper flares. She wants to strike him. "I don't want a ticket. I need to go *backstage*."

"A pass, miss, is what you need."

"How do I get one?"

"That gentleman over there, behind the ticket desk."

She steps away. There are ushers at every door. She hasn't time for this. As she nears the desk, the man attending it steps away. On the desk is a stack of papers. Annis grabs one, folds it. Steps to another usher and brandishes the paper. "My pass for backstage."

Instead of nodding her through, he reaches for the paper. As he does, she ducks past him and races through the door.

"Hey! You can't—"

His words are muffled as soon as the door closes. The darkness surrounds her, lit only by the illuminated stage yards away. She scurries left and takes the farthest aisle down that snakes along the wall. Behind her she can hear a disturbance—whispers of the ushers, a hissed call for her to stop. At the end of the aisle is a door. A sign that reads NO ADMITTANCE blazes in the darkness. She pulls it open, rushes through.

There is better light on the other side, but only just. She's in the bowels of the stage area. A large room, high ceiling, ropes and pulleys above. Applause from the audience, a hooted cry. The farther back she goes, the more people: propmen in shirtsleeves rolled to elbows, actors in finery with powdered faces. They ignore her.

Ben will be in the wings awaiting a scene change. Which side? A man at a small lectern lit with a gas lamp, pencil behind his ear, looks to the stage.

"Excuse me, I'm looking for Ben Hargrave. He changes scenes?"

He looks at her over his glasses and frowns. "Might I ask who you are?"

"His sister. There's been an emergency."

"It will have to wait. He's needed—"

"I understand. Please just tell me where I can find him."

"Other side. You must take the crossover—"

Annis doesn't let him finish. She races upstage, turns right at the crossover, and runs. By the time she reaches stage left, she is winded. Two young men stand beside a flat, poised to push it on stage. Neither is Ben.

"Ben Hargrave. Can you tell me where he is?"

The nearest eyes her with interest, his mouth twisting in a smirk. "I expect the nearest pub."

She doesn't understand. "He works here. You must know him."

"I do, but like I said, check the nearest pub. He left an hour ago. Hasn't been back. We're one short thanks to him."

It takes her a moment to understand what he's saying. *Ben isn't here. He left.* Her mouth goes dry, and she begins to shake.

"You all right?"

A weight settles on her, squeezes at her heart. The man is speaking again but she can't hear him for the ringing in her ears. The second man approaches, says something she can't hear either.

The next thing she knows, she's in a chair. She can't keep a lid on the sob in her throat and she lets it go. Her hand presses to her mouth.

Someone crouches at her ear. "You remember me don't you, Miss Hargrave?"

A wizened man crouches at her ear. He looks familiar. But she doesn't want to talk to him. Not now, not—

"Grady, from Chestnut Street Theatre?" His eyes worry over her. "Now may not be a good time, but a gift is a gift." He presents a tiny box tied with a bright crimson ribbon. "A man asked me to give you this. Said you'd come looking for Ben and I was to make sure you got it."

She looks at it as if it will bite her. Confusion presses down on her. Ben is gone. There is no link to this box and her brother. It's a token of Nathaniel's fondness for her, a surprise. And yet as she reaches for it, she knows it doesn't make sense.

It isn't a box, but a piece of paper folded many times over. She tugs the ribbon, unfolds the paper. Words scurry like spiders across the sheet.

> Come at dark. The Pit is waiting. Tell anyone and he's dead.

A burst of lightning discharges in her belly. She is rising when something drops to the floor. She squats down and picks it up. A stone attached to a chain. It flashes once, as if to remind her what it is, then goes dark. She drops it as if she's been stung.

And then she is scurrying through the wings: pushing past crates, scenery, clothing on horizontal bars. Her boot catches the corner of a pallet, and she trips, hands splayed for a fall but manages to keep upright. The door just ahead is marked EXIT.

She crashes through it and scrambles out into the dusk.

# GRETA

## PHILADELPHIA, FEBRUARY 1842

Night thickens around Annis, a darkness so impenetrable it's as if black paint has been mixed in the air. All the way to the college, the certainty that the Wolf means for her to die is a shroud that covers her, ever tightening, ever constricting, so it's harder and harder to breathe. How will he do it? Bash in her skull, drown her in a barrel of water? No. Deep down she knows —as sure as she knows something sick and corrosive lies within him—Greta's fate will be hers.

A knife to the throat, quick and ruthless. It's what excites him.

He never laid eyes on Ben in New York, but Annis spoke of him that day in the park. After the Wolf got their address from Kiersley, he followed them. That's how he knew Ben worked at the theatre.

She sees it all clearly now. He has laid his scheme so carefully, so meticulously. Even as terror thrums through her, she sees the brilliance of it. Using the blue pearl as a means to trace her. Summoning her using Ben as bait. The Wolf knows, without question, she will forfeit her life to save her brother.

She is light-headed with the knowledge that this is her new

reality: Ben is his prisoner, and he will die if she doesn't follow the Wolf's instructions. But what tears at her as she runs is that Ben may die even if she does.

*Perhaps he's dead already.*

Suddenly, she is filled with an immobilizing hopelessness so complete, her legs seize. She stops and doubles over, heaving deep breaths. She expels a sob. Never in her life has she felt so alone. Hours ago, she'd had a beau. A future. It had all been a shiny mirage built on naiveté and hope. She swipes at her tears with a sleeve and is hit with a sudden chill.

Standing six feet from her, undulating in the dark, is Greta. She shimmers with her own light—like a weak candle, faint yet perceptible.

The despair in Annis gives way to rage. "You," she spits. "I've had enough of you. No need to gloat now. You'll get your revenge soon enough. He's got, he's got..." She can't say it. It's too much.

But Greta doesn't look smug. Her pretty mouth turns down and her eyes shine with tears of her own. A memory flashes: Greta at Nathaniel's workshop, the frenzy of her movements. The sense that she'd been trying to tell her something. Another flash, and there is Greta behind Kiersley at the pawnshop when Annis handed over the pearl—the transaction that had as good as delivered her into the Wolf's hands.

And then, in that shipwreck moment, Annis understands. "You haven't been trying to scare me. You've been warning me he's coming."

A furious nod. Greta's skirts sway and her hands fold to her chest in a gesture of empathy. Then she beckons Annis with outstretched arms, shifts her body to convey she must keep going along the pavement.

Annis takes a step closer. "You know. You know he has Ben."

Another nod. Greta motions again, urges Annis forward.

"Ben will live, won't he? Tell me that." Greta lifts her shoulders in a shrug. "You don't know. But he's alive, isn't he? That's why you're hurrying me."

Greta's nod is a balm to Annis' tortured mind. Her brother breathes still. The Wolf will triumph, but Ben will live. He must.

She begins to run, following Greta through the darkness. This section of Tenth Street is deserted. There are few carriages, no pedestrians. At last, they turn a corner and Jefferson College looms large. She's never seen it at night before, never noted how much of the block it commands. A gaslight at the curb throws waxy light at the entrance, but there is no one waiting there. Annis stumbles with giddiness toward it. All the panes are black. That is, until she catches a vague glow in the lower panes of the second story windows of the Pit. She wouldn't have seen it if she wasn't looking.

The hallway is dark when the door closes behind her. Greta has disappeared, but Annis feels her close. She creeps along, one hand sliding along the wall as she goes. When her fingers discover the doors to the Pit, she halts and presses an ear to the wood. Not a sound inside. She takes a deep breath and opens one of the doors.

# RETURN

## PHILADELPHIA, FEBRUARY 1842

The boy lies on the surgical table, and Gabriel tests to make sure the cinches are tight. The chloroform-soaked rag had done the trick; the boy had dropped like a stone and hasn't moved since.

High above, gas hisses in fluted bowls. The circle of light pushes at the blackness. Two nights before, he'd seen the sign on the door: THE PIT. Gabriel had entered and knew at once from the echoes of his footsteps it was a large space. He'd gazed up to its heights but the lantern light only bled into indiscernible black. Once he'd stepped further into the room, he'd glimpsed the table, the cabinet of instruments, the pegs from which dangled leather aprons. Walking the perimeter, lantern raised, he'd seen the rows of benches.

It had come to him then what this place was. An operating theatre.

How inappropriate its name. The Pit was not a hole but a *stage*. Gabriel had been filled with the wonder of it, that fate had led him not just to her, but *here*. This was an arena where physicians performed their particular kind of magic: stitching wounds, setting bones, cutting away the malignant. His skin had prickled and his hair stood on end, and he had known then that this was the space to summon the wench.

The setup had all the hallmarks of a show and he, Gabriel Marchand, was nothing if not a showman.

He might be William Shakespeare himself with his theatre in the round—the Globe—where each audience member had an equal, unobstructed seat. Of course, there will be only one spectator tonight. But not for long. Gabriel rubs his hands together. The wench—his trophy, his prize—will become part of the act.

*The climax. Yes.*

He smiles at his double entendre and adjusts himself in his trousers. He has hunted so long for her. Time is collapsing. Months of searching have come down to weeks, then days. Only dusk separates them now.

But he must check his hunger and concentrate. Everything must go according to plan.

An icy draft slithers through the chamber from a source he cannot determine. The candle flames gutter in the candelabrum on the opposite side of the stage. Fortunately, he need not depend on candlelight alone. The night he discovered the Pit, it had taken him some time to determine how to turn on the gas (from a lever on the wall) and light the bowls (using the long stick resting below the lever), but in the darkness and eerie quiet with only a lantern to guide him, he'd mastered the secrets of it. The cabinet was stocked with the morbid tools of the butcher trade. The knives and saws and needles arranged in neat rows had twinkled in the gaslight like lost stars. If these were his props, a leather apron would be his costume. This is how destined this night is—he hadn't even needed to supply his own accoutrements! Everything he needs is here, as if this moment had been prearranged by some unseen hand long ago.

Gabriel smiles wickedly into the cabinet glass, sees his

pointy-toothed rictus leering back. For a moment, he looks like an animated skull. The contours of the bones beneath his skin are visible. The hollows at his temples and under his cheekbones are caved in and shadowed. Pain shoots from his scar, searing as a hot poker, and is gone.

He turns from the glass. The whiskey has gone to his head but only the sharp edges of it sate him. His attention flicks to the bottle on the table. Beside it, his prisoner remains under the spell of the chloroform. *Excellent.*

He strokes the boy's brow, the tender flesh warm against his fingers. The lad is so like his sister: hair the same hue, dark lashes framing blue eyes. How easy it had been to capture him. He'd pushed a note to a lackey entering through the theatre's back entrance an hour before. A short missive telling the boy to come quickly, his sister had suffered an accident. That it was signed by the doctor for whom the wench works conveyed the proper amount of urgency. A falsehood, but the boy came running through the same back entrance minutes later and Gabriel was waiting. He assured him the doctor had sent him, that he knew a shortcut to the school and he must follow Gabriel if he wished to make good time. When they turned down a particularly dingy alley, the boy hesitated.

"This way," Gabriel coaxed, working his face into a visage of sympathy. "We must hurry. There isn't much time."

Oh, the terror on the lad's face! When they arrived at the fence, Gabriel assured him they must climb over it. His moment arrived when the lad stepped toward it. Gabriel came from behind and pressed the rag to his nose and the boy collapsed. The wheelbarrow was there, disguised among the refuse. It had been laborious work getting the boy into it (so tall and gangly, this one) but once done it was a matter of covering him with the tarp and wheeling him the block to the college. Gabriel had even worn the clothes of a laborer to disguise himself. He was merely one of the cogs keeping the streets clear of debris and horse dung. No one paid him the slightest attention.

When he arrived at the school, there was a sign on the door announcing it was closed. Just as he figured, the doctors had closed the building for the day. Now that it was after hours, it was as usual: no one was about, every window was dark. They hadn't thought—out of naiveté, shock?—to place a guard on the premises. After all, what were the chances of the murderous ghoul striking twice in the same place?

A groan from the table and Gabriel's recollections fade.

"You are quite safe, my boy." Blue eyes flutter open, find him in the room. "You are at Jefferson College. You fainted in the alley. A doctor is coming shortly to have a look at you." The boy's head tosses from side to side, and he attempts to lift himself from the table, but the leather straps around his shoulders, torso, wrists, and ankles impede him. A moan is all that evinces from him, for his mouth is stuffed tight with a rag.

The boy stills and stares at him, and Gabriel drops his artifice. "Well, I suppose the gag has called my bluff." A chuckle. "The bad news is no doctor is coming. I lured you here on a lie. But fear not, there is good news. There's been no accident. Your sister is quite well. In fact, she's coming here. To you." He tilts his head, considers the boy as if he were a child. "Tell me, did she speak of me? The brilliant magician whose acquaintance she met last year in New York, the one from whom you ran?" The boy's brow knits in confusion. "No?" Gabriel makes a tsking sound. "A pity. That knowledge might've saved you from accompanying me down that despicable alley."

Another moan and the boy's eyes flare in their sockets.

"Now, now. I really must insist you remain calm." He brushes at the boy's brow again and the lad flinches, his attention rooted on his scar. Gabriel laughs. "Oh, yes. Have a good look. I shall tell you how I came to have it and who so savagely dealt it to me. But allow me to lay the groundwork first, yes?" He begins to circle the surgical table, fingers steepled, steps slow and measured. "My father was my first victim. I was about the age you are now I expect when I killed him." Details spill from the corridors of his mind. The day he'd stumbled into his father at the tavern, that rancid smile that mocked him. He was no more a magician than Gabriel a prince. "The night I met my father, I saw what he was—a low-born scoundrel. I searched for him for years, thinking him a great man. Well, when he turned his lip up at me and sneered, do you know what I did? I followed him to his rented room and lit fire to his building. It went up in seconds. I can still remember the screams."

Gabriel stops to consider the boy and notices the sheen of sweat on his brow, his labored breathing. "Ah, you begin to understand what I am capable of."

He pats the boy's shoulder and resumes his walk around the table. "I went home to my mother." Flashes like lightning strikes: their airless room, his mother in bed, the reek of gin. He'd approached like a cat but she'd awakened. The weeping sore festering around her nose—the pox rotting her from the inside out—sickened him, but it was the bones of her shoulders and neck that captivated him in that moment. So tiny and birdlike. *Gabriel? What is it? Why do you look at me so?* That filthy sheet she clutched to her breast like it would save her. Then, a sort of dawning as she smelled the smoke on him and took in his expression. *What have you done?*

"I told her, plainly and without artifice, I'd found my father and killed him with the strike of a match. And before she could ask why, or plead, or cry, or retch, I placed my hands around her neck and squeezed until she, too, was dead."

Beside the boy is a long knife grabbed from the surgical cabinet. He places it above the boy's face to give him a long look at the blade. He flinches when it flashes in the gaslight and Gabriel laughs.

The gas hisses and the candles shiver. The air has gone frigid and still. He is suddenly filled with an ache over the loss of Augustus, the man who had taught him nearly everything he knows about magic. Goose flesh ripples over him and Gabriel is seized with the impression that the flickering dark pressing at him is the weight of his own guilt, that somewhere in the seats above Augustus waits for him. He presses at his eyelids until spots form across his vision. He grabs the whiskey, knocks back another mouthful, wipes at his mouth with a sleeve.

"I gather you are wondering what this has to do with your sister. I met her at Scudder's Museum in New York where I was performing as a magician. She was there viewing the exhibits. Such a dangerous thing, a young lady alone. Why, any unscrupulous fellow might come along and bend her ear." His laugh jags the air, and he lays down details like scaffolding, each layer building on the other—the ticket to his act that he'd given her, their chance meeting at the park, his offer of a job because their mother's death had pitched them into a future unknown.

"She followed my assistant and me after we left the museum one night. I suppose the little vixen had come to tell me she wanted the job." The room sways and Gabriel brings a hand to his forehead. What was the assistant's name? Oh, no matter. She'd shown her true self: a woman of loose morals just as his mother and all the others had been. But they are dead now. All of them. He'd saved them from themselves, each one.

Gabriel takes another swig of whiskey and for a moment, he is on a carousel spinning. Two candelabra flicker at the edge of the stage. Above him, two interlocking rings of light. He clutches the table, waits for the room to settle. He has the sense he's skipped over parts of the story, bungled it, but cares not a whit. What's important is what he tells the boy next.

"My assistants soured, like cherries on the turn. Pure in the beginning, but they became like my mother—vulgar and loose. And so I saved them, you see, from their polluted selves." He leans forward with the knife, places it against the boy's throat, and whispers, "I shall tell you a secret. Burning and strangulation are no longer my methods of choice. It's a knife to the throat that arouses me. I dispatched my assistant in my cellar that night, one clean slash. Your sister saw me do it." The boy strains his wrists against the straps and Gabriel grins. "Oh, I haven't brought you here only for you to escape."

His face is inches from the boy's. "I believed your sister virtuous, yet she flew at me from her hiding place in the cellar like a harridan. *That* is how I got this." He draws a finger down his scar, wishes one of the boy's hands were free so he could feel the ruined flesh too.

Then Gabriel hears it. The sound of the outer door opening. A breeze rushes past and the candles gutter.

She is here. The wench has arrived.

# THE BEAST

A shaft of yellow light shines down on the surgical table to which Ben has been strapped. Standing beside him is the Wolf. Annis' heart pitches in her chest. To the left, near the wall that circles the stage, candles flit in an arced candelabrum. All else is cloaked in darkness.

"Come in, come in," the Wolf says, with the enthusiasm of a host greeting a guest at his door. "Step into the light where I can see you. Don't be shy."

The words are courteous but there is an undercurrent beneath them that sets her heart cantering. She remembers the Wolf's gallantry at Scudder's, how duped she'd been by his manners when underneath lurked a killer, a fiend. Something about his voice is different too. She takes another few steps into the pitching gaslight. Ben flinches on the table and tries to look at her but his bindings prevent it. She can see no visible injuries, but God knows what the beast has inflicted on him.

*But he's alive.*

Gabriel bares his teeth in a smile. He is emaciated. She can clearly see the bones of his face. His clothes—a laborer's, not the flashy togs of a showman—hang on him. Black shoulder-length hair a riot of greasy curls, skin the pallor of day-old milk. But what lunges at her is the scar. So thick and ropey, it casts a shadow across his cheek.

"So good of you to come rescue your brother, but then I reckoned you would. He's the only flesh and blood you have left, is he not?"

The words are like a splinter shoved beneath a fingernail and she winces. The Wolf notes it, his eyes shining with suppressed glee. It hits her then what it is about his voice that sounds odd. He's not speaking with a French accent. That, and so much else about him, had been a ruse.

"Let him go. It's me you want, not him."

"Oh, I wholeheartedly concur." He gives her a crooked grin and there is something in it that humiliates her to the core. "But as Shakespeare himself declared, timing is everything." He turns to the cabinet and fingers the tools there. "Such an interesting array of instruments and in such fine condition. Recently sharpened, and the shine!" He holds a knife to the light, fits the blade to his palm and makes a quick, shallow slice. Blood beads in a line. He selects a saw and turns around to the table.

Annis' breathing catches and she takes another step forward. Questions snap at the edges of her. Why hadn't she thought to bring a weapon? How can she prevent Ben from harm when the distance between them feels like an ocean?

"You must admit, our meeting here is perfect." He gestures to the room. "The *theatre* of it, and the props! How could you have known all those months ago that racing to Philadelphia—and you did race for your life fearing I was right behind you, I imagine—would end here?"

"Let him *go*." Annis' anger surprises her. She has come in defeat, rehearsed lines on the way—*take me in exchange for him. I'll do anything, anything*—but now something spreads its roots through her. Not courage; she's terrified. But the notion, perhaps, to fight.

And there it is: she will not make her death easy for him. She will die, but she'll go out like a lion, not a lamb. But first, he must free Ben.

"I've come as you asked. Now let him go." Another step. Ben thrashes on the table. She sees that his mouth has been stuffed with a rag and the realization only stokes her rage. How dare this monster lay a hand on him.

The teeth of the saw come down to rest against Ben's Adam's apple. Annis gasps.

"I told your brother our history. He knows you are responsible for this." He runs a finger down the ruin of his cheek. "I nearly died." A pause. "No apology? Tsk, tsk. What an ill-mannered chit you are." He tosses the saw in the air with one hand and catches it with the other, managing to keep his fingers from the blade. Then he places the saw at Ben's neck again. "I went into hiding, you know. Imagine my surprise when I saw nothing in the papers about the disappearance of a young woman who'd worked for a respected magician, a magician who had a month's worth of bookings at Scudder's who had simply disappeared. Of course, it had happened before—the sudden disappearance of a young woman in my employ."

His eyes twinkle knowingly, and it hits her like thunder. Greta was one of many. For a moment, all she can hear is the rush of her own blood.

"That was the beauty of the assistants I chose. I selected women who needed help because they were on their own. They were estranged from family or had none. Would it surprise you to know I was doing them a favor by getting them off the streets? It should hardly come as a shock. I offered the same to you."

"You killed them."

Something ripples over the Wolf's features transforming his

face to a visage so diabolical, it reminds her of the twisted, sinister grin of a gargoyle. "They betrayed me, every last one."

"How many?" Annis can barely breathe.

A shrug. "It doesn't matter. No one marked their loss."

"The young man at the theatre that night looking for his sister did. I wager there were more."

He waves the comment away. "Bah, he had no proof." He considers the saw, angles the blade so it catches the light. "The last was different, of course. You witnessed what I'd done. You didn't go to the authorities. Why?"

"I didn't think they'd believe me. I knew you would cover your tracks quickly, and I had no proof."

The Wolf's lips curl. He mimes a sawing motion above Ben's neck then sets the saw against the flesh again. He presses, once, and tiny beads of blood appear where the teeth have bitten into the flesh. Ben moans, his eyes wild.

"Stop, please. You're scaring him." Her hands come up.

Gabriel takes a gulp from a whiskey bottle and Annis wonders how much he's had, if she can use it to her advantage.

"You recognized it was *me* who was in control. That I was to be feared. Wise, but it won't save you." The liquid black of his irises sears her, and the acrid stench of the alcohol comes to her in a wave. "I saw you with your swain yesterday. Sitting atop that desk with his hands all over you. You're as impure and vile as my mother was."

A memory swims to her, one of the many details that night in the cellar she has locked inside her. What had the Wolf said? *My mother was dying of the pox, but I saved her. I can save you too.* Annis hadn't understood until now. His mother was likely the origin of his mania. A twisted version of the truth about her, a version upon which he's assigned himself the role of savior. He fashions himself a hero, granting redemption only he can give. Suddenly, she sees him for what he is. Not the mighty Wolf, but a mere man. A deluded lunatic who has fed on the misfortune of others who never deserved the fate he'd given them.

*I will never call you the Wolf again. I will never give you that much power.*

Marchand exchanges the saw for a long knife on the table. "The time has come. I will untie him, but only if he refuses to make trouble. Do you hear, boy? If you run or fight me, I shall kill you or your sister, whoever is nearest at hand." His laugh is as high-pitched as a girl's. He makes quick work of the straps and Ben gets up from the table. Marchand then backs Ben up against the cabinet, placing the tip of the knife under his chin. "Now, wench, it's your turn. Lie down or I'll run him through."

"Let him leave. I won't lie down until you do."

"And I shall kill him if you don't. The table. *Now.*"

A small, upward thrust of the knife. Ben winces as the tip of the blade punctures him. A drop of blood falls to the floor. Her brother's eyes flick to hers. In that tiny moment, it's an unspoken message, clear as glass: *Fight. Don't let him get away with this.*

She steps to Marchand and it's all she can do to lie down without shaking. The metal surface is slick beneath her. *Smooth and slick.* Her mind manages to scrabble hold of a plan.

Marchand takes another pull from the bottle and motions Ben to step closer to the table with him. "Strap her down good and tight or there will be more of your blood on the floor."

Marchand is now close enough to reach out and touch and Annis fights the revulsion rising up in her. "I'm so sorry, Ben." She works to make her voice sound weak, to signal to Marchand that he's won. "You must be strong. It will be all right." Her words have the desired effect. Marchand chuckles as if defeat is in his grasp. He doesn't seem to notice that her words contradict the quick, steely burn of her eyes as she locks them with Ben's.

Now's the time. Once she's lashed to the table, she's done for.

Before Ben can reach for the straps, she bends her legs at the knee and spins, feet pivoting to Marchand. Planting her boots firmly on his stomach, she straightens her legs and kicks against him. With a look of surprise, Marchand attempts to right himself, then tries to swipe her legs with the knife, but his movements are clumsy as he loses his footing. The lower half of her body is now off the table, her hands gripping the edge, using it as leverage to force Marchand back with kick after kick. With all her might she pushes, the soles of her boots now planted on Marchand's chest. He stumbles back into the cabinet, and it's as if Annis is once again in the cellar, once again using the weight of her body to topple him.

A *whoosh* of air exits his chest. The whiskey bottle crashes to the floor. The wooden structure teeters, a pane of glass cracks and then another. Instruments tumble from shelves. All the while, Ben struggles to prize the knife from his fingers.

Marchand roars and then, suddenly, inexplicably, they are plunged into darkness.

# STIRRINGS IN THE DARK
## PHILADELPHIA, FEBRUARY 1842

Marchand's howl, grunts, glass breaking, instruments clanging to the floor—it is chaos. Annis feels what she thinks is Ben colliding with the edge of the table just as she's about to set her feet down and run, but her arm is seized and she is slammed against Marchand. Even in the darkness, she knows it's him. Her nostrils fill with the sour tang of sweat and putrid breath. He wraps his arm around her throat and for an instant she thinks he will kill her then, in the dark, no one to know of her passing but Marchand himself.

She claws at his arm to loosen it, to catch a breath, but his feet are moving. With Annis in a choke hold, glass grinding underfoot, they sidle from the cabinet toward the direction of the benched seats. Only then does Marchand loosen his hold. As she catches her breath, she finds the chamber isn't entirely dark. Though the gas ring above has been extinguished, the candelabrum on the other side of the stage remains lit. Barely enough to light the few feet around it, but in the black abyss, it's something.

"Who did you tell, wench?" Gabriel snarls. "We had an agreement."

A rasp of sound near the double doors. A match sparks to life. A face appears in the murk above it. It's Dr. Mütter.

"She didn't tell me anything," the doctor says. "I came here to check on things and found the door unlocked. No one does business here without my knowledge, so I knew there was mischief about."

Marchand chuckles. "How noble of you, Doctor...?"

"Mütter."

"Ah, the estimable man who hired the wench to produce art —although I use the term loosely. I've seen the monsters here, the deformities of limb and such. Calling them *art* is rather too much, isn't it? Yet, how very gallant of you to set them aright by butchering them on the table before a rapt audience." Marchand chortles as if he's told a joke. "Well, since we're doing introductions, I am La Grande Merveille. Not so long ago I was a magician, a bewitcher of audiences myself. In different circumstances, I might have delighted you before a crowd of your peers. My conjuring days, I regret to say, are long gone thanks to this chit. I gather she's not mentioned a thing about our acquaintance, has she?"

"She has not," is the reply. Mütter's match goes out and he lights another.

"How disappointing. But then if she had, she would've had to tell you far too much of her rather unsavory actions since March of last year. I can't think you'd have hired her if you knew."

Mütter takes a step forward, the match flame pitching shadows across his features.

"*Stop*," Marchand barks, his jocularity gone. "I have a knife at her throat." His arm tightens around Annis' neck, and she makes a small cry. "Speak for the good doctor. Tell him."

Marchand releases his hold a bit, but Annis clamps her mouth shut. She will not perform for him. But his hand is suddenly clamped around her neck, the pressure so fierce, a swell of dizziness takes her.

"I'm here, doctor. Ben—"

"The boy will not move," Marchand says, and she feels his body rotate, as he rounds on the darkness. "It would be foolish of either of you to approach. Which one of you will be responsible for her death?"

He is elated; she can hear it in his voice. Mütter may have caught him unawares, but it is Marchand who wields the power. As long as he has her and the knife, they are helpless against him. And the darkness is his ally. He would like nothing better than to kill them all and leave the Pit a bloodbath for the students to stumble on in the morning. For an instant she imagines it, the young men coming through the doors, the blood, the bodies lying twisted and slashed.

Annis blinks, wills her eyes to pick out anything to use against him, but it's no use. The surgical tools that spilled from the cabinet are too far away. Besides, apart from the few feet around the candelabrum, it's black as tar. Except for Mütter's match. When he runs out, what then? He can't possibly come at Marchand from the dark without serious injury to himself.

In the next instant, two things happen: Mütter's match goes out and behind them, there's a faint noise. A breeze flits through the chamber as if one of the upper doors that lets out onto the benched seats has opened. Marchand turns to the sound; he's heard it too. Has the doctor brought someone with him? Dr. Pancoast perhaps, or a constable?

"Ben will remain where he is," Dr. Mütter replies, striking another match.

There is something about the way he's used his voice that makes Annis wonder if he's trying to distract Marchand or perhaps instruct someone above. They need to keep Marchand talking. If he's talking, he isn't killing.

"That's right," Annis says with force. "Ben, don't be stupid. Stay where you are. Marchand won't think twice about using the knife. I've seen it done." Underneath her words, she'd heard the faint creak of wood above. Has Ben used the steps from the stage to get up to the seats?

*Go. Leave and don't look back. Save yourself.*

"Ah, you begin to understand me," Marchand purrs at her ear. A shiver navigates her spine and the pent-up terror she has tried to keep in check for so long sets her limbs trembling. Marchand laughs. "Tell me, doctor," he calls, "did you know your hired strumpet came to Philadelphia to hide? She was an orphan, a nobody. A month or two, perhaps, from the streets. I've seen it dozens of times—girls with golden dreams who end up two-penny whores. Eventually they succumb to their plight, bodies as riddled with drink as they are the pox. I offered her a job in my show to keep her afloat and how did she repay me?" Annis feels the knife point at her cheek and gasps. "The bitch came at me with a knife. Sliced me open like a fatted calf. While I lay bleeding nearly to death, she fled here."

"I wager there's a good deal you've left out, providing anything you've said is true," Mütter says dryly. "I can't fathom the Miss Hargrave I know harming anyone. While we're on the subject, why Mariah Santos? Did you know her?"

*Yes, Mütter is engaging him. It's a distraction.*

"Not at all. She was merely a means by which to terrify your artist. A calling card, if you will."

Another creak. A footfall from above or is she imagining it?

Marchand's attention turns to the seats again and Annis shifts in his arms. "Who's there? Show yourself."

Silence.

When she turns back to Mütter, she finds that he has stepped a few feet closer. *He's trying to back him to the seats. Someone's up there.*

Marchand retreats a few steps. They are at the six-foot wall that borders the stage; she can feel the edge of it with her skirts. There is nowhere for Marchand to go unless he uses the steps to the benches, but does he know where they are, that they even exist?

Mütter's match goes out.

"Step to the candles where I can see you and stay there," Marchand hisses. "No tricks. It won't take but an instant to kill her and the blood will be on your hands."

Dr. Mütter steps into the flickering light of the candelabrum. He still wears his coat and topper, one hand thrust into a pocket. His eyes search for them in the darkness. "My driver is summoning the Night Watch. You won't get far with her, so I suggest you let her go. It will be easier to slip their grasp if you're alone."

"Perhaps," Marchand replies. "Unless you're lying. What do you think, my pet? Is the doctor as good as his word?" The knife's tip on her cheek stills her. Her thoughts careen. What answer will calm him, what response will set her free? She feels the prick then, the trickle of blood down her cheek, and she sucks in a sob. Anguish floods through her to her every edge.

Mütter tenses. "If you harm her, the brunt of the law will be upon you. Do you hear? There will be no refuge for you anywhere."

Marchand cackles. "You contradict yourself, doctor. Which is it? Will I slip their grasp or be shackled?"

"The difference is clear to me," Mütter replies, his words clipped. "Flee now and give yourself a chance. But bring ruin upon Miss Hargrave and there will be no place to hide. I shall see to it myself—"

The doctor's words grow faint as Annis listens for another sound behind them. Marchand speaks, his words lost to her. These are her last moments—Marchand will never let her go.

He'll kill her now or take her with him. The throb at her cheek is gone, but it has left behind a clarity, as if the nip of the knife has washed clean her mind. Annis is tired of Marchand's games, tired of hiding, of being afraid. Her resolve returns. She won't allow this madman to kill her so casually, so quickly. She will fight until the bitter end and, God willing, Dr. Mütter and Ben can slip away to safety.

Marchand's arm is still wrapped around her neck. Before fear can overcome her, she bites down hard on his forearm. He howls, loosening his grasp just enough for her to drop to her feet. Then she is skittering on all fours to get away.

"I'm free!" she screams.

A crunch, the crash of limbs, a scuffle. Someone *was* above and they've made contact with Marchand. A jump of light to her right. Mütter has hoisted the candelabrum and is bringing it near. With each step, more of the stage is illuminated until at last, the light spills over two figures—one Marchand, the other...

The breath leaves Annis' chest. Nathaniel.

The men are locked together, spinning like tops. The whir of limbs, teeth, Marchand's wild eyes. Nathaniel's hand works to rid his foe of the knife, but while he is strong, Marchand is fast. They tumble end over end. Ben stands watching, poised to use a knife he's found, but the duo is too quick for him to take a stab at Marchand. Finally, Nathaniel manages to get the better of him. He lands on top, knees pinning Marchand's arms to the floor, one hand holding the knife to his throat.

"You worthless piece of scum!" Nathaniel shouts. "I'll kill you. How dare you lay a hand on her."

Marchand's eyes glint with malice. "Ah, the whore's paramour. How tragically quaint."

A mechanical click and Annis turns. To her astonishment, Mütter holds a pistol and it's trained on Marchand. "Let him go,

Nathaniel," he says. "The Watch is on their way. He's not worth it." Nathaniel doesn't move. His hand tenses around the knife.

"Nathaniel," Annis says. "Please. Dr. Mütter is right."

The tension goes out of him and with great reluctance, Nathaniel pulls himself to his feet.

"Stand up," Mütter says with a twitch of the pistol. "What am I to call this creature?"

"Gabriel Marchand," Annis says. The words hang in the air like a taint.

"On your feet, Marchand," Mütter barks. "Slow and steady."

The beast does as he's told, runs a hand through his mess of hair. In the light of the candles, his scar is blanched white, a reminder of the savagery Annis inflicted on him in the cellar that dreadful night of death. When she catches Nathaniel's eye, she finds him looking at her with such tenderness it hurts.

*I lied to you. I should have told you everything.*

Then she sees that Nathaniel's arm is bleeding. Her heart hitches and she is stepping to him when Marchand lunges. She sees him in that instant laid bare: the twisted ruthlessness of his scar, the pointed daggers of his teeth.

The crack of the pistol. Marchand's eyes widen and he stops, looks down at himself. A red bloom swells on his chest and he falters, takes a teetering step back.

It's suddenly freezing. Annis' breath clouds the air, and she knows Greta has come at last.

# GHOSTS OF PERSONS PAST
## PHILADELPHIA, FEBRUARY 1842

Time slows for Gabriel, dips in on itself. He can scarcely credit it: the thrilling pulse of power as he sprang for the whore, and then the inexplicable pain. His vision dims, his heartbeat clamors in his ears. Red seeps from him. Seeps more.

A frigid gust of wind stirs around him. Light shimmers, moves. In the glow of the candelabrum, figures flit, awash in golden light: girls, women. So many of them, dancing in a ring around the candles. He knows them for what they are—his victims. Gabriel has forgotten their names, but never their faces, never their fear.

And yet. They aren't frightened now. In the center a fair young woman is seated, head bent over needlework. His mother. So young and pretty, before hardship hollowed her out. Gabriel remembers. Long ago, she'd been his everything and he, hers. A dark-haired man enters the circle. Tall, slender, much like himself. Gabriel watches him take his mother's hand, kiss it, and he is rewarded with a blush from her.

"Father?"

On the figures bob and Gabriel finds that he is shivering. Where is his coat? He looks down at himself and discovers he has collapsed to the floor. Where is he, what madness is this? He rubs his eyes but the people—no, *ghosts*, that is what they are—remain. They are happy. He has brought them this. There is no shame in it. He saved them, he knows he did.

Then, as if an invisible stroke of the clock has come down, they stop. A man flits toward Gabriel. Whiskered, dressed in a royal-blue frock coat. His eyes rake him, scorn in their depths.

*Augustus. The first Grande Merveille.*

"No, no," Gabriel pleads, cowering. "I didn't mean it, I—" He is shunted to a rented room with a dying fire. A carcass of a roast duck picked clean, the smell of cloved oranges. He knows what's coming. "No, I don't want to see it. I, I won't look."

He shuts his eyes against the memory, but the picture dances unfettered against his eyelids. He watches his younger self tell Augustus of his wish to join him on stage as his equal. On pins and needles he is, but he's expectant of a bright future. Gabriel has worked so hard for this. Then Augustus speaks and dashes it all. *I've no need for a partner. If you wish to elevate yourself, you'll do it with your own hard work and money. Your own tricks.* Augustus laughs and pours wine as if Gabriel's dream is nothing but a joke.

Oh, the rage, the bitter bloom of it. He flies at Augustus, places his hands around the older man's throat, and squeezes and squeezes until his mentor, his friend, sinks back into the chair. Flashes: rolling Augustus' body in canvas, dumping it in a nearby ditch.

He opens his eyes and the scene vanishes. He is again before the candelabrum, the specter of Augustus glaring down at him. Gabriel is dizzy, sick and weak, but manages to say, "I'm sorry. I didn't mean to do it."

Gabriel is sobbing now, his nose running, and still the ghosts of those he's taken watch. They begin to advance, and he brings a hand up to protect himself, to shut them out. His heart is slowing, his vision going. Beside Augustus is a young woman in pale blue. His last assistant. She's mouthing something again and again. He knows what it is. He remembers now. Her name was, is—

"Greta." There. He's said it. Now she—they—will leave him. He's remembered her. That's all she wants. And yet, still they come. With each step, shadows gather at the edges of him. The light is going.

A sudden, terrible dawning. They aren't happy he killed them; they are celebrating his doom. Dancing on his grave.

He takes in sips of air, wills himself to keep breathing, until he no longer has the energy and there is nothing but the darkness and those filthy wretched girls to take him.

# LOOSE ENDS
## PHILADELPHIA, FEBRUARY 1842

A half hour later, Annis sits before the fire in Mütter's office wrapped in a blanket. Ben sits in a chair across from her, staring at the hearth.

"Claret," Mütter says, coming to them with small glasses. "I think you both need it."

A strange familiarity settles over her: the fire, the drink, the horror of another of Marchand's acts. Annis takes a sip but barely tastes it. Her hands aren't steady so she rests the drink on her lap, her fingers curled around it. Behind her, Nathaniel is a calm presence, his hands on her shoulders.

There is an uncomfortable stretch of silence and then Ben says in a low voice, "He sent a note to me. I thought it was from you, Dr. Mütter. Your signature was at the bottom. The note said Annis had had an accident and I was to come to the school. When I exited the theatre, Marchand was there. He said I was to follow him. And then..." His voice breaks off and a tear travels down Annis' cheek.

*What I have done to him.*

"Take your time," Mütter says. He sips from his own glass and looks between them.

"He took me down an alley. A shortcut, he said. He pressed something to my face. The next thing I remember I was strapped to the table in the Pit."

"Chloroform most probably," Mütter says grimly.

"This is all my fault." They turn to her.

Nathaniel comes around to face her and sinks to his knees. "I very much doubt that."

"And so do I," Mütter says.

Nathaniel urges her to take a sip of claret, and she does. "You weren't yourself at my workshop, Annis. Naturally, you were shaken about Mariah, but I knew there was more to it than you were letting on. You seemed to be trying very hard to convince me all was well. I needed to see you again to convince myself I was overreacting and so I went to the theatre. When I got there, I asked to go backstage. An usher made a flippant comment about how the backstage was very popular this evening. I asked him for an explanation, and he told me a frantic young lady had made a rude attempt to get past him shortly before and when he refused her, she dashed past him.

"I knew then it was you." Nathaniel's voice cracks, emotion in it. "And I knew something terrible had happened. After I explained I knew you and I believed you were in grave danger, the usher permitted me through. It was clear, after making some inquiries, you and Ben had left. Although not together, which didn't make sense."

"You found Marchand's note," Annis says.

"Yes. It was on the floor where you'd dropped it. A necklace too. I pocketed both and made my way here." He takes her hand. "I have never felt so helpless in my life, Annis. I knew you and Ben were in trouble and I hoped it wasn't too late. Thank heaven the note made it plain where you'd gone."

"He found me at the clinic entrance," Mütter says, picking up the story. "I'd come to have a look around. I, too, had an uneasy feeling. Nathaniel showed me the note and we hastily made a plan. Thank heaven I had the foresight to bring a pistol. When I entered the Pit, I saw a man with a knife to Ben's throat demanding he strap you to the table. I cut the gas to foil him, but in so doing I rendered my pistol worthless in the dark."

The fire pops in the hearth. Seconds tick. It's time for Annis to speak. *I owe them this. I put them all at risk.*

Slowly and as clearly as she can, she winds back time and tells them of those spring days a year ago in New York City when her mother died and left them nothing, Uncle Desmond refused to take her and Ben in, and she met a Frenchman named Gabriel Marchand who promised her a job in his magic show. She relays, in excruciating detail, the evening when she followed Greta and Marchand to his home, hid in the cellar wardrobe, and witnessed him viciously slit Greta's throat. Just as Mariah's had been. Each memory is like a gutting, ripped from her like the roots of a noxious plant.

"He found me in the wardrobe—I couldn't keep back my sobs. We struggled and I ended up with the knife. And I, I cut him." She bursts into tears, shoulders shaking. Nathaniel wraps his arms around her and pulls her forward in the chair to him. When she is more composed, she releases herself and leans back. "We weren't safe after that. I was afraid he would find me and get his revenge. We had to leave the city."

"You didn't go to the police?" Ben asks. He is so pale, so fragile, incredulity etched strikingly on his face.

"I had no proof, Ben. Marchand was very clever. I knew he would cover his tracks." She takes a sip of claret to fortify herself. "But that's not the only reason. I... speaking out would have called attention to our lack of a guardian. We had no relatives, no place to go, no money. I thought if we vanished, we could stay together. I didn't want you to go to the Orphan's Asylum or be adopted, perhaps. I didn't want us separated, but the truth of it is, I couldn't bear the idea of being without you." Ben covers his face with his hands and turns to the fire, doing his best to mask his sobs. At least he knows now why they left New York in such a hurry. "Forgive me. I could have saved you from this if I'd only been brave enough to let you go."

"It would seem, Miss Hargrave," Mütter says ruminatively, "that your fear of Marchand was greater than your faith in the authorities."

Annis has never looked at it quite that way. "I suppose so." She stares down at the glass in her hands. "I see it so clearly now, Marchand gaining my trust. I think it was the same with Greta. He admitted tonight there were others who met Greta's same end. Other women who were alone and vulnerable and became his assistants." She shudders, thinking of Marchand's perverse elation when he'd murdered Greta. "He believed they became unchaste over time and that he had to save them from themselves."

"By killing them," Nathaniel says. His face is flushed, his jaw clenched.

Annis nods. "I know now I shouldn't have run." She tells them that this is what hurts the most, that because of her persistence in hiding the truth, Ben had been swept into the mess, becoming Marchand's toy. As had Mariah. "I deceived you, Dr. Mütter, and you too, Nathaniel. I knew who killed Mariah and I said nothing."

"You were frightened, Miss Hargrave," the doctor says gently. "And you were trying to protect your brother."

"And myself." She lays a hand against Nathaniel's cheek. "What if Constable Bradcliff had arrested you for Mariah's murder?"

"You *did* protect me," Nathaniel says. "The best way you could." He doesn't go any further; he doesn't need to. By affirming they had been together last evening, she'd established his innocence.

"I confess," Mütter says, moving a hand over his face, "I'm still confounded as to how Marchand traced you here."

Annis swallows, her throat tight. "I kept some of Mother's jewelry after she died. Ben and I needed it to live on, at least until we found suitable work. I sold some of it for train tickets and later, for rent and furnishings. Mother's most prized piece, the one worth the most, was a necklace. A rare blue pearl."

Nathaniel reaches into his trousers and pulls out the necklace. "This?"

"Yes." She takes it from him and lays it in her lap where it reflects the dancing flames. "For the last week or so, I've been looking for a new apartment, a surprise for Ben, and I needed—"

Her brother turns to face her. "Oh, Annis."

It's hard to look at him, this caved-in boy she'd tried to protect but only endangered and hurt.

"After our mother died, I happened to bump into Marchand again. I was wearing the pearl and he remarked on it. I told him how rare it was and I had to sell it to keep Ben and me afloat." She looks between Nathaniel and Mütter. "It was the last of Mother's jewelry and I pawned it."

Mütter stiffens. "The pawnbroker who was killed?" She nods, a fresh bank of tears brimming. "Marchand must have been writing pawnshops far and wide."

Annis nods. "Mr. Kiersley was insistent I leave an address on the paperwork. It makes sense now. He must have already received a letter from Marchand asking about the necklace." She takes a deep breath and with a trembling voice, says, "Now, you see, it isn't only Mariah, but Mr. Kiersley too."

Nathaniel rises to his feet and rakes a hand through his hair. "That blasted demon."

"Greta, too," Annis says, her voice breaking. "I didn't save her. I didn't save any of them."

Nathaniel places his hands on the armrests of her chair and leans in. "You mustn't blame yourself. Marchand was evil. Deranged. He was killing long before you met him. From what I understand, if you'd never met him he'd have found another assistant. He'd have killed Greta eventually. It was his pattern. Please understand that."

"But Mar—"

"Miss Hargrave," Mütter interjects. "Mrs. Santos and Mr. Kiersley were in his way. Collateral damage, if you will. You never could have foreseen he would find you, much less harm them. No one could have."

"He's right, Annis," Ben says. "You couldn't have known. I wish you'd confided in me, but your intentions were good, always good." He smiles a little and she feels a swell of love for him.

"You were alone in that cellar, Annis," Nathaniel says. "You had no weapon to fight him but your courage." His green eyes blaze with tenderness. "You did all you could. Your quick thinking saved your life."

"I couldn't agree more," Mütter says. "You must put the guilt you have for not coming to Greta's aid behind you. I commend you for getting away and trying to keep yourself and Ben out of harm's way. It was a noble thing to have done."

Despite her guilt, she feels a lightening in her chest. That they don't abhor her for the mistakes she's made—mistakes that endangered them—is a windfall she'd never foreseen. She is truly blessed to have them in her life, all of them. It feels incomprehensible to her that none of them had been harmed. For this, she is grateful too.

"My driver should be returning soon with the Watch," Mütter says. "Nathaniel and I will go downstairs and wait for their arrival. The two of you make yourselves comfortable. It may be a long night, but the worst of it is over." He nods with a small smile and heads for the door.

Nathaniel plants a soft kiss on her forehead, the affection in his eyes as soft as a caress.

When they are gone, Annis comes to Ben and then they are hugging each other tight. She doesn't think she has ever loved her brother more than in this moment.

While he pokes at the fire and she resumes her seat, she thinks of Greta. She'd thought herself alone in the matter of Marchand, surrounded on one side by a merciless fiend and on the other, a ghost bent on taking her revenge. But Greta had been her ally from the beginning. So, too, had Dr. Mütter, Nathaniel, and Ben. Annis had just been too foolish to see it.

And the ghosts swirling in the light of the candelabrum? They had been too obvious, too many in number for Ben, Dr. Mütter, and Nathaniel not to have remarked on them by now. Because they have not, she knows only she and Marchand had seen them.

In the beginning, Greta had shown herself to warn her. In the end, Marchand's other victims appeared too. Why? So that she could bear witness to how many of them there had been, perhaps.

But in her heart she knows they wanted to show her that justice had been achieved at last.

# PART 4

The Museum of the Institution affords essential aid to the student, by its various anatomical, pathological, and obstetrical preparations and drawings, as well as by the diversified specimens of genuine and spurious articles, and plates, drawings, &c. for illustrating the materica medica. These, with the numerous and varied specimens that have been recently added from the private collections of the members of the faculty, render the Museum and Cabinets more rich and effective for the purpose of Medical Instruction than they have ever been.

—excerpt, advertisement for Jefferson Medical College for the 1841–1842 academic year

# AT THE WHARF
## PHILADELPHIA, MAY 1842

Three months later

When Annis and Nathaniel turn the corner onto Sansom Street, Jefferson Medical College sits waiting in the weak May sun. A crowd stands before the entrance, the line petering out halfway down the block. Ladies are dressed in spring pastels, the men in shades of cool gray and camel. As they near the entrance, the porter opens the door and waves them past the queue.

The hall is crowded with people talking in small groups and Nathaniel tucks her arm more securely around his and navigates them through. At the door, her brother stands regally in a navy frock coat, his honey blond hair neatly combed.

"Ben," says Nathaniel, "you look the very picture of a gentleman."

"Do you think?" Ben makes a face and yanks at the cloth at his neck. "This cravat is killing me. Annis tied it too tight."

"Nonsense," Annis says, but the seriousness in her tone is

belied by the fondness in her eyes. "If you want to play the part, you have to look it, too." She considers him, head tilted. "I wager you'll have outgrown that coat by fall. Perhaps I should have purchased a gently used one."

"Oh, but it's grand," Ben says, running his hand down a sleeve. "I've never seen the like." He straightens. "And besides, the opening today is an aus... aus..."

Annis quirks a brow. "Auspicious occasion?"

"That's the word." He sobers. "The Mütters are here. The doctor's been asking for you both, so I won't keep you." He winks at Annis, opens the door, and gestures for them to step through.

"This will go to his head," Annis whispers as they enter. "He's been preening like a peacock ever since I gave him that coat."

"Well, if Dr. Mütter has anything to say about it, he'll have one in every shade." Nathaniel's eyes brim with affection and Annis feels a surge of pleasure. There are days when she can barely believe how fortunate she is to be alive.

Greeting them is a roar of chatter. A haze of pipe smoke swirls overhead, lit by the sun streaming from the windows. Gone is the storage room with its shrouded exhibits, its bursting crates. There is order now, a sign that reads JEFFERSON COLLEGE MUSEUM hanging resplendent over all. Everywhere there is something for the eye to feast upon. The walls are covered in framed illustrations (many of them Annis'). Cabinets form aisles to be browsed, displays of every variety to be discovered, taken in, assessed. There are bones, dried organs, wet specimens in jars of brine. What isn't organic has been rendered in papier-mâché, wax, plaster, and wood and they are no less remarkable.

The day before, the museum opened to the students after Mütter delivered a lively speech in the Pit about the evolution of medical science. Annis had watched from the upper tier, her whole body vibrating from the thunderous applause at the conclusion.

"Not bad for an opening." Dr. Pancoast scans the room, nods to a few people in greeting. "Mütter was correct. Making the museum accessible to the public was the right thing to do. I feared some of the ladies might faint from some of the more... gruesome specimens. Alas, they appear to be quite fascinated."

Dr. Mütter had been clear at the outset that, in part, the museum's role was to familiarize the public with the wonder that is the human body, the working of which physicians understood or, in some cases, were just beginning to comprehend. As for the curiosities that set patients apart from the norm, Mütter wished to demonstrate that all people had a common, shared humanity. Putting curiosities on display didn't exploit the souls who walked with these irregularities in life, they normalized them by laying their distinctions bare: an oddly shaped bone was no more or less than that, a tumor could be removed, a gall stone extracted, a cleft palate seamed. Birth defects and aberrations due to irregular growths or the result of accidents could be explained, understood, and ever increasingly rectified through Mütter's groundbreaking *chirurgies plastiques*. The doctor and his museum—it would forever be his in Annis' mind—were unmaking the monsters.

"It doesn't appear the college will suffer a whit," Nathaniel says.

While Jefferson still maintained a healthy roster of students, the board had been concerned last winter. Accounts of the brutal slaying of a patient and the shooting of a madman on the premises hit the papers immediately. To preserve the college's reputation, the faculty had been tight-lipped. With so few facts for the press to report, the public's focus soon waned.

Ironically, it was that very silence that fed the student rumor mill, which still ran like a virus within Jefferson's walls. The stories were so outlandish (the patient had been beheaded; the man shot was half monster, half man) they took on the air of penny dreadfuls. If anything, the murders had lent Jefferson a macabre sort of fame and the board expected enrollment to grow the next academic year.

Because Marchand's body was never claimed, his corpse was made available for dissection. As chair of anatomy, Dr. Pancoast refused—in part to curtail more gossip, in part to assure Annis that no shred of Marchand remained within Jefferson's walls. "We must," he'd remarked dourly, "let that stinking corpse lie."

"Ah, Miss Hargrave, Nathaniel," Dr. Mütter says, sidling up, his wife beside him. He's dressed in a frock coat of pastel blue. A white carnation blooms from his breast pocket. "So good of you to come."

"We wouldn't miss it," Annis says. "Ever since my interview, I've been dying to see the museum come to fruition." She takes in Mary's peach taffeta gown. "You look lovely."

"I shall give you the name of my dressmaker," Mary replies. "She's nothing short of a magician." For a brief instant, an uncomfortable pause stretches, as if Marchand has appeared and bared his teeth. "Forgive me," she says, cheeks pinking. "A poor choice of words."

Annis refuses to let the moment sour. She's lived in fear of Gabriel Marchand far too long to allow him to hinder her happiness. "Think nothing of it. The lady knows how to select the best colors for her customers and that *is* magic."

Dr. Mütter nods. "Indeed."

From the solemnity of his tone, it's clear the doctor isn't commenting on his wife's dressmaker, and it pleases Annis that he knows the length to which she has worked to overcome her past.

"I thank you both for helping bring this dream alive," Mütter says. His eyes scan the room. "I've long wished for an organized repository of materials for the faculty to use in instruction and a space in which the students can come and browse the displays to their hearts' content."

"Yes," Dr. Pancoast says. "He's been going on about a museum for so long he finally wore the board down." Mütter chuckles. "What? Do I speak out of turn?"

"Not at all," Mütter replies. To Annis he says, "Your drawings of the space were instrumental in helping them *see* it. The cabinets, too, Nathaniel. Precisely what I envisioned— imposing, beautifully crafted, decorative without being excessively so—it's the specimens themselves that attract the eye! In fact, I have a list for you, young man—friends who wish to make additions in their homes in the way of furniture." Mütter reaches in his breast pocket and pulls out a slip of paper. "While I know the cabinets are rather rudimentary compared to your typical pieces, I've bragged about your secretaries and bookcases to the extent that the names on this paper will keep you busy a good long time."

Nathaniel inclines his head. "I'm very grateful, doctor."

"As for you, Miss Hargrave," Mütter says, eyes sparkling, "I know I have said so already, but the work you've done has gone a long way in documenting our collection, not to mention my surgical techniques for our book." His voice is laced with tenderness, and he offers up the next words delicately. "I hope you are content here. There's a good deal more illustrating to be done."

Annis feels the prick of tears and just manages to nod. She doesn't want to embarrass herself by getting weepy, but she recognizes the bubbly feeling in her chest for what it is: bliss. Mütter had hired her, a woman, to draw for him. He'd seen her talent, trusted it. Where would she and Ben be if he hadn't?

What if she'd never been in Washington Park that cold December day peddling her sketches? It's good to be seen, to be valued for doing the only thing she's ever wanted to do: make art.

"Let them walk the floor," Mary says, as if she senses Annis' emotion. "Go on. Don't let us keep you."

And so they disengage themselves and walk each row. Every piece is labeled with a card and they read one after the other, fascinated by the descriptions, rapt by what they see. Some specimens Annis recognizes because she's drawn them; most are new and await her careful study. There is *aneurism of the aorta* (a wooden model of a heart with enlarged parts dyed red, blue, black, and white), *bladder stones* (pea-sized and displayed in a tiny bell jar), *right inguinal hernia* (a wax model showing the portion of a groin with a bulb-like growth under the skin), *bezoar* (a hair ball extracted from the gastrointestinal tract), *uterus with fetus* (papier-mâché, showing growth of the baby months one to nine), *tumor of the cerebrum* (floating in a jar with a mass projecting from the gray, grooved surface of a brain).

When they come upon a cluster of people in the middle of an aisle, they wait for browsers to move on and edge closer. Displayed on a marble pillar is the wax head of Madame Dimanche, enclosed inside her glass box. Her thick brown horn protrudes from her forehead like a devil's claw. The card reads *cornu cutaneum removed after six years of growth.*

"Is it real?" Nathaniel asks in a low tone.

"She lived, yes. Mütter uses her as a lesson in humility." Nathaniel looks a question. "She was shunned in her village. Once her horn was removed..." She shrugs.

"Let me guess. People no longer feared her?" His brow furrows. "I can well understand."

Annis squeezes his hand. "Come with me, there's some place I need to go."

The public landing is so picturesque, Annis wants to paint it. What colors would she mix for the ladies' parasols, the shimmering coat of the Irish setter? White gulls pitch and wheel in an azure sky and below, on the Delaware River, ships toss gently from their moorings.

"You look as though you want to eat it," Nathaniel says. He tucks a stray curl behind her ear. "Shall we go back to your studio for your paints?"

How well he knows her. "No. There's something I'd like—I need—to do first."

He waits, his green eyes taking her in. *I shall never do them justice,* she thinks. *Verdigris isn't quite right. There is no shade that could match them.* She could work the rest of her life attempting to perfect the color and be adversely baffled and content doing it.

She takes his hand and walks to the end of the pier. A gull cries overhead. The sun sparkles on the water like hundreds of tiny diamonds. She reaches into her purse and withdraws the necklace. The pearl is heavy in her palm. There's one last thing about it she must tell him.

"My father purchased it in a shop in Wales. It was cheap, he said. Priced far below its value. The jeweler wanted it gone because he thought it was cursed. Papa didn't believe a word of it. He gave it to my mother, and it became her favorite jewel."

She tells him then, eyes misted with tears, about how her mother demanded she be buried in all her jewelry and how, after Annis learned their uncle wouldn't take them and how destitute they were from her mother's reckless gambling, she'd stolen the jewelry off her mother's dead body.

Nathaniel pulls her around to face him. "Stolen? Your mother left you no choice. You realize that, don't you? That you had to take her jewels was her doing, not yours." He tries to wrap her in his arms, but she pulls away.

"No, I need to tell you all of it." When she looks down at the necklace, it flashes in her palm and goes dark. "I sold all Mother's jewelry except this. It's cursed. I didn't believe it at first, but I do now."

"Cursed how?"

"You get attached, covet it, and misfortune happens. I pawned it, remember. I wanted it *back*."

"It was the last of your parents you had left, Annis," Nathaniel says, cupping her cheek. He shrugs, thinking. "But maybe there's something to it. Marchand used it to find you. Constable Bradcliff's pieced it all together."

The constable has been busy. He'd found where Mariah had been staying in the city and returned her belongings to her husband, and he informed his counterparts in New York of Marchand's murders in Philadelphia. They had, in turn, quickly linked him to his professional persona, La Grande Merveille, and his performances at Scudder's. From there, it was a matter of working backward through Marchand's roster of shows to uncover a pattern of missing girls—all of whom were in some measure on their own and in need of work. Slowly, the girls who'd died by Marchand's hand were getting their due.

Annis wept for days, weeps still, for Mariah and Greta. For all the women whose lives had been cut short she will never know.

"My father died so suddenly," Annis says, "and Mother's spending habits ruined us. Once I took possession of the pearl, everything that happened with Marchand fell into place." She'd felt shattered in the Pit as she envisioned Ben's death and her own. But now, having unburdened herself with secrets she never should have kept, she feels herself possessed with a new resilience. A fortitude that will carry her through. She'd needed the pearl once, but never would again.

She raises her arm and, with all the strength she possesses, hurls the necklace into the river. It flies in an arc, winking once, twice until it pierces the water with a small splash and is gone. She is almost light-headed with the relief that washes over her.

"Better now?"

"Immeasurably."

"Promise?"

"Yes." They face each other, fingers entwined. The Irish setter barks. A pair of women pass and shoot them harsh looks, but Annis doesn't care a jot.

"If anything had happened to you, I don't know what I'd have done, Annis." Nathaniel raises his hand, strokes her cheek with his thumb.

It's a gesture that is as natural as breathing to him and she thinks, *I love everything about this man.* "You would have lived, Nathaniel."

"Yes, but you aimed to desert me—desert *us*—and I never would've known the reason. The ogre people thought me in the days I hid half my face behind a mask? I would've become that man."

She touches his scar lightly with her finger. She's come to adore it, though she doesn't think he'd believe it if she said as much. "I should've confided in you."

"You don't need to say it again. I know." Nathaniel's hands come around her waist and he tugs her closer. "Trust me, Annis. I'm here for you. Always." He takes her hand, places it on his heart. "Feel that? It beats for you. Only you." A muscle twitches in his jaw. "I have the strong urge to kiss—"

She laughs. "Here?"

He cradles her hands at his chest. "Why not? Though I'd

like to do a good deal more than that." His pupils darken and for an instant she sees a bit of the rake in him. "But as the public landing isn't the place and I can't abide the slap you would surely give me..." She laughs again, so suffused with happiness she feels weightless. "I shall settle for a kiss. For now." He leans in.

Annis pulls back. "Not yet." Disappointment flickers across his face and she rushes on. "I want to thank you for agreeing to apprentice Ben."

"Ah." A smile plays at his lips, and she sees that he understands she's led him to this topic deliberately. "Need I repeat it? It's not a favor I'm doing you or Ben. I need an apprentice; I have for years. Ben likes working with wood and he's good at it. If I'm honest, he's probably better than I was at his age. The work suits him. As my apprentice, he's bound to me for several years, of course, until—"

"He becomes a journeyman."

"Yes." He rests his forehead against hers.

They have arrived at last to the crux of it. She knows what he's going to say. Knows, too, that years from now, she will remember this moment with the sounds of the gulls and the scent of the sea in the air.

"An apprentice receives training, and room and board from his master," Nathaniel says. "As I've mentioned, an apprentice ordinarily becomes a member of the master's household. You remember this?"

"Yes." Nathanial had said this months before when Ben started his carpenter's training under him. But Ben hadn't been ready to leave Annis. In truth, Annis had needed Ben too. They craved time together, just the two of them, to talk about everything that had happened. It was important to Annis that Ben understood that, while she'd acted rashly, she'd done it for his protection and her wish to keep them together.

"It's time Ben came to live with me," Nathaniel says, and his eyes hold more than what he's saying.

"I know."

"I love you, Annis. I've loved you since you ran from me in the storage room." He cradles her face in his palms.

As difficult as it had been, confessing all that had happened in New York—her blind trust of Marchand, that night in the cellar—had slowly brought about a change in her. By unshackling the truth, the horror began to feel like something she survived instead of something to be kept deeply hidden. The heaviness inside her began to lift.

It comes to her then, what Uncle Desmond had written in his letter all those months ago. *It is through hard work and tenacity that the phoenix rises stronger from the ashes.* How cruel the words had been and yet, he'd been right.

Annis has, in the last few months, painted herself over with white, struck a new canvas. She is ready to coat herself in vibrant hues, brush on the colors of a new life. A wondrous one. She is poised for all the good things to come.

———

They stand at the pier. The pretty, slender girl with hair the color of honey. The tall, well-muscled man with broad shoulders. He speaks and the girl nods vigorously and then he is sweeping her up in his arms and spinning circles. The woman in blue smiles. At least she thinks she does. These days, she feels less and less. She has become barely discernible. Months ago, she'd shimmered for the girl as the girl lay crying, and she'd grinned and waved, and blew a kiss. They'd both known it was goodbye.

A gull screams overhead, the water sparkles, the breeze shifts. It's time to go to a better place. Her work here is done.

The ends of her are going, her edges disappearing. She is a wisp of a wisp. She feels herself thinning, thinning to nothingness until the very last of her is no more.


# THE END

ALSO BY TONYA MITCHELL

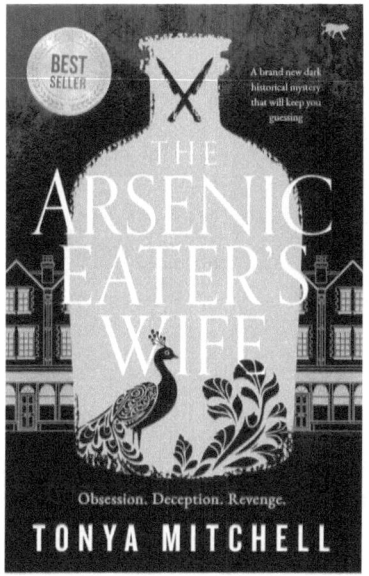

*The Arsenic Eater's Wife*

**A woman is accused of killing her husband, but is she guilty? Inspired by a true historical case, this spellbinding novel will keep you guessing until the final heart-stopping revelation...**

BUY NOW

# AUTHOR'S NOTE

The University of Pennsylvania School of Medicine was the first medical school in the United States. It was founded in 1765, a decade older than the country itself. It would be another sixty years before Jefferson Medical College was established. In its first year, Jefferson enrolled an impressive 107 students—not bad for a school that, in its nascent years, had to rent a theatre for space in which to teach. Soon, due to its impressive faculty, innovative lecture courses, and an ever-increasing roster of students, it was a formidable rival of the University of Pennsylvania. Notably for the time, Jefferson promised the all-important cadaver to each student, which was crucial in the study of the body. By 1841, the chairs of the various departments—including surgery, anatomy, obstetrics, and pharmacology (called *materia medica*)—were occupied by some of the most brilliant minds in medicine. Dr. Thomas Mütter, who was then thirty years of age and had only been practicing medicine for ten, was elected to the prized chair of surgery. He was the youngest among his peers. It's clear the board saw something special in him from the start.

Mütter was a curious, forward-thinking doctor. A medical

degree wasn't enough. After graduating from the University of Pennsylvania at age twenty, he went to Paris and trained under the best surgeons in a new field of surgery the French were calling *la chirurgie radicale*. Under the great Guillaume Depuytren and Jacques Lisfranc de St. Martin, Mütter watched in amazement as these skilled men performed *les chirurgies plastiques*. These were innovative procedures done on patients who were born with or developed physical deformities, or were the victims of battle or accidents. Mütter's training in Paris changed the course of his life. He now knew what he wanted to specialize in: reconstructive surgery. Before he left the city, he purchased the wax model of Madame Dimanche, which he unveils to a rapt audience of students in one of the scenes of the book. The model was one of the first, and arguably one of the most remarkable, items in his collection.

Mütter did, with British surgeon Robert Liston, publish a book of surgery in 1846. However, it was almost immediately obsolete due to the introduction of ether as an anesthetic (ether was first used in the dental profession). Ironically, the very thing that had outdated Mütter's book became his new cause. He was the first surgeon in Philadelphia to use ether (on a man with a tumor of the cheek). At last there was a way to safely eliminate pain during surgery. Mütter enthusiastically incorporated the administration of ether into his surgical curriculum.

Mütter regretfully stepped down from his position at Jefferson Medical College in 1856. Consumption had plagued him for years and his health was declining fast. As his condition worsened in the last years of his life, he wondered what would become of his collection of medical oddities—some 2,000 specimens—he'd amassed over the years. He wanted them displayed in a museum for doctors and students. Naturally, his first choice was Jefferson College, as the school's anatomical museum—the opening of which is a scene in the book—had existed there for fifteen years. The issue was space. Eventually, the College of Physicians of Philadelphia (not a school but a professional organization) agreed to accept Mütter's collection.

Tragically, Mütter died of consumption in 1859. He was only forty-eight years of age. Two years later, the College of Physicians started construction on the building that would become the Mütter Museum. It opened in 1863. Dr. Joseph Pancoast, who memorialized Mütter in a speech after his death, remained his truest friend to the end. In a time before even germ theory existed, it's remarkable that some of Mütter's surgical methods are still relevant. For example, the Mütter flap —a skin grafting procedure used on burn victims—is still used today.

Annis Hargrave is fictional. But certainly a young woman who, based on unfortunate circumstances, finds she must support herself is not. Multiple drawings of Mütter's patients and surgical techniques survive. The artist's name is lost to history. He was almost assuredly male. For the story's sake, I decided to make the illustrations the work of a young woman. Annis Hargrave was born.

As for the cursed pearl Annis pawns, the color had to be blue. Blue pearls are among the rarest in the world. The color and contours of the pearl in the story are similar to the silver blue white south sea variety, but I took its air of mystery from La Pelegrina, a famous thirty-three-carat, pear-shaped pearl. It appears in an 1894 painting around the neck of Russian Princess Zinaida Nikolaevna Yusupova.

Nathaniel Dixon is loosely based on Nathaniel Dickey, a twenty-five-year-old young man who suffered from cleft palate. Weeks before surgery, Mütter massaged the muscles of Dickey's face, readying him for surgery. Mütter's students watched in astonishment in the Pit as he deftly sewed his patient's lip and roof of mouth closed. This was without anesthesia, as ether wasn't in use yet. Mütter's remarks about how brave Dickey had been was something I couldn't resist adding to the story. However, since cleft palate surgery would've required more extensive healing, I decided to create Nathaniel Dixon who would suffer from a less complex facial tumor. That he became Annis' love interest was a surprise to me. Cleft palate and clubfoot (from which the fictional Mariah Santos suffers) were among the most common of Mütter's reconstructive surgeries.

The despicable Gabriel Marchand is my invention. I relied on the self-portrait by Gustave Courbet called *The Desperate Man* for Marchand's physical appearance. The depiction of a dark, tortured soul with wild eyes and unruly raven hair seemed perfect for the villain. The details of young Gabriel's work at the slaughterhouse collecting bones came out of my research on how bone char (or dust) was used in cane sugar refining (and still is, believe it or not). As for Marchand and Annis' first encounter, I was excited to find a unique attraction that was a perfect setting: Scudder's American Museum. The wonders described within are taken from a pamphlet circulating at the time. Marchand's "second sight" and "ethereal suspension" stunts are based on Jean-Eugene Robert-Houdin's tricks.

If you'd like to know more about Mütter's collection, I highly recommend a visit to the Mütter Museum in Philadelphia. It's a fantastic portal into early medical history. Though it has changed locations a few times, the museum remains the repository for Mütter's extensive collection. Most of the wax models, organs in jars, and bones Annis sketches in her studio were things I viewed at the museum when I was researching the book. The museum's selection continues to evolve as newer items are added (like glass slides of Albert Einstein's brain and an iron lung from the polio era).

For an impressive tale of Mütter's life and Jefferson College itself, I highly recommend Cristin O'Keefe Aptowicz's *Dr.*

*Mütter's Marvels.* It's nonfiction that reads like a novel. From this book I pulled rich details, such as Mütter's colorful mode of dress, his ambidextrous abilities during surgery, and the addition of the umlaut (the two dots) over the "u" in his surname. He was born Mutter (rhymes with butter) but changed it to Mütter (pronounced Moo-ter) because he liked the sophisticated way the French surgeons pronounced it. In my opinion, with or without the umlaut, Dr. Thomas Mütter was a noble man who helped hundreds of patients lead a normal way of life.

His work remains a testament to the human condition and what he tried so hard in life to achieve: the alleviation of human suffering.

# ACKNOWLEDGMENTS

This book wouldn't exist if I hadn't picked up a copy of *Dr. Mütter's Marvels*. A warm thank you to the author, Cristin O'Keefe Aptowicz, for introducing me to Mütter, his curious collection, and the groundbreaking college where he taught and served as chair of surgery until he died. Without her colorful prose and the numerous illustrations of patients with physical abnormalities Mütter remedied with his *chirurgies plastiques*, I would never have crafted the story that became *Needle and Bone*. Her book was an excellent launching point into more research into early 19th century medical history in the United States.

I'd like to thank my early beta readers, Jenny Graman and Jacqui Paul, for their careful diligence, suggestions, and encouragement along the way. You asked all the right questions to help make this book what it is. Kim Taylor Blakemore, Alan Hlad, and Susan Kraus kept me on the straight and narrow in weekly accountability meetings. I never wanted to go into those sessions without having made my word count goal—because you almost always did and who was I to slack? Jenny Quinlan of Historical Editorial also helped make this book shine before I submitted it to Bloodhound. As always, I cherish your thoughtful comments and Zoom chats where we discuss all things story and how best to improve mine.

I'm very grateful to Bloodhound Books for not only continuing to support my writing endeavors but enthusiastically marketing them to an audience of historical gothic lovers. Betsy,

Fred, Abbie, and Tara, thank you for answering my questions, polishing my manuscript, keeping me on schedule, and producing covers and back cover copy to die for.

Nearer to home a special thank you to my sons—Thomas, Nicholas, and Christopher—for putting up with my historical obsessions (sometimes I'm not in the room but off on some dark plot point in the 19th century). Most of all, deep thanks to Ron for his encouragement and being my biggest champion.

# BOOK CLUB GUIDE

1. The blue pearl necklace plays a key role in helping Marchand find Annis. Do you think it was cursed, or do you think it was simply bad luck that befell its owners?

2. Do you think Annis should have told Ben the real reason they were leaving New York City in such a rush? Have you ever kept something from someone you love to protect them?

3. Annis had a complicated relationship with her mother. Do you think Beulah Hargrave would have been happy to see her children settled and content in Philadelphia at the end?

4. Did it surprise you that Dr. Mütter hired a woman to be the college's artist? Why do you think he did?

5. Were you surprised, as Annis was, that the ghost of

Greta was trying to warn her rather than spook her? Do you believe in ghosts?

6. Would you have been comfortable working among the so-called "monsters" who came for treatment to Jefferson Medical College? Do such people have more freedoms today? Do you think they are more understood by the public than they were in 1841?

7. Gabriel Marchand had a tragic upbringing that shaped his feelings about many things, including his parents. Do you think this was due to his past or was there something more in Marchand that made him resort to evil?

# ABOUT THE AUTHOR

Tonya Mitchell writes gothic historical fiction. She is the author of *The Arsenic Eater's Wife*. Her debut, *A Feigned Madness,* won the Reader Views Reviewers Choice Award and the Kops-Fetherling International Book Award for Best New Voice in Historical Fiction. She is a member of WFWA, HNSNA, and the Authors Guild. She lives in the US.

For more: https://www.tonyamitchellauthor.com/

# A NOTE FROM THE PUBLISHER

**Thank you for reading this book**. If you enjoyed it please do consider leaving a review on Amazon to help others find it too.

**We hate typos**. All of our books have been rigorously edited and proofread, but sometimes mistakes do slip through. If you have spotted a typo, please do let us know and we can get it amended within hours.

**info@bloodhoundbooks.com**

www.ingramcontent.com/pod-product-compliance
Lightning Source LLC
Chambersburg PA
CBHW030531190726
48283CB00006B/1869